THE PENGUIN CLASSICS

FOUNDER EDITOR (1944–64): E. V. RIEU

EDITORS:

Robert Baldick (1964–72), C. A. Jones (1972–4), Betty Radice

MOLIÈRE was the stage name of Jean Baptiste Poquelin, the son of a wealthy merchant upholsterer. He was born in Paris in 1622. At the age of twenty-one he resigned the office at Court purchased for him by his father and threw in his lot with a company of actors, to found the so-styled 'Illustre Théâtre'. The nucleus of the company was drawn from one family, the Béjarts. Armande, the youngest daughter, was to become his wife.

Failing to establish themselves in Paris, the company took to the Provinces for twelve years. When in 1658 they returned to the capital it was with Molière as their leader and a number of the farces he had devised as their principal stock in trade. Invited to perform before Louis XIV, Molière secured his staunch patronage. In 1659 *Les Précieuses ridicules* achieved a great success, which was confirmed by *L'École des femmes* three years later. With *Tartuffe*, however, Molière encountered trouble; it outraged contemporary religious opinion and was forbidden public performance for several years. *Don Juan* also had a controversial history. *Le Misanthrope*, first played in 1666, is generally accorded to be the peak of Molière's achievement. Among plays that followed were *L'Avare*, *Le Médecin malgré lui*, *Les Femmes savantes*, *Amphitryon*, and *Le Bourgeois Gentilhomme*, one of the comedy-ballets to which Lully contributed the music.

By 1665 the company had become *La Troupe du Roi*, playing at the Palais-Royal. While taking the part of Argan in *Le Malade Imaginaire*, Molière was taken ill, and he died the same evening. The Troupe survived, however, to become one of the forerunners of the *Comédie Française*.

JOHN WOOD was born in 1900 and went to Manchester University. After some years in teaching and adult education, he spent his working life in educational administration. Concern with the relevance of the arts in education, combined with personal predilection, led to involvement with theatre and with the work of Molière in particular, as producer and translator. He has also translated *The Miser and other Plays* and *Beaumarchais – The Barber of Seville* and *The Marriage of Figaro* for the Penguin Classics.

Molière

THE MISANTHROPE

AND OTHER PLAYS

Translated with an Introduction by

JOHN WOOD

PENGUIN BOOKS

Penguin Books Ltd, Harmondsworth, Middlesex, England
Penguin Books Inc., 7110 Ambassador Road, Baltimore, Maryland 21207, U.S.A.
Penguin Books Australia Ltd, Ringwood, Victoria, Australia
Penguin Books Canada Ltd, 41 Steelcase Road West, Markham, Ontario, Canada
Penguin Books (N.Z.) Ltd, 182–190 Wairau Road, Auckland 10, New Zealand

—

These translations first published 1959
Reprinted 1961, 1962, 1963, 1965, 1966, 1968, 1969, 1970, 1971, 1973,
1974, 1975

—

Copyright © John Wood, 1959

—

Made and printed in Great Britain
by Cox & Wyman Ltd,
London, Reading and Fakenham
Set in Monotype Garamond

*The terms for the performance of these plays may
be obtained from the
League of Dramatists, 84 Drayton Gardens,
London SW10 9SD
to whom all applications for permission should be made*

What is there left for us
that have seen the newly discovered
stability of things changed from
enthusiasm to a weariness . . .
but to rediscover an art of the
theatre which shall be joyful,
fantastic, extravagant,
whimsical, beautiful, resonant and
altogether reckless. . . .

W. B. YEATS

To René Varin

Contents

Introduction

A SUMMARY of Molière's life and career with an estimate of his achievement as playwright and actor was given in the introduction to an earlier volume in this series.* Comment is therefore restricted now to the plays included here and their immediate background. Taken as a selection of Molière's work complete in itself, they include three of the greatest plays (two of which are in verse in the original), an example of the shorter comedy-ballets, and a farce which displays the dramatist's supreme mastery of this medium. With the five plays already published they comprise a majority of the works which retain their interest and significance.

THE MISANTHROPE

The Misanthrope was first produced in 1666 when Molière was forty-four. His rise to fame had been long delayed, but when it came it was meteoric. In the eight years since his return to Paris he had produced a dozen new plays and his company had set new standards of comedy and acting in comedy. He was the most popular comic actor of the day, enjoying the favour of the King and the plaudits of the town, but success had provoked a formidable reaction from rivals and critics and those who felt the edge of his satire. *L'École des Femmes* the most celebrated of his works up to this time, had achieved a resounding success, but it had been bitterly criticized as vulgar, immoral, beneath contempt by orthodox literary standards; *Dom Garcie de Navarre*, Molière's attempt to write a tragi-comedy in the grand manner, had been an unmitigated failure and, at the time when he was, one assumes, already engaged on *The Misanthrope* he had run into serious trouble with the first version of *Le Tartuffe*. It was forbidden public production: *Dom Juan*, written to fill the gap, was an immediate popular success, but it also fell under interdict, was taken off after fifteen performances, and never again played in Molière's lifetime. The dramatist's career had reached a critical stage. It was at this juncture, in the thick of the struggle for *Tartuffe* beset by his enemies, his health already impaired, harassed and unhappy in his personal life, fighting

* Molière: *The Miser and Other Plays – The Would-be Gentleman, Love's the Best Doctor, The Miser, That Scoundrel Scapin,* and *Don Juan.*

for the very survival of his theatre, that he produced a new and wholly original play. It is his greatest achievement, a deliberate masterpiece, a calculated, considered reply to the besetting forces of criticism and adversity, an assertion and justification of his genius. It is as if he had said, 'Literary usage insists that a play of any pretension to importance shall conform to the classical unities, that it shall deal with people in an elevated social *milieu*, that it shall avoid all suspicion of grossness in theme or vulgarity in treatment, that it shall be in verse and in five acts – very well! I will for the occasion conform to the unities although I have elsewhere derided them; I will submit my play to the restrictions of time, place, and theme; I will renounce the whole stock-in-trade of traditional farce, cuckolds and pedants and doctors, old men with young wives, lovers setting crabbed age at defiance, comic valets aping or deceiving their masters, vulgar provincials with ridiculous accents, *bourgeois* with pretentious ideas; I will make no use of ridiculous incidents, nor play of coincidence and contrivance, nor horseplay, nor *gauloiseries*, neither *machines* to excite wonder nor music and dancing to give sensuous pleasure. I will show you a picture of a refined and cultivated society, men and women of breeding and fortune in the most congenial surroundings the age can afford; I will endow them with wit and beauty and grace in just distribution and proper proportion, and you shall see in them the contrasts between what men are and what they pretend to be, what they aspire to do and what they have it in them to achieve. You shall hear them saying one thing and meaning another, mark them jostling for advantage while proclaiming disinterest, vying with each other in vanity and hypocrisy, in heartlessness and indifference to virtue when they encounter it; you shall behold the limitations of breeding and manners and learning exposed, and to these puppets, these creations of my own observation and vision, I will give such resemblance of life that though you smile at their follies you shall not escape grieving, though you laugh, your hearts shall be moved to compassion for the hollowness of their world. Finally, my comic hero shall be at one and the same time a figure of fun and a man of intelligence and feeling, a puppet of circumstance and an individual whose dilemma you shall recognize as your own.'

The play pushes the comic vision of reality to ultimate lengths, or, as some feel, beyond into regions which tragedy alone comprehends. It is a masterpiece of that rare theatre where feeling and intelligence are fused in delight, wise, compassionate, and gay, one of those works which, as Donneau de Visé put in words one hesitates to translate, '*font rire dans l'âme*'.

Judged in terms of the box office *The Misanthrope* was only a moderate success and has remained so. It has never equalled *Tartuffe* in popularity and even among its admirers it has always provoked a discriminating praise. It could hardly be otherwise, balanced as the play is on a fine edge of comedy, making little concession to sensation and still less to sentiment. It may be, as has been suggested, that the comedy of the play was less equivocal in the seventeenth century than now, that though we have outlived Romanticism we still do not see true love unrequited as quite so axiomatically funny as audiences did then. What is certainly true is that time has brought changes in the attitude to society itself: we may not follow Rousseau in seeing Alceste as a truly good man beset by society and betrayed by a conformist Philinte, but we do tend to regard society and the individual as inevitably in opposition in a way that is foreign to the ideas of Molière's age. Again, few people today could look on Célimène with quite the chivalrous eye of so recent a critic as Meredith. Each generation has had its own attitude to the play and its characters, with differing views of the nature of the issues involved. What remains is an abiding recognition of the play's truth to life. We are engaged, if no more deeply than in sympathetic amusement, in Alceste's dilemma; we recognize the compulsion under which he is acting if not the degree of it; the human problems have not changed fundamentally though 'atrabiliousness' is translated into 'nervous sensibility', and misanthropy has become despair of the rationality of existence itself: vanity, affectation, and self-love are constants though their manifestations may change.

The strength of the play lies in the convincing vitality of the characters. Alceste is alive from his first salvo of irritation to his last sad acceptance of the inevitable. The verbal vehemence of the part is tremendous: the words tumble out in torrents of eloquence, precious jargon, and high-flown constructions mixed or alternating with bursts of curt dogmatic assertion and negation: the impulse comes from the depths of his neurasthenic constitution – the 'bile' alternately aroused and subsiding. There is a constant and comic conflict between this impetuous urge and the constraint of manners and decency. In this Alceste is seen at his worst with his friends, at his best with his enemies; it takes a whole scene to bring him to the flash point with Oronte, whereas with Philinte he will go off at half-cock at any time; to Arsinoé he shows a consideration born of dislike, to Célimène an impatience founded on love. That, contradictory though it may seem, is one reason why we like him. He is really sincere, hard though he would find it to be otherwise, and this is a virtue shared with only one other character: his love is a genuine passion even if it is immoderately expressed and absurd in its demands: he *is* indifferent to material considerations though he prides himself unduly upon it: he *is* free from hypocrisy, deceit, and untruthfulness, laughable though his self-deception may be. Unlike Célimène, unlike the *Marquis*, unlike Philinte, unlike anyone else in the play except Éliante he has not let sophistication atrophy his feelings. He may have a liver but he still has a heart.

Célimène is unique among Molière's women. Elsewhere they are young or old, charming or sensible, vulgar or shrewd, scheming or good – with one characteristic quality only or one or two in combination. Célimène is an epitome of woman in sophisticated society; the facets of her character are legion. She is young, beautiful, witty, intelligent, charming, wealthy, well-born, and worldly wise, the mistress of all social graces. She is in herself the plot and motivation of the play. The heart of the action lies in the revelation of her character and Alceste's progress towards acceptance of what follows from it. We see her wit and intelligence in action, her charm exercised, her *médisance* fully displayed: we are shown the deadly weapons she can use when she chooses; finally we see the coquette overreach herself, worldly wisdom unmasked, the essential woman revealed, loveless, unloving, unlovable, and having encountered her rival we know what she herself will become. She is the justification of Alceste's misanthropy, the expression of Molière's own. How then, it may be asked, can the play be regarded as comic, how can such a spectacle be tolerable? Because *we* are kept aware from the first of Célimène's limitations: we are, as it were, forewarned not to share Alceste's illusions; his extravagance keeps us detached as well as amused; it prevents our becoming unduly involved. We know, and are never long allowed to forget, the incompatibilities which are inherent in Célimène and Alceste. In the end, when they go their several ways, we know that they have not, in any real sense, ever met. Alceste is wrapped up in his own private fantasy, Célimène in the display of her characteristic propensities. Of the others only Philinte is completely observed. Set in intimacy with, but in contrast to, Alceste, fundamentally different in his emotional make-up and attitude to life, he provides the counterpoint to Alceste's major theme. For him life is as easy as it is hard for Alceste, society as tolerable (in spite of his disclaimer) as for his friend it is detestable. Yet they are indissolubly linked – even the end of the play does not separate them – in a union that transcends the immediately dramatic relationship, or the parallel in real life of Swift, say, and Dr Delany. They are the conforming protesting elements which are at war in every man of sensibility who has to find a *modus vivendi* with society. Alceste is, one suspects, a near relation to the irascible Molière, absorbed in the business of producing his play, whom we see self-portrayed in *L'Impromptu de Versailles*, but Molière the court chamberlain, the purveyor of royal entertainments, the adroit courtier who penned the third Petition on Tartuffe, must have had much in common with Philinte.

Arsinoé is as clearly observed in hatred as Éliante in love, but neither is revealed in the round: the three *marquis* – Oronte, Acaste, and Clitandre – are individually no more than variations on the theme of self-love; together they are the chorus of the external world. Though the secondary characters are brilliantly observed, they are not allowed to detract from the attention which is concentrated on the two great protagonists – and of them, Célimène, necessary and central though she may be to the action, gives place to Alceste. The play is true to its title and when Alceste's erratic but inevitable progress towards the acceptance of reality ends, when he sees at last that he is 'not destined for such a union', the play is done. It is the most perfect of *dénouements*, the most natural, the most inevitable: there is no need for contrivance or eloquence or music at the close: Célimène and her counterparts have taken their leave one by one; Éliante and Philinte are in themselves of no particular concern: we have seen all that there is to see and we too can go.

TARTUFFE

Molière presented his new comedy *Tartuffe* in May 1664 before the King at Versailles as one of a series of plays, ballets, and spectacular diversions extending over several days. Louis was twenty-six years of age, only recently emancipated from the political tutelage of Mazarin and the restraining influence of his mother. At that moment he was passionately involved with Louise de la Vallière, in whose honour (with the Queen and the Queen Mother also present) the celebrations were being held. A play which made fun of bigotry and hypocrisy may well have been *à propos*: it is even possible that the theme was suggested by him.

The play then performed was not *Tartuffe* as we know it: probably it was a cruder, more purely farcical version in three acts only. From Molière's own account it appears that the play underwent revision to make it less offensive to religious susceptibilities. That revision was expedient is clear from the fact that though the King was said to approve of the original play he did not consider it suitable for public performance. It seems possible that it did not amuse the Queen Mother. If she did in fact disapprove, Louis' long hesitation in authorizing public performance of the play would be more explicable. What is beyond doubt is that *Tartuffe* offended the powerful and secret society – *La Compagnie du Saint-Sacrament*. That Molière had directly attacked them seems unlikely, particularly in a play written for a frivolous occasion. He may not even have known of their existence as an organization. On the other hand, he would know them as individuals. It is certain that people who took a prominent part in resistance to the play were members of the Company.

The long period – no less than five years – during which his play lay under proscription was one of desperate anxiety for its author and his company. It meant an immediate, constant, and crippling loss of money. New plays were essential for the relatively limited audiences of Paris and the Court. Molière depended directly, if not absolutely, on royal favour – any suggestion of equivocal attitude on the part of the King affected his prestige and threatened the very survival of his theatre. Moreover, on certain issues which arise in *Tartuffe* Molière seems to have some considerable degree of personal engagement. The tone of the play, the prefaces, and the first two petitions taken with that of parts of *Dom Juan* is too markedly embittered when prudery and hypocrisy are in question to leave much room for doubt that the author was at odds with particular prudes and hypocrites as well as those vices in general. There is a carry over of the same feeling even into the more calm and assured pages of *The Misanthrope*. Hypocrites who get on by devious means are the enemies of Alceste. Arsinoé, it has been suggested already, was not drawn dispassionately. It may be that *Tartuffe* was a miscalculation of some kind, that Molière did not realize himself, at the outset, how hard it hit the forces opposed to him, or the degree in which it could offend truly religious people and not merely those who paraded their piety (or how hard discrimination is in these matters): alternatively, he may have misunderstood the King's attitude, or it may in fact have been equivocal. The desperation with which Molière conducted the defence of his play, the wonderful relief on the day of 'its resurrection' are shown in the three petitions. Readers will judge for themselves whether he seems to protest perhaps overmuch.

The play as we know it bears signs of its vicissitudes. Act II is thought to be almost entirely a later interpolation with perhaps much of Act V; Act I shows the marks of a reshaping in speeches transferred to Toinette from Cléante without much attempt to suit them to character. Yet in spite of revision* there are passages which still retain sufficient edge to make one understand why the play provoked such resentment. Molière says that, in deference to protests, he made clear that his Tartuffe was a man of the world, that he dressed him as such, and made his own intentions quite clear, but he still allows Tartuffe to voice deadly sophistries which closely accord with views attributed if not to the Church itself to important sections within it. It has been suggested that in the original version Tartuffe was a priest: others have taken the view that Molière dare not in that age have put a priest on the stage,

---

* Or because of it? Did Molière while pruning the play also heighten the effect of certain speeches to express the bitterness which suppression had engendered?

but the reference to 'Men of our sort' who 'burn with discreeter fires' whose 'secrets are for ever sure' who 'to those who trust us' offer 'love without scandal, satisfaction without fear' would have greater point if the speaker were at least in minor orders. In so far as it might refer merely to the more hypocritical among men of the world it is less effective.* Moreover, if the play is to be regarded, as Molière claims it is, as a scourge of public vice, it is a defect that Tartuffe is revealed in the end as so inveterate and thorough-going a scoundrel. The satire on hypocrisy would be more effective if the hypocrites were what Molière alleges them to be – securely ensconced in society rather than adventurers such as Tartuffe turns out to be.

All such considerations, however, are concerned with the play as read. In the theatre its impact is immediately comic. Tartuffe himself is a titanic creation, one who makes our own 'Heap of Infamy' seem by comparison a mere cringing shadow. He is comic in the contrast between his sensuality and his ascetic pretensions, in the extremes of his arrogance as moralist and in his subjection as lover, in his perversion of virtuous maxims to selfish ends, but he is dominating, menacing, larger than life, comic but hateful. It takes a *deus ex machina* to remove him. Molière in his preface justly says that he makes his villain unmistakable, but a criticism of the play which was made then and is still made is that he makes 'the good man whom he opposes to him' ridiculous. It is a point to which Molière does not reply – perhaps because he considers Cléante made sufficient answer in the play. For him, as for Montaigne whom Cléante paraphrases, even virtue, if we embrace it with an over-greedy and violent desire, may become harmful. Over-greedy and violent embrace is a good definition of Orgon's piety; it is as self-centred or self-indulgent as Alceste's love or Argan's hypochondria or Don Juan's libertinism. It was no aberration, but consistent with his obsession that he should sacrifice wife, daughter and possessions to indulge it.

The play in its final form was played for the first time at the *Palais Royal*, Molière's own theatre, in February 1669. It had an

* It would of course involve a difficulty in so far as the proposed marriage with Mariane is concerned – but this may well have been a late interpolation.

immediate and prodigious success, running for twenty-eight successive performances, and it continued to be the most frequently performed and remunerative of Molière's plays in his lifetime and afterwards.

THE IMAGINARY INVALID

Tartuffe and *The Misanthrope* mark the peak of Molière's achievement. He never surpassed them, but in the seven years between *The Misanthrope* and *The Imaginary Invalid* he produced no less than fourteen plays and they include some of his best and most characteristic work. Among them none, unless it be *The Would-be Gentleman*, is more joyous, more expressive of his ebullient energy, his mingled compassion and delight in the spectacle of human frailty and folly than this last play, born of his own suffering, and produced when he must have been aware that his illness was mortal. Three years earlier Molière had been lampooned in a work, *Élomire Hypochondre*, which accused him specifically of thinking he was in the throes of consumption, whereas in fact his illness was imaginary. Perhaps he now took his enemies at their word; perhaps he was taking arms against his own troubles to end them in laughter. Certainly the play deals with his own dilemma. Nothing was ever more tragically true to life. Argan is faithful to fact and to fantasy. He is what every man who has been in the grip of major illness knows himself to be in greater or less measure; between dire suffering and hypochondria there is the narrowest of boundaries. What is unique, passing belief almost, in this play is the unflagging, unconquerable gaiety with which he turns his own condition to the same comic account as he had already done the foibles of others. If Molière is without mercy on doctors, he is no less ruthless with patients, and Argan is no less the typical patient because his ills are so largely imaginary. The theme of doctor and patient is one which he inherited from traditional farce; he had already used it on many occasions: here for the first time it provides the plot and material of a major play and a great character study. Argan is in the line of Molière's finest creations. He is far more than a type of his obsession, worlds away from the dupes of the early farces. Though we see him revealed in a series of farcical relationships – with himself (or his other self), his servant, his daughter, his wife, his doctor, it is clear that he is no fool apart from his foible: he engages our sympathy. The parallel with *The Would-be Gentleman* is close. It would seem that Molière, here as there, felt the conventions of comedy, even farcical comedy, too narrow; that he found that the theme released stores of imaginative energy which could only be fully expressed by calling on the sister muses of music and dancing. The play is far less a thing than he intended or achieved if it is treated only as a farcical comedy. It is a *comédie-ballet*, a form of art which was Molière's own, his development of theatre in its fullest and most popular sense. In its pure form it did not survive him: something of what he intended may be experienced in opera, and in musicals and spectacular revue, but his solution of the problem of fusing allied but separate arts had the advantage that it did not necessarily require actors who could sing, singers who could act, or dancers with any obligations other than to their own art. The most perfect realization of comedy-ballet is *The Would-be Gentleman*, where the interludes of music and dancing arise naturally from the scenes they succeed and link together. In *The Imaginary Invalid* the relevance of the interludes is less obvious and indeed it is commonly assumed that the play is sufficiently presented and Molière's intention achieved if they are omitted – provided there is some kind of burlesque finale. Even the *pastorale* in Act II rarely receives adequate musical treatment, though it is clear from its quality (in spite of Cléante's disclaimer) that Molière intended it to be perfect of its kind. The first interlude, an early example of Italianate opera in miniature, is beautifully conceived in both dramatic and musical terms. Charpentier's score is delightful. Moreover, apart from their value as entertainment in themselves the interludes, with their emphasis on the transience of love, youth, and beauty, add a commentary on the theme of the play. They remind us that whatever unnatural restrictions the Argans of the world may impose the senses will not be denied.

> *Ah, follow love's pleasures!*
> *Ah, follow love's pleasures*
> *Its delights are delicious*
> *Though its trials be hard.*

The burlesque finale sweeps the play along to a triumphant conclusion. When played as Molière conceived it, as a comedy mingled with music and dancing, the work leaves the audience with an impression of unmixed delight. Profoundly serious though its implications may be, Molière presented it as entertainment and herein lies its lasting quality. It is theatrical in the widest and fullest sense, fresh, vivid, brilliant, and brimming with life, an example, a reminder and justification of that theatre which Yeats postulates in the passage quoted at the front of this volume.

THE LANGUAGE AND STYLE OF THE PLAYS

The outstanding characteristic of Molière's style is its vigour. Reference has been made to Alceste's verbal energy, but the same quality pervades his work as a whole. Sganarelle, for example, in *A Doctor in Spite of Himself*, is as loquacious as Alceste is eloquent, and his loquacity drives the farce along as Alceste's outpourings sustain the impetus of the greater play. In *The Imaginary Invalid*, Toinette provides, in the direct language of the people, a continuous commentary of common sense, derisory of self-indulgence, sentiment, self-interest, and pretentiousness as personified and revealed in Argan, Angélique, Béline, and the Diafoiruses.

With rare exceptions, due usually to external factors, as in the first act of *Tartuffe*, Molière's characters speak the language peculiar and appropriate to them. The nobility, as represented in *The Misanthrope*, use the contemporary language of preciosity, but they resort also, as such people do in real life, to current colloquial forms. Acaste, for example, explains in terms of pure preciosity that others may *burn* for unyielding *beauties*, *languish* at their feet, submit to their *rigours* with *constancy* . . . seek to obtain by assiduous courtship the *favours* they don't get and don't even deserve, but when he puts his own case he resorts to metaphors of the market place – 'Men of my stamp . . . are not given to giving their love *upon trust*, *doing* all the *paying* themselves . . . we have our *value* . . . and to keep the *scales* even there should be *give* and *take* on both sides.'

The effects of alternations of elevation of diction and preciosity of vocabulary (when the socially becoming emotions are in question, i.e. love and courage) with directness, not to say rudeness, as real nature will out, may at times seem incongruous but they are true to life, to character, and to comedy. Célimène is more vigorous than ladylike when she says of Bélise (literally – not as translated) 'one has to sweat all the time to find something to say to her'. Her first reference to Arsinoé. 'What does the woman want with me?', is not the language of aristocratic condescension but of brutal reality between equals – the mask of social convention being removed. The *bourgeois* characters speak a straightforward, colloquial French with occasional vulgarities or homely touches, swift-moving and highly effective for stage purposes.

This spare forceful speech may have been the direct expression of Molière's own nervous energy but it is a language wonderfully appropriate to farce and farcical comedy where so much depends on the immediate impact of the words, on a maintenance of tension, and, above all, on pace.

In the verse plays Molière uses metre and rhyme to accentuate the rhythmical and musical qualities of the speech, to give the effect of brilliance appropriate to the scene, as in *The Misanthrope*, and to provide a witty, ironic, or comic counterpoint to the sentiments expressed. Much of this is inevitably lost in a prose translation and it is small consolation that it is possible to eliminate some of the minor but recurring tautologies, the odd words which are put in to rhyme or to eke out the line. The effect of translation, in *The Misanthrope* in particular, is to make the speech more direct than in the original, the more so since much of the preciosity has no tolerable modern equivalent. What one has sought to do is to preserve the rhetorical line of the speeches, the sense of mounting rhythms, of successions of phrase upon phrase, sentence on sentence (not always or necessarily wholly coherent when Alceste is the speaker), the exciting theatrical eloquence characteristic of the classical French theatre. In *Tartuffe* the transfer to prose may reveal, more than one would wish, a certain overweighting of the rhetoric, some failure in Molière's usually clear definition of character by speech, and some repetition due no doubt to the reshaping of Acts III and IV.

Molière was much criticized in his own age for his neologisms, his so-called barbarities of style, and his slip-shod constructions. The short answer, if answer is needed, is that he was not writing to be read or considered at leisure on the page. Printing was still primarily a means of protecting the author's rights in the play. His was a language to be spoken and heard in the theatre. Moreover, as he often mentions himself, he worked under conditions characteristic of the theatre – that is, in haste and not as he wished but as he was commissioned. Furthermore, the critical view of anything new in vocabulary or construction so characteristic of literary and academic France tends inevitably to carry less weight in the theatre and particularly in comedy, which is and must remain, if it is to survive, a popular art. Molière did not hesitate to introduce or invent new words or to give old words new meanings. His sense of fun comes out in nonsense and in deformations of language, in dialect and provincialisms, in the mock Turkish of *The Sicilian* and the bogus Latinity of *The Imaginary Invalid*. Some things he never aspired to. He was a skilled versifier, a poet in his attitude to life, in his conception and management of his themes, but he does not write poetry. There is none of the play of imagery and fancy which gives an additional dimension to Shakespearean comedy, nor, at the other extreme, does he seek to achieve the distillation of feeling through words which distinguishes Racinian tragedy. His style has nothing of the elaborated brilliance or the deliberate wit which is the mark of Congreve, Sheridan, or Wilde. His characters achieve few *bons mots* and none which are not essential to the revelation of character.

THE MUSIC OF THE COMEDY-BALLETS

The music of the two comedy-ballets is, for the most part, extant and available in print. That of *The Sicilian*, as for all Molière's plays except *The Imaginary Invalid*, was composed by Jean Baptiste Lully. The collaboration of dramatist and composer was of the closest and the results most felicitous; the styles of play and music are perfectly attuned. A piano transcription by Schaeffner from the original notation by Floridor is included in Vol. v of the Payot edition of Molière's collected works (Paris 1929). It includes the music for the second interlude, i.e. the dance of the slaves, Hali's song, Don Pedro's reply, and the dance of the Moors only. Another transcription by Sauzay, published by Firmin-Didot (Paris 1881), includes the *Pastorale* from the first scene of the play with the so-called second interlude mentioned above. Music for the finale and possibly an introduction may still exist but there appears to be no record of publication.

By the time of *The Imaginary Invalid* Molière's relations with his colleague had deteriorated. Lully was using his growing influence with the King to obtain a monopoly of performance not only of all music he had composed but of the words written for it. Furthermore, he was granted the power to limit the number of musicians to be employed in any performances but his own. Molière therefore turned to a young Frenchman, Marc Antoine Charpentier (1634–1702). The music he wrote for the play is available in print with one minor exception, though in a rather scattered form. That for the first of the two alternative Prologues is published by Durand (Paris 1907) in a piano transcription by Büsser under the title of *La Couronne des Fleurs*. The music for the play proper (excepting only the First Interlude but including Overture, Pastorale in Act II, songs and dances of the Second Interlude, and the burlesque Finale) edited by Saint Saëns is also published by Durand (Paris 1952). Music for the First Interlude transcribed and edited by Tiersot was published by Heugel under the title of *Polichinelle* (Paris 1925). Because the music of Charpentier was not preserved by Floridor it was long overlooked and neglected. Other music was written in the eighteenth and nineteenth centuries and is still often used instead of that originally commissioned. Charpentier's music has not the immediate appeal of Lully's but it is beautiful of its kind and of the kind which Molière intended. One can say from experience that it repays the trouble of seeking it out.

The text used as the basis for translation is that prepared by Michaut for the *Collection Nationale des Classiques Français* and published by the Imprimerie Nationale in 1947.

The plays as originally published observed the convention still respected in French editions and most English translations of sub-division into scenes defined by entrance and exit of a principal character. This serves no purpose now except for reference and it has been abandoned here in favour of conventional division into acts.

My thanks are due to Dr W. T. Gairdner for help and advice at all stages of this translation and to Dr Edward Allam for his version of the Italian songs in the First Interlude of *The Imaginary Invalid*.

J.W.

The Misanthrope

LE MISANTHROPE

CHARACTERS IN THE PLAY

ALCESTE, in love with Célimène
PHILINTE, his friend
ORONTE, in love with Célimène
CÉLIMÈNE, Alceste's beloved
ÉLIANTE, cousin of Célimène
ARSINOÉ, friend of Célimène
ACASTE }
CLITANDRE } Marquises
BASQUE, Célimène's manservant
DU BOIS, Alceste's manservant
OFFICER OF THE MARSHALS OF FRANCE

Scene: Célimène's house in Paris

Act One

PHILINTE, ALCESTE

PHILINTE. What is it? What's the matter?

ALCESTE. Oh, please go away.

PHILINTE. But – I ask you once again what fantastic idea . . .

ALCESTE. Let me alone, I tell you, and get out of my sight.

PHILINTE. You might at least hear what people have to say without getting annoyed.

ALCESTE. I *will* get annoyed and I *won't* hear a word.

PHILINTE. I don't understand you when these sudden fits of temper come over you. Friends as we are, I'm one of the first . . .

ALCESTE. I'm your friend? Get that out of your head! Until now I have professed myself such, but after what I have just seen of you I do so no longer. I'll have no share in a corrupted affection.

PHILINTE. You consider I'm really to blame then, Alceste?

ALCESTE. You ought to be mortally ashamed of yourself. What you did was beyond all possible excuse, absolutely shocking to any honourable man. I see you loading a fellow with every mark of affection, professing the tenderest concern for his welfare, overwhelming him with assurances, protestations, and offers of service and when he's gone and I ask who he is – you can scarcely tell me his name! Your enthusiasm dies with your parting. Once we are alone you show that you care nothing about him. Gad! What a base, degrading, infamous thing it is to stoop to betraying one's integrity like that. If ever I had had the misfortune to do such a thing I'd go and hang myself on the spot in sheer self-disgust.

PHILINTE. Well, personally, I don't see that it's a hanging matter, so I'll ask you to be good enough to allow me to mitigate your sentence and not hang myself this time, if you don't mind.

ALCESTE. Oh! It's no occasion for joking!

PHILINTE. Seriously then, what do you expect one to do?

ALCESTE. I expect you to be sincere and as an honourable man never to utter a single word that you don't really mean.

PHILINTE. But when a fellow comes along and shows such pleasure in seeing you, surely you must repay him in kind, respond to his enthusiasm as far as you can, return offer for offer, exchange vow for vow?

ALCESTE. No! I can't bear these despicable mannerisms that so many of your men of fashion put on. There's nothing I hate more than the contortions of these protestation mongers, these affable exchangers of fatuous greetings, polite mouthers of meaningless speeches – who bandy civilities with all comers and treat everyone, blockhead and man of sense and discernment, alike. What satisfaction can there be in having a man express his consideration for you, profess friendship, faith, affection, esteem, and praise you up to the skies when he'll hasten to do as much for the first worthless scoundrel he comes across? No, No! No man with any self-respect wants that sort of debased and worthless esteem. There's precious little satisfaction in the most glorious of reputations if one finds that one has to share it with the whole universe. Esteem must be founded on some sort of preference. Bestow it on everybody and it ceases to have any meaning at all. Surrender to the foolish manners of the age and, by Gad, you are no friend of mine! I spurn the all-embracing, undiscriminating affection which makes no distinction of merit. I want to be singled out and, to put it bluntly, the friend of all mankind is not my line at all.

PHILINTE. But surely, as a man of the world one must observe such outward forms of civility as use and custom demand.

ALCESTE. No, I tell you! We should have no mercy whatever on such shameful traffic in simulated friendship. I want us to be men and say what we really mean on all occasions. Let us speak straight from the heart and not conceal our feelings under a mask of vain compliment.

PHILINTE. But surely there are circumstances in which complete frankness would be ridiculous or intolerable. With all due respect to these austere standards of yours there *are* times when it's well to conceal what one really feels. Would it be right and proper to go round telling people just what one thinks of them? Supposing there's a person one dislikes or finds disagreeable, is one to tell him so?

ALCESTE. Yes!

PHILINTE. So you would tell old Amelia how ill it becomes her to pose as a beauty at her time of life? How disgusting it is to see her painting and powdering as she does?

ALCESTE. Undoubtedly!

PHILINTE. And Dorilas, what a bore he is! that there isn't a single person at court who isn't tired of hearing him tell of his martial deeds and the glories of his family?

ALCESTE. Certainly!

PHILINTE. You are joking!

ALCESTE. Not in the least! This is an issue on which I'll spare no one. I have seen and suffered too much. Court and city alike provoke me to fury. It fills me with depression – reduces me to utter despair to see men living as they do. I meet with nothing but base flattery, injustice, selfishness, treachery, villainy everywhere. I can bear it no longer. It infuriates me. I mean to fling my gauntlet in the face of the whole human race!

PHILINTE. This philosophic rage is a bit overdone. It makes me laugh to see you in these gloomy fits of yours. I always think that – brought up together as we were – we are like the brothers in *The School for Husbands* whose . . .

ALCESTE. Oh! For goodness sake spare me your futile comparisons!

PHILINTE. No, seriously, give up these violent tirades. The world won't change its ways for anything you may do. And since you're so fond of frankness, let me tell you plainly that this foible of yours makes you a general laughing stock. You just make yourself look ridiculous by getting so incensed against the manners of the age.

ALCESTE. Egad! So much the better! So much the better!

That's all I ask. It's a good sign and I welcome it, I find mankind so odious that I should hate to have it approve of me.

PHILINTE. You are very hard on human nature!

ALCESTE. Yes, I am coming to loathe it.

PHILINTE. And are all poor mortals without exception to be included in this aversion? Isn't there a single living creature . . .

ALCESTE. No. It's universal. I hate all mankind, some because they are wicked and perverse, others because they tolerate wickedness – because they don't show the unrelenting detestation that virtue owes to vice. Look what inexcusable indulgence people extend to the arrant scoundrel I'm at law with! The rogue's plain to be seen beneath the mask! Everyone knows what he is! He may turn up his eyes and assume the accents of humility but he only imposes on strangers. We know that the despicable cur has got on in the world by the dirtiest of means, that his dazzling success is a reproach to true merit and makes virtue blush; whatever shameful honours may be paid to him in public no one really respects him. Call him an infamous rogue, a damnable scoundrel, and all the world agrees! No one will contradict you – and yet his cringing hypocrisy gains him acceptance everywhere. People receive him; they smile on him and he worms his way in everywhere. If there's a job to be canvassed you'll see him triumph and better men passed by. Gad! It breaks my heart to see how men compound with vice! There are times when a sudden longing comes over me to seek some solitary place and flee the approach of men.

PHILINTE. Good Lord! Let us worry less about the manners of the age and make more allowance for human nature. Let us judge it less severely and look more kindly on its faults. What is needed in society is an accommodating virtue. It's wrong to be too high principled. True reason lies in shunning all extremes; we should be wise in moderation. This rigorous passion for the antique virtues runs counter to the age and customary usage. It demands too much perfection of mere mortals. We need to move with the times and not be too inflexible, and it's the height of folly to take upon oneself the burden of the world's correction. I notice, as you do, a hundred times a day, things which could to advantage be done differently, but whatever I happen to see I don't show my irritation openly, as you do. I take men as they are, school myself to bear with what they do, and, in my opinion, my self-possession is no less philosophical than your intemperate spleen.

ALCESTE. And can nothing disturb this famous self-possession of yours, most rational of philosophers? Suppose a friend betrayed you, suppose someone plotted to lay hands on your estate, or endeavoured to besmirch your reputation – would you regard it all with equanimity?

PHILINTE. Yes, I look upon these faults which you are so concerned about as defects inseparable from human nature: it disturbs me no more to find men base, unjust, or selfish than to see apes mischievous, wolves savage, or the vulture ravenous for its prey.

ALCESTE. So I am to see myself betrayed, torn to pieces, robbed with never a . . . Gad! Such arguments are so futile, I'll talk no more!

PHILINTE. Upon my word! You'd do better to be silent. Rail less against your adversary and give some attention to your lawsuit.

ALCESTE. I'll do no such thing. On that my mind's made up.

PHILINTE. What influence do you intend to bring to bear upon your behalf?*

ALCESTE. Reason, Justice, the rightness of my cause.

PHILINTE. Won't you call on any of the judges then?

ALCESTE. No! Is my cause dubious or unjust?

PHILINTE. No, but your opponent's intrigue can do you harm and . . .

ALCESTE. No. I'm determined not to move a single step. Either I'm in the right or in the wrong.

* Literally 'who is to solicit' – i.e. visit the judge as was customary at the time.

PHILINTE. I wouldn't count on that.

ALCESTE. I won't budge an inch.

PHILINTE. You have a powerful adversary. He can bring great influence to bear . . .

ALCESTE. No matter.

PHILINTE. You may find you are mistaken.

ALCESTE. So be it. I'll await the outcome.

PHILINTE. But . . .

ALCESTE. I shall have the pleasure of losing my case.

PHILINTE. But surely . . .

ALCESTE. This case will show me whether people can really have the effrontery, be so wicked, so villainous, so corrupt, as to do me injustice openly before the eyes of all the world.

PHILINTE. What a man!

ALCESTE. I should be prepared to lose my case, whatever it cost me, to have the satisfaction of putting that to the test.

PHILINTE. Really, Alceste, people would laugh if they heard you talk like that.

ALCESTE. So much the worse for them.

PHILINTE. But do you find this rectitude that you are always insisting on, this absolute integrity you set such store by, in the lady you are in love with? It astonishes me that although you are so much at odds, as it seems, with the whole human race, you have found, in spite of everything that makes it odious to you, one member of it who has power to charm you. What surprises me still more is the strange choice on which your affections have come to rest. Éliante is a model of sincerity and she has some inclination for you; the virtuous Arsinoé looks on you with a most tender regard, but you refuse your heart to them for Célimène to toy with it – Célimène whose coquetry and love of scandal seem to accord so closely with the manners of the age. How does it come about that, hating these characteristics as you do, you can tolerate their embodiment in her? Are they no longer faults when they appear in so fair a shape? Don't you see them or do you find excuses for them?

ALCESTE. No. My love for this young widow doesn't blind

me to her faults. Notwithstanding the passion she inspires in me I'm the first to see and to condemn them. And yet, do what I may, I have to confess my frailty. She bewitches me. In vain I see her faults: vainly I condemn them. She makes me love her in spite of myself. Her charms are irresistible and I'm sure my love will reclaim her from these follies of the age.

PHILINTE. If you do that you will indeed do much! You think that she loves you then?

ALCESTE. Heavens, yes! I shouldn't love her if I didn't think so.

PHILINTE. But if she has made clear that she loves you how does it come about that you are so concerned about your rivals?

ALCESTE. Because true love demands an undivided affection in return. That's my sole purpose in coming here now – to open my heart to her on that very issue.

PHILINTE. Well, if the decision rested with me it would be her cousin Éliante I should aspire to. She loves you and her affection is constant and sincere. She would be a far better and more suitable choice for you.

ALCESTE. That's true. So the voice of reason tells me every day. But then love's not ruled by reason.

PHILINTE. I tremble for your love. Your hopes may well prove . . .

[*Enter* ORONTE.]

ORONTE. I learned downstairs that Éliante had gone out shopping and Célimène as well but as they told me that you were here I came up to inform you, Sir, in all sincerity, of the extraordinarily high opinion I have of you and the ardent desire I have long felt to be numbered among your friends. Yes, I dearly love to accord recognition where it is due, Sir, and I long to be united with you in the bonds of friendship. I assume that the sincere friendship of a man of my rank and quality is not to be rejected.

[*During this speech* ALCESTE *appears completely abstracted and seems not to notice that* ORONTE *is addressing him.*]

ORONTE. It is to you, Sir, if you please, that my remarks are addressed.

ALCESTE. To me, Sir?

ORONTE. To you, Sir. Have you any objection?

ALCESTE. Not in the least but I'm very much surprised. I wasn't expecting such an honour.

ORONTE. The fact, Sir, that I hold you in such esteem should not surprise you. Your claims are universally acknowledged.

ALCESTE. Sir...

ORONTE. You enjoy a reputation without parallel in this country.

ALCESTE. Sir...

ORONTE. Yes, in my opinion you are a man of quite outstanding distinction.

ALCESTE. Sir...

ORONTE. May it be the last word I ever utter if I'm not speaking the truth! And now – permit me, Sir, in confirmation of my sentiments, to embrace you most heartily and solicit a place in your affection. Your hand on it, if you please! You promise me your friendship?

ALCESTE. Sir...

ORONTE. What! You decline?

ALCESTE. Sir, you do me too much honour, but friendship is not quite so simple a matter. Indeed it's a profanation of the word to use it on every occasion. It is a relationship which should spring from discerning and deliberate choice. We should be better acquainted before we commit ourselves. Our dispositions may well be such that we should repent of the bargain.

ORONTE. By Jove! Spoken like a man of sense and I admire you all the more for it. Let us then leave it to time to establish this felicitous relationship between us. Meanwhile I am entirely at your service. If there is anything I can do for you at court I am known to cut some figure with His Majesty, I have his ear and he treats me with the greatest possible consideration. Once again then – count on me entirely. And now, since you are a man of taste and discrimination, may I venture to show you, by way of establishing our relationship, a sonnet I composed a little while ago? I want your opinion as to whether I should do well to publish it.

ALCESTE. Sir, I'm quite the wrong person to give a decision on such a matter. Pray be good enough to excuse me!

ORONTE. But why?

ALCESTE. It's a failing on my part that I tend to be a little more frank in these things than I should.

ORONTE. But that's what I want! I should have cause for complaint if, when I had gone so far as to ask you to give me your honest opinion, you failed to do so or kept anything back from me.

ALCESTE. Well then, I agree, since you will have it so.

ORONTE [*reading*]. . . . 'Sonnet' . . . it is a sonnet. 'Hope . . .' the lady in question has deigned to give some encouragement to my hopes . . . 'Hope . . .' There's nothing at all elaborate about it – just a few simple lines . . . tender and full of feeling. [*He looks at* ALCESTE *at each pause.*]

ALCESTE. We shall see.

ORONTE. 'Hope . . .' I don't know if you'll consider the style sufficiently easy and polished or whether the choice of words will please you –

ALCESTE. We shall see, Sir.

ORONTE. What's more you ought to know that I didn't spend more than a quarter of an hour on it.

ALCESTE. Let us hear it, Sir. The time spent on it is quite immaterial.

ORONTE. 'Hope doth assuage 'tis true, one's pain
And for a while brings consolation
But, Phyllis, wherein lies the gain
If Hope be followed by Frustration?'

PHILINTE. A charming beginning!

ALCESTE [*aside*]. What! You have the audacity to admire that!

ORONTE. 'Some kindness once you did afford;
Less would have been sufficient proffer,
Kinder had been the cruel word
If Hope was all you meant to offer.'

PHILINTE. Oh! Very nicely phrased indeed!

ALCESTE [*aside to* PHILINTE]. Vile Flatterer! How can you praise such rubbish?

ORONTE. 'Since on Eternity I needs must wait
And fruitless passion be my fate
Death now remains my one resort,
Your fond regrets afford me no comfort
Hope may beguile the heart's distress
But Hope deferred begets blank hopelessness.'

PHILINTE. Oh! A lovely ending – charming! Admirable!

ALCESTE. A plague on your ending. The devil take such pestilent nonsense. *You* need ending – or mending!

PHILINTE. I never heard lines more gracefully turned.

ALCESTE [*aside*]. Good Lord!

ORONTE [*to* PHILINTE]. You flatter me Sir. Perhaps you think . . .

PHILINTE. No, I'm not flattering you in the least.

ALCESTE [*aside to* PHILINTE]. Then what *are* you doing, you scoundrel?

ORONTE [*to* ALCESTE]. And now, Sir, you remember what we agreed. Please give me your candid opinion.

ALCESTE. Well, Sir – it's always a delicate matter . . . you see when it comes to questions of taste we all like to be flattered . . . but as I was saying only the other day to a person whose name I won't mention, on looking over some lines he had composed, a gentleman should always be at pains to control that itch for scribbling to which we are so prone; one should keep a tight rein on any desire one may have to advertise such trivial diversions or in eagerness to display one's work one runs a risk of cutting a pretty poor sort of figure.

ORONTE. Are you trying to tell me that I was wrong in wanting to . . .

ALCESTE. No, I'm not saying that . . . but what I went on to tell him was how deadly the effect of pedestrian writing can be, how it only needs a foible of that sort to ruin a man's reputation and though one may have a hundred good qualities, people only notice one's weaknesses.

ORONTE. Are you saying there's something wrong with my sonnet?

ALCESTE. No, I'm not saying that but . . . to put him off writing I pointed out the harm this sort of craving had done to some very worthy people in our own time.

ORONTE. Do I write badly? Am I to assume I resemble them?

ALCESTE. No, I'm not saying that . . . but what I *did* say to him finally was this – do you really *need* to write poetry and if so, why the deuce must you rush into print? The only people who can be excused for letting a bad book loose on the world are the poor devils who *have* to write for a living! Take my word for it, resist the temptation, conceal what you do from the public, and don't go and prejudice the honourable reputation you enjoy at the Court – however much people may urge you to do so – for the sake of receiving at the hands of some grasping printer the wretched and ridiculous title of author. That's what I tried to impress on him.

ORONTE. That's all very well. I think I understand what you mean, but may I not be told what there is in my sonnet that . . . ?

ALCESTE. Frankly – the only thing to do is to put it away and forget it. You have formed your style on bad models. The expressions you use are not natural. What's the meaning of 'and for a while brings consolation'? or 'be followed by frustration'? and 'Kinder had been the cruel word'? or 'Hope deferred begets blank hopelessness'? This figurative style people pride themselves so much on is false and meretricious. It's just play upon words – sheer affectation! It isn't a natural way of speaking at all. I find contemporary taste appalling in this respect. Our ancestors, crude and unpolished as they were, did very much better. I prefer to any of the stuff people admire so much nowadays an old ballad such as . . .

> If King Henry said to me
> 'Here's Paris, my rich town and fair;
> All this and more I'll give to thee

> Gin thou wilt leave thy dear,'
> I'd up and say to King Henry
> 'Keep thou thy gold and gear!
> What care I for thy fair Paris
> Gin I am with my dear?'

The rimes may be crude and the style old-fashioned but don't you see how much better it is than all this trumpery stuff that's so revolting to one's common sense? Don't you feel that this is the voice of true love speaking?

> If King Henry said to me
> 'Here's Paris, my rich town and fair;
> All this and more I'll give to thee
> Gin thou wilt leave thy dear,'
> I'd up and say to King Henry
> 'Keep thou thy gold and gear!
> What care I for thy fair Paris
> Gin I am with my dear?'

That's just what a man who was really in love would say. [*To* PHILINTE *who is laughing*] Yes Sir, you may laugh, but whatever your wits and your critics may say I prefer that to the solemn flourishes and superficial polish that everyone makes such a fuss about.

ORONTE. For my part, I still maintain that my lines are excellent.

ALCESTE. You have your reasons for your opinion, but you must permit me to think otherwise.

ORONTE. It's sufficient for me that other people think well of them.

ALCESTE. Because they are skilled in dissimulation. I am not.

ORONTE. So you think you have a pretty good share of discernment?

ALCESTE. I should, if I saw anything in your verses!

ORONTE. I shall manage very well without your approval.

ALCESTE. I'm afraid you will have to.

ORONTE. I should like to see you try to compose something on the same theme.

ALCESTE. I might well have the misfortune to do equally badly, but I should take care not to show other people the result.

ORONTE. You speak with a good deal of assurance, Sir. Such self-opinion . . .

ALCESTE. I suggest, Sir, that you pursue your search for flattery elsewhere.

ORONTE. Come, my little friend . . . don't be so high and mighty.

ALCESTE. Upon my word, Sir, I shall do as I please, for all your huge . . .

PHILINTE [*coming between them*]. Now gentlemen! That's enough! Pray leave it at that!

ORONTE. Ah! I'm at fault I admit. I'll take my leave. [*To ALCESTE ironically*] I am, Sir, your most devoted.

ALCESTE [*ironically*]. And I, Sir, your most obedient.

[*Exit ORONTE.*]

PHILINTE. Well, there you are! That's where your precious sincerity has landed you! A nice awkward business you have on your hands now! I saw perfectly well that Oronte wanted to be flattered and . . .

ALCESTE. Don't talk to me!

PHILINTE. But . . .

ALCESTE. Leave me!

PHILINTE. It's too . . .

ALCESTE. Go away!

PHILINTE. If I . . .

ALCESTE. Say no more!

PHILINTE. But what . . .

ALCESTE. I won't hear a word!

PHILINTE. But . . .

ALCESTE. What, again?

PHILINTE. You insult . . .

ALCESTE. Oh God! That's enough of it. Don't follow me about [*Going*].

PHILINTE. Oh! Don't be absurd. I'm not going to leave you. [*He follows.*]

Act Two

ALCESTE. May I speak frankly, Madam? Then I'm very far from being pleased with the way you behave. I begin to find it intolerable. I can see that we shall have to break off our relationship. Yes, it would be deceiving you to tell you anything else. We shall undoubtedly come to a breach sooner or later. Even if I gave you my word to the contrary a thousand times over I shouldn't be able to stand by it.

CÉLIMÈNE. So it seems that you wished to see me home in order to scold me.

ALCESTE. I'm not scolding you but you have a way of according your affection too freely to anyone who happens to come along. You have too many admirers for ever hanging round you and I just cannot bear it.

CÉLIMÈNE. So you blame me for having admirers? Can I prevent people from finding me attractive? When they are good enough to go to the trouble of coming to see me am I to take a stick and drive them from my door?

ALCESTE. No, Madam. It's not a stick that you need – only to be less tolerant towards their advances. I know you can't help being attractive wherever you are but your attitude encourages those who fall under the spell of your glances; your indulgence to those who surrender completes the conquest your beauty began; the alluring hopes you hold out keep them dancing attendance upon you. If you were less free with your favours you would reduce the ranks of those who languish and sigh for you. You might, at any rate, tell me how your friend Clitandre comes to enjoy your favours so markedly; upon what qualifications, what sublime virtue, may one ask, is your regard for him founded? Is it the length of his little finger-nail that has won your esteem? Have you, like the rest of the fashionable world succumbed to the egregious merits of his blond periwig? Is it perhaps the wide frills at his knees or his accumulation of ribbons you find so enchanting? Has he endeared himself by the charms of his massive *Rhingrave** while playing the role of devoted slave to you? Or is it his laugh or that falsetto voice of his that has found the secret of pleasing you?

CÉLIMÈNE. How unfair of you to take umbrage on his account. You know perfectly well why I keep in with him! Can't you see that he can procure me the interest of his friends in my lawsuit as he has indeed promised to do?

ALCESTE. Resign yourself to the loss of your case. Don't try to ingratiate yourself with a man whose rivalry is so offensive to me.

CÉLIMÈNE. You are becoming jealous of the whole universe.

ALCESTE. Because the whole universe enjoys your favours.

CÉLIMÈNE. But shouldn't the very fact that I distribute my favours so widely afford some reassurance to your unquiet heart? Wouldn't you have more reason for being offended if you saw me bestowing them on one person?

ALCESTE. But I ask you – what advantage have I – whom you reproach for being so jealous – over any of them?

CÉLIMÈNE. The satisfaction of knowing that you are loved.

ALCESTE. And what reason have I to cherish any such belief?

CÉLIMÈNE. I think when I have gone so far as to tell you so, such an avowal should be sufficient.

ALCESTE. But what assurance have I that you aren't perhaps saying just as much to others at the same time?

CÉLIMÈNE. A pretty compliment from a lover, I must say! And a nice opinion you have of me! Very well! To relieve you of any such concern I here and now unsay all that I said before. Now no one can deceive you but yourself. Let that content you.

ALCESTE. Heavens above! Why do I have to love you? If I could only be heart-whole once more, how thankful I should be for the blessing! I make no secret of it – I have done

---

* Rhingrave: a kind of wide breeches much be-ribboned, originally intended for riding but at this period a fashionable extravagance so called from the supposed originator *circa* 1660.

everything I possibly can to break this cruel infatuation but so far all to no purpose. It must be for my sins that I love you as I do.

CÉLIMÈNE. Love such as yours is unique indeed!

ALCESTE. Yes. There I can defy the whole world! *My* love is beyond all imagining. No man has ever loved as I do!

CÉLIMÈNE. And you certainly have a novel way of showing it! You love people so that you can quarrel with them. The only expression you can find for your passion is in reproaches. I have never heard of a lover who grumbled and scolded as you do.

ALCESTE. But it rests entirely with you to put an end to the trouble. Let us be finished with all these contentions, I beseech you. Let us be entirely open with each other and see if we can stop . . .

[*Enter* BASQUE.]

CÉLIMÈNE. What is it?

BASQUE. Acaste is downstairs.

CÉLIMÈNE. Very well. Show him up.

ALCESTE. What! Am I never to have a word with you alone? Must you always be willing to receive people? Can you never bring yourself to say you are not at home for one single moment?

CÉLIMÈNE. Would you have me offend him?

ALCESTE. You consider people's feelings too much for my liking.

CÉLIMÈNE. He's the sort of man who would never forgive me if he knew that his presence was unwelcome.

ALCESTE. And why should that trouble you?

CÉLIMÈNE. Heavens! The goodwill of such people is important. He's one of those who have acquired, goodness knows how, the privilege of making their opinions heard in court circles. One finds them butting in to every conversation. Though they can do you no good they may do you harm. Whatever support one may have elsewhere one should never get embroiled with that noisy crowd.

ALCESTE. In short you'll always find reasons for keeping on

good terms with everyone – whoever they may be and whatever they may do. You are so careful to avoid . . .

[*Re-enter* BASQUE.]

BASQUE. Clitandre is here as well, Madam.

ALCESTE. Oh, of course, he would be! [*Makes to go.*]

CÉLIMÈNE. Where are you running off to?

ALCESTE. I'm going.

CÉLIMÈNE. Stay.

ALCESTE. Why should I?

CÉLIMÈNE. *Do* stay.

ALCESTE. I can't.

CÉLIMÈNE. *I* want you to.

ALCESTE. It's no use. These conversations only bore me. It's asking too much of me to endure them.

CÉLIMÈNE. But I want you to. I want you to!

ALCESTE. No. It's impossible.

CÉLIMÈNE. Very well then. Go! Be off! Do as you please!
[*Enter* ÉLIANTE, *followed by* CLITANDRE *and* ACASTE.]

ÉLIANTE. The two Marquises are coming up too. Did no one come to tell you?

CÉLIMÈNE. Yes. [*To* BASQUE] Chairs for the company. [*To* ALCESTE] Haven't you gone?

ALCESTE. No Madam. I intend to make you declare yourself – for their satisfaction or mine.

CÉLIMÈNE. Hush!

ALCESTE. Today you shall make clear your position.

CÉLIMÈNE. Are you out of your senses?

ALCESTE. Not a bit! You shall show where you stand.

CÉLIMÈNE. Oh!

ALCESTE. On one side or the other.

CÉLIMÈNE. Is this a joke?

ALCESTE. No, you shall make your choice. I have been patient too long.

CLITANDRE. Egad Madam! I have come straight from the Louvre. Cléonte has been making a perfect fool of himself there at the levée. Has he no friends who could in charity enlighten him as to how to behave?

CÉLIMÈNE. He certainly does himself no credit in company. His manner is always very conspicuous and when one sees him again after an interval is seems even more strange.

ACASTE. Talking of strange fellows I have just had a dose of one of the most tiresome of the lot – I mean that garrulous chap, Damon! He kept me out of my chair for an hour, if you please, and in the blazing sun too!

CÉLIMÈNE. How he *does* talk! He contrives to say nothing at the most inordinate length and I can never make any sense of what he is talking *about*. It is all just so much noise.

ÉLIANTE [*to* PHILINTE]. Not bad for a beginning. A nice way of pulling one's acquaintances to pieces!

CLITANDRE. Now what about Timante? Don't you think he's an admirable character?

CÉLIMÈNE. The complete mystery man! He throws you a distracted glance in passing for he's always so busy though he has nothing to do! Any information he has to impart is accompanied by signs and grimaces – the fuss he makes is quite overwhelming! He's for ever interrupting the conversation because he has some secret to whisper to you but there's never anything in it. He makes a sensation out of the merest trifle and everything, even his 'good morning', has to be whispered in your ear.

ACASTE. And Géralde, Madam?

CÉLIMÈNE. Oh! That pretentious bore! He can never throw off his lordly manner. He moves in none but the highest circles and never mentions anybody below the rank of Duke, Prince, or Princess. He's obsessed with rank and family and can talk of nothing but horses and hunting and dogs. He 'thees and thous' people of the most exalted position, so much so that he has forgotten the use of the ordinary forms of address.

CLITANDRE. They say he's on very good terms with Bélise.

CÉLIMÈNE. That stupid creature – she's dreary company I must say! I suffer agonies when she comes to see me. It's one continual struggle to find something to say. She's so utterly unresponsive that she just kills all conversation.

You clutch at all the usual topics in an endeavour to break down her stupid silence but it's not the least use – the fine weather or the rain, how cold it is or how hot it has been – before long you've exhausted them all and her visit, unbearable enough anyway, becomes more and more awful as it drags out its hideous length. You may ask the time and yawn twenty times over but she'll no more stir than a block of wood.

ACASTE. And what do you think of Adraste?

CÉLIMÈNE. Too conceited for words! The man's blown up with his own self importance. He has a perpetual grievance against the court because he thinks he's not sufficiently appreciated there. There's never an appointment made or a place or preferment offered that isn't an injustice to his own idea of himself.

CLITANDRE. And young Cléon? Everyone who is anybody congregates at his house nowadays. What do you say about him?

CÉLIMÈNE. That he owes his reputation to his cook. People go there for the sake of his table.

ÉLIANTE. He does go to the trouble of providing good food.

CÉLIMÈNE. Yes, if only he didn't serve up his own company with it! His stupidity takes a good deal of stomaching. To my mind it entirely spoils the entertainment he offers.

PHILINTE. Damis, his uncle is highly esteemed. What do you say about him, Madam?

CÉLIMÈNE. He's a friend of mine.

PHILINTE. I think he's a sound, sensible, fellow.

CÉLIMÈNE. Yes, but what annoys me is that he *will* be so dreadfully clever. He's so high and mighty and always so obviously trying to be witty. Since he's taken it into his head to show what a smart fellow he is there's just no suiting his taste – he's so difficult to please. He's out to find fault with everything anyone writes and thinks that to praise is beneath the dignity of a man of taste and intelligence, that to find something to criticize is evidence of learning, that only fools allow themselves to admire things or be amused, and that he demonstrates his superiority to everyone else by disapproving of all contemporary work. Even in ordinary conversation either he'll find something to cavil at or the subject will be so far beneath his notice that he'll just fold his arms and look down in pity from the height of his own wisdom on everything that anyone says.

ACASTE. Damn it! That's got him to the life.

CLITANDRE. You are wonderful at hitting people off.

ALCESTE. Ay! Stick to it, friends, like the true courtiers that you are! You spare no one. Everyone suffers in turn but let any one of them appear on the scene and you would all rush to meet him, offer him your hands in fulsome greeting, and protest your eternal devotion.

CLITANDRE. But why pick on us? If what has been said offends you – it's the lady here you should address your reproaches to.

ALCESTE. No! Confound it! I blame you. It's your laughter that encourages her to these slanderous sallies. Your wicked flattery feeds her satirical humour. She would find less satisfaction in her mockeries if you withheld your approval. Flatterers are always to blame for the vices which prevail among mankind.

PHILINTE. Why such concern for people whom you could condemn yourself for the very same reasons?

CÉLIMÈNE. But surely the gentleman must be allowed to contradict! Would you have him reduced to sharing the common opinion? Nature has endowed him with a spirit of contrariety. Isn't he to take every opportunity of displaying it? He can never agree with other people's opinions. He must always maintain the contrary view. He would think he was cutting a very ordinary figure if he were found to agree with anyone else. He's so fond of contradicting that he frequently takes up an argument against himself and opposes his own sentiments as soon as he hears other people expressing them.

ALCESTE. Ay, Madam, the laugh's on your side, there's no doubt about that! You may safely indulge your satire against me.

PHILINTE. But it is true that you are always up in arms against everything people say. You admit, yourself, to being equally intolerant, whether it's praise or blame they are offering.

ALCESTE. Ay! Confound it! Because people *are* wrong, because there's always justification for being annoyed with them, because they are invariably as misguided in their praise as they are rash in their condemnation.

CÉLIMÈNE. But . . .

ALCESTE. No, Madam, no. I'll say it if it kills me. You take a delight in things I find intolerable and it's downright wicked of these people to be encouraging the very habits they blame you for.

CLITANDRE. Well, I don't know about that. I'm bound to say I've always thought the lady perfection itself.

ACASTE. To me she's everything that's charming and graceful. If she has any faults I haven't noticed 'em.

ALCESTE. But *I* notice them and, far from shutting my eyes to them, she knows I'm at pains to reproach her with them. The greater one's love for a person the less room for flattery. The proof of true love is to be unsparing in criticism. For my part I would banish any lover so mean spirited as to submit to my opinions and feebly and obsequiously pander to my extravagances.

CÉLIMÈNE. Then if you had your way as to how lovers behaved one would have to demonstrate one's affection by adjuring all tenderness and railing at one's beloved as the supreme testimony of one's regard!

ÉLIANTE. That isn't really how love works at all. You find that a lover always justifies his own choice. He's blind to all faults. . . for him everything in the loved one is lovable. Her very blemishes he counts as perfections or contrives to find flattering names for; should she be pale it's the pale beauty of the jasmine flower; she may be swarthy enough to frighten you, but for him she's an adorable brunette; if thin, she's slender and graceful; if fat, she has a queenly dignity; the slattern, slight though her attractions may be, passes for a 'careless beauty'; let her be tall she'll have a goddess's majesty; the dwarf's compact of all the virtues under Heaven! So haughtiness appears as proper pride, cunning as cleverness, chatter as cheerfulness, and folly as good nature. The dumb preserve a decent modesty! So the true lover worships the very faults of his beloved.*

ALCESTE. Well for my part I maintain . . .

CÉLIMÈNE. Suppose we drop the subject now and take a turn in the gallery. What? Are you going, gentlemen?

CLITANDRE }
ACASTE } By no means, Madam.

ALCESTE [*to* CÉLIMÈNE]. You seem very much concerned lest they should go. [*To* CLITANDRE *and* ACASTE] Go at your leisure gentlemen, but I warn you I shall stay until you do.

ACASTE. Unless the lady is inconvenienced I can remain all day.

CLITANDRE. Provided I return for the hour of His Majesty's retiring, I have no business that need call me away.

CÉLIMÈNE [*to* ALCESTE]. You think this amusing, I suppose?

ALCESTE. Not in the least; but we'll see whether I'm the one you wish to go.

[*Enter* BASQUE.]

BASQUE [*to* ALCESTE]. There's a man would like to speak to you on business which he says admits of no delay.

ALCESTE. Tell him I have no business of such urgency.

BASQUE. He has a long pleated coat with gold braid all over it.

CÉLIMÈNE [*to* ALCESTE]. Go and see what it is or else have him come in.

ALCESTE [*to the* OFFICER *as he enters*]. Come in, Sir. What is it you want?

OFFICER. I want a word with you, Sir.

---

* The speech is a paraphrase of a passage in Lucretius's *De Natura Rerum* which Molière is said to have translated. Its dramatic justification is a little doubtful unless it be to give Éliante something to contribute to the scene.

ALCESTE. Speak up then and let me hear it.

OFFICER. The Marshals of France, whose commands I bear, require you to appear before them, Sir, immediately.

ALCESTE. Who? Me, Sir?

OFFICER. You, Sir. In person.

ALCESTE. For what purpose?

PHILINTE. It's that absurd squabble with Oronte.

CÉLIMÈNE [*to* PHILINTE]. What's this?

PHILINTE. Oronte and he had words about some trifling verses which he didn't think much of. They want to nip the quarrel in the bud.

ALCESTE. I won't stand for any miserable compromise.

PHILINTE. But you must obey the summons. Come, get ready.

ALCESTE. What sort of agreement do they intend to impose on us? Will these gentlemen condemn me to approve the lines we quarrelled about? I won't go back on what I have said. I think they are dreadful.

PHILINTE. If you would only be a little more . . .

ALCESTE. I won't budge an inch. They are execrable!

PHILINTE. You must try to be reasonable. Come along.

ALCESTE. I'll go but nothing will make me retract.

PHILINTE. Let us go and put in an appearance.

ALCESTE. Short of His Majesty's express command to approve the verses all the fuss is about I shall never cease to maintain, egad, that they are bad and that the fellow deserves to be hanged for writing such miserable stuff. [*To* CLITANDRE *and* ACASTE *who are laughing*] Confound it gentlemen! I was not aware that I was so amusing.

CÉLIMÈNE. Go quickly and obey the summons.

ALCESTE. I am going, Madam, but I shall come back immediately to finish our discussion.

Act Three

CLITANDRE, ACASTE

CLITANDRE. You seem highly pleased with yourself, my dear Marquis. Everything amuses you and you haven't a care in the world. Tell me frankly now – do you really believe that you have good reason for looking so cheerful?

ACASTE. Egad! When I examine myself closely I can't see any reason for dissatisfaction. I'm wealthy, I'm young, I come of a house which can with some reason account itself noble; by virtue of my birth and the precedence it gives me I believe there are very few posts for which I'm not well placed. As to valour – which we should, of course, put before everything else – I think I may say in all modesty that I'm known not to be wanting in that respect. I have shown that I can pursue an affair of honour with sufficient vigour and boldness. Brains I have beyond question, with good taste sufficient to pass judgement and give an opinion on everything without need of study, to sit on the stage and play the expert at first nights (occasions I dote on) and give a rousing lead to the audience at all the fine passages that deserve their applause. I'm pretty adroit, have a good carriage and good looks, particularly fine teeth, and a very fine figure: as for knowing how to dress – well, not to flatter myself unduly, I defy anyone to compete with me there. I'm as popular as any man can be, beloved of the fair sex, and stand well with His Majesty . . . with such advantages, my dear Marquis, I think a man might feel pleased with himself anywhere.

CLITANDRE. Yes, but finding easy conquests elsewhere, as you do, why is it that you sigh in vain here?

ACASTE. Me? Sigh in vain? Egad! I'm not the sort of man to put up with a woman's indifference nor am I inclined to! It's all very well for fellows who are wanting in any sort of grace or distinction whatever to burn for unyielding beauties, languish at their feet, and submit to their rigours with constancy. They may resort to sighing and tears in the endeavour to obtain by assiduous courtship the favours they don't get and don't even deserve, but men of *my* stamp, my dear Marquis, men of *my* stamp are not given to bestowing their love upon trust and doing all the paying themselves. No, No! Rare though the merits of the fair sex may be I contend that we, Heaven be praised, have our value as they have, and that it isn't reasonable that any of them should enjoy the honour of a love such as mine without it costing her anything. At least, to keep the scales even, there should be some give and take on both sides.

CLITANDRE. You think then, Marquis, that you stand pretty well here?

ACASTE. I have some grounds for thinking so.

CLITANDRE. Believe me, you should rid yourself of any such illusion. You are flattering yourself, my dear fellow – it's sheer self-deception!

ACASTE. Oh! Of course I'm flattering myself!

CLITANDRE. But what reason have you for thinking you are so fortunate?

ACASTE. I flatter myself!

CLITANDRE. On what basis are your hopes founded?

ACASTE. Self-deception!

CLITANDRE. Have you some certain proof?

ACASTE. I tell you, I deceive myself.

CLITANDRE. Has Célimène given you some secret assurance?

ACASTE. No, I'm cruelly used!

CLITANDRE. Do answer me, please!

ACASTE. I meet with nothing but rebuffs.

CLITANDRE. Oh! Have done with your foolery and tell me! What reason has she given you to hope?

ACASTE. I'm the unlucky one. You are the happy man. She detests me. One of these days I shall have to go and hang myself.

CLITANDRE. Well now, Marquis, shall we come to an understanding as to how we conduct our courtship in future? If one of us can show proof of preference in Célimène's favour, let the other give way to him as the successful suitor and so rid him of a troublesome rival.

ACASTE. Egad! Now that's talking! I heartily agree to that arrangement. But hush! Here she . . .

[*Enter* CÉLIMÈNE.]

CÉLIMÈNE. Still here?

CLITANDRE. It's love that detains us, Madam.

CÉLIMÈNE. I heard a carriage below. Do you know who it is?

CLITANDRE. No.

[*Enter* BASQUE.]

BASQUE. Arsinoé is coming up to see you, Madam.

CÉLIMÈNE. What does the woman want with me?

BASQUE. Éliante is talking to her downstairs.

CÉLIMÈNE. What can she be thinking about? Who on earth asked her to come here?

ACASTE. She has the reputation of being the most virtuous of women. She's so pious that . . .

CÉLIMÈNE. Yes, but it's all sheer hypocrisy! She's completely worldly at heart. Her sole interest is in hooking a man – so far without any success – so she just can't restrain her envy when she sees anyone else with admirers. Because her own sorry charms are ignored she's forever up in arms against the blindness of the age, trying to conceal the hideous emptiness of her existence beneath a pretence of virtue and modesty and consoling herself for her waning attractions by branding as sinful the pleasures she hasn't the chance to enjoy. But a lover would be very acceptable to the lady. She even has a fancy for Alceste and regards the attentions he pays me as an insult to her. According to her it's an act of robbery on my part! So her barely concealed spite and jealousy find vent in underhand attacks on me at every opportunity. It all seems utterly stupid to me. She's really the silliest, most tiresome . . . [*Enter* ARSINOÉ] Ah! What happy chance brings you here? I have been really worried about you.

ARSINOÉ. I have come about something I thought I had a duty to tell you.

CÉLIMÈNE. I'm so pleased to see you. [*Exeunt* CLITANDRE *and* ACASTE, *laughing.*]

ARSINOÉ. It's just as well that they've gone.

CÉLIMÈNE. Shall we sit down?

ARSINOÉ. No, there's no necessity, Madam. Since friends have a particular duty to each other in matters which may concern them most nearly, and because nothing concerns one more than one's honour and good reputation – I have come to show my friendship for you by telling you of something which touches your own honour. Yesterday I was with some extremely God-fearing people when, the conversation turning upon you, your behaviour and the sensation it causes were, unhappily, not considered commendable. The crowds of men whom you permit to visit you, your flirtations, and the scandal to which they give rise, found all too many critics and were more severely condemned than I would have wished. You may imagine which side I endeavoured to take! I did what I could to defend you and made every excuse for you on the ground that you meant no harm by such things: I offered to go bail for your goodness of heart but, you know, there *are* things which, with the best will in the world, one cannot defend. I was obliged to agree that your behaviour did bring some discredit upon you, that it created an unfortunate impression, that all sorts of unpleasant stories were going the rounds, and that, if you were so minded your whole manner of life could well be less open to criticism. Not that I really believe your virtue to be compromised. Heaven preserve me from thinking any such thing! But people are ready to seize upon the slightest shadow of misconduct and it isn't enough to live blamelessly in one's own estimation. You are, I believe Madam, too sensible not to take this advice in good part or to believe that I have any motive other than concern for your welfare.

CÉLIMÈNE. On the contrary, I'm greatly beholden to you . . . most grateful for what you have told me and, so far from taking it ill, I propose to return the favour immediately by giving *you* information which equally concerns your own reputation. Just as you showed your friendship by telling me what people were saying about me, so I in turn will follow your well meant example and tell you what they are saying of you. At a house where I was paying a call the other day I met some exceptionally virtuous people who were discussing what constituted the good life, and the conversation turning on you, Madam, your severe principles and ostentation of piety were not accounted models of behaviour: the affected gravity of your demeanour, your everlasting sermons on morals and propriety, your habit of exclaiming and pulling a face at the least semblance of indecency to which an innocently ambiguous word may give rise, your high opinion of yourself and your pitying condescension for everyone else, your perpetual moralizing and the sour censoriousness with which you condemn things which are in reality innocent and pure – all this, if you will permit me to speak frankly, was quite unanimously condemned. 'What is the use', they said, 'of her modest demeanour, her virtuous outward appearance, if everything else contradicts it? She's meticulous about saying her prayers and yet she beats her servants and she's always behind with their wages: she makes great parade of her piety in devout circles and yet she paints her face and would fain pass for a beauty: she insists on nudity being veiled in pictures but she's not averse to the reality!' Of course I took your part against the whole company and roundly charged them with slandering you, but they were all at one in opposing me and their conclusion was that you would do well to concern yourself less with other people's behaviour and more with your own; that we should examine ourselves thoroughly before condemning others, that strictures on our neighbours have more effect if our own lives are exemplary, and that if it comes to the point it's far better to leave such things to those to whom Heaven has entrusted the responsibility for them. I believe that you also are too sensible a person not to take my counsel in good part or to believe that I have any other motive than concern for your welfare.

ARSINOÉ. One inevitably lays oneself open in offering any reproof but I did not expect this sort of reply. I perceive from the bitterness of your tone that my warning, though given in all sincerity, has wounded you deeply.

CÉLIMÈNE. On the contrary, Madam, it would be a good thing if such mutual exchanges became customary. Yes, if we were prepared to be honest we might rid ourselves of much self-deception. It rests entirely with you to say whether we continue these friendly offices with the same enthusiasm as we have begun and make a point of repeating to each other everything that we hear – you of me and I, Madam, of you.

ARSINOÉ. Oh! I shall never hear anything about you. I'm the one who has all the faults.

CÉLIMÈNE. Madam, I believe there's nothing people can't contrive to praise or condemn and find justification for doing so, according to their age and their inclinations. There's a season for love-making and another equally appropriate to being straitlaced and one may as well choose the latter when one's hey-day is passed – it may serve to conceal some of life's disappointments! I don't say that I shan't follow your example one day – there's no saying what one will come to in the course of the years but you must agree that twenty is not the age for being prim.

ARSINOÉ. Really! You pride yourself on a very slight advantage! You make a terrible fuss about your youth, but whatever the difference in our ages may be it doesn't amount to so much that you need make such a song about it. What's more I don't know why you are getting so excited or what reason you have for attacking me in this fashion.

CÉLIMÈNE. Nor do *I* know why you are always making a set at me. Must you be forever venting your disappointments on me? Can I help it if men take no notice of you? If they find me attractive and insist on paying me the very attentions you would like to see me deprived of – what can

I do? It isn't my fault. You have a clear field. I'm not preventing you from attracting them.

ARSINOÉ. Dear me! Do you think I worry about the number of admirers you so pride yourself on? Or that one can't perfectly well guess the price they demand for their attentions? Would you have us believe, things being what they are, that your good qualities alone bring them thronging around you, and that they are content to burn with pure love and court you for your virtues alone? People aren't blinded by your subterfuges: the world's not deceived! *I* know women endowed with every quality to inspire love who nevertheless don't attract suitors. Hence we can draw the conclusion that men's affections aren't gained without making considerable advances, that they don't love us just for our beautiful eyes, and that all their attentions have to be paid for. So don't be so puffed up with pride in your trivial triumphs! Moderate that arrogant opinion of your own charms which makes you so contemptuous of others! If one envied your conquests in the least I fancy one could do as the others do – and if one were equally careless of restraint, show you that lovers can be had for the asking.

CÉLIMÈNE. Have them then, by all means! Let us see how you do it. Show us the secret . . . try to make yourself attractive and . . .

ARSINOÉ. Let us break off this discussion or it may try our tempers too far. I should have taken my leave already had my carriage not kept me waiting.

CÉLIMÈNE. You may stay as long as you please. There's no occasion for hurry. I won't weary you with ceremony but leave you to better company. The gentleman who has just arrived most opportunely will take my place and entertain you better than I can. [*Enter* ALCESTE.] Alceste, I must go and write a note which I can't very well postpone. Stay with this lady and she'll the more easily excuse my incivility. [*Exit* CÉLIMÈNE.]

ARSINOÉ. It seems that she wishes me to entertain you for a few minutes, while I'm waiting for my carriage to arrive. She could have offered me no greater pleasure than an opportunity of conversing with you. Of course, we all admire men of outstanding abilities but there is something about you – some mysterious influence which makes me deeply concerned for your interests. I only wish the Court would turn a more propitious eye on your merits. You have reason for complaint. It infuriates me to see time go by and nothing at all done for you.

ALCESTE. For me, Madam? On what grounds could I make any claim? What services am I supposed to have rendered the State? What have I done, may I ask, that is so outstanding that I have reason to complain that the Court does nothing for me?

ARSINOÉ. Not all those on whom the Court looks with favour have rendered such distinguished service. Opportunity is needed as well as ability and in fact your talents and abilities ought to be . . .

ALCESTE. Good Lord! Let us say no more about my abilities, I beseech you! Why should the Court worry about them? The Court would have enough to do – more than enough if it took to unearthing people's abilities!

ARSINOÉ. Outstanding abilities come to light of themselves. Yours are highly spoken of in many quarters. I may say that only yesterday I twice heard you praised in most influential circles by people of great consequence.

ALCESTE. Why Madam! They praise everyone nowadays. This is an age which shows no discrimination whatever in that respect! Everybody is endowed with brilliant gifts and in equal degree! It's no longer any distinction to find one's self praised: one's sickened of eulogies. They throw them round wholesale. Why! My valet has been mentioned in the *Gazette*!

ARSINOÉ. Nevertheless I wish an office at Court made more appeal to you. Your talents would be seen to greater advantage. If you showed the slightest inclination that way I could pull strings for you. I have good friends whom I could ask to use their influence on your behalf and smooth the way for you.

ALCESTE. And what would you have me do there, Madam?

My temperament is such that I should keep well away from there. I am not suited by nature to the atmosphere of the court. I don't feel I have the qualities necessary for success there. My main gift is for frankness and sincerity. I have no ability for bamboozling people with words. A man who can't hide what he thinks shouldn't stay too long in such places. Away from the Court one no doubt misses the influence and the honours it dispenses nowadays but in forgoing those advantages one at least avoids the humiliation of making a fool of oneself and suffering many a cruel rebuff, or having to praise Mr Such a One's verses, dance attendance on Madam So and So, or put up with the inanities of our inimitable Marquises.

ARSINOÉ. Well, since you prefer it, suppose we leave the subject of the Court, but I can't help deploring your love affair. If I may say so I could have wished your affections had been more wisely bestowed. You deserve a happier fate. The lady you are so enamoured of isn't worthy of you.

ALCESTE. Kindly remember when you are saying such things, Madam, that the lady in question is your friend.

ARSINOÉ. Yes, but it really does go against my conscience to let her continue to wrong you. It distresses me to see the position you are in. I warn you. She's deceiving you.

ALCESTE. That's very kind of you, Madam. Information of that kind is most acceptable to a lover.

ARSINOÉ. Yes, although she's my friend, I maintain that she's unworthy of an honourable man's love. Her affection for you is all mere pretence.

ALCESTE. That may well be. We can't see into other people's hearts, but you might in charity have refrained from putting such thoughts into my head.

ARSINOÉ. If you prefer not to be undeceived I need say no more. It's easy enough.

ALCESTE. No. In a case like this whatever one risks hearing can't be as bad as remaining in doubt, but I would rather you told me nothing except what you can prove.

ARSINOÉ. Very well. That's good enough. You shall be fully

enlightened. I won't ask you to believe anything but your own eyes. Conduct me to my house and there I'll give you proof undeniable of the lady's unfaithfulness. Should you then have eyes for another's charms it may be possible to offer you some consolation.

Act Four

ÉLIANTE, PHILINTE

PHILINTE. No, I never did meet such an obstinate fellow nor a case where it was so hard to reach an understanding. They tried every way to shift him but it was no use. There was no getting him to change his opinion. I don't suppose so strange a problem ever exercised their Lordships' wisdom before. 'No, Gentlemen,' he said. 'I will not withdraw. I'll agree to anything you like but that. . . . What is he offended at? What does he reproach me with? Suppose he doesn't write well, is it any discredit to him? What does my opinion matter that he should have taken it so much amiss? One can be a gentleman and still write wretched verse. One's honour's not involved in these things. I consider him an admirable person in every way, a man of breeding, courage, ability – anything you like but a very poor poet indeed. If you wish I'll praise his retinue, his style of living, his horsemanship, his skill in arms or in dancing, but as for his verse – no! There he must excuse me. If one can't manage to do better than that one should leave verse alone – unless one's condemned to do it on pain of death!' In the end the utmost he could be persuaded to say by way of concession or amends – and he thought he was being very conciliatory – was 'I'm sorry, Sir, to be so difficult to please and I do most heartily wish, in consideration for you, that I could have thought better of your sonnet.' Whereupon they made them shake hands and left it at that.

ÉLIANTE. Yes, his behaviour *is* peculiar but I must say I

admire him for it. There's something in its way noble and heroic in this sincerity he so prides himself on. It's a rare virtue in these days. I only wish there were more people like him.

PHILINTE. Well, the more I see of him, the more surprised I am by this passion for Célimène in which he is so deeply involved. I can't imagine what he thinks he's doing to be falling in love at all being the sort of fellow he is, still less how your cousin comes to be the one to capture his fancy.

ÉLIANTE. It just shows that love isn't always a matter of temperamental affinities. All the usual ideas of mutual sympathy are proved wrong in this case.

PHILINTE. And do you believe, from what you can see, that she loves him?

ÉLIANTE. It's hard to say. How is one to judge whether she is really in love? She's not entirely sure of her feelings herself. Sometimes she's in love without knowing it and at other times she fancies she's in love when she isn't at all.

PHILINTE. I fear our friend will have more trouble with this cousin of yours than he imagines. If he felt as I do he would turn his attentions in quite a different direction. He would be better advised if he took advantage of the affection you feel for him.

ÉLIANTE. Well, I make no bones about it – I think one should be honest in such matters. I don't oppose his love for Célimène; on the contrary I encourage it. If it rested with me he would marry the lady of his choice but if, as may well happen, his suit didn't succeed and Célimène bestowed her hand elsewhere, I might bring myself to accept his addresses, and none the less so because someone else had already refused them.

PHILINTE. And I for my part, Madam, do nothing to oppose his high regard for you. He could tell you himself, were he so minded, what I have gone out of my way to say to him on this question. If, however, they were once united and you, in consequence were not in a position to receive his addresses, then I should do all I could to win for myself those signal favours you now accord him. I should count myself happy, if, he having renounced them, you transferred them to me.

ÉLIANTE. You are joking, Philinte.

PHILINTE. No, Madam, I say it in all sincerity. I await the opportunity of offering you my entire devotion. All my hopes turn towards that happy moment.

[*Enter* ALCESTE.]

ALCESTE. Ah Madam, avenge me! Avenge an injury which is more than my constancy can bear.

ÉLIANTE. What is it? Whatever can have upset you so?

ALCESTE. Something beyond mortal experience! A calamity more overwhelming than anything within the order of nature! It's all up! My love – I don't know how to say it!

ÉLIANTE. Try to calm yourself a little.

ALCESTE. Merciful Heavens! Why should such graces go with such odious, such criminal baseness?

ÉLIANTE. But what can have . . . ?

ALCESTE. It's the end of everything. I'm . . . I'm betrayed, and utterly undone! Célimène . . . who would have believed such a thing . . . Célimène has deceived me. She's faithless after all!

ÉLIANTE. Have you some good reason for believing this?

PHILINTE. May it not be some ill-conceived suspicion? Your jealous temper runs at times to imagining things.

ALCESTE. Confound it! Mind your own business Sir! What more certain proof of her treachery could there be than to have, here in my pocket, a letter written in her hand? Yes Madam, a letter written to Oronte – that's the evidence of my betrayal and her shame . . . Oronte whose advances I thought she shunned . . . of all my rivals the one I feared least!

PHILINTE. A letter may well give a wrong impression. Sometimes it isn't as compromising as it seems.

ALCESTE. You again, Sir! Pray let me alone and give your attention to your own concerns!

ÉLIANTE. You should try to control yourself. The trouble . . .

ALCESTE. Madam, the remedy lies with you. It's to you I

turn now for healing of this bitter blow. Avenge me on this ungrateful and perfidious kinswoman of yours who has so basely betrayed my constant love. Avenge a deed which must fill you with horror.

ÉLIANTE. I avenge you? How?

ALCESTE. By accepting my love. Take it, Madam! Take the heart she has betrayed. That's how I can punish her – by dedicating to you in ardent sacrifice my vows, my profoundest love, my care, respect, and duty.

ÉLIANTE. You may be sure I feel for you in your distress. I don't in the least undervalue the love you offer me but it may be there's less harm done than you suppose. You may get over this desire for vengeance. When we suffer at the hands of one we love we make many a plan we never carry out. Strong as the reasons for breaking off relations may appear – it's of no avail – guilt in the loved one soon turns to innocence again, resentment quickly vanishes: we all know what lovers quarrels are!

ALCESTE. No, no, Madam. No! The injury's too deep. There's no going back. I'm breaking with her. Nothing can alter my decision. I couldn't forgive myself if I ever loved her again. Here she is! My rage redoubles at the sight of her. I'll charge her with the offence, confound her utterly, and then bring to you a heart entirely freed from her perfidious charms.

[*Exeunt* PHILINTE *and* ÉLIANTE. *Enter* CÉLIMÈNE.]

ALCESTE. Oh, Heavens! Can I control my feelings now?

CÉLIMÈNE. Why! Whatever's the matter with you? Why these sighs? What do these black looks mean?

ALCESTE. That all the horrors the mind can conceive are nothing in comparison with your perfidy! That fate, Hell, Heaven in its wrath never produced a thing so vile as you.

CÉLIMÈNE. This is certainly a remarkable method of love making!

ALCESTE. Ah! Don't make a joke of it! This is no time for laughter. Far better blush, for you have cause enough! I have proof positive of your treachery. It's what my premonitions indicated and it was not for nothing that I was alarmed. My suspicions – which you found so odious – directed me to the very evil that my eyes have now beheld. Despite all your precautions, your cunning in deceit, my guiding star revealed to me what I had cause to fear! But don't assume that I shall suffer the humiliation of finding myself abused and not seek my revenge! I know that our affections are beyond our own control, that love strikes where it will, that hearts cannot be won by force; that each is free to choose to whom it will surrender: nor should I have had any reason for complaint if you had spoken frankly: if you had rejected my addresses from the first I should have had no quarrel save with fortune, but to flatter my hopes with a false assurance of your passion, that was an act of treachery, of perfidy, for which no punishment could be too severe: it justifies my going to any lengths. Yes, yes, after such a deed you may well fear that anything may happen! I am no longer myself: rage overwhelms me! Under the impact of this deadly blow my passion is no longer subject to the constraints of reason! I yield to the impulse of my righteous wrath. I'm not answerable for what I do!

CÉLIMÈNE. Why are you raving like this? Have you taken leave of your senses?

ALCESTE. Yes, yes indeed! When I first set eyes on you and had the misfortune to imbibe the poison that is destroying me; when I thought to find sincerity in those treacherous charms which cast so false a spell upon me!

CÉLIMÈNE. What treachery have you to complain of?

ALCESTE. Ah! The duplicity! How skilled her heart is in deceit! But I have the means at hand to bring it to the test. Cast your eyes on this and admit to your own writing! This letter coming to light is all that is needed to confound you. This is the evidence to which there's no reply.

CÉLIMÈNE. So that's what is troubling you!

ALCESTE. Don't you blush to see this document?

CÉLIMÈNE. Why should I blush?

ALCESTE. What! You have the audacity to persist in your deceit? You'll disown it because it bears no signature?

CÉLIMÈNE. Why should I disown a letter in my own hand?

ALCESTE. Can you look upon it and not blush for the wrong it does me. Why! The whole tone of the letter convicts you!

CÉLIMÈNE. You are, indeed, a strangely foolish man!

ALCESTE. What! You still persist in face of this convincing proof? Isn't this revelation of your feeling for Oronte sufficient reason for my resentment and your shame?

CÉLIMÈNE. Oronte? Who said the letter was addressed to him?

ALCESTE. The people who handed it to me today. But supposing I were willing to grant it might have been addressed to someone else, should I have any less reason to complain? Would it make you less guilty towards me?

CÉLIMÈNE. But if the letter were addressed to a woman what harm would it do you? What would there be wrong in that?

ALCESTE. Ah! That's a clever trick! An admirable excuse! I confess, I never thought of that! Of course I'm perfectly convinced! How *dare* you resort to such a barefaced fraud? Do you think people have no sense at all? But do go on! Let's see what further shifts you'll use to sustain so palpable a lie, how you'll manage to make out that so passionate a letter could be from one woman to another. Reconcile – if you are to cover your inconstancy – what I am going to read . . .

CÉLIMÈNE. No, indeed I won't. I consider it ridiculous on your part to presume to such authority and dare to say such things to my face!

ALCESTE. Now, now. Don't fly into a temper! Just try and explain what these expressions mean.

CÉLIMÈNE. No, I'll do no such thing. You can think what you like about it. It matters little to me.

ALCESTE. Show me, I beseech you, that such a letter could really be intended for a woman and I'll be satisfied.

CÉLIMÈNE. No, it's to Oronte. I'd rather you thought that. I delight in his attentions, enjoy his conversation, esteem his qualities – I'll agree to anything you like. Go on, pursue your quarrel, don't let anything deter you . . . so long as you plague me no longer.

ALCESTE. Heavens! Could there ever be anything so cruel? Was lover ever treated in such fashion? Why! Here am I with every justification for being infuriated with her – I'm the one making the complaint and yet I get the blame! She drives me to the extremity of grief and suspense, leaves me to believe the worst – and glories in it! And yet I haven't the strength of mind to bring myself to break the chains that bind me to her, to steel my heart to show my proud contempt for this unworthy object of my too fond desires! [*To* CÉLIMÈNE] Perfidious creature! How well you know how to turn my weaknesses against me and exploit to your own purposes the fatal and excessive love those faithless eyes inspire! At least deny a crime which is more than I can bear! Cease this pretence that you are guilty! Prove to me, if it is possible, the innocence of your letter! My love will lend a helping hand. Endeavour to seem true to me in this and I'll endeavour to believe you so.

CÉLIMÈNE. No, no! You are mad when you are in these jealous fits, and don't deserve the love I have for you. What – I should like to know – what could make me stoop to the baseness of deceiving you? Why – if my affections were given to another, should I not frankly tell you so? Doesn't the fact that I chose to assure you of my feelings towards you protect me from such suspicions? How can they have any weight in face of such a confession? Is it not an insult to me that you give credence to them? When it is asking so much of a woman's heart that she should bring herself to confess her love; when the honour of the sex – ever at war with our passions – is so strongly opposed to such admissions, how can a lover doubt so solemn an assurance with impunity? Isn't he to blame if he's not content with what one can only utter at all after a great inward struggle? No, no! Such suspicions deserve to arouse my anger! You aren't worthy of the consideration I have shown you! I'm a fool! I'm vexed at my own simplicity. I *ought* to bestow my affections elsewhere and give you reason for legitimate complaint.

ALCESTE. Ah, traitress! Strange indeed is my weakness for you! No doubt your honeyed words are intended to deceive but no matter, I must accept my destiny! My very soul depends upon your love. I must probe your heart's recesses to the uttermost and see whether you will really be so base as to betray me.

CÉLIMÈNE. No, you don't love me as you should.

ALCESTE. Ah! My love is beyond all comparison! Such is my desire to make it manifest to all the world that I could even wish misfortune might befall you – yes, I would have you unloved, reduced to misery or born to indigence, without rank or birth or fortune so that I might in one resounding act of loving sacrifice repair the injustice of your fate and enjoy the joy and satisfaction of knowing that you owe everything to my love.

CÉLIMÈNE. A strange way of showing your goodwill! Heaven grant you may have no such opportunity! But here comes Master Du Bois – and most comically arrayed.

[*Enter* DU BOIS.]

ALCESTE. What's the meaning of this get-up? Why the appearance of alarm? What's the matter?

DU BOIS. Master . . .

ALCESTE. Well?

DU BOIS. Here be strange goings-on indeed.

ALCESTE. What is it?

DU BOIS. A sad state we be in now, Master.

ALCESTE. What do you mean?

DU BOIS. Shall I say it out loud?

ALCESTE. Yes, and waste no time about it!

DU BOIS. Be there no one here as . . .

ALCESTE. Why can't you get on with it? Speak, will you!

DU BOIS. Master, we must beat a retreat.

ALCESTE. What?

DU BOIS. We must decamp – and make no bones about it!

ALCESTE. Why?

DU BOIS. I tell you we must get out of this place.

ALCESTE. What for?

DU BOIS. No time for farewells, Master.

ALCESTE. Why are you talking like this?

DU BOIS. Why Master? Because we must pack and be off.

ALCESTE. Ah! Explain what you mean you blockhead or I'll make your head sing for it.

DU BOIS. Master, a man with a face as black as his coat came right into the kitchen and left us a paper – a paper so scrawled over a chap'd have to be as crafty as the Devil himself to read it. 'Tis about your lawsuit I make no manner of doubt, but Old Nick himself couldn't make head nor tail of it.

ALCESTE. Very well then, you rascal, what has the paper to do with our going away?

DU BOIS. That's what I'm here to tell you, Master. An hour later a gentleman that often comes to see you arrives and wanting you urgent like, and not finding you at home, charges me, very civil, to tell you – knowing that I be your faithful servant – to tell you that . . . now wait a minute, what was his name?

ALCESTE. Never mind his name, you dog, tell me what he said.

DU BOIS. He's a friend of yours, anyway, Master. We'll leave it at that. He told me that you are in danger here and like to be arrested if you stop.

ALCESTE. But why? Did he give no reason?

DU BOIS. No, he just asks me for ink and paper and writes you a letter. I don't doubt it'll tell you all you are wanting to know.

ALCESTE. Give it to me then!

CÉLIMÈNE. What's behind all this?

ALCESTE. I don't know but I mean to find out. [*To* DU BOIS] Have you got it yet you blundering fool?

DU BOIS. [*after a long search*]. 'Pon my word, Master, I left it on the table.

ALCESTE. I don't know what prevents me from . . .

CÉLIMÈNE. Don't be angry. Go and find what it all means.

ALCESTE [*going*]. Try as I may, it seems the fates conspire to prevent me from talking with you. Permit me nevertheless to see you again before the evening is out.

Act Five

ALCESTE, PHILINTE

ALCESTE. I tell you my mind's made up.

PHILINTE. But however serious the blow may be, do you really need to . . .

ALCESTE. No, you can talk and argue as much as you like; nothing can make me go back on what I have said. There's too much baseness in the world today: I'm determined to withdraw from all contacts with mankind. Why! Honour, probity, equity, the law itself were all against my opponent, the justice of my cause was acknowledged everywhere: I was confident I was in the right and, in the event, I was deceived. Justice was on my side, and yet I lost my case! Thanks to the direst falsehood a rogue, whose scandalous history is notorious, emerges triumphant! Honesty goes down before his perfidy. He does me in and yet finds means to justify himself. By dint of sheer hypocrisy, of open and most palpable fraud, right is overthrown and justice perverted! Then to crown his villainy he obtains a writ against me and, not content with the wrong thus done me – there's an abominable book in circulation, a work it's criminal even to read, one for which no punishment could be too severe – and the scoundrel has the audacity to attribute the authorship to me! And on top of all that, I find Oronte going round whispering against me and spitefully lending support to the imposture, Oronte who has the reputation at Court of being an honest man, one I have always treated with frankness and sincerity. Yet he needs must come pestering me for an opinion on his verses, and because I treat him honourably and will neither dissemble nor betray the truth – he joins in accusing me of a crime I haven't committed! Now he's become my bitterest enemy! He'll never forgive me for not liking his sonnet. Egad! That's human nature for you! That's what vanity leads men to! That's the measure of their good faith, their love of virtue, the sort of honour and justice that you find among them! No, no! The vexations they are devising for me are beyond all endurance. Let's flee this jungle, this thieves' alley of a world! Since you live like wolves among yourselves you shall never include me among you!

PHILINTE. I think your intentions are a little rash. Things aren't so bad as you make out. The charges your adversary makes against you haven't gained sufficient credence to lead to your arrest. The falsity of his story is self-evident and his actions may yet recoil upon himself.

ALCESTE. On him? Little he need fear on that account! He's a licensed scoundrel. Far from his reputation suffering from this affair you'll see that tomorrow it will stand higher than before.

PHILINTE. Nevertheless, the fact remains that people have attached little importance to the malicious rumours he has been spreading around. So far you have nothing to fear on that account. As for your lawsuit – you have cause for complaint but you can easily appeal against the decision and . . .

ALCESTE. No, I'll accept it. Bitterly as the verdict may wrong me I'm far from wanting to see it squashed. It shows all too plainly how right may be abused. I'll have it go down to posterity as outstanding evidence – a signal proof of the wickedness of our generation. It may cost me twenty thousand francs but those twenty thousand francs give me the right to rail against the iniquity of human nature and cherish an undying hatred for it.

PHILINTE. But after all . . .

ALCESTE. But after all – your concern is superfluous! What can you possibly find to say? Will you even have the audacity to justify to my face the dreadful things that have happened?

PHILINTE. On the contrary I'll agree to anything you please. The world *is* governed by intrigue and self-interest; fraud *does* carry all before it nowadays. Men *ought* to be different from what they are. But is the prevalence of injustice among them a reason for withdrawing from their society? The defects of human nature afford us opportunities of exercising our philosophy, the best employment of our virtues. If all men were righteous, all hearts true and frank and loyal what use would our virtues be? Their use lies in enabling us to support with constancy the injustices others inflict upon us. Even as the noble mind . . .

ALCESTE. Yes, my good Sir, you talk admirably I know! You are never at a loss for arguments but your eloquence is a waste of time. Reason bids me retire from the world for my own good. I lack sufficient control over my tongue. I can't answer for what I may say: I might involve myself in troubles innumerable. Leave me without further ado to await Célimène. I need her consent to what I intend to do. I'll see now whether she really loves me. This is the moment that will put it to the proof.

PHILINTE. Let us go up to Éliante's room and wait until she comes.

ALCESTE. No. I have too much on my mind. You go and see her and leave me to this dark corner and my gloomy thoughts.

PHILINTE. That's odd company for you! I'll go and get Éliante to come down.

[*Exit* PHILINTE. *Enter* CÉLIMÈNE *and* ORONTE.]

ORONTE. Yes Madam, it's for you to decide now whether you wish to tie the knot that will make me entirely yours. I must have absolute assurance of your love. This is not an issue on which a lover can bear to be kept in uncertainty. If the ardour of my passion has moved you, you should not hesitate to let me know it. The proof I now demand is that you permit Alceste's attentions no longer, that you sacrifice him to my love, and, in short, banish him from your house this very day.

CÉLIMÈNE. But what has turned you so much against him? I have often heard you speak highly of him.

ORONTE. There's no point in explaining that, Madam. It's a question of knowing what *your* feelings are. Pray make your choice. Take one or the other of us. I'm in your hands.

ALCESTE [*emerging from his corner*]. Ay, Madam, the gentleman is right. You *must* make your choice. His question accords with my own desires. I am moved by a like ardour, a similar concern. *My* passion too requires an unequivocal sign from yours. Things can go on no longer as they are. The time has come for you to declare yourself.

ORONTE. I have no wish to prejudice your fortunes in any way, Sir, by an inopportune intrusion of my own affection.

ALCESTE. Nor have I the least desire, Sir, call it jealousy or what you will, to share her affection with you.

ORONTE. If she feels that your love is preferable to mine . . .

ALCESTE. If she's capable of the slightest regard for you . . .

ORONTE. I renounce any further pretensions to her hand.

ALCESTE. I swear I'll never see her again.

ORONTE. Madam, it's for you to speak without constraint.

ALCESTE. Madam, you need not fear to say where you stand.

ORONTE. All you need is to tell us where your affections lie.

ALCESTE. All you need is to come to the point and choose between us.

ORONTE. What! Can you really find it difficult to make a choice?

ALCESTE. What! Are you wavering? Can you be in any doubt?

CÉLIMÈNE. Heavens! What an ill-timed demand! How unreasonable you both are! I'm quite capable of making my choice. My heart's not wavering; I'm not in any doubt. Nothing is simpler than to make a choice, but what I do find most embarrassing, I must admit, is to declare my preference before the two of you. I feel that one should not have to say such disagreeable things before the people concerned. One can give sufficient indication of one's preference without being forced to throw it in a person's face. Some gentler form of intimation should be enough to convey to a lover the ill success of his attentions.

ORONTE. No, no! I have nothing to fear from a frank statement. There's no objection on my part.

ALCESTE. As for me – I demand it! I insist on its being made openly here and now. I have no desire to see you soften the blow. You are always anxious to keep in with everybody. No more delay! No more uncertainty! You shall explain exactly where you stand. If you won't I shall take that as a decision in itself. I shall know, so far as I'm concerned, what interpretation to put upon your silence. I'll presume the worst.

ORONTE. I'm most grateful to you for putting it so strongly, Sir. I say the same.

CÉLIMÈNE. How tiresome you are with these unreasonable demands. I ask you, is it fair to put such a question? Haven't I explained my reluctance? But here comes Éliante. I'll ask her to be judge.

[*Enter* ÉLIANTE *and* PHILINTE.]

CÉLIMÈNE. Cousin, I'm being persecuted by these two gentlemen who seem to have agreed on a common course of action. They both demand, with equal insistence, that I declare which of them has the prior place in my affections, and that I make an open pronouncement forbidding one or the other of them to pay his addresses to me in future. Did you ever hear of such a thing in all your life?

ÉLIANTE. Don't ask me about it! You may find you have come to the wrong person. I'm for those who speak their minds.

ORONTE. It's no use your refusing, Madam.

ALCESTE. Your evasions will get no support from her.

ORONTE. You really must come down on one side or the other.

ALCESTE. You need only continue to keep silent.

ORONTE. One single word will end the argument for me.

ALCESTE. *I* shall understand if you say nothing at all.

[*Enter* ARSINOÉ, ACASTE, CLITANDRE.]

ACASTE. Madam, we have a little matter we should like to clear up with you if you don't mind.

CLITANDRE. It is most fortunate, gentlemen, that you should be here, since you also are concerned.

ARSINOÉ. You will be surprised to see me, Madam, but it's these gentlemen who are responsible. They came and complained to me about something I couldn't bring myself to credit. I have too high an opinion of your character to believe you could ever be guilty of such a dreadful thing. Rejecting the evidence they showed me, strong though it appeared to be, and overlooking our little disagreement in the interests of friendship, I agreed to accompany them here and see you clear yourself of this calumny.

ACASTE. Yes, Madam, kindly show us how you can contrive to justify this. Did you write this letter to Clitandre?

CLITANDRE. Did you address this tender missive to Acaste?

ACASTE [*to* ORONTE *and* ALCESTE]. This writing is not unknown to you gentlemen. The civilities she has extended to you have no doubt made the hand familiar but this is worth the trouble of reading. [*reads*] 'What a strange man you are to condemn me for my cheerfulness and reproach me with never being so happy as when I am away from you. Nothing could be more unfair and unless you come soon and ask my pardon I'll never forgive you so long as I live. Our great lubberly Viscount . . .'
It's a pity he's not here!
'Our great lubberly Viscount whom you complain of first isn't at all the sort of man to appeal to me. I have never had any opinion of him since I saw him spitting into a well for fully three-quarters of an hour for the pleasure of making rings in the water. As for the little Marquis . . .'
That's me, gentlemen, not to flatter myself unduly . . .
'As for the little Marquis who was so assiduous in attendance upon me yesterday, he's a person of no significance whatever and he's as poor as a church mouse. Now, the man with the green ribbons . . .'
[*To* ALCESTE] It's your turn now, Sir.
'The man with the green ribbons does sometimes amuse me with his bluntness and his churlish ill humour but there

are times when I find him the most tiresome person imaginable. Then there's the man with the waistcoat . . .'*
[*To* ORONTE] This is your bit.

'The man with the waistcoat who has taken it into his head that he's a wit and is determined to be an author in spite of what anyone says, I just can't bother to listen to him. I find his prose as dull as his verse so do please understand that I don't always enjoy myself as much as you think, that I miss you most dreadfully at all the functions I'm obliged to attend, and that it's very much more pleasant to be with someone one likes.'

CLITANDRE. And now for myself. [*reads*] 'You mention your friend Clitandre who's so given to playing the languishing lover, but he's the last man in the world I could have any fancy for. He's mad to persuade himself that one loves him; you are as bad to believe that one doesn't love you. Be sensible, exchange opinions with him, and come and see me as often as you can and help me to put up with the misery of being pestered by him.'

[*To* CÉLIMÈNE] A very fine pattern of virtue we have before us here, Madam. No doubt you know the name normally given to such persons. That's enough! We'll all go and publish abroad this splendid picture of you as you really are.

ACASTE. There is much I could say to you – and with justification but I don't consider you worth getting angry about. I'll show you that little Marquises can find consolations superior to anything you have to offer.

[*Exeunt* ACASTE *and* CLITANDRE.]

ORONTE. To think that you could pull me to pieces like that after all that you've written to me! And you offer the same specious promises of love to everyone in turn! Ay! I was too easily fooled but it shan't happen again. You have done me a service in letting me see you as you really are. I'm heart-whole once again and I have the satisfaction of

* Man with the waistcoat – 'Homme à la Veste' was changed in the edition of 1682 to 'Homme du Sonnet' – the Sonneteer.

knowing that the loss is yours. [*To* ALCESTE] Sir, I offer no further obstacle to your suit. You may come to terms with the lady. [*Exit*.]

ARSINOÉ. This really is the most disgraceful business I ever heard of! I just can't contain my indignation. Was there ever such behaviour! I'm not concerned about the others, but this gentleman whom you were fortunate enough to attract, a most honourable and worthy man who worshipped the very ground that you trod on, deserved . . .

ALCESTE. Madam, kindly leave me to look after my own affairs and don't meddle with what doesn't concern you. No purpose would be served by your taking up my quarrel. I'm in no position to repay your zeal on my behalf. You aren't the person my thoughts would turn to if I sought to avenge myself by transferring my affections elsewhere.

ARSINOÉ. Do you imagine, Sir, that I have any such idea? Why should I be so anxious to have you? You have too high an opinion of yourself if you entertain any such impression! This lady's leavings are not a commodity I should prize as highly as all that! Pray come to your senses and don't have such a high and mighty opinion of yourself! People like me are not for the likes of you. Better go on sighing for her. I should love to see so suitable a match. [*Exit*.]

ALCESTE [*to* CÉLIMÈNE]. Well. I have held my peace in spite of everything. I have let them all have their say before me. Have I restrained myself long enough? May I now . . . ?

CÉLIMÈNE. Yes, you may say anything now. You have a right to complain and reproach me with any crimes you choose. I'm in the wrong and I admit it. I'm too ashamed to put you off with excuses. The anger of the others I despised, but you I admit I have wronged. Your resentment is justified. I know how much I must appear to blame, how everything points to my having betrayed you. You have indeed good reason to hate me. Do so. I consent.

ALCESTE. Ah! But can I do it, false creature? Can I overcome my fondness for you? Try as I may to hate you shall I find it in my heart to do so? [*To* ÉLIANTE *and* PHILINTE] You see what an ignoble love can do! I call you both to witness my frailty but, let me confess it, I shall go further yet! You'll see me push my weakness to the uttermost limit and show how wrong it is to call any of us wise – how there's some touch of human frailty in every one of us. [*To* CÉLIMÈNE] Yes, perfidious creature, I'm willing to forget your misdeeds. I'll contrive to excuse or condone them as youthful frailties into which the evil manners of the age have led you – provided you'll agree to join me in my plan of fleeing from all human intercourse and undertake to accompany me forthwith into the rustic solitude to which I have sworn to repair. Thus, thus and only thus, can you make public reparation for the harm done by your letters. Thus after all the scandal so abhorrent to a noble mind I may be permitted to love you still.

CÉLIMÈNE. Me? Renounce the world before I'm old and bury myself in your wilderness!

ALCESTE. Ah! If your love would but respond to mine what would the rest of the world matter? Can I not give you everything you desire?

CÉLIMÈNE. The mind shrinks from solitude at twenty. I don't feel I have the necessary fortitude to bring myself to take such a decision. If the offer of my hand would content you I would consent and marriage . . .

ALCESTE. No! Now I abhor you! This refusal is worse than all that has gone before. Since you can't bring yourself to make me your all in all as you are mine, I renounce you! This dire affront frees me from your ignoble fetters for ever.

[*Exit* CÉLIMÈNE. ALCESTE *addresses* ÉLIANTE.]

Madam, a hundred virtues adorn your beauty. In you alone have I found sincerity. I have long esteemed you – permit me to continue to do so still but forgive me if, beset as I am with troubles, I do not aspire to the honour of your hand. I feel myself unworthy of it and I begin to realize that I'm not destined for such a union, and that a heart which another has refused would be too poor a tribute to offer you . . . and in fact . . .

ÉLIANTE. Continue to think that if you wish. I am in no anxiety to bestow my hand but, without needing to trouble myself unduly, I think your friend here might contrive to accept it if I asked him to.

PHILINTE. Ah, Madam! I could ask no greater honour. For that I would sacrifice my life itself.

ALCESTE. May you ever continue to cherish such feelings for each other and so come to savour true content. Betrayed on all sides, injustice heaped upon me, I mean to escape from this abyss of triumphant vice and search the world for some spot so remote that there one may be free to live as honour bids. [*Exit.*]

PHILINTE. Come, Madam, let us go and do all we can to persuade him to give up this foolish plan.

The Sicilian *or* Love the Painter

LE SICILIEN *ou* L'AMOUR PEINTRE

CHARACTERS IN THE PLAY

ADRASTES, a young Frenchman, in love with Isidore
DON PEDRO, a Sicilian, in love with Isidore
ISIDORE, a Greek girl, slave to Don Pedro
CLIMÈNE, sister* of Adrastes
HALI, Adrastes' servant
A MAGISTRATE
MUSICIANS
SLAVES
MOORS
LACKEYS

Scenes I and III   *A public square in Messina*
Scene II   *Inside the house of Don Pedro*

* There is no reference to this relationship in the play. Climène, designated as Zaide in later editions, is in fact another slave girl.

Scene One

[*Enter* HALI *with musicians.*]

HALI. Hush! Don't come any further. Wait here till I call you [*To himself*]. It's as black as an oven, a real Scaramouche sky tonight. There isn't the slightest glimmer of a star showing anywhere. What a contemptible thing it is to be a slave! Never able to live your own life, always at the beck and call of a master, at the mercy of his whims and his fancies, and obliged to shoulder his burdens as if they were your own! Mine insists on my sharing his present worries so, because he's in love, there can be no rest for me night or day . . . but there are torches approaching. Here he comes, I expect.

ADRASTES [*preceded by two lackeys each carrying a torch*]. Is that you Hali?

HALI. Who else could it be? I can't imagine anyone but you and me raking the streets at this time of night, Master.

ADRASTES. Nor can I imagine there's anyone else whose heart is tortured as mine is. To have to contend with the indifference or caprices of a woman one loves is nothing. One has at least the pleasure of bewailing one's lot and the right to feel sorry for oneself, but never to be able to find a single opportunity for exchanging a word with the object of one's adoration, never to be able to learn from her lips whether the love that her eyes have inspired is acceptable or not – that, to my mind, is the worst of all possible frustrations. And that's what I'm reduced to by the intolerable jealousy of this fellow who maintains such everlasting watch and ward over my charming Greek girl and never moves a step without keeping her close at his side.

HALI. But surely there are more ways than one of expressing one's love. My impression is that your eyes and hers have found means of saying plenty of things to each other these last few months.

ADRASTES. It's true that our eyes have spoken – often enough – but how is one to know whether the language

79

has been rightly interpreted – on either side? How can I know whether she really understands what my looks would convey? Or that hers say what I think they do?

HALI. You must find some other means of communication.

ADRASTES. Have you the musicians at hand?

HALI. Yes.

ADRASTES. Bring them here. [*To himself*] I'll have them sing until dawn. We shall see if their music will bring her face to the window.

HALI. Here they are. What shall they sing?

ADRASTES. Whatever they think best.

HALI. Then they shall sing the trio they sang to me the other day.

ADRASTES. No, that's not what I want.

HALI. Ah Master – it's in a lovely major key.

ADRASTES. What the deuce do you mean? Major key?

HALI. I am all for the major key, Master. You must agree that I know what I'm talking about. The major key's charming; there's no true harmony without it. Just listen to this trio.

ADRASTES. No. I want something gentle and sentimental, something to lull me into a sweet and dreamy meditation.

HALI. I see that you are for the minor key. But there are means of satisfying both of us. They shall sing you a passage from a little play which I have seen them rehearsing. Two shepherds are suffering the pains of unrequited love. They are in a wood and each comes forward in turn to make his lamentations – in the minor key – recounting one to another the cruelties of their mistresses, whereupon in comes a jolly shepherd who makes fun of them – in an admirable major key of course.

ADRASTES. All right. Let's have a look at it.

HALI. Here's a very suitable place for a stage and a pair of torches to light the play.

ADRASTES. You stand beside the house so that at the least noise within I can have the torches put out.

[*Singers as* PHILÈNE *and* TIRCIS.]

FIRST SINGER [PHILÈNE].

        Forgive me rocks and stones that I disturb your
           solitude
        And trouble your repose with my inquietude;
        Ye crags, be not impatient of my lay!
        Did you but know the pain which on my heart
           doth weigh,
        Unfeeling though you be,
        You must needs pity me.

SECOND SINGER [TIRCIS].

        The gladsome birds at break of day
        Awake the woodlands with their roundelay
        While I, alas, awake to my pain
        To grief, sighs, and sorrow again,
        Ah dearest Philène!

PHILÈNE.   Ah dearest Tircis!

TIRCIS.   Oh, pity my pain.

PHILÈNE.   Alas, my lost bliss.

TIRCIS.   Ever deaf to my suit is ungrateful Climène.

PHILÈNE.   Clarissa to me will accord no promise.

TOGETHER.   Oh Love without pity – oh Love in-humane,
        Oh passion that ever our hearts doth con-
           strain,
        Why condemn us forever to loving in vain?

THIRD SINGER [SHEPHERD].

        How foolish are lovers
        To love thus in vain!
        When true love's requited
        How light is the chain!
        And if love be slighted
        Why constant remain?

        To many a beauty
        I pay faith and duty
        If she be so inclined;
        But should she prove unkind –
        If she should show her claws and scratch
        Why then – in me she'll find her match!

FIRST AND SECOND TOGETHER.
>Alas! No happiness lies thus
>For us. No happiness for us!

HALI. Master! I heard a noise inside.

ADRASTES. Away quickly, all of you; put out the lights.

DON PEDRO [*coming out in his nightcap and dressing gown with a sword under his arm*]. I have been hearing singing outside my door for some time. They certainly aren't doing that for nothing! It's dark but I must try to find out who it can be.

ADRASTES [*stealing out – loud whisper*]. Hali!

HALI. What?

ADRASTES. Did you hear anything more?

HALI. No. [DON PEDRO *is behind them listening.*]

ADRASTES. Am I not to speak to my beloved Greek girl for a single moment in spite of all our efforts? Is this jealous scoundrel, this accursed Sicilian to keep me apart from her for ever!

HALI. I only wish the devil would fly away with him for all the trouble he's given us, the insufferable blackguard that he is! If we had him here how I should enjoy paying him out with a thrashing for all the trouble his jealousy has put us to.

ADRASTES. And we really must find some means, some device, some trick to catch the brute. I just can't accept failure now. If only I could –

HALI. Master, I don't know what it means, but the door's open. If you like I'll steal in quietly and see what's happening. [DON PEDRO *retires into the doorway.*]

ADRASTES. Yes do – but don't make a noise. I won't be far away. Heaven grant that it's my charming Isidore!

DON PEDRO [*giving* HALI *a slap on the cheek*]. Who goes there!

HALI [*giving him one back*]. Friend!

DON PEDRO. Hallo there! Francis, Dominic, Simon, Martin, Peter, Thomas, George, Bartholomew! Come at once! My sword, my buckler, my halberd, my pistols, my muskets, my guns. Quick! Hurry! Come! Kill! Give no quarter! *He goes inside – A silence.*

ADRASTES. I don't hear anyone stirring! Hali! Hali!

HALI [*hiding in a corner*]. Master?

ADRASTES. Where are you hiding?

HALI. Have those fellows come out?

ADRASTES. No. Nobody's stirring.

HALI [*coming out of hiding*]. If they do they'll be for it!

ADRASTES. What! Are all our schemes to come to nothing? Is this jealous fool to have the laugh on us still?

HALI. No. My temper's up now and my honour's involved. I won't have it said that anyone can get the better of me. It's a reflection on my reputation for rascality to have set-backs of this kind – it's time I showed the qualities Heaven has bestowed on me!

ADRASTES. If only there were some way of letting her know either by letter or by word of mouth the affection I have for her and finding out what her feelings are. Then one might easily find means of . . .

HALI. Just leave it to me. I'll try such a variety of tricks that one or other is bound to succeed. Come along; day's breaking. I'll go and find my men and keep watch here until our jealous friend comes out. [*Exeunt.*]

[DON PEDRO *and* ISIDORE *come out.*]

ISIDORE. I can't imagine what pleasure you can find in waking me up so early. It doesn't go very well, it seems to me, with your plan of having my portrait painted today. Rising at break of day hardly makes for a fresh complexion and a sparkling eye!

DON PEDRO. I have business which requires me to go out at this hour.

ISIDORE. But I should have thought your business could have done without my presence and you could have allowed me to enjoy the pleasure of staying in bed without inconvenience to yourself.

DON PEDRO. Yes, but I like to have you with me all the time. It's just as well to be on one's guard against inquisitive people. There's already been someone singing under your window.

ISIDORE. Yes, the music was admirable.

DON PEDRO. Was it intended for you?

ISIDORE. I'm willing to believe it since you suggest it.

DON PEDRO. And do you know who provided the serenade?

ISIDORE. No, but I'm grateful to him, whoever he was.

DON PEDRO. Grateful to him!

ISIDORE. Of course. He was trying to please me.

DON PEDRO. So you like people to make love to you, then?

ISIDORE. Very much. I never take it unkindly.

DON PEDRO. And you are grateful to all those who venture to do so?

ISIDORE. Of course.

DON PEDRO. Well that's candid enough!

ISIDORE. What's the use of trying to hide it? Whatever pretence one may make one is always glad to be loved. Homage to one's charms is never displeasing. Whatever people may say, to inspire love is a woman's greatest ambition, believe me. It's the one thing women care about and there's no woman so proud that she doesn't rejoice at heart in her conquests.

DON PEDRO. Well if it gives you pleasure to see people in love with you please understand that it gives me – who love you – no pleasure at all.

ISIDORE. I don't see why not. If I were in love with anyone nothing would please me better than to see everyone love him. What better evidence could there be of the wisdom of one's choice? Ought we not to congratulate ourselves when the one whom we love is found lovable?

DON PEDRO. Every man to his own way of loving but that isn't mine. I should be very glad if people didn't think you quite so beautiful and if you want to please me you won't try to appear too much so in other men's eyes.

ISIDORE. What! Are you jealous?

DON PEDRO. Yes! Jealous as a tiger or as the devil himself if you like. I want you all to myself. I object to every smile, every glance that other men get from you. All these precautions I'm taking are intended to cut you off from admirers and keep your love to myself. I can't bear that anyone should rob me of even the smallest particle.

ISIDORE. Very well then, let me tell you something! You go about things quite the wrong way. Affection is very insecure when you seek to retain it by force. I assure you that if I were a young man and in love with a woman who was in another man's power I would try every means of making him jealous and force him to keep constant watch on her. It would be an admirable way of furthering his cause. He couldn't fail to profit from the resentment and anger whch constraint and servitude create in a woman's heart.

DON PEDRO. So that if a man were to make advances to you he would find you ready to listen to him? Eh?

ISIDORE. I'm not saying anything about that. But it is a fact that women dislike having their freedom curtailed and it's risking trouble to show that you are suspicious of them and keep them under constraint.

DON PEDRO. You show little gratitude for all that you owe to me. I should have thought that a slave I had freed and intended to marry –

ISIDORE. What obligation have I to you if you make me exchange one kind of slavery for another even more irksome, if you allow me no freedom at all and weary me – as you do – by keeping perpetual watch over me.

DON PEDRO. But it's all because I love you so much –

ISIDORE. If that's how you love me, kindly be so good as to hate me.

DON PEDRO. You are in a very disagreeable humour this morning but I'll put it all down to irritation at being awakened so early.

[*Enter* HALI *dressed as a Turk. He makes elaborate obeisances to* DON PEDRO.]

DON PEDRO. A truce to your ceremonies. What do you want?

HALI [*getting between* DON PEDRO *and* ISIDORE, *he turns to* ISIDORE *at each sentence he addresses to* DON PEDRO, *making signs to indicate his master's plan*]. Signor – with the permission of the signora – I am to tell you – with the permission of the signora – that I have come to see you – with the

permission of the signora – to ask you – with the permission
of the signora – to be good enough – with the permission
of the signora –

DON PEDRO. With the permission of the signora – come over
here. [*Puts himself between* HALI *and* ISIDORE.]

HALI. Sir, I am a virtuoso.

DON PEDRO. I have nothing to give you.

HALI. That's not what I mean. I am in the singing and
dancing business and I have trained a few slaves who now
wish to find a master who likes that sort of thing. Knowing
you to be a man of means, I would like to ask you to see
them and hear them with a view to buying them if they
please you or recommending them to someone among
your acquaintance who might like to do so.

ISIDORE. We should certainly see them. It will be amusing.
Ask them to come in.

HALI. *Chala Bala.* This is a new song, the very latest thing.
Listen please. *Chala Bala.*

[*Enter slaves. One of them* sings to* ISIDORE.]

> By ardour driven, where'er she be,
> A lover seeks his dear one
> But her – he may not see
> For jealousy
> Has her in keeping
> With watch unsleeping –
> What fate more cruel ever
> Could befall a lover?
> [*To* DON PEDRO.]
> Chiribirida ouch alla
> Me poor Turkish wallah
> You employ me today
> Me workee – you pay
> Me make good cuisine – a
> Rise early matina

* The stage direction to the edition of 1668 is *Hali sings* but the
partition, or original libretto, gives the song to a slave – a more convenient arrangement unless the actor taking the part of Hali is a singer.

> Me good cook and clean – a
> Parlara – please say
> If you buy me – today?

[*Dance of slaves. Slave sings again. To* ISIDORE.]

> Pity his fate, forlorn estate
> Thus parted from his dear one
> Let her vouchsafe
> Him cause for hope;
> Let her bright eyes
> Transform his sighs;
> He'll show love mocks
> At bars and locks.

[*To* DON PEDRO *as before. Second dance of slaves.*]

DON PEDRO [*sings*].

> Learn now my smart fellows
> What means this your song
> It means that I'll beat you
> Back where you belong!

> Chiribirida ouch alla!
> Right well you'll be paid
> By my bastonnade
> Right well you'll be paid
> By my bastonnade!

[*He drives them off.*]

DON PEDRO. What a pack of scoundrels. Come along. Let's
go inside. I have changed my mind. Moreover it's getting
rather cloudy. [*To* HALI *who appears again*] You scoundrel!
Just let me catch you at it again!

HALI. All right then! My master adores her and his sole
desire is to declare his love to her. If she consents he'll
make her his wife.

DON PEDRO. Yes, but I shall look after her.

HALI. We shall get her – in spite of you.

DON PEDRO. What! You villain –

HALI. We shall get her, I say, show your teeth as you may!

DON PEDRO. If I once –

HALI. You can keep watch as much as you like but I have taken my oath on it – we shall get her away from you.

DON PEDRO. Leave that to me – I'll catch you easily enough.

[DON PEDRO *goes indoors*.]

HALI. No! We'll do the catching! The master shall marry her. That's already decided. [*Alone*] We'll succeed this time if I die in the attempt.

[*Enter* ADRASTES *with lackeys*.]

ADRASTES. Well, Hali, how are our affairs progressing?

HALI. Master, I have made one attempt but . . .

ADRASTES. Don't worry. I have found quite by chance just what I wanted. I'm to have the pleasure of seeing the lady in her own house. I happened to call to see Damon the artist and he told me that he was going to paint the portrait of this adorable young lady today. He's an old friend of mine and he was willing to help me to attain my purpose so here I am in his place with his letter of introduction. I have always been fond of painting, you know, and – contrary to the usual custom in France which forbids a gentleman to be able to do anything useful – I can handle a brush. So I shall be able to see the lady at my leisure. I don't doubt that our jealous friend will be there all the time and prevent our saying all the things we should like to, but with the help of a young slave girl I have prepared another scheme to rescue her from the clutches of her keeper if only I can win her consent.

HALI. You leave it to me. I'll give you an opportunity of talking to her. [*Whispers to* ADRASTES] I can't have it said that I had no hand in the business. When are you going?

ADRASTES. This very moment. I have got everything ready.

HALI. I'll go and get ready too.

ADRASTES. I don't want to lose any time. How I'm longing to see her!

Scene Two

A room in Don Pedro's house

DON PEDRO, ADRASTES, TWO LACKEYS

DON PEDRO. And what may you be seeking here, sir?

ADRASTES. I am seeking the gentleman of the house, Don Pedro.

DON PEDRO. At your service.

ADRASTES. Pray, be good enough to read this letter.

DON PEDRO [*reads aloud*]. 'I am sending a young Frenchman to paint the portrait for you. He has been good enough to undertake the task at my request and he is beyond question an exceptionally good man for work of this kind. I thought I couldn't do better than send him along to do the portrait of the young lady you admire. Whatever you do, don't mention any question of payment. He's the sort of man who would be offended – he has no interest in these matters beyond the pursuit of fame and reputation.' Well, sir, this is a great honour you do me and I'm very much indebted to you.

ADRASTES. My only ambition is to be of service to people of standing and distinction.

DON PEDRO. I'll go and summon the lady.

[*Enter* ISIDORE.]

DON PEDRO [*to* ISIDORE]. This is a gentleman whom Damon has sent to us. He has kindly undertaken to paint you. [*To* ADRASTES, *who kisses* ISIDORE *by way of salutation*] My good sir, that form of greeting is not customary in this country.

ADRASTES. It's customary in France, sir.

DON PEDRO. The French custom may be very well for French women but for ours – it is a little too familiar.

ISIDORE. I am delighted with the honour you do me though it's a little unexpected and I must confess I hardly looked for so illustrious a painter.

ADRASTES. Any painter would be proud to undertake such

89

a commission. I have no great ability but the subject is, in this case, an inspiration in itself. There is scope for achieving something really delightful when one's working from such an original.

ISIDORE. The subject is but so-so, but the skill of the painter will no doubt make up for its deficiencies.

ADRASTES. There are none that the painter is aware of. His sole aspiration is to do justice to the grace and beauty which he sees before him.

ISIDORE. If your brush is as flattering as your tongue your picture won't be much like me.

ADRASTES. Nature, madam, in creating the original left no possibility of flattery open to the painter.

ISIDORE. Nature, whatever you may say won't –

DON PEDRO. That's quite enough, if you please – let us cut out the compliments and come to the picture.

ADRASTES [*to lackeys*]. Come, bring the things here.

[*They bring in the necessary equipment.*]

ISIDORE [*to* ADRASTES]. Where do you wish me to sit?

ADRASTES. Here – this is the most suitable place. We get the light to the best advantage.

ISIDORE [*after taking her seat*]. Like this?

ADRASTES. Yes. A little higher if you please. A shade more to this side. The body turned so. Head up a little so as to show the beauty of the neck. This a little more exposed [*he's referring to her bosom*]. Good. There, a little more; a trifle more yet.

DON PEDRO [*to* ISIDORE]. You take a lot of getting into position. Why don't you sit properly?

ISIDORE. This is all quite new to me. It's for the gentleman to pose me as he thinks fit.

ADRASTES [*sitting down*]. That's very good indeed. You pose beautifully. [*Turning her a little towards him*] So, if you please. The attitude of the sitter is everything.

DON PEDRO. Indeed!

ADRASTES. A little more to this side. Keep your eyes turned towards me, please – keep them fixed on mine.

ISIDORE. I am not one of those women who demand a portrait which isn't them at all and are pleased with the artist only if he makes them appear altogether too beautiful to be true. To satisfy that sort of sitter there need only be one portrait for all, for they all want the same things, a complexion all lily and roses, a shapely nose, a small mouth, a pair of wide-set sparkling eyes and above all a face no larger than one's hand, however big it be in reality. What *I* ask of you is a portrait which shall be a real likeness so that there's no need to ask who it is.

ADRASTES. It would be difficult to imagine anyone asking that of yours for your features are unique. How delightful, how charming they are! But what a risk one runs in trying to paint them!

DON PEDRO. The nose seems a bit large to me.

ADRASTES. I read somewhere how Apelles was once engaged on a portrait of one of the mistresses of Alexander the Great and in the course of painting her he fell madly, indeed desperately, in love with her – so much so that Alexander generously surrendered her to him. [*To* DON PEDRO] I could follow Apelles' example here and now but you wouldn't, perhaps, follow Alexander's. [DON PEDRO *makes a grimace*.]

ISIDORE [*to* DON PEDRO]. How typically French! Frenchmen have an unlimited capacity for gallantry and indulge it on every occasion.

ADRASTES [*to* ISIDORE]. One's intuition is seldom at fault in these things and you are too intelligent not to understand the real meaning of what I am saying. Even if Alexander were here and your lover, I couldn't refrain from telling you that I have never beheld anything so beautiful as what I see now and that . . .

DON PEDRO. My good sir, I think you are talking too much. It takes your attention from your work.

ADRASTES. No. Not in the least. I always talk when I'm painting. A little conversation stimulates the imagination and maintains the requisite vivacity in the face of the sitter.

[*Enter* HALI *dressed as a Spaniard*.]

DON PEDRO. What does this fellow want? Who lets people come up here without announcing them?

HALI [*to* DON PEDRO]. I have entered without ceremony but that is a freedom permitted between gentlemen. Am I known to you, Sir?

DON PEDRO. No sir.

HALI. I am Don Gilles d'Avalos. The history of Spain is witness to my fame.

DON PEDRO. And do you want something from me?

HALI. Yes. I want your advice on a point of honour. I know that in affairs of this kind it would be difficult to find a gentleman of greater authority than you. But pray let us draw to one side a little.

DON PEDRO. This is quite far enough.

ADRASTES [*looking at* ISIDORE]. She has blue eyes.

HALI [*drawing* DON PEDRO *away from* ADRASTES *and* ISIDORE]. Sir, I have received a slap in the face. You know what a slap is when it's given with an open hand full in the middle of the cheek. I have taken this slap much to heart and I am undecided whether, in order to avenge the affront, I should fight him or have him assassinated.

DON PEDRO. Assassination's quicker. Who is he?

HALI. Let us speak quietly if you please. [*Detaining him in conversation in such a way that he cannot see* ADRASTES.]

ADRASTES [*on his knees beside* ISIDORE *while* DON PEDRO *is talking to* HALI]. Yes, my charming Isidore, my eyes have been telling you of my love for the past two months, and it seems that you have understood their message. I love you beyond anything else in the world. I have no thought, no purpose, no desire, but to be yours for the rest of my life.

ISIDORE. I don't know whether you are telling the truth but you are very persuasive.

ADRASTES. But have I persuaded you sufficiently for you to feel some affection for me?

ISIDORE. My only fear is that I may feel too much.

ADRASTES. Enough, dear Isidore, to consent to the scheme I have told you of?

ISIDORE. I cannot yet say.

ADRASTES. But what are you waiting for?

ISIDORE. To make up my mind.

ADRASTES. Ah, but when one is really in love one soon makes up one's mind!

ISIDORE. Very well then, yes, I consent.

ADRASTES. Then do you consent to do it immediately?

ISIDORE. Does the time matter once one has taken the decision?

DON PEDRO [*to* HALI]. That's my opinion, sir, and I'll be taking my leave of you.

HALI. Sir, should you ever receive a slap, I'm a good counsellor too and I'd be glad to help you in return. [*Exit.*]

DON PEDRO. I will let you go without seeing you to the door – that's a freedom permitted between gentlemen.

ADRASTES [*to* ISIDORE]. No, nothing can ever efface from my heart these tender proofs . . . [*To* DON PEDRO] I was looking at this dimple on her chin. At first I thought it was a mole. But that's enough for today. We'll finish it another time. [*To* DON PEDRO, *who wishes to see the portrait*] No, don't look at it yet. Have it put away please. [*To* ISIDORE] And you, madam, don't, I beseech you, give way. Keep up your spirits so that we may complete the work we have in hand.

ISIDORE. I'll keep up my spirits you may be sure.

[ADRASTES *goes.*]

ISIDORE. Well I don't know what *you* say but he seems to me a very gentlemanly person indeed. One must admit that the French have a polish and gallantry that other nations lack.

DON PEDRO. Maybe, but the trouble with them is that they become too free in their manners and far too fond of paying compliments to every woman they come across.

ISIDORE. That's because they know what women like.

DON PEDRO. Yes, but what women like men *dis*like very much. Nobody wants to see his wife or his mistress made love to under his very nose.

ISIDORE. They only do it for fun.

Scene Three

[*Enter* CLIMÈNE, *wearing a veil.*]

CLIMÈNE. Ah, my good sir, please save me from my infuriated husband. His jealousy is beyond belief; it goes to
unimaginable lengths. He insists that I always wear a veil
and because he found me with my face partly exposed he
snatched up a sword and I had no alternative but to throw
myself on your protection and ask your support against
his injustice. But here he comes. I beseech you, sir, save me
from his fury.

DON PEDRO [*indicating* ISIDORE]. Go in there with her and
fear nothing.

[*Exeunt* CLIMÈNE *and* ISIDORE. *Enter* ADRASTES.]

DON PEDRO. Why, sir, it's you, is it? So much jealousy in
a Frenchman? I thought only we Sicilians were capable of
such feeling.

ADRASTES. The French invariably excel in everything they
undertake. When we go in for jealousy we are twenty times
worse than any Sicilian. The wretch thinks she has found a
safe refuge in your house but you, I am sure, will appreciate
my feelings and allow me to give her what she deserves.

DON PEDRO. No, stop, I implore you. Such a trifling offence
doesn't justify all this fury.

ADRASTES. The seriousness of the offence lies not in what
she has done but in the defiance of my orders – the merest
trifle becomes a crime when it's forbidden.

DON PEDRO. But from what she says it would seem that she
has done nothing intentionally wrong. I beg you to be
reconciled again.

ADRASTES. Ha! So you take her part, you who are so
scrupulous in such matters!

DON PEDRO. Yes, I take her part and if you wish to please me
you will forget your anger and be reconciled to each other.

I ask it as a favour and I will receive it as a proof of the friendship I would have between us.

ADRASTES. Since you put it that way I can't refuse. I'll do as you wish.

[ADRASTES *retires to one end of the stage.*]

DON PEDRO. Hello, you can come out! I've made peace with your husband. You did well to come to me.

CLIMÈNE. I'm deeply grateful to you but I'll go and put on my veil. I mustn't appear before him without it.

[ADRASTES *returns*]

DON PEDRO. She'll be back in a moment. I assure you that she was most relieved when I told her that everything was settled.

[*Enter* ISIDORE *wearing* CLIMÈNE'S *veil.*]

DON PEDRO [*to* ADRASTES]. Since you have agreed to put aside your resentment allow me to join your hands and implore you to live in harmony, *for my sake*.

ADRASTES. Yes, I promise that I'll live with her in love and harmony *for your sake*.

DON PEDRO. I'm deeply grateful. I shall always remember it.

ADRASTES. I give you my word, Signor Don Pedro, that I shall cherish her – *in consideration for you*.

DON PEDRO. You are too kind. [*They go.*] It's always nice to be able to exercise a pacifying influence and to bring things to a happy conclusion. Hello, Isidore, you can come out.

[CLIMÈNE *enters.*]

DON PEDRO. What does this mean?

CLIMÈNE [*without her veil*]. What does it mean? It means that a jealous man is a monster who's universally hated, that there isn't a soul anywhere who wouldn't be delighted to play a trick upon him for the mere pleasure of doing it, that all the locks and bars in the world can't keep people apart, that one must appeal to their hearts by affection and kindness, that Isidore is in the keeping of the man she loves, and that you have been made a fool of.

[*She goes out.*]

DON PEDRO. Shall Don Pedro suffer this mortal insult? No. No. Never! Not if I know it! I'll go and call in the law to bring the villain to justice. There's a magistrate lives here – Hello [*knocks on door*].

MAGISTRATE. Your servant. Don Pedro. You've come just at the very moment I wanted to see you.

DON PEDRO. I have come to complain of a wrong that's been done to me.

MAGISTRATE. I have arranged the most charming masquerade.

DON PEDRO. I have been tricked by a scoundrelly Frenchman.

MAGISTRATE. You have never, in all your life, seen anything finer.

DON PEDRO. He has carried off a slave girl I had set free.

MAGISTRATE. They are all in Moorish costume and they are wonderful dancers.

DON PEDRO. You'll hear whether it's the sort of insult that can go unpunished.

MAGISTRATE. Wonderful costumes made specially for the occasion.

DON PEDRO. I demand your assistance in the name of the law.

MAGISTRATE. I do want you to see it. They are going to rehearse now for the public performance later.

DON PEDRO. What on earth are you talking about?

MAGISTRATE. I'm talking about my masquerade.

DON PEDRO. And I am talking about my lawsuit.

MAGISTRATE. I'm not interested in any business but pleasure today. Come along, gentlemen. Come along! Let us see how it will go.

DON PEDRO. A plague on the fool and his masquerade!

MAGISTRATE. The devil take both him and his complaints!

[*Enter dancers in Moorish costume. Their dance ends the play.*]

Tartuffe *or* The Impostor

LE TARTUFFE *ou* L'IMPOSTEUR

Preface

This is a comedy about which a great deal of fuss has been made and it has long been persecuted. The people it makes fun of have certainly shown that they command more influence in France than any of those I have been concerned with before. Noblemen, pretentious women, cuckolds, and doctors have all submitted to being put on the stage and pretended to be as amused as everyone else at the way I portrayed them, but the hypocrites would not stand for a joke: they took immediate alarm and found it strange that I had the audacity to make fun of their antics or to decry so numerous and respectable a profession. For them it was an unforgivable crime and they united in furious attacks on my play. They were at pains not to retaliate on the points which touched them most nearly – they were too cunning for that, too wordly-wise to disclose their real feelings. Following their laudable custom they used the cause of Godliness to conceal their own interests and according to them *Tartuffe* is a play which offends against true religion. It is an abomination from beginning to end, fit only to be consigned to the flames: every single syllable is a blasphemy: the very gestures of the actors are criminal, a mere wink, a nod of the head, the slightest move right or left conceals some mysterious significance which they contrive to explain to my disadvantage.

It availed me nothing that I submitted the play to the criticism of my friends and to the judgement of the public: the alterations I contrived to make, the opinion of the King and Queen who saw it performed, the approbation of great princes and ministers who publicly honoured it with their presence, the testimony of good and worthy men who found profit in it – all these things went for nothing. They are not prepared to change their opinions and they still continue to incite their fanatics to denouncing me daily in public, heaping pious insults upon me, and charitably consigning me to perdition.

I should care very little for anything they might say were it not for their cunning in making enemies for me among men I respect and enticing into their ranks genuinely good people whose faith they abuse, people whose concern for the interests of true religion makes them all the more receptive to the impressions they seek to inculcate. This is what compels me to defend myself. It is to the truly devout people everywhere that I would like to justify the theme of my play. I implore them not to condemn it unseen and unread, to divest themselves of all prejudice, and not to lend support to the fanaticism of those who ape and dishonour their virtues.

People who will take the trouble to examine the play in good faith will see, beyond question, that my intentions were innocent throughout, that it in no wise tends to hold up to ridicule things to which reverence is due and that I have handled it all with the delicacy which the subject demands and used all my skill and taken every possible precaution to distinguish the hypocrite from the truly devout man. To this end I employed two whole acts in preparing for the entrance of my villain. The audience is never for a moment in doubt about him: he is recognizable at once by the distinguishing marks I have given him and from first to last he never utters a word or performs one single action which does not clearly indicate to the audience that he is a scoundrel in direct contrast to the truly good man I set in contrast to him.

I am fully aware that these gentlemen endeavour to suggest in reply that the theatre is not the place for discussing these matters but I ask them, with all due deference, on what do they base this convenient assumption. It is a proposition founded on pure supposition for which they adduce no proof whatever: there is no question that one could prove to them, without difficulty, that the theatre of the Ancients had its origins in religion and formed an integral part of their religious ceremonies; that our neighbours the Spaniards never celebrate any festival of the Church without plays being included; and that even among our own people the drama owes its origins to the efforts of a religious fraternity who still own the *Hôtel de Bourgogne*, a building given to them with the intention that the most important mysteries of our Faith might there be presented; that one can still find plays printed in Gothic type under the name of a doctor of the Sorbonne* and not to go so

* Molière is referring to a particular one – *The Mystery of the Passion* of Jean Michel.

far afield, that the sacred plays of Monsieur de Corneille which won the admiration of all France have been performed there in our own time.

If the purpose of comedy be to chastise human weaknesses I see no reason why any class of people should be exempt. This particular failing is one of the most damaging of all in its public consequences and we have seen that the theatre is a great medium of correction. The finest passages of a serious moral treatise are all too often less effective than those of a satire and for the majority of people there is no better form of reproof than depicting their faults to them: the most effective way of attacking vice is to expose it to public ridicule. People can put up with rebukes but they cannot bear being laughed at: they are prepared to be wicked but they dislike appearing ridiculous.

I am reproached with having put expressions of piety into the mouth of my impostor. But how was I to avoid it if I wished to present the character of a hypocrite? It is sufficient, it seems to me, that I made clear the wicked motives that impelled him to these utterances and that I deleted certain sacred terms which it would have been painful to hear him misuse. Ah! But in the fourth act he propounds a pernicious system of morality! But has this system of morality not already been dinned into our ears? Does my play introduce anything new? Can one really fear that sentiments so generally detested will have any influence on men's minds? Do they become dangerous by the mere fact of being voiced on the stage? Are they likely to acquire authority by being heard from the lips of a scoundrel? It does not seem in the least likely and the fact is that one either has to approve of my play, *Tartuffe*, or condemn plays in general.

This is exactly what some people have been endeavouring to do for some time past: never has there been such an outcry against the theatre: I cannot deny that there have been Fathers of the Church who have condemned plays but, on the other hand, it must be conceded to me that there have been others who treated them more leniently and such division of opinion destroys the authority on which these people seek to base their censure: all that one can infer from this diversity of views among men of similar degrees of enlightenment is that they have looked at the question differently:

some have considered drama in its pure form, others have seen it in degraded versions and confounded it with disgraceful spectacles rightly condemned as sheer exhibitions of vice.

If, however, the discussion were directed as it should be, to things themselves and not the names applied to them – since most differences of opinion arise from misunderstandings and from using the same terms for things which are in fact utterly different – we need only strip off the veil of equivocation, and consider what a play really is, to see whether or not it is deserving of condemnation. We shall find, beyond question, that, since it is nothing more or less than a form of poem which ingeniously seeks to reprove men's errors by lessons presented in an agreeable form, we cannot in justice condemn it and, if we are willing to listen to the testimony of Antiquity on the point, we shall find that the most famous philosophers, those who professed the most austere views, eulogized the Drama: we shall hear how Aristotle devoted time and thought to the theatre and took the trouble to lay down principles for the writing of plays: we shall learn that some of the noblest and greatest men of those times were proud to have written plays themselves and that others did not disdain to recite their works publicly: that Greece showed her esteem for the Art of the Theatre by the magnificent prizes she awarded and the superb buildings she erected in its honour: that in Rome too this same Art was accorded outstanding honours, and I am not referring to the debauched and licentious Rome of the Caesars but to the disciplined Rome under the wise rule of the Consuls when the Roman virtues were still in full vigour.

I admit that there have been periods when the theatre became decadent and corrupt, but what is there in this world that escapes corruption? There is nothing so innocent but men can defile it, no art so salutary but its intentions can be reversed, nothing so good in itself that it cannot be turned to evil uses. Medicine is a valuable art, one universally esteemed for its benefits, yet there have been periods when it fell into disrepute; the art of healing has not seldom become the art of the poisoner. Philosophy is Heaven's gift to mankind, bestowed upon us as a means of bringing our minds to the knowledge of a Divine Being by the contemplation of the wonders of nature, but we know quite well that its purposes have often been perverted and employed in support of ungodliness. Even the holiest of things are not secure from man's corrupting influence: we see piety abused daily by scoundrels and turned to criminal uses but for all that, we do not fail to make the necessary distinctions, we do not make false deductions and confuse the essential goodness of the things men corrupt with the evil in the minds of those who corrupt them. We discriminate in any art between evil practices and sound intentions. Just as we would not think of forbidding the practice of Medicine because it was once banished from Rome, nor of Philosophy because it was at one time publicly condemned in Athens, so we should not seek to put the theatre under proscription because at certain periods it fell under censure. There was once justification for such censures but they do not apply now. They were directed to evils which were in evidence at the particular time: we should not seek to apply them in different circumstances nor gratuitously extend them and so confound innocence with guilt. The theatre of those days was a wholly different thing from the one we now seek to defend. We must beware of confusing one with the other. They are like two people whose ways of life are entirely opposed. They have nothing in common with one another except the name. It would be a dreadful injustice to condemn the virtuous Olympia because there was another Olympia who was a courtesan. Judgements of that sort would certainly cause a great deal of trouble in society. Nothing would escape condemnation. Moreover, since there are so many things which are daily abused to which we do not apply such rigorous standards we ought to extend a similar tolerance to the theatre and give our support to those plays in which there is manifest evidence of instruction and honest intention.

I am aware that there are people who are so squeamish that they cannot bear any sort of play whatsoever: they say that the better the play the more harm it does; that the passions depicted are all the more affecting for being virtuous ones and that people are unduly excited by such performances. I do not see that it is any great crime to be moved at the sight of an honest passion. This complete insensibility to which they would have us aspire is indeed a high standard of virtue! I doubt whether such perfection lies within the power of human nature and I am not sure that it is not better to work for the refinement and control of men's passions rather than seek their total extinction. I admit there are places which one can frequent to greater advantage than the theatre and if everything not conducive to the service of God and our Salvation is to be regarded as reprehensible, then certainly the theatre must be included and I take no exception to its being condemned with the rest. Assuming, however, as is indeed the case, that intervals in the exercise of devotion are permissible and that people need some relaxation, then I maintain that there is none more harmless than the theatre. I have been over long. Let us finish with a great Prince's comment on the play *Tartuffe* itself.

A week after performance of this play was forbidden a play was given at Court called *Scaramouche the Hermit*. As he was coming away the King said to the great nobleman I have in mind, 'I would like to know why people who are so scandalized by Molière's play have no word to say about *Scaramouche*.' To which the Prince replied, 'The reason is this: *Scaramouche* makes fun of religion and sacred things in which these gentlemen have no interest at all: Molière's play holds *them* up to ridicule. That's what they can't stand.'

FIRST PETITION

ADDRESSED TO THE KING
CONCERNING THE PLAY

Tartuffe

Sire,

The duty of comedy being to correct men's errors in the course of amusing them, I thought that there was nothing I could do to greater advantage, in the exercise of my profession, than attack the vices of the age by depicting them in ridiculous guise and hypocrisy being, beyond question, one of the most prevalent and most pernicious among them, the idea occurred to me, Sire, that I should render no small service to all good men among your subjects, if I wrote a play attacking hypocrites that would draw attention to the studied posturing of the ultra-godly and the covert rascality of these false coiners of devotion who seek to ensnare their fellow men by means of a counterfeited zeal and a sophistical charity.

I have, Sire, written this play with all the care and circumspection, I believe, that the delicacy of the subject demands and, the better to preserve the esteem and respect which one owes to sincerely pious people, I have been at pains to make clear the real nature of the character I was depicting. I have left no room for uncertainty: I have omitted everything which might lead anyone to confuse good with evil and I have employed, in the portrayal, precisely those colours and essential characteristics which are best calculated to make a veritable and downright hypocrite immediately recognizable.

Nevertheless all my precautions have been in vain. People have profited, Sire, from the delicacy of your scruples in everything that concerns religion and managed to approach you on the one side where you are vulnerable – I refer to your respect for sacred things. The Tartuffes have surreptitiously contrived to find favour with Your Majesty and the people whom the picture portrays have managed to suppress it, salutary though it was in intention, and accurate though the likeness was admitted to be.

Severe as was the blow of having my work suppressed, my disappointment has been softened by the way Your Majesty made clear your personal views on the question. I felt, Sire, that Your Majesty deprived me of all ground for complaint when you had had the goodness to say that you yourself found nothing to object to in this play you were forbidding me to perform in public.

Notwithstanding this gracious pronouncement of the greatest and most enlightened of monarchs, notwithstanding the approbation shown by His Grace the Papal Legate and the greater part of his fellow prelates all of whom, in the private readings of my work which I have given in their presence, have found themselves in agreement with Your Majesty: notwithstanding all this, I say, a book has just been published by a certain parish priest which flatly contradicts these august testimonies. Your Majesty can say what you like; the Legate and his colleagues may give what judgement they please – my play, which he has never seen, is, according to him, a diabolical work and I myself am no less diabolical: I am a fiend in human shape, an atheist, a blasphemer, deserving of exemplary punishment. It is not enough that the flames should expiate my offence publicly; that would be letting me off too cheaply: the charitable zeal of this worthy, god-fearing man is not content to stop there: he would deny me God's mercy itself and demands in the most absolute terms that I should be damned to all eternity: and no argument about it.

This book has been presented to Your Majesty and you can doubtless judge yourself how trying it is for me to find myself exposed daily to the insults of these gentlemen: how harmful such calumnies will be to my public reputation, should they be allowed to pass uncorrected, and how concerned I must be to clear myself of this slander and demonstrate to the public that my play is not at all what it is made out to be. I shall, therefore, say nothing, Sire, about what is, I feel, required in the interest of my reputation or in justification of the innocence of my work in the eyes of the world: with monarchs as enlightened as you, Sire, there is no need to elaborate one's requests. They perceive, like God, what our needs are and know better than we do what should be accorded to us. It is sufficient for me to commit my interests to Your Majesty's keeping and I respectfully await whatever you may be pleased to ordain.

(*August* 1664)

SECOND PETITION

PRESENTED TO THE KING IN CAMP BEFORE THE TOWN OF LILLE IN FLANDERS

Sire,

It is indeed an act of temerity on my part to come and importune a great monarch in the midst of his glorious conquests but, my position being what it is, where am I to find protection, Sire, except where I am now seeking it? Whose aid can I solicit against the authority of the power which is bearing so hardly upon me unless it be that of the source of all power and authority, the just dispenser of absolute commands, the sovereign judge and master of all?

Preface

My play, Sire, has not so far reaped the advantage here in Paris of the favour Your Majesty accorded it. In vain I have produced it under the title of *The Imposter* and disguised the leading character beneath the garb of a man of the world; it has availed me nothing that I have given him a small hat, flowing locks, a ruff, and a sword, decked him out in lace, toned the play down in many places, and rigorously deleted everything which I thought could furnish a shadow of pretext to the celebrated originals of the portrait I have chosen to draw. All this has proved useless. The cabal have renewed their hostility on the basis of their own crude preconceptions. They have found means to influence people who, in all other matters, boast that they are not wont to let themselves be influenced. No sooner did my play appear than it was struck down by a power which must be respected and all I could do in the circumstances to protect myself from the storm was to say that Your Majesty had been so gracious as to allow me to perform the play and that it had not occurred to me that I need ask permission from anyone else since it was by your decree alone that it had originally been forbidden.

I do not doubt, Sire, that the people whom I depict in my comedy will use every means of influencing Your Majesty and will try to enlist on their side, as they have done before, the truly good men who are the more easily deceived in that they judge others by themselves. These people are skilful in depicting their intentions in the most favourable colours but, whatever pretence they may make, it is not the interests of religion they have at heart – that much they have sufficiently shown from the plays they have so often allowed to be presented in public without protest. But these plays merely attacked piety and true religion about which they are little concerned: my comedy was directed at them and turned them to ridicule and that is something they will not permit. They cannot forgive me for publicly tearing the veil from their impostures. Beyond question they will not fail to inform Your Majesty that my play has shocked everybody. But the plain truth, Sire, is that what has really shocked all Paris is the prohibition of it; that the most scrupulous judges have esteemed its performance a salutary influence and that what has caused surprise is that persons of known probity should pay such deference to those who deserve to be universally regarded with horror, and are themselves so opposed to the true piety of which they make profession.

I await respectfully such decision as Your Majesty may deign to give on the matter but one thing is beyond question, Sire, that it is useless for me to think of writing any more for the theatre if the Tartuffes are to gain the day, for if they do, they will assume the right to persecute me more than ever and contrive to find something to condemn in the most innocent works of my pen.

May your bounty deign to accord me protection, Sire, against their venomous rage and so enable me, when you return from your triumphant campaign, to afford Your Majesty diversion after the fatigues of your conquests, provide you with innocent pleasures after your noble exertions, and bring a smile to the countenance of the Monarch before whom Europe trembles.

(*August* 1667)

THIRD PETITION

PRESENTED TO THE KING

Sire,

A worthy physician, whose patient I have the honour to be, has promised to keep me alive for another thirty years if I can obtain him a certain favour from Your Majesty and he is willing to enter into a legal undertaking to that effect. I told him that, so far as his undertaking was concerned, I did not ask so much of him and I should be satisfied if only he would undertake not to kill me. The favour in question, Sire, is a Canonry in the Chapel Royal of Vincennes vacant through the death of . . . .

Might I venture to ask this additional favour of Your Majesty on the very day of the great resurrection of *Tartuffe*, restored to life by your bounty? I am by this first favour reconciled with the devout and I shall by the second make peace with the doctors. For myself it is undoubtedly too much to ask at one and the same time but perhaps not too much for Your Majesty's generosity and I respectfully await the answer to my petition with some slight measure of hope.

(*February* 1669)

CHARACTERS IN THE PLAY

MADAME PERNELLE, mother of Orgon
ORGON
ELMIRE, his wife
DAMIS, his son
MARIANE, his daughter, in love with Valère
VALÈRE, in love with Mariane
CLÉANTE, brother-in-law of Orgon
TARTUFFE, a hypocrite
DORINE, maid to Mariane
MR LOYAL, a tipstaff
FLIPOTE, maid to Madame Pernelle
AN OFFICER

The scene is Orgon's house in Paris

Act One

[*Enter* MADAME PERNELLE *and* FLIPOTE, ELMIRE, MARIANE, CLÉANTE, DAMIS, DORINE.]

MADAME PERNELLE. Come, Flipote, come along. Let me be getting away from them.

ELMIRE. You walk so fast one can hardly keep up with you.

MADAME PERNELLE. Never mind, my dear, never mind! Don't come any further. I can do without all this politeness.

ELMIRE. We are only paying you the respect that is due to you. Why must you be in such a hurry to go, mother?

MADAME PERNELLE. Because I can't bear to see the goings-on in this house and because there's no consideration shown to me at all. I have had a very unedifying visit indeed! All my advice goes for nothing here. There's no respect paid to anything. Everybody airs his opinions – the place is a veritable Bedlam!

DORINE. If . . .

MADAME PERNELLE. For a servant you have a good deal too much to say for yourself, my girl. You don't know your place. You give your opinion on everything.

DAMIS. But . . .

MADAME PERNELLE. You, my lad, are just a plain fool. I'm your grandmother and I'm telling you so! I warned your father a hundred times over that you showed all the signs of turning out badly and bringing him nothing but trouble.

MARIANE. I think . . .

MADAME PERNELLE. Oh Lord, yes! You are his little sister, and you put on your demure looks as if butter wouldn't melt in your mouth – but it's just as they say, 'Still waters run deep'. I hate to think of what you do on the sly.

ELMIRE. But mother . . .

MADAME PERNELLE. My dear, if you'll allow me to say so you go about these things in the wrong way entirely. You ought to set them an example. Their own mother did very much better. You are extravagant. It distresses me to see the way you go about dressed like a duchess. A woman who's concerned only with pleasing her husband has no need for so much finery, my dear.

CLÉANTE. Oh come, after all madam . . .

MADAME PERNELLE. As for you, sir, I have the greatest esteem, affection, and respect for you as the brother of Elmire but if I were in her husband's place I should entreat you never to set foot in the house. You keep on advocating a way of life which no respectable people should follow. If I speak a little bluntly – well, that's my way. I don't mince matters. I say what I think.

DAMIS. Your Mr Tartuffe is undoubtedly a very lucky man . . .

MADAME PERNELLE. He's a *good* man and people would do well to listen to him. It enrages me to hear him criticized by a dolt such as you.

DAMIS. What! Am I to allow a sanctimonious bigot to come and usurp tyrannical authority here in the very house? Are we to have no pleasure at all unless his lordship deigns to approve?

DORINE. If we took notice of him we should never be able to do anything without committing a sin. He forbids everything – pious busybody that he is!

MADAME PERNELLE. And whatever he forbids deserves to be forbidden. He means to lead you along the road to Salvation. My son ought to make you all love him.

DAMIS. No, grandmother, neither my father nor anyone else could make me have any liking for him. It would be hypocrisy for me to say anything else. His behaviour infuriates me at every turn. I can only see one end to it. It'll come to a row between this scoundrel and me. It's bound to.

DORINE. It really is a scandalous thing to see a mere nobody assuming a position of authority in the house, a beggar without shoes to his feet when he first came, all the clothes he had to his back not worth sixpence, and getting so far above himself as to interfere with everything and behave as if he were the master.

MADAME PERNELLE. Mercy on us! It would be a lot better if the whole place *were* under his pious instruction.

DORINE. You imagine he's a saint but, believe me, he's nothing but a hypocrite!

MADAME PERNELLE. Listen to her talking!

DORINE. I wouldn't trust myself with him without good security or his man Laurence either.

MADAME PERNELLE. I don't know what the servant is really like, but the master's a good man, that I *will* warrant. The only reason you dislike him and are so set against him is that he tells you all the truth about yourselves: it's sin that rouses his wrath. Everything he does is done in the cause of the Lord.

DORINE. Hm! Then why is it – particularly just recently – that he can't bear to have anyone coming about the place? What is there sinful in calling on someone in an ordinary straightforward way that he should make such a hullabaloo about it? Shall I tell you what I think – between ourselves – [*she indicates* ELMIRE] I believe he's jealous on account of the mistress. Upon my word I do!

MADAME PERNELLE. Hold your tongue and mind what you are saying! He's not the only one who takes exception to visitors. All these people coming here and causing a disturbance, carriages for ever standing at the door, and swarms of noisy footmen and lackeys make a bad impression on the whole neighbourhood. I'm willing to believe that there's no harm in it really, but it sets people talking and that's not a good thing.

CLÉANTE. And do you propose, madam, to stop people talking? It would be a poor affair if we had to give up our best friends for fear of the silly things that people might say about us and even if we did, do you think you could shut everybody's mouth? There's no defence against malicious tongues, so let's pay no heed to their tittle-tattle; let us try to live virtuously and leave the gossips to say what they will.

DORINE. It's our neighbour, Daphne, and that little husband of hers who have been speaking ill of us, isn't it? Folk whose own behaviour is most ridiculous are always to the fore in slandering others. They never miss a chance of seizing on the least glimmering suspicion of an affair, of gleefully spreading the news and twisting things the way they want folk to believe. They think they can justify their own goings-on by painting other people's behaviour in the same colours as their own and so hope to give an air of innocence to their intrigues or throw on other people some share of the criticism their own actions only too well deserve.

MADAME PERNELLE. All this talk is beside the point. Everybody knows that Orante's life is an example to everybody. She's a God-fearing woman and I hear she strongly condemns the company that comes here.

DORINE.* She's a wonderful example – a really good woman! It's quite true that she leads a strict sort of life but it's age that has made her turn pious. We all know that she's virtuous only because she has no alternative. So long as she was able to attract men's attentions she enjoyed herself to the full, but now that she finds her eyes losing their lustre she resolves to renounce the world which is slipping away from her and conceal the fading of her charms beneath an elaborate pretence of high principles. That's what coquettes come to in the end. It's hard for them to see their admirers desert them. Left alone and unhappy, the only course left to them is to turn virtuous. Their righteous severity condemns everything and forgives nothing. They rail against other people's way of life – not in the interests of righteousness but from envy – because they can't bear that anyone else should enjoy the pleasures which age has left them no power to enjoy.

MADAME PERNELLE [*to* ELMIRE]. These, daughter, are the sort of idle stories they serve up to please you. I have to hold my tongue when I'm at your house for Mistress Chatterbox here holds forth all day long. Nevertheless I will have my turn. What I say is that it was the wisest thing my

* This is one of the speeches thought to have been originally given to Cléante.

son ever did to take into his house this holy man whom the Lord sent just when he was needed, to reclaim your minds from error. For the good of your souls you should hearken to him for he reproves nothing but what is deserving of reproof. This giddy round of balls, assemblies, and routs is all a device of the Evil One. In such places one never hears a word of godliness, nothing but idle chatter, singing, and nonsensical rigmaroles: often enough the neighbours come in for their share and slander and gossip go the rounds. Even sensible heads are turned in the turmoil of that sort of gathering, a thousand idle tongues get busy about nothing and, as a learned doctor said the other day, it becomes a veritable tower of Babylon where everybody babbles never-endingly – but to come to the point I was making. [*Pointing to* CLÉANTE] What! The gentleman is sniggering already is he? Go find a laughing-stock elsewhere and don't – [*To* ELMIRE] Daughter, good-bye. I'll say no more, but I'd have you know I have even less opinion of this household than I had. It will be a long time before I set foot in here again. [*Giving* FLIPOTE *a slap*] Hey you! What are you dreaming and gaping at? God bless my soul! I'll warm your ears for you. Come slut. Let's be off.

[*Exeunt all but* CLÉANTE *and* DORINE.]

CLÉANTE. I won't go out in case she starts on me again. How the old woman . . .

DORINE. It's a pity she can't hear you talking like that! She'd tell you what she thinks about you, and whether she's of an age that you can call her 'old woman' or not!

CLÉANTE. Didn't she get worked up against us – and all about nothing! How she dotes on her Tartuffe!

DORINE. Oh! It's nothing compared with her son. If you'd seen him you'd agree he was much worse. During the late disturbances he gained the reputation of being a reliable man and showed courage in the King's service, but since he took a fancy to Tartuffe he seems to have taken leave of his senses. He addresses him as brother and holds him a

hundred times dearer than wife or mother, daughter or son.
The man's the sole confident of all his secrets and his
trusted adviser in everything. He caresses and cossets him
and he couldn't show more tenderness to a mistress. He
insists on his taking the place of honour at table, and
delights in seeing him devour enough for half a dozen. He
has to have all the tit-bits and if he happens to belch it's
'Lord, preserve you!'* In short, he's crazy about him. He's
his all in all, his hero: he admires everything he does, quotes
him at every turn, his every trivial action is wonderful and
every word he utters an oracle. As for Tartuffe, he knows
his weakness and means to make use of it. He has a hundred
ways of deceiving him, gets money out of him constantly
by means of canting humbug, and assumes the right to take
us to task. Even his lout of a servant has taken to instructing
us, comes and harangues us with wild fanatical eyes, and
throws away our ribbons, patches, and paint. The other
day the dog tore up with his own hands a handkerchief
he found in the *Flowers of Sanctity*. He said it was a
dreadful thing to sully sacred things with the devil's trap-
pings.

[*Re-enter* ELMIRE *and* MARIANE.]

ELMIRE. You are lucky to have missed the harangue she
delivered at the gate. But I caught sight of my husband and
as he didn't see me I'll go and wait for him upstairs.

CLÉANTE. I'll await him here to save time. I only want to
say good morning.

[*Exeunt* ELMIRE *and* MARIANE.]

DAMIS. Have a word with him about my sister's marriage.
I suspect that Tartuffe is opposing it and that it's he who is
driving my father to these evasions. You know how
closely concerned I am. Valère and my sister are in love
and I, as you know, am no less in love with his sister,
and if . . .

* *Molière's note.* It is a servant speaking.

DORINE. Here he comes.

[*Enter* ORGON.]

ORGON. Ah, good morning, brother.

CLÉANTE. I was just going. I'm glad to see you back again. There isn't much life in the countryside just now.

ORGON. Dorine – [*to* CLÉANTE] a moment brother, please – excuse me if I ask the news of the family first and set my mind at rest. [*To* DORINE] Has everything gone well the few days I've been away? What have you been doing? How is everyone?

DORINE. The day before yesterday the mistress was feverish all day. She had a dreadful headache.

ORGON. And Tartuffe?

DORINE. Tartuffe? He's very well: hale and hearty; in the pink.

ORGON. Poor fellow!

DORINE. In the evening she felt faint and couldn't touch anything, her headache was so bad.

ORGON. And Tartuffe?

DORINE. He supped with her. She ate nothing but he very devoutly devoured a couple of partridges and half a hashed leg of mutton.

ORGON. Poor fellow!

DORINE. She never closed her eyes all through the night. She was too feverish to sleep and we had to sit up with her until morning.

ORGON. And Tartuffe?

DORINE. Feeling pleasantly drowsy, he went straight to his room, jumped into a nice warm bed, and slept like a top until morning.

ORGON. Poor fellow!

DORINE. Eventually she yielded to our persuasions, allowed herself to be bled, and soon felt much relieved.

ORGON. And Tartuffe?

DORINE. He dutifully kept up his spirits, and took three or four good swigs of wine at breakfast to fortify himself against the worst that might happen and to make up for the blood the mistress had lost.

ORGON. Poor fellow!

DORINE. They are both well again now so I'll go ahead and tell the mistress how glad you are to hear that she's better. [*Exit.*]

CLÉANTE. She's laughing at you openly, brother, and, though I don't want to anger you, I must admit that she's right. Did anyone ever hear of such absurd behaviour? Can the man really have gained such influence over you as to make you forget everything else, so that after having rescued him from poverty you should be ready to . . .

ORGON. Enough brother! You don't know the man you are talking about.

CLÉANTE. I grant you I don't know him, but then, to see what sort of fellow he is, one need only . . .

ORGON. Brother, you would be charmed with him if you knew him. You would be delighted beyond measure . . . he's a man who . . . who . . . ah! A man . . . in short, a man! Whoever follows his precepts enjoys a profound peace of mind and looks upon the world as so much ordure. Yes, under his influence I'm becoming another man. He's teaching me how to forgo affection and free myself from all human ties. I could see brother, children, mother, wife, all perish without caring that much!

CLÉANTE. Very humane sentiments, I must say, brother!

ORGON. Ah! Had you seen how I first met him you would have come to feel for him as I do. Every day he used to come to church and modestly fall on his knees just beside me. He would draw the eyes of the whole congregation by the fervour with which he poured forth his prayers, sighing, groaning, kissing the ground in transports of humility. When I went out he would step in front of me to offer me the Holy water at the door. Having learned from his servant – a man who follows his example in every way – who he was and how needy his condition, I offered him alms, but he would always modestly return a part. 'Too much,' he'd say, 'too much by half. I'm not worthy of your pity.' When I wouldn't have it back he'd go and bestow it on the poor before my very eyes. At length Heaven inspired me to give him shelter in my house, since when all things seem to prosper here. He keeps a reproving eye upon everything and, mindful of my honour, his concern for my interests extends even to my wife. He warns me of those who make eyes at her and is ten times more jealous for her than I am myself. You wouldn't believe the lengths to which his piety extends: the most trivial failing on his own part he accounts a sin: the slightest thing may suffice to shock his conscience – so much so that the other day he was full of self-reproach for having caught a flea while at his prayers and killed it with too much vindictiveness.

CLÉANTE. Gad! You are crazy, brother, that's what I think – or are you trying to pull my leg with a tale like this? What do you intend all this foolery . . .

ORGON. Brother, what you are saying savours of atheism. You *are* somewhat tainted with it at heart. As I have warned you a dozen times you'll bring some serious trouble upon yourself.

CLÉANTE. That's the way your sort of people usually talk. You would have everyone as purblind as yourselves. If one sees things clearly one's an atheist: whoever doesn't bow the knee to pious flummery is lacking in faith and respect for sacred things. No, no! Your threats don't frighten me! I know what I'm talking about and Heaven sees what's in my heart. We are not all duped by humbugs. Devotion, like courage, may be counterfeit. Just as, when honour puts men to the test, the truly brave are not those who make the biggest noise, so the truly pious, whose example we should ever follow, are not those who make the greatest show. What! Would you make no distinction between hypocrisy and true religion? Would you class both together, describe them in the same terms, respect the mask as you would the face itself, treat artifice and sincerity alike, confound appearance and reality, accept the shadow for the substance, base coin for true? Men, in the main, are strangely made. They can never strike the happy mean: the bounds of reason seem too narrow for them: they must needs overact whatever part they play and often ruin the noblest things because they will go to extremes and push them too far. This, brother, is all by the way –

ORGON. Yes, yes, there's no doubt you are a most reverend doctor. You have a monopoly of knowledge, you are unique in wisdom and enlightenment, Sir Oracle, the Cato of our age. In comparison the rest of us are fools –

CLÉANTE. No brother. I'm no reverend doctor; I've no monopoly of knowledge. I merely claim to be able to discriminate between false and true. Just as I know no kind of man more estimable than those who are genuinely religious, nothing in the whole world nobler or finer than the holy fervour of true piety, so I know nothing more odious than those whited sepulchres of specious zeal, those charlatans, those professional zealots, who with sacrilegious and deceitful posturings abuse and mock to their heart's content everything which men hold most sacred and holy; men who put self-interest first, who trade and traffic in devotion, seek to acquire credit and dignities by turning up their eyes in transports of simulated zeal. I mean the people who tread with such extraordinary ardour the godly road to fortune, burning with devotion but seeking material advantage, preaching daily the virtues of solitude and retirement while following the life of courts, shaping their zeal to their vices, quick, revengeful, faithless, scheming, who when they wish to destroy, hide their vindictive pride under the cloak of religion. They are the more dangerous in that they turn against us in their bitter rage the very weapons which men revere and use the passion for which they are respected to destroy us with a consecrated blade. One sees all too much of falsehood such as this. Yet the truly devout are easy to recognize. Our own age offers us many a glorious example, brother. Look at Ariston, Periander, Oronte, Alcidamus, Polydore, Clitander! Their claims no one can deny: theirs is no braggart virtue, no intolerable ostentation of piety; their religion is gentle and humane: they don't censure our actions: they would consider such strictures arrogant: leaving pride of eloquence to others they rebuke our conduct by their own: they don't assume from appearances that others are in fault: they are always ready to think well of people. No '*cabales*' for them, no intrigues! their whole concern is to live virtuously: they show no anger against sinners: they reserve their hate for sin itself: nor do they take upon themselves the interests of Heaven with a zeal beyond anything that Heaven itself displays. These are my sort of men: this is how one should conduct oneself: this is the example one should follow! Your man, however, is of another kind. You vaunt his zeal in all good faith but I think you are deceived by false appearances.

ORGON. My dear brother-in-law, have you finished?

CLÉANTE. Yes.

ORGON [*going*]. I'm much obliged to you.

CLÉANTE. One word, brother, please. Let us leave this topic. You remember that you promised Valère your daughter's hand?

ORGON. Yes.

CLÉANTE. And you named a day for the happy event.

ORGON. True.

CLÉANTE. Why then defer the ceremony?

ORGON. I don't know.

CLÉANTE. Have you something else in mind?

ORGON. Maybe.

CLÉANTE. Do you intend to break your word?

ORGON. I never said so.

CLÉANTE. There is nothing, I believe, to prevent your keeping your promise.

ORGON. That's as may be.

CLÉANTE. Why such circumspection in giving an answer. Valère has asked me to come and see you.

ORGON. God be praised!

CLÉANTE. What am I to tell him?

ORGON. Whatever you please.

CLÉANTE. But I need to know your intentions. What do you mean to do?

ORGON. The will of Heaven.

CLÉANTE. But, speaking seriously, Valère has your promise –
are you standing to it or not?

ORGON. Good-bye. [*Exit.*]

CLÉANTE. I fear he is going to be disappointed in his love.
I must warn him of the way things are going.

Act Two

ORGON, MARIANE

ORGON. Mariane.

MARIANE. Yes, father.

ORGON. Come here. I want a word with you in private.

MARIANE. What are you looking for? [*He is looking into a closet.*]

ORGON. I'm looking to see that there's no one to overhear
us. This little place is just right for eavesdropping. Now,
we are all right. I've always known that you have an
obedient disposition Mariane, and you've always been very
dear to me.

MARIANE. I am very grateful for your fatherly affection.

ORGON. I'm pleased to hear you say so, my girl – and if you
want to deserve it you should be at pains to do what I want.

MARIANE. That is my most earnest wish.

ORGON. Very well. What have you to say about our guest,
Tartuffe?

MARIANE. What have I to say?

ORGON. Yes, you! Mind how you answer.

MARIANE. Oh dear! I'll say anything you like about him.
[*Enter* DORINE, *unobserved; she takes up her position behind*
ORGON.]

ORGON. That's very sensible. Then let me hear you say, my
dear, that he is a wonderful man, that you love him, and
you'd be glad to have me choose him for your husband,
Eh?

[MARIANE *starts in surprise.*]

MARIANE. Eh?

ORGON. What's the matter?

MARIANE. *What* did you say?

ORGON. What?

MARIANE. I must have misheard you.

ORGON. How d'ye mean?

MARIANE. Who is it, father, I'm to say I love and be glad to have you choose as my husband?

ORGON. Tartuffe!

MARIANE. But, father, I assure you I don't feel like that at all. Why make me tell such an untruth?

ORGON. But I mean it to be the truth and it's sufficient for you that it's what I have decided.

MARIANE. What, father! You really want me to . . .

ORGON. My intention, my girl, is that you should marry Tartuffe and make him one of the family. He shall be your husband. I have made up my mind about that and it's for me to decide . . . [*Seeing* DORINE] What are *you* doing here? You must be mighty curious, my lass, to come eavesdropping like that.

DORINE. I don't really know master how the rumour arose – whether it's guesswork or coincidence, but when I heard about this marriage I treated it as a joke.

ORGON. Why? Is it unbelievable?

DORINE. So much so that I *won't* believe it though you tell me yourself.

ORGON. I know how to make you believe it.

DORINE. Yes, yes, but you are telling us it as a joke.

ORGON. I'm telling you what's going to happen and before long too!

DORINE. Oh, rubbish!

ORGON [*to* MARIANE]. It's no joking matter I tell you!

DORINE. No! Don't you believe your Papa! He's teasing!

ORGON. I'm telling you . . .

DORINE. It's no good. We shan't believe you.

ORGON. If I once get annoyed.

DORINE. All right! We believe you then and so much the worse for you. Why! How can you, master! You with all the appearance of a sensible man – and a venerable beard like you have – how can you be so silly as to . . .

ORGON. Listen! You have got into the habit of taking liberties lately. I tell you, my girl, I don't like it at all!

DORINE. Do let us discuss it without getting cross, master, please. You really must have made it all up for a joke. Your daughter isn't at all the right person to marry a bigot and he ought to have other things to think about. Anyhow, what use is such an alliance to you? With all the money you have why go and choose a beggar for a son-in-law?

ORGON. Be quiet! If he's poor that's all the more reason for respecting him. Understand that! His is an honourable poverty. That's beyond question. It should raise him above material consequence for he's allowed himself to be deprived of his means by his indifference to temporal matters and his unswerving attachment to the things which are eternal. My help may be able to afford him the means to escape from embarrassment and enter into his own possessions again – lands which are quite well known in his part of the country. Moreover, whatever his present condition may appear to be, he's certainly a gentleman.

DORINE. Yes. That's what *he* says, but that kind of boasting doesn't go very well with his piety. A man who chooses the saintly life shouldn't crack up his birth and family so much. The humble ways of piety don't go well with such-like ambitions. Why take pride in that sort of thing? But there, you'd rather not discuss that. Let's leave the question of his family and talk about the man himself! Could you really bear to hand over your daughter to a fellow like that? Shouldn't you consider what's due to her and what the consequences of such a marriage might be! Let me tell you that when a girl isn't allowed her own choice in marriage her virtue's in jeopardy: her resolve to live as a good woman depends on the qualities of the husband she's given. Those whose wives are unfaithful have often made them what they are. There are some husbands it's not easy to remain faithful to and whoever gives a girl a husband she detests is responsible to Heaven for the sins she commits. Just think then what perils this scheme of yours may involve you in!

ORGON [*to* MARIANE]. Well, I declare, I have to take lessons from her as to how to do my own business!

DORINE. You couldn't do better than follow my advice.

ORGON. Let's waste no more time on such nonsense, my girl. I'm your father and I know what's good for you. I had promised you to Valère, but apart from the fact that he's said to be a bit of a gambler I suspect him of being a free thinker. I don't see him at church much.

DORINE. I suppose you'd have him run there at the very moment you get there yourself like some folk who only go there to be noticed.

ORGON. I'm not asking for your opinion. [*To* MARIANE] Moreover Tartuffe stands well with Heaven and that surpasses all earthly riches. This marriage will give you everything you could wish for, a perpetual source of pleasure and delight. You'll live together loving and faithful just like two babes – like a pair of turtle doves. No differences will ever arise between you and you'll be able to do just what you like with him.

DORINE. Will she? She won't do anything with him but make him a cuckold, believe me!

ORGON. Sh! What a way to talk!

DORINE. I tell you he has all the looks of one – he's born to it, master, and all your daughter's virtue couldn't prevent it.

ORGON. Stop interrupting me! Just hold your tongue and don't be for ever putting your nose in where you have no business.

DORINE. I'm only telling you for your own good, master. [*Every time he turns to speak to his daughter she interrupts.*]

ORGON. You don't need to trouble. Just be quiet!

DORINE. If it wasn't that I'm fond of you . . .

ORGON. I don't *want* you to be fond of me.

DORINE. Yes, but I'm *determined* to be fond of you – whether *you* like it or not.

ORGON. Tcha!

DORINE. I'm concerned for your good name, and I won't have you making yourself the butt of everyone's gibes.

ORGON. Will you never be quiet?

DORINE. I could never forgive myself if I let you make such an alliance.

ORGON. Will you be quiet, you reptile, with your impudent . . .

DORINE. Ah! Fancy a godly man like you getting angry!

ORGON. Yes! This ridiculous nonsense is more than my temper can stand. I insist on your holding your tongue.

DORINE. Right, but I shan't *think* any the less because I don't say anything.

ORGON. Think if you like but take care you don't talk or . . . that's enough. [*Turning to* MARIANE] I've weighed everything carefully as a wise man should . . .

DORINE. It's maddening not to be able to speak. [*She stops as he turns his head.*]

ORGON. Without his being exactly a beauty Tartuffe's looks are . . .

DORINE. Yes! A lovely mug hasn't he?

ORGON. Such . . . that even if his other advantages don't appeal to you . . . [ORGON *turns and faces* DORINE, *looking at her with arms folded.*]

DORINE. She *would* be well off wouldn't she? If *I* were in her place no man would marry me against my will – not with impunity. I would show him, ay, and soon after the ceremony too, that a woman has always ways and means of getting her own back.

ORGON. So what I say hasn't any effect on you at all?

DORINE. What are you grumbling about? I'm not talking to you.

ORGON. Then what *are* you doing?

DORINE. I'm talking to myself.

ORGON. Very well. [*Aside.*] I shall have to give her a backhander for her impudence yet. [*He stands ready to box her ears.* DORINE *every time he looks at her stands rigid and without speaking.*] You can't do otherwise, my girl, than approve what I have in mind for you . . . and believe that the husband

... I have chosen for you. ... [*To* DORINE] Why aren't you talking to yourself now?

DORINE. I've nothing to say to myself.

ORGON. Not a word even?

DORINE. Not a word thank you!

ORGON. But I was waiting for you ...

DORINE. I'm not so silly as that!

ORGON. Well now, my girl, you must show how obedient you are and fall in with my choice.

DORINE [*running away*]. I'd scorn to take such a husband! [*He takes a slap at her and misses.*]

ORGON. She's a thorough pest is that girl of yours! If I live with her any longer I shall do something I shall be sorry for. I'm in no state to go on now. I'm so incensed at her impudence I shall have to go outside to recover myself.

[*Exit* ORGON.]

DORINE. Have you lost your tongue? Do I have to do all the talking for you? Fancy letting him put a ridiculous proposal like that to you and never saying a word in reply!

MARIANE. What would you have me do in face of the absolute power of my father?

DORINE. Whatever is needed to ward off the danger.

MARIANE. But what?

DORINE. Tell him one can't love at another's bidding; that you'll marry to suit yourself, not him; that *you* are the person concerned and therefore it's *you* the husband has to please not him; and that, if he has such a fancy for his precious Tartuffe, he can marry him himself and there's nothing to stop him.

MARIANE. I confess that a father's authority is such that I have never had the temerity to say anything.

DORINE. Well, let us get down to business. Valère has made proposals for you. I ask you, *do* you love him or don't you?

MARIANE. You do my love great injustice, Dorine. How can you ask such a question? Haven't I opened my heart to you many and many a time? Don't you know how much I love him?

DORINE. How do I know that you meant what you said or that the young man really appeals to you?

MARIANE. You do me grievous wrong to doubt it, Dorine. I've shown my true feelings all too clearly.

DORINE. So you *do* love him, then?

MARIANE. Indeed I do.

DORINE. And, so far as you know, he loves you too?

MARIANE. I believe so.

DORINE. And you both want to be married?

MARIANE. Assuredly!

DORINE. Then what do you mean to do about this other proposal?

MARIANE. To die by my own hand if they force me to submit to it.

DORINE. Splendid! That's something I never thought of! You only need die and you are finished with your troubles. There's no doubt that's a wonderful remedy. That sort of talk infuriates me!

MARIANE. Oh dear, you are tiresome, Dorine. You have no sympathy at all for other people's troubles.

DORINE. I've no sympathy with folk who talk nonsense and are as faint-hearted as you are when it comes to the point.

MARIANE. But what do you expect me to do. If I'm timid . . .

DORINE. What lovers need is determination.

MARIANE. And have I wavered in my love for Valère? Surely it's for him to deal with my father.

DORINE. What! If your father's the fantastic creature he is – if he's plumb crazy over his precious Tartuffe and breaks his promise about the marriage he had decided on, is your lover to be blamed?

MARIANE. But can I reveal by flat refusal and open defiance how much I'm in love? Can I, whatever Valère's qualities may be, abandon the modesty of my sex and my filial duty? Do you want me to expose my feelings for all the world to see and . . .

DORINE. No. No. *I* don't want anything. I see that you want to marry Mr Tartuffe and, now I come to think about it, it would be wrong of me to dissuade you from such an alliance. Why should I oppose your inclinations? It's a most suitable match. Mr Tartuffe! Ha! Ha! It's not an offer to be despised, is it? Come to think of it Mr Tartuffe's a fine fellow. It's no small honour to be his better half. Everybody defers to him already. He's a man of family – where he comes from, and a fine looking fellow to boot – with his red ears and his red face. You would be sure to live happily with a husband like that.

MARIANE. Heavens!

DORINE. How delightful to be married to such a fine-looking husband!

MARIANE. Oh, please stop talking like this, and suggest some means of avoiding the marriage. It's enough. I give in. I'm ready for anything.

DORINE. No. No, a daughter must do as her father tells her even if he wants her to marry a monkey. You are very lucky. What are you complaining of? You'll be carted off to his little provincial town, and find it swarming with his relations. What fun you'll have meeting them all! You'll be taken straight into local society, visit the bailiff's wife and the councillor's lady, and they'll accord you the honour of letting you sit down with them as an equal, perhaps! In carnival time you'll be able to look forward to a ball with a grand orchestra, to wit a couple of bagpipes, and now and again Fagotin the monkey, and a marionette show. If only your husband . . .

MARIANE. Oh! I can't endure it! Why don't you help me?

DORINE. No, you must excuse me!

MARIANE. Oh Dorine, *please* . . .

DORINE. No it must go through now – you deserve it!

MARIANE. Dear Dorine . . .

DORINE. No.

MARIANE. If my confessions of love . . .

DORINE. No. Tartuffe is your man, you shall have your fill of him.

MARIANE. You know that I've always trusted in you. Help me to . . .

DORINE. No, no! I give you my word – you shall be thoroughly Tartuffed!

MARIANE. Very well, since my miserable lot doesn't move you, leave me alone with my despair. There my heart will find relief. I have one infallible remedy for my troubles. [*She makes to go.*]

DORINE. Hey there! Come back. I won't be angry any more. I must take pity on you in spite of everything.

MARIANE. I assure you, Dorine, if they put me to this cruel torment it will be the death of me.

DORINE. Don't distress yourself. We'll find some means of preventing it. But here comes your Valère.

[*Enter* VALÈRE.]

VALÈRE. I have just heard a fine piece of news. Something I was quite unaware of!

MARIANE. What is it?

VALÈRE. That you are to marry Tartuffe.

MARIANE. That is certainly my father's intention.

VALÈRE. But your father . . .

MARIANE. He's changed his mind. He has just put the new proposal to me now.

VALÈRE. What, seriously?

MARIANE. Yes, seriously. He's determined on the match.

VALÈRE. And what is your intention?

MARIANE. I don't know.

VALÈRE. That's a fine answer! You don't know?

MARIANE. No.

VALÈRE. No?

MARIANE. What do you advise me to do?

VALÈRE. What do I advise you to do? I advise you to take him!

MARIANE. *You* advise me to do that?

VALÈRE. Yes.

MARIANE. You really mean it?

VALÈRE. Of course. It's a splendid offer – one well worth considering.

MARIANE. Very well, sir. I'll take your advice.

VALÈRE. I don't doubt you'll find little difficulty in doing so.

MARIANE. No more than you in offering it.

VALÈRE. I gave it to please you.

MARIANE. And I'll follow it – to please you.

DORINE [*aside*]. We'll see what will come of this!

VALÈRE. So this is how you love me! You were deceiving me when . . .

MARIANE. Don't let us talk of that please! You told me frankly that I should accept the husband I was offered. Well then, that's just what I intend to do – since you give me such salutary advice.

VALÈRE. Don't make what I said your excuse! You had already made up your mind. You're just seizing on a frivolous pretext to justify breaking your word.

MARIANE. That's true. You put it very well.

VALÈRE. Of course! You never really loved me at all.

MARIANE. Alas! You may think so if you like.

VALÈRE. Yes, yes. I may indeed: but I may yet forestall your design. I know on whom to bestow both my hand and my affections.

MARIANE. Oh! I don't doubt that in the least, and the love which your good qualities inspire . . .

VALÈRE. Good Lord! Let's leave my good qualities out of it. They are slight enough and your behaviour is proof of it. But I know someone who will, I hope, consent to repair my loss once she knows I am free.

MARIANE. Your loss is little enough and, no doubt, you'll easily be consoled by the change.

VALÈRE. I shall do what I can you may be sure. To find oneself jilted is a blow to one's pride. One must do one's best to forget it and if one doesn't succeed, at least one must pretend to, for to love where one's love is scorned is an unpardonable weakness.

MARIANE. A very elevated and noble sentiment, I'm sure.

VALÈRE. Of course and one that everyone must approve. Would you have me languish for you indefinitely, see you throw yourself into the arms of another and yet not bestow elsewhere the heart that you spurn?

MARIANE. On the contrary, that is just what I want. I only wish it were done already.

VALÈRE. That's what you would like?

MARIANE. Yes.

VALÈRE. You have insulted me sufficiently. You shall have your wish . . . [*makes a move to go*] and immediately!

MARIANE. Very well.

VALÈRE [*turning back*]. At least remember that it is you yourself who are driving me to this extremity.

MARIANE. Yes.

VALÈRE. And that in what I am doing, I am only following your example.

MARIANE. My example, so be it!

VALÈRE. Very well! You shall have just what you asked for.

MARIANE. So much the better!

VALÈRE. You'll never see me again.

MARIANE. Capital!

VALÈRE [*goes but when he reaches the door he returns*]. Eh?

MARIANE. What?

VALÈRE. Didn't you call?

MARIANE. Me? You are dreaming.

VALÈRE. Good. I'm going then. Good-bye!

MARIANE. Good-bye!

DORINE. I think you must be out of your senses to behave in this absurd fashion. I've let you go on squabbling to see how far you would go. Here, Mr Valère! [*She takes him by the arm.* VALÈRE *pretends to resist.*]

VALÈRE. What do you want, Dorine?

DORINE. Come here!

VALÈRE. No, no. I'm too angry. Don't try to prevent me doing what she wants.

DORINE. Stop!

VALÈRE. No, no. It's all settled.

DORINE. Ah!

MARIANE. He can't bear the sight of me. He's going because I'm here. I'd better get out of his sight. [DORINE *leaves* VALÈRE *and runs to* MARIANE.]

DORINE. The other one now! Where are you off to?

MARIANE. Let me go!

DORINE. Come back!

MARIANE. No, no, Dorine. It's no good your trying to stop me.

VALÈRE. I can see that she hates the very sight of me. Far better I should spare her the embarrassment.

DORINE [*leaving* MARIANE *and running to* VALÈRE]. You again. The devil take you before I let you go. Stop this silly nonsense and come here both of you. [*She drags them both in.*]

VALÈRE. What are you trying to do?

MARIANE. What do you want?

DORINE. To bring you together again and get you out of this mess. [*To* VALÈRE] You must be crazy to quarrel like this!

VALÈRE. Didn't you hear how she spoke to me?

DORINE. You must be out of your mind to get so annoyed.

MARIANE. But didn't you see what happened? Didn't you see how he treated me?

DORINE [*to* VALÈRE]. Sheer silliness on both sides. She wants nothing better than to be yours – I can witness. [*To* MARIANE] He loves nobody but you and desires nothing better than to be your husband – I'll stake my life on it.

MARIANE. Then why did he give me the advice he did?

VALÈRE. Why did you ask me for advice on such a question?

DORINE. You are both quite mad. Here – give me your hands, both of you. [*To* VALÈRE] Come along, you.

VALÈRE [*giving his hand to* DORINE]. What good will that do?

DORINE [*to* MARIANE]. Now yours.

MARIANE [*giving her hand*]. What's the use?

DORINE. Heavens! Be quick. Come on! You love each other better than you think.

VALÈRE [*to* MARIANE]. Come, don't do it with such an ill grace. Don't look at a fellow as if you hated him. [MARIANE *turns towards* VALÈRE *and gives a little smile.*]

DORINE. The truth is all lovers are a bit touched!

VALÈRE. Ah! But hadn't I some cause for complaint? You must admit it was cruel of you to take such pleasure in giving me such a horrible piece of news.

MARIANE. But you – aren't you the most ungrateful of men?

DORINE. Let's leave the argument to another time and think how we can prevent this dreadful marriage . . .

MARIANE. Tell us what we are to do.

DORINE. We'll try everything we can. Your father can't be serious and it's all sheer rubbish, but you had better pretend to fall in with his nonsense and give the appearance of consenting so that if it comes to the point you'll more easily be able to delay the marriage. If we can only gain time we may set everything right. You can complain of a sudden illness that will necessitate delay; another time you can have recourse to bad omens – such as having met a corpse or broken a mirror or dreamt of muddy water. Finally, the great thing is that they can't make you his wife unless you answer 'I will'. But I think, as a precaution, you had better not be found talking together. [*To* VALÈRE] Off you go and get all your friends to use their influence with her father to stand by his promise. We must ask his brother to try once again, and see if we can get the step-mother on our side. Good-bye.

VALÈRE [*to* MARIANE]. Whatever schemes we may devise you are the only one I really count on.

MARIANE [*to* VALÈRE]. I can't answer for what my father decides but I will never marry anyone but Valère.

VALÈRE. Ah, how happy you make me! Whatever they may venture to . . .

DORINE. Ah? Lovers are never tired of blathering! Be off, I tell you.

VALÈRE [*making to go, then turning back*]. Still . . .

DORINE. What a talker you are! [*Pushing them both out*] You go this way and you that. Be off!

Act Three

DAMIS, DORINE

DAMIS. May I be struck dead on the spot – call me the most miserable blackguard alive if I let either fear or favour prevent me – if I don't think out some master stroke!

DORINE. For goodness sake, don't get so excited! Your father has only just mentioned it. People don't do everything they intend to. There's a deal of difference between talking about a thing and doing it.

DAMIS. I must put a stop to the dog's machinations! I'll have something to say to him!

DORINE. Oh, go easy! Leave your stepmother to deal with both him and your father. She has some influence with Tartuffe. He takes notice of her. I'm not sure that he isn't sweet on her. I wish to Heaven he were! That would be a lark! As a matter of fact it's on your account that she's sent for him: she intends to sound him about this marriage you are so worried about: she means to find out what he has in mind and make him see what trouble it would cause in the family if he encouraged the idea. His servant said he was at his prayers so I wasn't able to see him, but he said he'd be coming down soon. So please go away and leave me to wait for him.

DAMIS. I'll be present at the interview.

DORINE. No. They must be alone.

DAMIS. I won't say a word.

DORINE. That's what *you* think! We all know how excitable you are and that's just the way to spoil everything. Off you go.

DAMIS. No I must see it. I won't lose my temper.

DORINE. How tiresome you are. Here he comes. Do go.

[*Enter* TARTUFFE.]

TARTUFFE [*seeing* DORINE]. Laurent, put away my hair shirt and my scourge and continue to pray Heaven to send you grace. If anyone asks for me I'll be with the prisoners distributing alms.

DORINE. The impudent hypocrite!

TARTUFFE. What do you want?

DORINE. I'm to tell you . . .

TARTUFFE. For Heaven's sake! Before you speak, I pray you take this handkerchief. [*Takes handkerchief from his pocket.*]

DORINE. Whatever do you mean?

TARTUFFE. Cover your bosom. I can't bear to see it. Such pernicious sights give rise to sinful thoughts.

DORINE. You're mighty susceptible to temptation then! The flesh must make a great impression on you! I really don't know why you should get so excited. I can't say that I'm so easily roused. I could see you naked from head to foot and your whole carcass wouldn't tempt me in the least.

TARTUFFE. Pray, speak a little more modestly or I shall have to leave the room.

DORINE. No. No. *I'm* leaving *you*. All I have to say is that the mistress is coming down and would like a word with you.

TARTUFFE. Ah! Most willingly.

DORINE [*aside*]. That changes his tune. Upon my word I'm convinced there is something in what I said.

TARTUFFE. Will she be long?

DORINE. I think I hear her now. Yes, here she comes. I'll leave you together.

[*Exit* DORINE. *Enter* ELMIRE.]

TARTUFFE. May the bounty of Heaven ever bestow on you health of body and of mind, and extend you blessings commensurate with the prayers of the most humble of its devotees!

ELMIRE. I'm very grateful for these pious wishes. Let us sit down. We shall be more comfortable.

TARTUFFE. Do you feel better of your indisposition?

ELMIRE. Very much. The feverishness soon left me.

TARTUFFE. My prayers have too little merit to have obtained this favour from on high; yet all the petitions I have addressed to Heaven have been concerned with your recovery.

ELMIRE. You are too solicitous on my behalf.

TARTUFFE. One cannot be too solicitous for your precious health. I would have sacrificed my own life for the sake of yours.

ELMIRE. That is carrying Christian charity rather far but I'm truly grateful for your kindness.

TARTUFFE. I do far less for you than you deserve.

ELMIRE. I wanted to speak to you in private on a certain matter. I'm please that no one can overhear us.

TARTUFFE. I too am delighted. I need hardly say how pleased I am to find myself alone with you. It's an opportunity which I have besought Heaven to accord me – vainly until this moment.

ELMIRE. What I want is that you should speak frankly and conceal nothing from me.

TARTUFFE. And my sole desire is that you should accord me the singular favour of allowing me to express all that is in my heart and assure you that anything I have said against those who were paying homage to your charms was not spoken in malice against you but rather that the intensity of my pious zeal and pure . . .

ELMIRE. I take it in that sense and believe that it arises from your concern for my salvation.

TARTUFFE. That is indeed so, madam, and such is the fervour of my . . . [*Squeezing her fingers.*]

ELMIRE. Oh! You're hurting me . . .

TARTUFFE. It comes from excess of devotion. I never intended to hurt you. [*Putting his hand upon her knee.*] I would rather . . .

ELMIRE. What is your hand doing there?

TARTUFFE. I'm feeling your dress. How soft the material is!

ELMIRE. Please don't I'm dreadfully ticklish. [*She pushes back her chair.* TARTUFFE *brings his closer.*]

TARTUFFE. What marvellous lace! They do wonderful work nowadays. Things are so much better made than they used to be.

ELMIRE. Very true, but let us return to our business. They say my husband intends to break his promise to Valère and give his daughter to you. Tell me, is it true?

TARTUFFE. He did mention something about it, but to tell the truth, madam, that isn't the happiness I aspire to. All my hopes of felicity lie in another direction.

ELMIRE. That's because you have no interest in temporal things.

TARTUFFE. *My* breast does not enclose a heart of flint!

ELMIRE. I'm sure your thoughts are all turned Heavenward. Your desires are not concerned with anything here below.

TARTUFFE. A passion for the beauties which are eternal does not preclude a temporal love. Our senses can and do respond to those most perfect works of Heaven's creation, whose charms are exemplified in beings such as you and embodied in rarest measure in yourself. Heaven has lavished upon you a beauty that dazzles the eyes and moves the hearts of men. I never look upon your flawless perfections without adoring in you the great Author of all nature and feeling my heart filled with ardent love for that fair form in which He has portrayed Himself. At first I feared lest this secret passion which consumes me might be some subtle snare of the accursed one. I even resolved to avoid your sight, believing you to be an obstacle to my salvation; but at length I came to realize, O fairest among women, that there need be nothing culpable in my passion and that I could reconcile it with virtue. Since then I have surrendered to it heart and soul. It is, I admit, no small presumption on my part to address to you this offer of my love, but I rely upon your generosity and in no wise upon my own unworthy self: my hopes, my happiness, my peace are in your keeping: on you my bliss or future misery depends: my future hangs on your decree: make me for ever happy if such be your will, wretched if you would have it so.

ELMIRE. A very gallant declaration but a little surprising I must confess! It seems to me you ought to steel yourself more firmly against temptation and consider more deeply what you are about. A pious man like you, a holy man whom everyone . . .

TARTUFFE. Ah! But I'm not less a man for being devout! Confronted by your celestial beauty one can but let love have its way and make no demur. I realize that such a declaration coming from me may well seem strange but, after all, madam, I'm not an angel. If you condemn this declaration of mine you must lay the blame on your own enchanting loveliness. From the first moment that I beheld its more than mortal splendours you have ruled supreme in my affection. Those glances, goddess-like and gracious beyond all description, broke down my stubborn heart's resistance, surmounted every obstacle, prayers, fasting, tears, and turned all my thoughts to love of you. My eyes, my sighs, have told you a thousand times what I am now seeking to express in words. If you should turn a kindly eye upon the tribulations of your unworthy slave, if in your generosity you should choose to afford me consolation and deign to notice my insignificance, then I would offer you for ever, O miracle of loveliness, a devotion beyond compare. Moreover, your honour runs no risk with me; at my hands you need fear no danger of disgrace; these courtly gallants that women are so fond of noise their deeds abroad; they are for ever bragging of their conquests, never receiving a favour but they must divulge it, profaning with blabbing tongues (which folk still put their trust in) the altar to which they bring their offerings. But men of our sort burn with discreeter fires; our secrets are for ever sure; our concern for our own reputation is a safeguard for those we love, and to those who trust us we offer love without scandal, satisfaction without fear.

ELMIRE. I have listened to what you say and your eloquence has made your meaning sufficiently clear, but are you not afraid that I might take it into my head to tell my husband of this charming declaration of yours and that such a disclosure might impair his friendly feelings for you?

TARTUFFE. I know you are too kind, that you will pardon my temerity, condone as human frailty the transports of a passion which offends you, and, when you consult your glass, reflect that I'm not blind and that a man is but flesh and blood.

ELMIRE. Others might perhaps take a different course but I prefer to show discretion. I shall say nothing to my husband, but in return I must ask one thing of you – that you give your support openly and sincerely to the marriage of Valère and Mariane, renounce the exercise of that improper influence by which you have sought to promote your own hopes at the expense of another and . . .

DAMIS [*coming out of the closet where he has been hidden*]. No, no! This must be made known! I was in there and heard everything. Heaven's mercy has brought me here to confound the arrogance of a villain who intends me harm: it has offered me the opportunity to be revenged upon his insolence and hypocrisy, to undeceive my father, and lay bare the soul of this scoundrel who talks to you of love!

ELMIRE. No, Damis, it is sufficient that he should mend his ways and endeavour to deserve the pardon I have promised him. I have given my word so don't make me break it. I'm not one to make a fuss: a wife makes light of follies such as these and never troubles her husband with them.

DAMIS. You may have your reasons for doing this but I have mine for doing otherwise. Your wish to spare him is absurd. He has already triumphed sufficiently over my just resentment with his insolence and humbug and made enough trouble among us. The scoundrel has ruled my father long enough and thwarted my love as well as Valère's. My father must be shown what a perfidious wretch he is and Providence now offers a simple means of doing it. I'm answerable to Heaven for this opportunity and it's too favourable to be neglected. Not to make use of it would be to deserve to lose it.

ELMIRE. Damis . . .

DAMIS. No. Pardon me – I must trust to my own judgement. I'm overjoyed. Nothing you say can dissuade me from the pleasure of revenge. I'll finish the business without more ado, and [*seeing* ORGON] here comes the instrument of my satisfaction.

[*Enter* ORGON.]

DAMIS. We have interesting news for you father. Something has just occurred which will astonish you. You are well repaid for your kindness! The gentleman sets a very high value on the consideration you have shown for him! He has just been demonstrating his passionate concern for you and he stops at nothing less than dishonouring your bed. I have just overheard him making a disgraceful declaration of his guilty passion for your wife. She in kind-heartedness and over-anxiety to be discreet was all for keeping it secret but I can't condone such shameless behaviour. I consider it would be a gross injustice to you to keep it from you.

ELMIRE. Well, I still think a wife shouldn't disturb her husband's peace of mind by repeating such silly nonsense to him; one's honour is in no wise involved. It's sufficient that we women should know how to defend ourselves. That's what I think and if you had taken notice of me you would not have said anything at all. [*Exit.*]

ORGON. Oh Heavens! Can what they say be true?

TARTUFFE. Yes, brother, I am a guilty wretch, a miserable sinner steeped in iniquity, the greatest villain that ever existed; not a moment of my life but is sullied with some foul deed: it's a succession of wickedness and corruption. I see now that Heaven is taking this opportunity of chastising me for my sins. Whatever crime I may be charged with, far be it from me to take pride in denying it! Believe what they tell you. Set no bounds to your resentment! Hound me like a felon from your doors! Whatever shame is heaped upon me I shall have deserved much more.

ORGON [*to his son*]. Ah! Miscreant! How dare you seek to tarnish his unspotted virtue with this false accusation?

DAMIS. What! Can a pretence of meekness from this hypocrite make you deny . . .

ORGON. Silence! You accursed plague!

TARTUFFE. Ah, let him speak. You do wrong to accuse him. You would do better to believe what he tells you. Why should you take such a favourable view of me? After all, do you know what I am capable of? Why should you trust appearances? Do you think well of me because of what I seem to be? No, no, you are letting yourself be deceived by outward show. I am, alas, no better than they think; everyone takes me for a good man but the truth is I'm good for nothing. [*Speaking to* DAMIS] Yes, my son, speak freely, call me deceitful, infamous, abandoned, thief, murderer, load me with names yet more detestable, I'll not deny them. I've deserved them all, and on my knees I'll suffer the ignominy, in expiation of my shameful life.

ORGON [*to* TARTUFFE]. Brother, this is too much. [*To his son*] Doesn't your heart relent, you dog!

DAMIS. What! Can what he says so far prevail with you that . . .

ORGON [*raising up* TARTUFFE]. Silence you scoundrel! [*To* TARTUFFE] Rise brother – I beg you. [*To his son*] You scoundrel!

DAMIS. He may –

ORGON. Silence!

DAMIS. This is beyond bearing! What! I'm to . . .

ORGON. Say another word and I'll break every bone in your body!

TARTUFFE. In God's name, brother, calm yourself. I would rather suffer any punishment than he should receive the slightest scratch on my account.

ORGON [*to his son*]. Ungrateful wretch!

TARTUFFE. Leave him in peace! If need be, I'll ask your pardon for him on my knees . . .

ORGON [*to* TARTUFFE]. Alas! What are you thinking of? [*To his son*] See how good he is to you, you dog!

DAMIS. Then . . .

ORGON. Enough!

DAMIS. What! Can't I . . .

ORGON. Enough, I say! I know too well why you attack him. You hate him. Every one of you, wife, children, servants, all are in full cry against him. You use every impudent means to drive this devout and holy person from my house: but the more you strive to banish him the more determined I am not to let him go. I'll hasten his marriage with my daughter and confound the pride of the whole family.

DAMIS. You mean to make her accept his hand?

ORGON. Yes, you scoundrel, and this very evening to spite you all. Ah! I defy the lot of you. I'll have you know that I'm the master and I'll be obeyed. Come, retract your accusation instantly, you wretch! Down on your knees and beg forgiveness!

DAMIS. Who? Me? Of a villain whose impostures . . .

ORGON. So you refuse, you scoundrel, do you? And abuse him too! A stick! Give me a stick! [*To* TARTUFFE] Don't try to restrain me! [*To his son*] Out of my house this instant and never darken my doors again!

DAMIS. Yes, I'll go but . . .

ORGON. Out! Leave the house! Be off! I disinherit you, you dog! And take my curse into the bargain.

[*Exit* DAMIS.]

ORGON. What a way to insult a holy man!

TARTUFFE. May Heaven forgive him the sorrow that he causes me! Ah, if you only knew how much it grieves me to see them try to blacken me in my brother's esteem —

ORGON. Alas!

TARTUFFE. The mere thought of such ingratitude is unbearable to me . . . it horrifies me . . . it wrings my heart so that I cannot speak . . . it will be the death of me.

ORGON [*weeping, runs to the door through which he drove forth his son*]. Scoundrel! I'm sorry I kept my hands off you and didn't fell you on the spot! [*To* TARTUFFE] Compose yourself brother. Don't give way to your feelings.

TARTUFFE. Let us put an end to these painful dissensions. When I see what troubles I cause here I feel that I must leave you, brother.

ORGON. What! Are you mad?

TARTUFFE. They hate me. I see now they are trying to make you doubt my sincerity.

ORGON. What does it matter? Do you think I listen to them?

TARTUFFE. But they'll not fail to try again. These same reports you have rejected now you may believe another time.

ORGON. No, brother, never!

TARTUFFE. Ah, brother, a wife can easily influence her husband's mind.

ORGON. No. No!

TARTUFFE. Let me go and by going hence remove all occasion for them to attack me.

ORGON. No. No. You shall stay. My very life depends upon it.

TARTUFFE. Well then if it be so, I must sacrifice myself. But if you would only . . .

ORGON. Yes?

TARTUFFE. Let it be so. We'll speak of it no more but I know now what I must do. Reputation is a brittle thing: friendship requires that I should forestall every whisper, every shadow of suspicion. I must forswear the company of your wife and you will never see . . .

ORGON. No! You *shall* see her in spite of them all. Nothing gives me greater joy than to annoy them. You shall appear with her constantly and – to show my defiance, I'll make you my sole heir. I'll make a gift to you in due form of all my goods here and now. My true, dear, friend whom I now take as my son-in-law, you are dearer to me than son or wife or kin. Will you not accept what I am offering you?

TARTUFFE. Heaven's will be done in all things.

ORGON. Poor fellow! Let us go and draft the document at once. And let the whole envious pack of them burst with their own vexation at the news!

Act Four

CLÉANTE, TARTUFFE

CLÉANTE. Yes, everyone is talking about it and, believe me, the sensation the news has made has done your reputation no good. This is an opportune time to tell you briefly and bluntly what I think about it. I won't go into details of the reports that are going about; setting them on one side and taking the matter at its worst, let us suppose that Damis did behave badly and that you were accused unjustly. Wouldn't it be the Christian thing to pardon the offence and forgo your revenge? Can you allow a son to be turned out of his father's house because of your quarrel with him? I tell you again – and I'm speaking frankly – that everybody thinks it shocking – people of all sorts, high and low alike. If you'll take notice of me you'll come to terms and not push things to extremes. Sacrifice your resentment as a Christian should and reconcile the son to his father again.

TARTUFFE. Alas! For my own part, I would willingly do so. I harbour no resentment against him, sir. I forgive him everything. I don't blame him at all. I would do anything I could for him and gladly, but the interests of Heaven forbid it. If he comes back here, then I must go. After such unheard-of behaviour any further relations between us would create a scandal. God knows what people might think of it! They would impute it to purely material considerations on my part and say that, knowing I was guilty, I feigned a charitable concern for my accuser; that in my heart of hearts I was afraid of him, and sought an arrangement with him to keep his mouth shut.

CLÉANTE. That's just putting me off with specious excuses. Your arguments are all too far fetched. Why should you take upon yourself the interests of religion? Can't God punish the guilty without assistance from us? Leave Him to look after his own vengeance. Remember rather that He ordains that we should forgive those who offend against us. When you are following orders from on high why worry about human judgements? What! Lose the glory of doing a good deed for trivial considerations of what people may think! No. No. Let us just obey Heaven's commands and not bother our heads about anything else.

TARTUFFE. I have already said I forgive him. That's doing what Heaven commands, but Heaven doesn't command me to live with him after the scandal and the insults put on me today.

CLÉANTE. And does it command you to lend an ear to his father's fantastic caprices? Or to accept the gift of possessions to which you have no rightful claim?

TARTUFFE. People who know me will not suspect me of self-interest. Worldly wealth makes little appeal to me. Its tawdry glitter doesn't dazzle me. If I resolve to accept the gift the father insists on offering me it's only because I fear that such possessions may fall into unworthy hands or pass to people who will use them for evil purposes and not employ them as I intend to do, to the glory of God and the good of my neighbour.

CLÉANTE. My good sir, put aside these delicate scruples! They'll get you into trouble with the rightful heir. Let him enjoy his possessions at his own peril without worrying your head about it; consider how much better it would be that he should make ill use of them than that you should find yourself accused of defrauding him! I'm only surprised that you could permit such a proposal without embarrassment. Does any of the maxims of true piety enjoin one to plunder a lawful heir? If Heaven has really inspired you with an insurmountable inability to live in the same house as Damis, wouldn't it be better that you should prudently withdraw rather than let a son be hounded from his father's house on your account in the face of all right and reason? Believe me, that would be showing some sense of decency and . . .

TARTUFFE. It is now half past three, sir. Certain pious obligations require my presence upstairs without delay. Excuse my leaving you so soon.

[*Exit* TARTUFFE.]

CLÉANTE. Ah!

[*Enter* ELMIRE, MARIANE, DORINE.]

DORINE. Please join with us in trying to help her, Sir. She's in dreadful distress. The betrothal her father has arranged for this evening has reduced her to despair. Here he comes. I beseech you, give us your help. Let us try by hook or crook to frustrate this wretched scheme which is worrying us all.

ORGON. Ah! I'm pleased to find you all here. [*To* MARIANE] I have something in this document to please you. You know what it is.

MARIANE [*on her knees*]. Father, in the name of Heaven which is witness to my unhappiness, and by everything that can move your heart, forgo your rights as a father and absolve me from the dire necessity of obeying you in this matter. Don't drive me, by harsh insistence on your rights, to complain to Heaven of being your daughter; don't condemn to misery the life you have bestowed upon me. If, contrary to the one dear hope I cherished, you now forbid me to give myself to the man I love, save me at least – on my knees I implore you – from the torment of belonging to a man I abhor! Don't drive me to some act of desperation by pushing your authority to the extreme.

ORGON [*moved*]. Steel your heart, man, now! No human weakness!

MARIANE. Your affection for him doesn't trouble me: show it to the full; give him your wealth and, if that's not enough, let him have mine. I consent with all my heart and freely give it to you, but at least don't include me with it. Rather let me spend such sad days as may remain to me within the austere walls of a convent.

ORGON. Oh yes! Of course, girls are all for going into convents as soon as their fathers' wishes conflict with their wanton designs! Get up! The harder you find it to accept him the better for your soul! Marry and mortify the flesh but don't plague me any more with your bawling and crying!

DORINE. But what . . .

ORGON. You be quiet! Mind your own business. I absolutely forbid you to say a single word.

CLÉANTE. If I might be allowed to offer you a word of advice . . .

ORGON. Brother, your advice is always excellent, most cogent, and I value it extremely, but I hope you will allow me to manage without it!

ELMIRE [*to her husband*]. I am at a loss to know what to say after what we have seen; I can only marvel at your blindness. You must be bewitched by the man – infatuated – to deny the truth of what we told you today.

ORGON. With all due deference to you I judge things as I see them. I know your indulgence for that worthless son of mine. You were afraid to admit that he had played a trick on this unfortunate man. But you took it too calmly for me to believe you. Had the accusation been true you would have been in a very different state of mind.

ELMIRE. Why should a woman have to behave as if her honour is imperilled by a mere declaration of love? Is there no answering but with blazing eyes and furious tongue? For my part I just laugh at such advances. I don't like all this fuss at all. I would rather we protected our good name by less violent means. I have no use for virtuous harridans who defend their honour with tooth and claw and scratch a man's eyes out at the slightest word. Heaven preserve me from that sort of rectitude! No woman need be a dragon of vindictiveness. A snub coolly and discreetly given is, I think, sufficiently effective in rebuffing advances.

ORGON. All the same, I know where I stand and I'm not going to be put off.

ELMIRE. I wonder more and more at this strange infatuation, but what would you say if I were actually to show you that we are telling you the truth.

ORGON. Show me?

ELMIRE. Yes.

ORGON. Rubbish!

ELMIRE. Supposing I could contrive a means of letting you see with your own eyes.

ORGON. The very idea!

ELMIRE. What a man you are! Do at least give an answer. I'm not asking you to take my word for it. Supposing that I arranged for you to see and hear everything from some point of vantage, what would you say then about this Godly man of yours?

ORGON. I should say nothing – because it just can't be done.

ELMIRE. This delusion has lasted too long. I have had enough of being accused of deceiving you. It's necessary now for my own satisfaction that I make you a witness to the truth of everything I have said and without more ado.

ORGON. Very well. I'll take you at your word. We'll see what you can do. Let me see how you make good your promise.

ELMIRE [*to* DORINE]. Ask him to come here.

DORINE. He's cunning. He may be difficult to catch.

ELMIRE. No. People are easily taken in by what they love and vanity predisposes them to deception. Have him come down. [*To* CLÈANTE *and* MARIANE] You two must retire.

[*Exeunt*]

ELMIRE. Help me to bring the table up. Now get under it.

ORGON. What!

ELMIRE. It's essential that you should be completely hidden.

ORGON. But why under the table?

ELMIRE. Oh, for Heaven's sake leave it to me! I know what I'm doing. You shall see in due course. Get under there and, mind now, take care that he doesn't see or hear you.

ORGON. You are asking a good deal of me, I must say, but I suppose I must see it through now.

ELMIRE. I don't think you'll have any cause to complain but I'm going to play a rather unusual role. Don't be shocked. [ORGON *is under the table*.] I must be allowed to say whatever I like – it will be to convince you as I promised. Since you reduce me to it, I intend to coax this hypocrite to drop his mask, to flatter his impudent desires and encourage his audacity. I shall lead him on merely for the purpose of opening your eyes and exposing him completely. I can stop as soon as you say you give in: things will only go so far as you wish them to go: it will be for you to call a halt to his insensate passion just as soon as you think he has gone far enough: you can spare your poor wife by exposing her to no more than is necessary to disabuse you. It's your affair, and it will be for you to decide . . . but here he comes. Keep in and take care not to be seen.

[*Enter* TARTUFFE.]

TARTUFFE. I was informed that you wished to speak to me here.

ELMIRE. Yes, I have a secret to tell you – but shut the door before I begin and have a good look round in case we should be overheard. We don't want another business like this morning's. I was never so surprised in my life. Damis made me terribly frightened on your account. You must have seen what efforts I made to check him and quieten him down. The truth is I was so taken aback that it never entered my head to deny his accusations, but there – thank Heaven it all turned out for the best! We are much more secure now in consequence. Your reputation saved us. My husband is incapable of thinking ill of you. He insists on our being together to show his contempt for idle rumour. So now I can be in here with you without fear of reproach and can reveal to you that I'm perhaps only too ready to welcome your love.

TARTUFFE. I find it difficult to follow your meaning, madam. Only a while ago you spoke very differently.

ELMIRE. How little you know the heart of woman if such a rebuff has offended you! How little you understand what we mean to convey when we defend ourselves so feebly! At such moments our modesty and the tender sentiments you arouse in us are still in conflict. However compelling the arguments of passion may be we are still too diffident to confess it: we shrink from an immediate avowal but our manner sufficiently reveals that in our heart of hearts we surrender: though our lips must in honour deny our true feelings, such refusals in fact promise everything. I realize that I am making a very frank admission: it shows little regard for womanly modesty but since I *am* speaking – should I have been so anxious to restrain Damis, should I have listened so indulgently, do you think, to your declaration of love, should I have taken it as I did if I had not welcomed it? Moreover, when I sought to make you renounce the marriage which had just been announced what was that intended to convey to you, if not that I took an interest in you and regretted the conclusion of a marriage which would force me to share an affection I wanted entirely to myself?

TARTUFFE. Ah, Madam, it is indeed delightful to hear such words from the lips of one I love! The honey of your words sets coursing through my whole being sensations more delicious than I have ever known before. My supreme concern is to find favour in your eyes. My hopes of bliss lie in your love. Yet you must forgive me if my heart still dares to entertain some doubt of its own felicity. Suppose what you are saying proved to be no more than a virtuous stratagem to induce me to abandon this impending marriage. If I may be allowed to put the matter frankly, I'll never trust these promises until I have been vouchsafed some small foretaste of the favours for which I yearn – that alone will reassure me and give me absolute confidence in your intentions towards me.

ELMIRE [*coughing to attract her husband's attention*]. Why must you go so fast? Would you have me reveal at once all that I feel for you? I have overstepped the bounds of modesty in confessing my feelings and yet it isn't enough for you! Can there be no satisfying you without going to ultimate lengths?

TARTUFFE. The less one deserves the less one dares to hope, and words are poor assurances of love. One cannot but mistrust a prospect of felicity: one must enjoy it before one can believe in it. Knowing how little I deserve your favours I doubt the outcome of my own temerity. I'll believe nothing until you give me proofs tangible enough to satisfy my passion.

ELMIRE. Heavens! What an importunate lover you are! I just don't know where I am. You quite overwhelm me – is there no denying you? Is there no evading your demands? Won't you even allow me a breathing space? How can you be so insistent, so peremptory, so merciless? How can you take such advantage of one's fondness for you?

TARTUFFE. But if you look upon my advances with a favourable eye, why refuse me convincing proof?

ELMIRE. How can I consent to what you ask without offending Him whose name is ever on your lips?

TARTUFFE. If fear of Heaven is the only obstacle to my

passion that is a barrier I can easily remove. That need not restrain you.

ELMIRE. But they threaten us with the wrath of Heaven.

TARTUFFE. I can dissipate these foolish fears for you. I know the way to remove such scruples. It is true that certain forms of indulgence* are forbidden but there are ways and means of coming to terms with Heaven, of easing the restraints of conscience according to the exigencies of the case, of redressing the evil of the action by the purity of the intention. I can instruct you in these secrets, Madam. Only allow yourself to be led by me. Satisfy my desires and have not the slightest fear. I will answer for everything and take the sin upon myself. You have a bad cough, Madam.

ELMIRE. Yes! I'm in great distress.

TARTUFFE. Would you care for a little of this liquorice?

ELMIRE. It's a most obstinate cold. I fear that all the liquorice in the world won't help me now.

TARTUFFE. It is certainly very trying.

ELMIRE. More so than I can say.

TARTUFFE. As I was saying then, your scruples can easily be removed. You are assured of absolute secrecy with me and the harm of any action lies only in its being known. The public scandal is what constitutes the offence: sins sinned in secret are no sins at all.

ELMIRE [*after coughing again*]. Very well then, I see that I must make up my mind to yield and consent to accord you everything you wish. It's no use hoping that anything less will satisfy or convey conviction. It's hard indeed to go to such lengths: it's very much against my will that I do so but since, it seems, I *have* to do it, since I'm not believed in spite of all I've said, since proofs still more convincing are required – I must resign myself to doing what's required of me. But if in consenting I offend, so much the worse for him who forces me to such extremity. The fault can surely not be accounted mine.

TARTUFFE. Yes, Madam, upon me be it and . . .

* *Molière's footnote* 'It is a scoundrel speaking.'

ELMIRE. Just open the door a moment and make sure that my husband isn't in the gallery.

TARTUFFE. Why worry about him? Between ourselves — he's a fellow one can lead by the nose. He glories in our association. I've got him to the stage where though he saw everything with his own eyes he wouldn't believe it.

ELMIRE. All the same, do go out a moment, please, and have a good look round.

ORGON [*coming out from under the table*]. Yes! I must admit it! The man's an abominable scoundrel! I can't get over it! I'm in a daze.

ELMIRE. But why come out so soon? You can't mean what you say! Get under the table again! It's not time yet. Wait till the very end and make quite sure. Don't trust to mere conjecture.

ORGON. No! No! Hell itself never produced anything more wicked.

ELMIRE. Good Heavens! You mustn't believe as easily as that. Wait until you are utterly convinced before you give in. Don't be too hasty! You might be mistaken! [*She puts her husband behind her.*]

[*Re-enter* TARTUFFE.]

TARTUFFE. Everything favours me, Madam. I've looked in all the rooms. There's no one there and now my rapture . . .

ORGON [*stopping him*]. Steady! You are letting your amorous desires run away with you. You shouldn't get so excited! Ah ha, my godly friend, you would deceive me, would you? How you give way to temptation! You meant to marry my daughter and yet you coveted my wife! For a long time I couldn't believe that it was really true and thought to hear you change your tune: but the proof has gone far enough. I'm convinced, and, for my part, I ask nothing further.

ELMIRE [*to* TARTUFFE]. It was very disagreeable to me to do it. I was driven to treat you like this.

TARTUFFE [*to* ORGON]. What! You believe . . .

ORGON. Come, let's have no more of it, please. Get out of the house without more ado.

TARTUFFE. My intention . . .

ORGON. That sort of talk won't do now. You must leave the house forthwith.

TARTUFFE. You are the one who must leave the house – you who talk as if you were master. This house is mine and I'll have you realize it. What's more, I'll show you how vainly you resort to these devices for picking a quarrel with me. You little know what you are doing when you insult me. I have the means to confound and punish your imposture, avenge the affront to Heaven, and make those who talk of making me leave the house regret it.

[*Exit* TARTUFFE.]

ELMIRE. What is he talking about? What does he mean?

ORGON. Alas! I don't know what to do. This is no laughing matter.

ELMIRE. Why? What . . .

ORGON. What he said makes me realize my mistake. My deed of gift begins to worry me.

ELMIRE. Your deed of gift . . . ?

ORGON. Yes, there's no going back upon it now, but there's something else that worries me.

ELMIRE. What is it?

ORGON. I'll tell you everything but I must go at once and see whether a certain casket is still upstairs.

Act Five

ORGON, CLÉANTE

CLÉANTE. Where are you off to?

ORGON. Alas! How do I know?

CLÉANTE. The first thing is to consider what's to be done.

ORGON. It's the casket that's worrying me. I'm more concerned about that than anything else.

CLÉANTE. Is there some important secret about the casket?

ORGON. Argas, my lamented friend, left it with me for safe keeping. He put it into my hands himself in the greatest secrecy. He selected me for this when he fled the country. It contains documents on which, he told me, his life and property depended.

CLÉANTE. Then why did you trust them to someone else?

ORGON. Because of a scruple of conscience. I went straight to this scoundrel and took him into my confidence. He persuaded me that it was better to let him have the casket for safe keeping so that in case of inquiry I could deny that I had it, and yet safeguard my conscience so far as giving false testimony was concerned.

CLÉANTE. You're in a difficult position it seems to me. Both the deed of gift and your action in confiding the casket to him were, if I may say so, very ill considered; he's in a position to lead you a pretty dance! What's more it was most imprudent to provoke him when he has such a hold upon you. You ought to have been more conciliatory in dealing with him.

ORGON. What! A fellow who could hide such double dealing, such wickedness, under the outward semblance of ardent piety, a man whom I took into my house as a penniless beggar. . . . No, that's finished with: I'll have no more to do with godly men. I'll hold them in utter abhorrence in future. I'll consider nothing too bad for them!

CLÉANTE. There you go again! No moderation in anything! You are incapable of being temperate and sensible; you seem to have no idea of behaving reasonably. You must always be rushing from one extreme to the other. You see your mistake now; you've learned that you were taken in by an assumed piety; but what's the good of correcting one error by an even greater one, and failing to make a distinction between a scoundrelly good for nothing and genuinely good men? Because an audacious rogue has deceived you by a pretentious assumption of virtue and piety must you go and think everybody is like him and that there are no truly devout people nowadays? Leave such foolish inferences to the unbelievers; distinguish between virtue and the outward appearance of it, don't be so hasty in bestowing your esteem, and keep a sense of proportion. Be on your guard if you can against paying deference to imposture but say nothing against true devotion, and if you must run to extremes, better err on the same side as you did before.

[*Enter* DAMIS.]

DAMIS. Is it true, father, that this scoundrel is threatening you, that he's insensible to every benefit, and that in his wicked and outrageous pride he is turning your own generosity against you?

ORGON. It is, my son, and a dreadful grief it is to me too.

DAMIS. Leave it to me! I'll crop his ears for him. No half-measures with a rascal like that! I'll undertake to rid you of him without delay. I'll settle the business! I'll deal with him.

CLÉANTE. That's typical young man's talk. Moderate your feelings for goodness sake! We live in an age and under a government where it goes ill with those who resort to violence.

[*Enter* MADAME PERNELLE.]

MADAME PERNELLE. What's all this? What are these strange goings-on I have been hearing about?

ORGON. Ay! Strange indeed and I've seen them with my own eyes too. This is the reward I get for my pains. In sheer kindness of heart I relieve a man in his misery, receive him into my house, treat him like a brother, load him with kindness, give him my daughter, everything I possess, and what does the infamous scoundrel do but foully endeavour to seduce my wife! Not content with that he has the audacity to turn my own benevolence against me and threatens to ruin me with the weapons my own unwise generosity has put into his hand, deprive me of my possessions, and reduce me to the beggary from which I rescued him.

DORINE. Poor fellow!

MADAME PERNELLE. My son, I just can't believe that he has been guilty of such wickedness.

ORGON. How d'ye mean?

MADAME PERNELLE. People are always envious of the righteous.

ORGON. Whatever are you talking about, mother?

MADAME PERNELLE. I mean that there are queer goings-on in this house and I know very well how much they hate him.

ORGON. What has their hatred to do with what I'm telling you?

MADAME PERNELLE. I told you a hundred times when you were a little boy.

> 'Virtue, on earth, is persecuted ever
> The envious die, but envy never.'

ORGON. But what has this to do with what has happened?

MADAME PERNELLE. They'll have made up a hundred idle tales about him.

ORGON. I've already told you that *I saw it all myself*.

MADAME PERNELLE. There are no limits to the malice of slanderous tongues.

ORGON. You'll make me swear, mother, I've told you I saw his wickedness with my own eyes.

MADAME PERNELLE. Malicious tongues spread their poison abroad and nothing here below is proof against them.

ORGON. This is ridiculous talk. I *saw* him, I tell you, *saw him* with my own eyes! When I say I saw him I mean I really did see it! Must I go on saying it? How many times am I to tell you? Must I bawl it at the top of my voice?

MADAME PERNELLE. Good Heavens, appearances can often be deceptive. One shouldn't judge by what one sees.

ORGON. You'll drive me mad!

MADAME PERNELLE. It's human nature to think evil of people. Goodness is often misinterpreted.

ORGON. Am I to interpret it as kindly solicitude when I see him trying to kiss my wife?

MADAME PERNELLE. One ought never to make accusations

without just cause. You should have waited until you were quite certain of his intentions.

ORGON. What the devil! How was I to be more certain? I should have waited, should I, until he. . . . You'll drive me to say something I shouldn't.

MADAME PERNELLE. No, no! He's far too good a man. I just can't imagine he meant to do what you are saying he did.

ORGON. Look here! If you weren't my mother – I don't know what I wouldn't say to you – I'm so angry.

DORINE. Serves you right, master; it's the way of the world. *You* refused to believe once and now she won't believe you.

CLÉANTE. We are wasting time with this nonsense which we ought to be using for making plans. We can't afford to go to sleep in face of the scoundrel's threats.

DAMIS. Why! Do you think he'll really have the audacity to carry them out?

ELMIRE. I can't think he would have a case. His ingratitude is too glaring.

CLÉANTE. I shouldn't rely on that. He'll find means to justify whatever he does to you. Intrigue has landed people in difficulties on less evidence than this before now. I repeat what I said before: when he was in so strong a position as he is, you should never have provoked him so far.

ORGON. True. But what could I do? The audacity of the villain was such that I wasn't master of my feelings.

CLÉANTE. I only wish we could patch up some sort of reconciliation.

ELMIRE. Had I known what a strong position he was in I would never have been a party to making such a fuss . . .

ORGON [*to* DORINE]. What does *this* fellow want? Go at once and see. I'm in a fine state for anyone to come to see me.

[*Enter* MR LOYAL.]

MR LOYAL. Good afternoon, dear sister. Pray let me speak with the master.

DORINE. He has company. I don't suppose he can see anyone just now.

MR LOYAL. I'm not for being troublesome. I don't think he'll
find *my* visit unsatisfactory. He'll be pleased with what I've
come about.

DORINE. Your name?

MR LOYAL. Just tell him that I'm here on behalf of Mr
Tartuffe and for his own good.

DORINE [*to* ORGON]. It's a man who's come on behalf of
Mr Tartuffe. He's very civil about it. He says that his
business is something that you will be pleased to
hear.

CLÉANTE [*to* ORGON]. We must see who the man is and
what he wants.

ORGON. Perhaps he's come to reconcile us. How should I
behave to him?

CLÉANTE. Don't show your resentment. If he's for coming
to an agreement you must listen to him.

MR LOYAL. How d'ye do, sir. May Heaven bless you and
confound all who seek to do you harm.

ORGON [*aside to* CLÉANTE]. This civil beginning confirms
my impression. It means a reconciliation.

MR LOYAL. I have always been very devoted to your family.
I was once in your father's service.

ORGON. I'm sorry not to recognize you. You must forgive
me but I don't know your name.

MR LOYAL. Loyal's the name. Norman by birth and bailiff
to the court; and let them envy me that want to. I can
rightly claim to have discharged my duty with credit this
forty year now, Heaven be praised, and now I've come, sir,
to serve this writ upon you, excusing the liberty.

ORGON. What! You've come to . . .

MR LOYAL. Now take it quiet, sir. It's only a writ, an order
to quit the house at once, you and yours, bag and baggage,
and make way for others, without delay and without fail
as herein provided.

ORGON. What, me? Leave the house?

MR LOYAL. That's it, sir, if you don't mind. This house is
now, as you be duly aware, good Mr Tartuffe's and no
argument about it. He's lord and master of your possessions

from now on by virtue of the deed that I be the bearer of. It's in due form and there's no disputing it.

DAMIS. What marvellous impudence!

MR LOYAL [*to* DAMIS]. I want nothing to do with you, sir. It's this gentleman I'm dealing with. He's reasonable and good to deal with and he knows too well what a good man's duty is to want to interfere with the course of justice.

ORGON. But . . .

MR LOYAL. Yes sir. I know you'd never resist authority, not on any consideration. You'll allow me to carry out my orders as a gentleman should.

DAMIS. You may as easily find yourself getting a hiding for all your black gown, Mr Bailiff.

MR LOYAL. Ask your son to hold his tongue, sir, or retire. I should be very sorry to have to report you.

DORINE. He should be *Dis*loyal, not Loyal, by the look of him.

MR LOYAL. I have a soft spot for godly men, sir, and I only took service of this writ in consideration for you sir, and just to be helpful and to stop the job falling to anybody who mightn't have the same feeling for you that I have and wouldn't have gone about things so considerate-like.

ORGON. And what could be worse than ordering a man out of his own house?

MR LOYAL. We are giving you time. I'll give a stay of execution till tomorrow. I'll just come and pass the night here with a dozen or so of my men without fuss or scandal. I must ask for the keys as a matter of form, of course, before you go to bed. I'll take pains not to disturb your rest and I'll see that there's nothing that isn't as it should be. But tomorrow morning you'll have to look slippy and clear everything out of here down to the last article. My men will help you. I've picked a handy lot so that they can get everything out for you. Nobody could treat you fairer than that and, seeing as I'm showing you every consideration, I ask the same from you, sir – that is, that you won't do nothing to hinder me in discharge of my duty.

ORGON [*aside*]. I'd willingly give the last hundred louis I possess for the pleasure of landing him a punch on his ugly snout!

CLÉANTE [*whispers to* ORGON]. Steady. Don't do anything foolish.

DAMIS. I can hardly restrain myself before such unheard-of insolence. I'm itching to be at him.

DORINE. That broad back of yours could do with a good dusting, Mr Loyal.

MR LOYAL. I could get you into trouble for talking like that, my lass. The law applies to women as well, you know.

CLÉANTE [*to* LOYAL]. That's enough, sir. We'll leave it at that. Give us the document and go.

MR LOYAL. Good day then. The Lord be with you all.

[*Exit* MR LOYAL.]

ORGON. Ay, and the Devil take you and him who sent you! Well mother, you see now whether I was right or not. On the other point you can judge from the writ. Do you realize now what a rascal he is?

MADAME PERNELLE. I don't know whether I'm on my head or my heels.

DORINE. You have no cause for complaint and no right to blame him. It all fits in with his pious intentions; it's all part of his love for his neighbour. He knows how possessions corrupt a man and it's pure charity on his part to rob you of everything that might stand in the way of your salvation.

ORGON. Be quiet! I'm always having to remind you!

CLÉANTE. Let us go and take counsel on what course to follow.

ELMIRE. Go and expose the ungrateful scoundrel! This last act of his must invalidate the deed of gift. His treachery must appear too obvious to permit him the success we fear.

[*Enter* VALÈRE.]

VALÈRE. I'm very sorry to bring you bad news, sir, but I'm obliged to do so because you are in most urgent danger. A very close friend who knows the interest I have reason to take in your welfare has violated the secrecy due to affairs of state and sent me intelligence, in confidence. The purport of it is that you must fly immediately. The scoundrel, who has so long imposed upon you, denounced you to the King an hour ago and, among various charges made against you, put into his hands a casket which belonged to a disaffected person whose secrets he contends you have kept in breach of your duty as a subject. I know no particulars of the offence with which you are charged but a warrant has been issued for your arrest and to ensure effective service of it Tartuffe himself is commanded to accompany the person who is to apprehend you.

CLÉANTE. And so he strengthens his hand! That's how he means to make himself master of your possessions.

ORGON. I must admit, the man really is a monster!

VALÈRE. The slightest delay may be fatal to you. I have my carriage at the door to take you away, and a thousand guineas which I have brought for you. We must lose no time: this is a shattering blow – there's no avoiding it except by flight. I offer you my services to conduct you to some place of safety. I'll stay with you until you are out of danger.

ORGON. Alas! How can I repay your kindness? But I must leave my thanks to another time. May Heaven allow me some day to return this service! Farewell! Take care all of you . . .

CLÉANTE. Go at once, brother. We'll see that everything necessary is done.

[*Enter* TARTUFFE *and an* OFFICER.]

TARTUFFE. Gently, sir, gently, don't run so fast. You don't need to go very far to find a lodging. You are a prisoner in the King's name.

ORGON. Villain! To keep this trick to the last! this is the blow whereby you finish me, the master stroke of all your perfidy!

TARTUFFE. Your insults are powerless to move me. I am schooled to suffer everything in the cause of Heaven.

CLÉANTE. Remarkable meekness indeed!

DAMIS. How impudently the dog makes mockery of Heaven.

TARTUFFE. Not all your rage can move me. I have no thought for anything but to fulfil my duty.

MARIANE. What credit can you hope to reap from this? How can you regard such employment as honourable?

TARTUFFE. Any employment must needs be honourable which proceeds from that authority which sent me hither.

ORGON. And do you not remember, ungrateful wretch, that it was my charitable hand which rescued you from indigence?

TARTUFFE. Yes, I am mindful of the assistance I received from you, but my first duty is to the interests of my King and that sacred obligation is so strong as to extinguish in me all gratitude to you. To that allegiance I would sacrifice friends, wife, kinsmen, and myself with them.

ELMIRE. Impostor!

DORINE. How cunningly he cloaks his villainies with the mantle of all that we most revere!

CLÉANTE. If this consuming zeal of which you boast is as great as you say, why didn't it come to light until he had caught you making love to his wife? Why didn't it occur to you to denounce him until your attempt to dishonour him had forced him to turn you out? If I mention the gift it isn't to deter you from doing your duty but, nevertheless, if you want to treat him as a criminal now, why did you consent to accept anything from him before?

TARTUFFE. Pray deliver me from this futile clamour, sir! Proceed to the execution of your orders.

OFFICER. Yes. I have indeed waited too long already and you do well to recall me to my duty. In fulfilment of my instructions I command you to accompany me forthwith to the prison in which you are to be lodged.

TARTUFFE. What? Me, sir?

OFFICER. Yes, you.

TARTUFFE. But why to prison?

OFFICER. I am not accountable to you. [*To* ORGON] Calm your fears, sir. We live under the rule of a prince inimical

to fraud, a monarch who can read men's hearts, whom
no impostor's art deceives. The keen discernment of that
lofty mind at all times sees things in their true perspective;
nothing can disturb the firm constancy of his judgement nor
lead him into error. On men of worth he confers immortal
glory but his favour is not shown indiscriminately: his love
for good men and true does not preclude a proper detestation of those who are false. This man could never deceive
him – he has evaded more subtle snares than his. From the
outset he discerned to the full the baseness of the villain's
heart and in coming to accuse you he betrayed himself
and by a stroke of supreme justice revealed himself as a
notorious scoundrel of whose activities under another name
His Majesty was already informed. The long history of his
dark crimes would fill volumes. In short, the King, filled
with detestation for his base ingratitude and wickedness to
you, added this to his other crimes and only put me under
his orders to see to what lengths his impudence would go
and to oblige him to give you full satisfaction. All documents he says he has of yours I am to take from him in your
presence and restore them to you and His Majesty annuls
by act of sovereign prerogative the deed of gift of your
possessions that you made to him. Moreover, he pardons
you that clandestine offence in which the flight of your
friend involved you: this clemency he bestows upon you
in recognition of your former loyal service and to let you
see that he can reward a good action when least expected,
that he is never insensible to true merit and chooses rather
to remember good than ill.

DORINE. Heaven be praised!

MADAME PERNELLE. Now I can breathe again.

ELMIRE. A happy end to all our troubles!

MARIANE. Who could have foretold this?

ORGON [*to* TARTUFFE]. So you see, you villain, you . . .

CLÉANTE. Ah! Brother forbear. Do not stoop to such
indignity. Leave the unhappy creature to his fate. Add
nothing to the remorse which must now overwhelm him.
Rather hope that he may henceforward return to the paths

of virtue, reform his life, learn to detest his vices, and so earn some mitigation of the justice of the King. Meanwhile, for your own part, you must go on your knees and render appropriate thanks for the benevolence His Majesty has shown to you.

ORGON. Yes, that's well said. Let us go and offer him our humble thanks for all his generosity to us. Then, that first duty done, we have another to perform – to crown the happiness of Valère, a lover who has proved both generous and sincere.

A Doctor in Spite of Himself

LE MÉDECIN MALGRÉ LUI

CHARACTERS IN THE PLAY

SGANARELLE
MARTINE, his wife
MR ROBERT, his neighbour
VALÈRE, a steward to Géronte
LUCAS, a country fellow
GÉRONTE
LUCINDE, his daughter
LÉANDRE, her lover
JACQUELINE, a foster-mother, Lucas's wife
THIBAUT, a peasant
PERRIN, his son

Scene

ACT I. *A wood*
ACT II. *A room in Géronte's house*
ACT III. *Géronte's garden*

Act One

[Enter SGANARELLE *and* MARTINE *quarrelling.]*

SGANARELLE. No, I tell you I'll have nothing to do with it and it's for me to say. I'm the master.

MARTINE. And I'm telling you that I'll have you do as I want. I didn't marry you to put up with your nonsensical goings on.

SGANARELLE. Oh! The misery of married life! How right Aristotle was when he said wives were the very devil!

MARTINE. Just listen to the clever fellow – him and his blockhead of an Aristotle!

SGANARELLE. Yes, I'm a clever fellow all right! Produce me a woodcutter who can argue and hold forth like me, a man who has served six years with a famous physician and had his Latin grammar off by heart from infancy!

MARTINE. A plague on the idiot!

SGANARELLE. A plague on you, you worthless hussy!

MARTINE. A curse on the day and hour when I took it into my head to go and say 'I will'!

SGANARELLE. And a curse on the cuckold of a notary who made me sign my name to my own ruin.

MARTINE. A lot of reason you have to complain, I must say! You ought to thank Heaven every minute of your life that you have me for your wife. Do you think you deserved to marry a woman like me?

SGANARELLE. It's true you did me a great honour and I had good cause to be satisfied with my wedding night but confound it! Don't set me talking about that – I might say things . . .

MARTINE. Such as?

SGANARELLE. No, let's leave it at that. We know what we know. That's enough. You were pretty lucky to come across me.

MARTINE. Lucky you call it to come across you – a man who has brought me down to the workhouse, a dissolute scoundrel, a dog who eats me out of house and home?

SGANARELLE. That's a lie. I drink as well as eat!

MARTINE. Who has sold every stick in the house.

SGANARELLE. Living on one's means, that is!

MARTINE. Who's taken the very bed from under me.

SGANARELLE. You'll get up all the sooner!

MARTINE. Who hasn't left a single thing in the whole place.

SGANARELLE. All the easier to move house.

MARTINE. And does nothing but gamble and drink from morning to night.

SGANARELLE. That's to keep up my spirits.

MARTINE. And what am I supposed to do with the family in the meantime?

SGANARELLE. Whatever you like.

MARTINE. I have four little children on my hands.

SGANARELLE. Put 'em on the floor.

MARTINE. They are crying for bread all the time.

SGANARELLE. Give 'em a whipping. When *I've* had my fill I'll have everyone in the house be content.

MARTINE. And do you intend, you sot, that things shall continue to go on like this?

SGANARELLE. Now wife, take it easy, do.

MARTINE. Am I to go on putting up with your insolence and debauchery for ever?

SGANARELLE. Don't let us get annoyed, my dear.

MARTINE. Do you think I don't know how to bring you to some sense of your duty.

SGANARELLE. What you *do* know, my dear, is that I'm not very long suffering and that I have a pretty strong arm.

MARTINE. I don't care what you do.

SGANARELLE. My dear little wifie, you are itching for trouble as usual.

MARTINE. I'll show you that I'm not afraid of you.

SGANARELLE. My dear better half, you really are asking for it.

MARTINE. Do you think I care for your threats?

SGANARELLE. I shall have to box your ears for you, sweetheart.

MARTINE. Drunken sot that you are!

SGANARELLE. I'll wallop you.

MARTINE. You great soaker!

SGANARELLE. I'll leather you.

MARTINE. You horrible creature!

SGANARELLE. I'll give you a drubbing!

MARTINE. Wretch! Villain! Twister! Scoundrel! Gallows bird! Beggarly, scoundrelly, rascally thief . . .

SGANARELLE [*picking up a cudgel and beating her*]. Ah! So you will have it.

MARTINE. Ow! Ow! Ow!

SGANARELLE. That's the right way to quieten you!

[*Enter* MR ROBERT.]

MR ROBERT. Hallo! Hallo! Hallo! Come, come! What's all this about? Disgraceful behaviour! Confound you, you scoundrel, fancy beating your wife like that!

MARTINE [*facing* MR ROBERT, *arms akimbo she gives him a slap*]. Suppose I want him to beat me.

MR ROBERT. Ah! Then I heartily agree –

MARTINE. What are you butting in for?

MR ROBERT. It was wrong of me.

MARTINE. Is it any business of yours?

MR ROBERT. You are right.

MARTINE. Just fancy! The impertinence! Wanting to stop husbands beating their wives!

MR ROBERT. I apologize.

MARTINE. What have you to do with it?

MR ROBERT. Nothing.

MARTINE. What right have you to poke your nose in?

MR ROBERT. None at all.

MARTINE. Mind your own business then.

MR ROBERT. I won't say another word.

MARTINE. I like being beaten.

MR ROBERT. All right.

MARTINE. It doesn't hurt you.

MR ROBERT. That's true.

MARTINE. You are a fool to come meddling with what has nothing to do with you. [*She gives him a slap.* MR ROBERT *now goes towards* SGANARELLE *who addresses him similarly, forces him to retreat, beats him with his cudgel, and puts him to flight.*

MR ROBERT. I beg your pardon friend, most sincerely. Carry on, beat her and thrash her to your heart's content. I'll give you a hand if you like.

SGANARELLE. No I don't want to.

MR ROBERT. Ah! That's different then.

SGANARELLE. I'll beat her or not as I choose.

MR ROBERT. Very good.

SGANARELLE. She's my wife, not yours.

MR ROBERT. Undoubtedly.

SGANARELLE. I don't take orders from you.

MR ROBERT. Of course not.

SGANARELLE. I don't want your help either.

MR ROBERT. Well, that suits me.

SGANARELLE. You are an idiot to interfere in other folks business. Remember what Cicero said about not putting the bark between the trunk and your finger.

[*He beats* MR ROBERT *and chases him out.*]

SGANARELLE [*turns to his wife and takes her hand*]. Suppose we make peace now. Your hand on it.

MARTINE. Oh yes! After you've beaten me like that!

SGANARELLE. That was nothing. Your hand.

MARTINE. I won't.

SGANARELLE. Eh!

MARTINE. No.

SGANARELLE. My dear little wife.

MARTINE. Not a bit of it.

SGANARELLE. Come on now.

MARTINE. No, I won't.

SGANARELLE. Come, come, come, come!

MARTINE. No! I'm annoyed and I mean it!

SGANARELLE. Bah! It was nothing! Come along!

MARTINE. Let me be.

SGANARELLE. Shake hands, I tell you.

MARTINE. You've treated me too badly.

SGANARELLE. All right then, I'll say that I'm sorry. Shake hands on it!

MARTINE. I forgive you. [*Aside*] But I'll pay you out for it yet.

SGANARELLE. It's silly of you to take any notice of it. These little things have to be now and then – they are a necessary part of a loving relationship and a few blows with a cudgel – between man and wife – only serve to restore zest to their affection. There now. I'm off to the wood and I promise you shall have a hundred faggots and more before the day's out.

[*Exit* SGANARELLE.]

MARTINE. Be off with you. I'm not forgetting my grievance whatever face I put on it. I'm just longing to find some means of paying you out for the beating you gave me. I know very well that a wife always has ways and means of getting her own back on her husband but that sort of punishment is too good for my precious gallows bird. What I need is a revenge that he'll feel a bit more or it will be no satisfaction for what I've had to suffer.

[*Enter* LUCAS *and* VALÈRE.]

LUCAS. Indeed to goodness, we'm taken on a deuce of a commission the pair of us. I can't see what we'm getting out of it neither.

VALÈRE. Well, what about it, old man? We have to obey the Master haven't we? And what's more we are both of us concerned for the health of the Master's daughter. Then again her marriage, which has been put off because of her illness, ought to be worth something to us. Horace is free with his money and he's like to succeed with his suit. She may have shown a fancy for this fellow Léandre, but her father would never consent to have him for a son-in-law.

MARTINE [*aside to herself*]. Can I find no way at all of getting my own back?

LUCAS [*aside to* VALÈRE]. But what sort o' fancy idea has he got into his head – now the doctors be run out of Latin?

VALÈRE. Sometimes if one goes on searching one can find the very thing one couldn't find at the start and often in some obvious place . . .

MARTINE [*still talking to herself*]. Yes I must have my own back whatever it costs. I can't get over that thrashing. I'm not going to swallow it . . . I . . . [*Bumps into* VALÈRE *and* LUCAS] Ah, gentlemen I beg your pardon. I didn't see you. I was racking my brains to find something that's worrying me.

VALÈRE. We all have our troubles in this world. We too are looking for something we should very much like to find.

MARTINE. Would it be anything I can help you with?

VALÈRE. Possibly. We are trying to find some clever man, some doctor, who might afford some relief to our master's daughter who has been attacked by a malady which has suddenly robbed her of the use of her tongue. Many physicians have exhausted all their skill on her behalf but one sometimes finds people who have remarkable secrets, special remedies of their own, who can achieve what others have failed to do. That's what we are looking for.

MARTINE [*aside*]. Here's a Heaven-sent way of getting my own back on my dog of a husband. [*To* LUCAS *and* VALÈRE] You couldn't have asked anyone better able to put you in the way of what you are looking for. We have a fellow here who's the most marvellous man in the world for hopeless diseases.

VALÈRE. And where, pray, can we find him?

MARTINE. You'll find him now somewhere over there busy cutting wood.

LUCAS. A doctor cutting wood!

VALÈRE. Perhaps you mean he's busy gathering herbs?

MARTINE. No. He's an extraordinary man. He takes a delight in that sort of thing. He's a strange, fantastic, crotchety sort of fellow. You would never take him for what he is. He goes about dressed in a most extraordinary fashion, often pretending to be ignorant and concealing his knowledge. He dislikes nothing so much as using the wonderful talents for healing which Heaven has given to him.

VALÈRE. It's a remarkable thing that great men have usually some kind of kink, some little grain of foolishness mixed with their learning.

MARTINE. This man's foolishness is beyond all belief. It goes to the length sometimes of preferring a thrashing to admitting his skill. I warn you, you'll never get anything out of him, he'll never admit he's a doctor if he's that side out unless you each take a stick to him and thrash him into admitting in the end what he'll begin by denying. That's what *we* do when we need him.

VALÈRE. What a strange aberration!

MARTINE. True. But in the end you'll find he'll do wonders.

VALÈRE. What is his name?

MARTINE. He's called Sganarelle. He's easy to recognize. He's a man with a big black beard. He's wearing a ruff and a yellow and green coat.

LUCAS. Green and yaller coat. He'm a parrot doctor then!

VALÈRE. And he really is as clever as you say?

MARTINE. Why! He's a man who can work miracles. Six months ago there was a woman given up by all the doctors. She had been taken for dead some six hours or more and they were arranging to bury her when they forced him to come – the man we are talking about. He looked at her and put a little drop of something-or-other into her mouth, whereupon she instantly got up from her bed and began walking round the room as if nothing had happened.

LUCAS. Ah!

VALÈRE. It must have been a drop of gold elixir.

MARTINE. May be! Then again, not three weeks ago a young boy of twelve fell from the top of the church tower and smashed his head, arms, and legs on the road. They had no sooner called this fellow in than he rubbed him all over with a certain ointment he makes and the boy immediately got to his feet and ran off to play marbles.

LUCAS. Ah!

VALÈRE. He must have the secret of the Universal Remedy.

MARTINE. No doubt about it!

LUCAS. Lummy! He'm the very man we be after. We mun go quick and seek un.

VALÈRE. Thank you very much for the help you have given us.

MARTINE. Mind you don't forget what I told you.

LUCAS. Cor' lumme! Leave that to us. If it be no more'n a matter o' thrash'n' un we be where we'm want'n' to be already.

VALÈRE. We are very lucky to have met her. I'm feeling very hopeful indeed.

[SGANARELLE *comes on stage singing, a bottle in his hand.*]

SGANARELLE. La! La! La!

VALÈRE. I hear someone singing and cutting wood.

SGANARELLE. La la la! Faith! That's enough work done to deserve a drink. Let me take a breather. . . . [*Drinks.*] This wood makes a man as thirsty as the very Devil.

[*Singing*]   See me lift my little bottle
Hear the gurgle in my throttle!
Ah! How folk would envy me,
Think how happy I should be
If every time I took a pull
I still found my bottle full.
Ah! How happy I should be
Alas! Why can't it really be?

Well, there we are. It's no good giving way to melancholy.

VALÈRE. It's the very man himself.

LUCAS. I think you be right. We'm bumped right into un.

VALÈRE. Let us have a closer look.

SGANARELLE [*noticing them, turns and looks first at one and then the other, lowers his voice and says*]. Ah! my little rogue. How fond I am of thee, my little bottle.

[*Sings*]   How folk would envy me
Think how . . .

What the devil do these fellows want?

VALÈRE. It's him all right.

LUCAS. He'm the very spit o' what she was a tell'n' on.

SGANARELLE [*aside*]. They are talking about me and looking

174

at me. What are they up to? [*Puts the bottle down. As* VALÈRE *bends forward in salutation,* SGANARELLE *thinks he means to take the bottle and puts it the other side of him.* LUCAS, *doing the same thing from the other side,* SGANARELLE *picks up the bottle again and holds it against his stomach with a lot of other by-play.*]

VALÈRE. Sir, is your name not Sganarelle?

SGANARELLE. What's that?

VALÈRE. I'm asking is your name not Sganarelle.

SGANARELLE [*looking first at* VALÈRE *then at* LUCAS]. Yes and no, according to what you want with him.

VALÈRE. We only want to show him every possible civility.

SGANARELLE. In that case I'm Sganarelle.

VALÈRE. We are delighted to meet you, sir. We have been recommended to you for something we are seeking. We have come to implore you to give us your assistance.

SGANARELLE. If it's anything in my line of business, gentlemen, I'm entirely at your service.

VALÈRE. Sir, you are too kind. But do be good enough to put on your hat, sir. You might find the sun troublesome.

LUCAS. Ay, cover thysel' up, Maister.

SGANARELLE [*aside*]. They're very polite, these fellows.

VALÈRE. Don't think it strange, sir, that we should come to you. Clever men are always sought after and we are well aware of your abilities.

SGANARELLE. It's true gentlemen that I'm the best man in the world at cutting faggots.

VALÈRE. Ah! sir . . .

SGANARELLE. I spare no pains. I do the job really well.

VALÈRE. That isn't what I'm referring to.

SGANARELLE. And what's more I sell 'em at a hundred and ten sous a hundred.

VALÈRE. Pray, don't let us talk about that.

SGANARELLE. I assure you I can't take any less.

VALÈRE. We know how things are, sir.

SGANARELLE. If you know how things are you know that's my price.

VALÈRE. This is all very well as a joke but . . .

SGANARELLE. It's no joke to me. I can't take any less.

VALÈRE. Pray don't let us go on like this.

SGANARELLE. You may get 'em for less somewhere else. There are faggots and faggots. But mine . . .

VALÈRE. Suppose we leave the topic, sir, and . . .

SGANARELLE. I swear you shan't have 'em for a farthing less –

VALÈRE. Really . . .

SGANARELLE. No, upon my conscience, that's what you'll pay for 'em. I mean what I say. I'm not given to over-charging.

VALÈRE. Does a gentleman like you, sir, really need to indulge in these clumsy pretences? Fancy descending to talking like this! Can a man of learning, a famous doctor like you really want to hide his identity from people and keep his great talents concealed?

SGANARELLE [*aside*]. He's mad!

VALÈRE. Pray, sir, don't attempt to deceive us.

SGANARELLE. How d'ye mean?

LUCAS. Bain't no sense in all this fiddle faddle. Us knows what us knows.

SGANARELLE. What d'ye know? What are you getting at? Who do you take me for?

VALÈRE. For what you are, a great physician.

SGANARELLE. Physician yourself. I'm not one and never was.

VALÈRE [*aside*]. This is how the fit takes him. [*To* SGANARELLE] Sir, pray don't go on denying it any further. Don't let us have to resort to regrettable extremities.

SGANARELLE. To what?

VALÈRE. To doing anything we should be sorry for.

SGANARELLE. Upon my word. Resort to anything you like but I'm not a doctor. I don't know what you are talking about.

VALÈRE [*aside*]. I can see we shall have to come to the remedy. [*To* SGANARELLE] Once again, sir, I do beg you to admit to being what you are.

LUCAS. 'Ods my life! Don't 'ee mess about no more but confess frankly-like that 'ee be a doctor.

SGANARELLE [*aside*]. This is getting annoying.

VALÈRE. Why deny what we know?

LUCAS. Why all this 'ere rigmarole? What use is it to 'ee?

SGANARELLE. Gentlemen! I can say it in one word as well as in a thousand. I am *not* a doctor.

VALÈRE. You are *not* a doctor?

SGANARELLE. No.

LUCAS. 'Ee bain't no doctor?

SGANARELLE. *No*, I tell you.

VALÈRE. Since you *will* have it. Here goes. [*They each take a cudgel and beat him.*]

SGANARELLE. Oh! Oh! Oh! Gentlemen. I'm anything you please.

VALÈRE. Why do you drive us to this violence, sir?

LUCAS. Why do 'ee put us to the pain of thrash'n' 'ee?

VALÈRE. I assure you that I couldn't regret anything more.

LUCAS. 'Pon my soul I be main sorry, that I be.

SGANARELLE. What the Devil is all this about? For goodness sake, gentlemen, is it a joke or are you both out of your minds that you will have it that I'm a doctor?

VALÈRE. What? Haven't you given in yet? Do you still deny you are a doctor?

SGANARELLE. Devil take me, if I am!

LUCAS. It bain't true 'ee be a doctor?

SGANARELLE. No. May the plague choke me. [*They begin to beat him again.*] Oh! Oh! Oh! All right then, yes, gentlemen, I agree, if you will have it so. I'm a doctor. I'm a doctor. Apothecary as well if you like. I'll agree to anything rather than get myself knocked about.

VALÈRE. Ah! That's better then. I'm pleased to find you coming to your senses, sir.

LUCAS. We be main joyful to hear 'ee a talk'n' that way.

VALÈRE. I do most heartily beg your pardon.

LUCAS. Excus'n' of the liberty we do be a-tak'n'.

SGANARELLE [*aside*]. Ah! I suppose I can't be mistaken. Can I have become a doctor without noticing it?

VALÈRE. You won't regret admitting what you are, sir. You'll certainly be well rewarded.

SGANARELLE. But, gentlemen, tell me – is there not some mistake? Is it quite certain I'm a doctor?

LUCAS. Ay. 'Pon my word, it be.

SGANARELLE. Honestly?

VALÈRE. Beyond question.

SGANARELLE. Devil take me if I knew it.

VALÈRE. Why, you are the cleverest doctor in the world.

SGANARELLE. Ha ha ha!

LUCAS. A doctor that 'ave cured I don't know how many diseases.

SGANARELLE. Good Lord!

VALÈRE. A woman was taken for dead six hours or more. She was just going to be buried when you brought her round with a drop of something or other and set her walking about the room.

SGANARELLE. Plague on it! Did I?

LUCAS. A little boy twelve years old – fell from the top o' the church tower, 'e went an' broke his head and legs and his arms 'e did and 'ee used some sort of ointment, I dunno what it was, and then the young lad gets to his feet and away he goes to play marbles.

SGANARELLE. The devil he did!

VALÈRE. There you are, sir, you'll have good reason for satisfaction with us. You'll get any fee you like if you'll come along with us.

SGANARELLE. I shall get any fee I like?

VALÈRE. Yes.

SGANARELLE. Ah! Then I *am* a doctor. Beyond any question. I had forgotten but I remember now. What's the problem? Where do we go?

VALÈRE. We'll take you. It's a case of a young lady who has lost her tongue.

SGANARELLE. Upon my word, I haven't got it.

VALÈRE [*aside*]. He will have his joke! [*To* SGANARELLE] Come along, sir.

SGANARELLE. Without my doctor's gown?

VALÈRE. We'll get you one.

SGANARELLE [*handing* VALÈRE *his bottle*]. Carry that, you.

I keep my juleps in there. [*Turning towards* LUCAS *and spitting*] You. Put your foot on that. Doctor's orders.

LUCAS. Odds my life. This be the right sort of doctor for me. I reckon he'll do the job – for a proper comic he be.

Act Two

GÉRONTE, VALÈRE, LUCAS, JACQUELINE

VALÈRE. Yes, sir, I think you'll be satisfied. We have brought you the greatest doctor in the world.

LUCAS. Ay! Marry! There bain't nobody to touch un. The rest of 'em, they bain't fit to clean his boots for un.

VALÈRE. He's a man who has performed the most miraculous cures.

LUCAS. Cured them as was dead and done for, 'e 'as.

VALÈRE. As I mentioned he's rather eccentric. His mind wanders at times and he's not quite himself.

LUCAS. Ay. He likes playing the fool. Folk do say – excuse my mentioning it, as how he'm a bit touched like.

VALÈRE. But in reality he's a thoroughly learned man, and he often says most remarkable things.

LUCAS. When he be so minded 'e can talk fine – ay – talk like a book!

VALÈRE. His fame is already spreading hereabouts and people are flocking to consult him.

GÉRONTE. I'm dying to see him. Bring him here at once.

VALÈRE. I'll go find him. [*Exit*]

JACQUELINE. Mark my word, Maister, this 'un will do just what t'others have done. I reckon 't will be just the usual tale. The best doctor ye could give your daughter – to my way of thinking would be a strapping young man for a husband – one as she had a fancy for.

GÉRONTE. Now now, Nursie dear, you will be interfering!

LUCAS. Thee 'old thy tongue, our Jacqueline. It bain't no business o' thine to be butt'n' in.

JACQUELINE. I'm a tell'n' 'ee, ay, and a dozen times over,

that all these 'ere doctors be a-doing 'er no earthly good. It baint rhubarb nor senna she be in need of. A good husband be the best sort of plaster for to cure a young woman's ailments.

GÉRONTE. Would any man want to burden himself with her in her present state of infirmity? When I wanted to marry her off didn't she set herself up against me?

JACQUELINE. I well believe that, for 'ee wanted to hand 'er over to a man she hadn't no love for. Why couldn't 'ee give 'er to this Maister Léandre that she had such a fondness for? She'd have obeyed 'ee quick enough then and I reckon he would take her as she is if you were minded to give un the chance.

GÉRONTE. He's not a suitable man for her. He hasn't the money the other one has.

JACQUELINE. He has a rich uncle and he's his heir.

GÉRONTE. These tales of money to come are all stuff and nonsense. There's nothing like having it in hand. It's a chancy business counting on other folk's money. Death doesn't always give much attention to the prayers of the noble company of heirs and assigns. You'll have time to get pretty long in the tooth if you are waiting for dead men's shoes.

JACQUELINE. Well, I have always heard tell that in marriage, like in everything else, contentment be worth more than riches. Fathers and mothers do always have this cursed habit of asking 'How much be he worth?' or 'How much have she got?' Old Gaffer Pete have married his daughter Simonetta to fat Thomas because he had a few more square yards of vineyard than that young Robin she had ta'en a liking for and look now how the poor creature be gone as yellow as a quince and have never been herself since. Take notice of that Maister, we only have our fun once in this world and I'd rather give my girl a good husband and the one she'd a liking for than all the wealth in China.*

GÉRONTE. Plague on it, Nurse, how you do go on! Do be

* Literally in the Beauce – famous among French provinces for its agricultural riches.

quiet. Worry yourself like that and you'll spoil your milk.

LUCAS [*slapping* JACQUELINE'S *shoulder*]. Ay indeed, hold thy tongue. Thou'rt an impertinent creature. The Maister knows what 'e be about and wants none of thy prating. Let 'ee look after suckling thy babe and don't 'ee do so much argufying. The Maister be his daughter's father and he be a good sensible man and knows what she needs.

GÉRONTE. Gently now, gently!

LUCAS. I be a-want'n' to put her in her place a bit, Maister. I be a teach'n' 'er the respect that is due to 'ee.

GÉRONTE. Yes, but you don't need to show her with your hands.

[*Enter* VALÈRE *and* SGANARELLE.]

VALÈRE. Get ready, sir. Here comes our doctor.

GÉRONTE. Sir, I'm delighted to see you here. We are in great need of your help.

SGANARELLE [*in doctor's gown and steeple hat*]. Hippocrates says . . . that we should both keep our hats on.

GÉRONTE. Hippocrates says so?

SGANARELLE. Yes.

GÉRONTE. In what chapter, please?

SGANARELLE. In his chapter on hats.

GÉRONTE. If Hippocrates says so we must do it.

SGANARELLE. My dear doctor – having heard of the remarkable things . . .

GÉRONTE. Whom are you addressing, pray?

SGANARELLE. You.

GÉRONTE. But I'm not a doctor.

SGANARELLE. You aren't a doctor?

GÉRONTE. No.

SGANARELLE [*taking a cudgel*]. Honestly? [*Beats him as he was beaten.*]

GÉRONTE. Honestly. Oh, oh, oh!

SGANARELLE. You are now. That's all the qualification I ever had.

GÉRONTE. What the devil sort of man have you brought here?

VALÈRE. I told you he was a droll sort of doctor.

GÉRONTE. I'll send him packing – him and his drollery.

VALÈRE. Don't take any notice of it, master. It's only his joke.

GÉRONTE. I don't like that sort of joke.

SGANARELLE. Sir, I ask your pardon for the liberty I have taken.

GÉRONTE. Don't mention it.

SGANARELLE. I'm sorry –

GÉRONTE. That's nothing.

SGANARELLE. About the cudgelling –

GÉRONTE. There's no harm done.

SGANARELLE. That I had the honour of giving you.

GÉRONTE. We'll say no more about it. I have a daughter who has fallen victim to a very strange malady.

SGANARELLE. I'm delighted, sir, that your daughter should be in need of my services. I heartily wish you had been in need of them as well – you and your whole family so that I could have shown how anxious I am to be of service to you.

GÉRONTE. I'm obliged for your sentiments.

SGANARELLE. I assure you that I say it in all sincerity.

GÉRONTE. You do me too much honour.

SGANARELLE. What is your daughter's name?

GÉRONTE. Lucinde.

SGANARELLE. Lucinde! A beautiful name for a patient – Lucinde!

GÉRONTE. I will just go and see what she's doing.

SGANARELLE. Who is that fine woman there?

GÉRONTE. She's the wet nurse to my youngest child.

SGANARELLE. 'Pon my word! She's a fine piece of goods. Ah Nurse, charming Nurse, my medicine is the very humble servant of your nursery-ship! I only wish I were the fortunate little nursling who [*he lays his hand on her bosom*] imbibes the milk of your kindness. All my skill, all my knowledge, all my capacities are at your service.

LUCAS. Ax'n' your pardon, Mr Doctor, pray let my wife be.

SGANARELLE. What!! Is she your wife?

LUCAS. Ay.

SGANARELLE [*making as if to embrace* LUCAS, *he embraces the nurse*]. Really. I didn't realize that. I'm very glad of it because of the affection I feel for both of you.

LUCAS [*pulling him aside*]. Go easy if 'ee don't mind.

SGANARELLE. I assure you I'm delighted that you are man and wife. I congratulate her on having such a husband as you [*makes as if to embrace* LUCAS *again but, passing under his arm throws himself on the wife*] and I congratulate you on your part, on having so handsome, so sensible, and so shapely a wife.

LUCAS [*pulling him away again*]. Lor lumme! Not so much of thy compliments I do beg of 'ee.

SGANARELLE. Don't you want me to share your appreciation of such a lovely conjunction of parts?

LUCAS. With me, as much as 'ee likes but with my wife a truce to thy ceremonies.

SGANARELLE. I have the happiness of both of you at heart [*same by-play as before*] and if I embrace you to show my satisfaction – I embrace her for the same reason.

LUCAS [*pulling him away again*]. Oh go on with 'ee! Mr Doctor what a way to behave!

[*Re-enter* GÉRONTE.]

GÉRONTE. They are going to bring my daughter in immediately.

SGANARELLE. I await her with all the resources of medical science, sir.

GÉRONTE. Where are they?

SGANARELLE [*touching his forehead*]. In here.

GÉRONTE. Excellent.

SGANARELLE [*wanting to fondle the nurse*]. But as I take an interest in all your household I must make a little test of your nurse's milk and examine her breasts.

LUCAS [*pulling him away and making him spin round*]. No, no. I baint having that.

SGANARELLE. It's the doctor's duty to examine the breasts of all foster-mothers.

LUCAS. Duty or no duty I baint stand'n' for it!

SGANARELLE. You have the audacity to oppose the doctor's orders. Get out!

LUCAS. I don't take no notice o' that.

SGANARELLE [*looking narrowly at him*]. I'll give you a fever.

JACQUELINE [*pulling* LUCAS *away and spinning him round*]. Get out of the way. Baint I old enough to defend myself if he does anything he oughtn't to?

LUCAS. I don't want him a touch'n' 'ee.

SGANARELLE. Fie! The dog's jealous for his wife!

GÉRONTE. Here's my daughter.

[*Enter* LUCINDE.]

SGANARELLE. Is this the patient?

GÉRONTE. Yes. she's my only daughter. It would break my heart is she were to die.

SGANARELLE. She mustn't do anything of the kind. She mustn't die without a doctor's prescription.

GÉRONTE. Come, a chair.

SGANARELLE. She's not a bad-looking patient. I think a strong healthy man might make something of her.

GÉRONTE. You've made her laugh, sir.

SGANARELLE. So much the better. It's an excellent sign when the doctor makes the patient laugh. Now what's the trouble? What's wrong with you? Where do you feel bad?

LUCINE [*replies by signs touching her mouth, head and chin with her finger*]. Haw, hee, ho haw!

SGANARELLE. Eh! What d'ye say?

LUCINDE [*gesturing as before*]. Haw he haw haw he ho!

SGANARELLE. What?

LUCINDE. Haw he ho.

SGANARELLE [*imitating her*]. Haw he ho haw ha. I don't understand you. What the deuce language is this?

GÉRONTE. That's exactly the trouble, sir. She's lost the power of speech and so far no one has been able to find what the reason is. It has caused her marriage to be post-poned.

SGANARELLE. But why?

GÉRONTE. The man she is to marry wishes to wait until she's recovered.

SGANARELLE. But who is this idiot who doesn't want his wife to be dumb. Would to God mine had the same trouble! I shouldn't be wanting her cured.

GÉRONTE. Nevertheless I beseech you, sir, to do everything you can to cure her affliction.

SGANARELLE. Oh! Don't you worry yourself. Tell me now, does she have much pain?

GÉRONTE. Yes, sir.

SGANARELLE. All the better. The suffering is very severe?

GÉRONTE. Very severe.

SGANARELLE. Splendid. Does she go – you know where?

GÉRONTE. Yes.

SGANARELLE. Freely?

GÉRONTE. I couldn't say.

SGANARELLE. And is it the normal sort of . . . ?

GÉRONTE. I know nothing about that.

SGANARELLE [*turning to the patient*]. Give me your hand. This sort of pulse indicates that your daughter is dumb.

GÉRONTE. Ah yes sir, that *is* her trouble. You've got it straight away.

SGANARELLE. Ha ha!

JACQUELINE. See, he guessed what the trouble was.

SGANARELLE. We great physicians know these things at once. An ignorant fellow would have puzzled his brains and said 'It's either this or that', but of course I put my finger on the trouble immediately and I inform you that your daughter is dumb.

GÉRONTE. Yes, but I would very much like you to tell me how it comes about.

SGANARELLE. Nothing could be simpler. It's because she has lost the power of speech.

GÉRONTE. Very good, but why has she lost the power of speech?

SGANARELLE. All the best authorities would tell you that it's due to an impediment in the use of her tongue.

GÉRONTE. Yes, but what do you think is the cause of the impediment in the use of her tongue?

SGANARELLE. What Aristotle said about this was . . . very interesting.

GÉRONTE. I well believe it.

SGANARELLE. Ah! He was a great man!

GÉRONTE. Undoubtedly.

SGANARELLE. A very great man indeed. A greater man than I am . . . by . . . that much! [*Raising his arm from the elbow.*] But to come back to what we were talking about. I consider that the impediment in the use of her tongue is caused by certain humours which we learned physicians call morbid – morbid, that is to say morbid humours – so that the vapours formed by the exhalations of influences which arise in the diseased region coming – so to speak – do you understand Latin?

GÉRONTE. Not a bit.

SGANARELLE [*drawing himself up in astonishment*]. You don't understand Latin?

GÉRONTE. No.

SGANARELLE [*accompanying his speech with various amusing gestures*]. *Cabricius arci thuram, catalamus, singulariter, nominativo haec Musa*, the Muse, *Bonus, bona, bonum. Deus Sanctus, est ne oratio Latinas? Etiam*. Yes. *Quare* – Why? *quia substantivo et adjectivum concordat in generi, numerum et casus.*

GÉRONTE. Ah. If only I had been a scholar!

JACQUELINE. There be a clever man for 'ee!

LUCAS. Ay, it be that fine I don't understand a word.

SGANARELLE. But these vapours I referred to, passing from the left side where the liver is to the right side where the heart is, it happens that the lungs which we call in Latin *Armyan* having communication with the brain which in Greek we call *Nasmus* by means of the hollow vein which we call, in Hebrew, *Cubile* encounter on the way the vapours aforesaid which fill the ventricles of the omoplate and because the said vapours – notice this particularly please –

and because the aforesaid vapours have a malignant
quality – do listen very carefully . . .

GÉRONTE. Yes.

SGANARELLE. Have a certain malignant quality – give me
your attention please.

GÉRONTE. I'm doing so.

SGANARELLE. Caused by the acidity of the humours
engendered in the concavity of the diaphragm, it so happens
that these vapours – *Ossabandus, nequeys, nequer, potarinum,
quipsa milus* and that's precisely what makes your daughter
dumb.

JACQUELINE. Ah! But that be well said, husband.

LUCAS. Would my clapper were that well hung!

GÉRONTE. It was very clearly explained, but there was just
one thing which surprised me – that was the positions of
the liver and the heart. It seemed to me that you got them
wrong way about, that the heart should be on the left
side, and the liver on the right.

SGANARELLE. Yes, it used to be so but we have changed
all that. Everything's quite different in medicine nowadays.

GÉRONTE. I didn't realize that. Forgive my ignorance.

SGANARELLE. Quite all right, you can't be expected to know
all that we know.

GÉRONTE. Of course not. But what do you think ought to
be done about this trouble of hers, sir?

SGANARELLE. What do I think ought to be done?

GÉRONTE. That's it.

SGANARELLE. My advice is to put her back to bed and make
her take some bread dipped in wine.

GÉRONTE. Why that, sir?

SGANARELLE. Because bread and wine mixed together have
a certain sympathetic virtue that's conducive to talking.
They give parrots nothing else, you know. That's how they
learn to talk.

GÉRONTE. That's true. What a great man! Quick! Some
bread and wine.

SGANARELLE. I'll come back and see how she is this evening.

[*To the nurse*] Wait a minute you. [*To* GÉRONTE] I must now administer a few little remedies to the nurse, sir.

JACQUELINE. Me? I'm well enough.

SGANARELLE. So much the worse. Nurse. So much the worse. A state of rude health gives great cause for concern. It would do you no harm to bleed you a little or administer you a nice emollient injection.

GÉRONTE. But this is a method I don't understand, sir. Why start blood letting when the patient's in good health?

SGANARELLE. The method is a salutary one. Just as one drinks as precaution against thirst so one should be bled in preparation for illnesses to come.

JACQUELINE [*going off*]. Faith. I reckon nothing o' that, I baint for making a chemist's shop of myself.

SGANARELLE. You are an obstinate patient but we'll find means of bringing you to reason. [*To* GÉRONTE] I give you good day, sir.

GÉRONTE. Wait a moment, please.

SGANARELLE. What do you want to do?

GÉRONTE. Give you some money, sir.

SGANARELLE [*holding his hand out behind him underneath his gown while* GÉRONTE *is opening his purse*]. I couldn't take it, sir.

GÉRONTE. Sir!

SGANARELLE. No.

GÉRONTE. Just a minute.

SGANARELLE. No, no, no!

GÉRONTE. Please.

SGANARELLE. You are joking.

GÉRONTE. Come, take hold.

SGANARELLE. No, I couldn't.

GÉRONTE. Eh?

SGANARELLE. I don't work for money.

GÉRONTE. I quite understand.

SGANARELLE [*having taken it*]. Is it full weight?

GÉRONTE. Yes.

SGANARELLE. I'm not a mercenary man.

GÉRONTE. I'm sure you aren't.

SGANARELLE. I'm entirely disinterested.

GÉRONTE. That's what I thought.

[*Exit.*]

SGANARELLE [*looking at the money*]. My goodness. That's not too bad. Provided . . .

[*Enter* LÉANDRE.]

LÉANDRE. Sir, I have been waiting for you a long time. I have come to implore you to help me.

SGANARELLE [*seizing his wrist*]. A very poor pulse.

LÉANDRE. I'm not ill, sir. That's not why I have come to you.

SGANARELLE. You aren't ill? Why the devil didn't you say so?

LÉANDRE. No. To put the whole thing in a nutshell, my name's Léandre and I'm in love with Lucinde whom you have come to see. I'm forbidden all access to her by her curmudgeon of a father, so I venture to ask you to help me to carry out a plan that I have thought of for getting a word or two with her. My whole life and happiness depend on it.

SGANARELLE [*feigning anger*]. What do you take me for? How dare you presume to ask me to serve your amours and debase the dignity of a doctor by lending myself to that sort of business.

LÉANDRE. Sir, don't make such a noise.

SGANARELLE [*pushing him away*]. I'll do as I choose. You are an impertinent fellow.

LÉANDRE. Go easy, sir.

SGANARELLE. An ill-mannered rascal.

LÉANDRE. Please.

SGANARELLE. I'll teach you that I'm not that sort of man. And that it's the height of insolence to . . .

LÉANDRE [*pulling out a purse and offering it to* SGANARELLE]. Sir.

SGANARELLE [*taking the purse*] . . . to think of employing me. I'm not talking about you. You are a decent fellow and I shall be delighted to help you. But there are some impertinent people about who come and take the wrong attitude altogether. I must say it annoys me.

LÉANDRE. I beg pardon, sir, for taking the liberty.

SGANARELLE. Don't mention it. What do you want?

LÉANDRE. I wanted to tell you that this illness which you are here to cure is all put on. The doctors have done the usual diagnosis and they've not hesitated to say how it arose. According to some, from the brain or the bowels, according to others from the spleen or the liver, but the fact is that the real cause is *love*. Lucinde only assumed the symptoms in order to avoid being forced into marriage with a man she detests. But let us get out of here in case people see us together. I'll tell you what I want you to do as we go along.

SGANARELLE. Come along, sir. You've made me more interested in this affair of yours than you could possibly imagine. Either the patient shall peg out or be yours or I'm no sort of doctor.

Act Three

LÉANDRE, SGANARELLE

LÉANDRE. I don't think I look too bad for an apothecary. The old man has scarcely ever seen me so the change of coat and wig should disguise me sufficiently.

SGANARELLE. No doubt about that.

LÉANDRE. All I need now is to know five or six words of medical jargon to spice my talk with and give me the air of a learned man.

SGANARELLE. Oh no, that isn't necessary. The costume's sufficient. I know no more than you do.

LÉANDRE. What?

SGANARELLE. The devil take me if I know anything about medicine! You are a good chap and I'm willing to confide in you just as you confided in me.

LÉANDRE. What! You are actually not . . .

SGANARELLE. No. They made me a doctor in the teeth of

my objections. I never set up to be as learned as all that. I didn't get beyond the bottom class at school. I don't know how they got the idea into their heads, but when I saw that they absolutely insisted on my being a doctor I decided to be one and let someone else take the consequences. But you wouldn't believe how the mistaken notion has spread and how crazy everybody is on taking me for a clever man. They are coming to see me from all up and down. If things keep on as they are I reckon I shall stick to Medicine for good. I find it's the best of all trades because whether you do any good or not you still get your money. We never get blamed for bad workmanship. We slash away at the stuff we are working on, and whereas a cobbler making shoes can't spoil a piece of leather without having to stand the racket himself, in our job we can make a mess of a man without it costing us anything. If we blunder it isn't our look out: it's always the fault of the fellow who's dead and the best part of it is that there's a sort of decency among the dead, a remarkable discretion: you never find them making any complaint against the doctor who killed them!

LÉANDRE. Yes, the dead are certainly very decent fellows in that respect.

SGANARELLE [*seeing people approaching*]. These people look as if they are coming to consult me. [*To* LÉANDRE] Go and wait for me near the young lady's house.

[*Exit* LÉANDRE. *Enter* THIBAUT *and* PERRIN.]

THIBAUT. Us be a-coming a-seeking 'ee, maister, my lad Perrin and me.

SGANARELLE. What's the matter?

THIBAUT. His poor old mother, Parette, she's a-been ill in bed these six months.

SGANARELLE [*holding his hand out for money*]. And what do you expect me to do about it?

THIBAUT. Us be a-want'n' 'ee to give us a bit o' some drug-gery to cure her.

SGANARELLE. But I need to know what is wrong with her.

THIBAUT. She be a sick of an hypocrisy, maister.

SGANARELLE. Hypocrisy?

THIBAUT. Ay. That's to say she be a-swelled up all over. They do be a-tell'n' me that 'tis a deal of seriosities she do have inside her. Her liver, her belly, and her spleen, as you might say, 'stead o' making blood make nothing but water. Then, more days than not, she has the quotigian fever with aches and pains in the muscles of her legs. Ye can hear flegms in her throat fit to choke her. At times she's that taken with syncups and conversions we think she be a goner. Us do have an apothecary in our village, all due respect to him, that have given her I don't know how many prescriptories and have cost me more than a dozen good crowns in enemas, excuse my mentioning it, and apistumes he's made her take, infections of jacinth and cordial portions but it was all, as you might say, summat an' noth'n'. He wanted to give her some sort of drug called Ametile wine but I was afraid, honestly, that it would send her to join her forebears, for they do say as how these great doctors have killed I don't know how many folk with that there discovery.

SGANARELLE [*still holding out his hand and moving it up and down to show he wants money*]. Come to the point, my man, come to the point.

THIBAUT. The fact is, maister, we be come to ask 'ee to tell us what to do.

SGANARELLE. I don't understand you at all.

PERRIN. My mother be sick, maister, and here be a couple of crowns us be a-bringing so as 'ee can give us some medicine for her.

SGANARELLE. Ah! I understand you. Here's a lad who speaks up and explains what he means properly. You say that your mother is ill of a dropsy, that her body is greatly distended, that she is feverish, has pains in her legs, and at times is liable to syncope and convulsions – that is to say fainting fits?

PERRIN. Ay, maister, that's just how it be.

SGANARELLE. I understood you immediately. Your father here doesn't know what he's talking about. Now you are asking me for medicine?

PERRIN. Yes, sir.

SGANARELLE. Something to cure her?

PERRIN. That's what I be meaning.

SGANARELLE. Right. Then you must give her this piece of cheese.

PERRIN. Cheese, maister?

SGANARELLE. Yes, it's a specially prepared cheese containing gold, coral, and pearls, with various other precious ingredients.

PERRIN. Us be main obliged to 'ee, maister, us'll go make her take some right away.

SGANARELLE. Go, and if she dies make sure you give her the best funeral you can.

[*Exeunt* PERRIN *and* THIBAUT.]
[*Enter* JACQUELINE *and* LUCAS – *upstage*.]

SGANARELLE. Here's my beautiful nurse. Ah! Nurse of my heart, I'm delighted to see you. The sight of you is as good as rhubarb, cassia, and senna for purging my system of melancholy.

JACQUELINE. Coo, Doctor, that be over fine talking for me. I don't understand all that there Latin of yours.

SGANARELLE. Be ill, Nursie, be ill, I beseech you. Fall ill for my sake. It would give me all the pleasure in the world to attend you.

JACQUELINE. Thank ye kindly, sir, but I'd rather not have to be cured.

SGANARELLE. How I pity you, fair nurse, for having such a tiresome, jealous husband as you have.

JACQUELINE. What would 'ee have me do, sir, 'tis a punishment for my sins, and as we make our beds so we mun lie on 'em.

SGANARELLE. What! A clod like that! A man who keeps watch on you all the time and won't let anybody speak to you.

JACQUELINE. Alas! 'Ee've seen noth'n' yet: 'tis only a small sample of his ill nature.

SGANARELLE. Is it possible? How can a man have the heart

to ill use a person like you! Ah! I know people, Nurse, and not so far away either, who would think themselves happy only to kiss your little tootsies! How does a handsome woman like you come to have fallen into the hands of a beastly, dull, stupid creature like . . . . Forgive my talking like that of your husband, Nurse.

JACQUELINE. Ah, sir. I know very well that he deserves every word of it.

SGANARELLE. Yes, he certainly does, Nurse, and what he deserves even more is that you should plant certain things on his head to punish him for his suspicions.

JACQUELINE. 'Tis true that if I only thought of what he deserved it might make me do some very strange things.

SGANARELLE. Upon my word! You'd do well to get your own back on him with somebody else. It would serve him right I assure you, and if I were lucky enough to be chosen I . . . [*At this moment they both notice* LUCAS *behind them listening to all that they say. They steal in opposite directions, the doctor with amusing by-play.*]

[*Enter* GÉRONTE.]

GÉRONTE. Hello there, Lucas. Have you seen our doctor anywhere about?

LUCAS. Ay, the deuce I have! And my wife with him as well.

GÉRONTE. Then where can he have gone to?

LUCAS. I dunno. I only know I wish him at the devil.

GÉRONTE. Be off and see what my daughter is doing.

[*Exit* LUCAS. *Enter* LÉANDRE *and* SGANARELLE.]

GÉRONTE. Ah! I was asking where you were, sir.

SGANARELLE. I was busy relieving myself of a little superfluous liquid in the courtyard. How is the patient?

GÉRONTE. Rather worse since she took your prescription.

SGANARELLE. So much the better. That means it's working.

GÉRONTE. Yes, but I'm afraid that it may choke her in the process.

SGANARELLE. Don't worry. I have remedies that make light of all illnesses. I'm waiting until she's at death's door.

GÉRONTE [*pointing to* LÉANDRE]. Who is the man you have brought with you?

SGANARELLE [*indicating in dumb show that he is an apothecary*]. He's . . . a . . .

GÉRONTE. What?

SGANARELLE. The man . . . [*dumb show*].

GÉRONTE. Eh?

SGANARELLE. Who . . . [*more dumb show*].

GÉRONTE. I understand you.

SGANARELLE. Your daughter will need him.

[*Enter* JACQUELINE *and* LUCINDE.]

JACQUELINE. Master. Your daughter wants a little stroll.

SGANARELLE. That'll be good for her. You, Mr Apothecary, go with her and take her pulse now and again while I discuss her symptoms with her father. [*He takes* GÉRONTE *aside and putting one arm on his shoulder holds him under the chin with the other so that he must look at him and can't turn to see what the others are doing.*] It's a very important and debatable point among learned doctors, sir, whether women are easier to cure than men. I would like you to listen to this if you please. Some say yes, others say no. I myself say both yes and no. Inasmuch as the incongruity of the opaque humours which arise from the nature and temperament of women are the reason for the usual dominance of the physical over the intellectual, we observe that the instability of these opinions depends on an oblique movement of the lunar cycle: and as the sun launching its rays on the concavity of the earth, finds . . .

LUCINDE [*to* LÉANDRE]. No. I'm utterly incapable of any change in my affections.

GÉRONTE. That's my daughter's voice! She's talking! Oh wonderful remedy! Oh most admirable of doctors! How grateful I am to you, sir, for this wonderful cure! What can I do for you in return for such a service?

SGANARELLE [*walking up and down the stage wiping his brow*]. It's been quite a troublesome case!

LUCINDE. Yes, father, I have recovered my speech, but I

have recovered it to tell you that I'll never have any husband but Léandre and that it's no use your wanting to give me Horace.

GÉRONTE. But . . .

LUCINDE. Nothing will ever shake my resolve.

GÉRONTE. What!

LUCINDE. It's useless to argue against it.

GÉRONTE. If –

LUCINDE. Nothing you say will do any good.

GÉRONTE. But –

LUCINDE. No paternal authority can make me marry against my will.

GÉRONTE. I have –

LUCINDE. I'll never submit to such tyranny.

GÉRONTE. There –

LUCINDE. I'll shut myself up in a convent rather than marry a man I don't love.

GÉRONTE. But –

LUCINDE [*in a deafening voice*]. No! No use at all! Nothing doing! You are wasting your time! I won't do it. That's final!

GÉRONTE. Oh, what a torrent of words. There's no doing anything with her. [*To* SGANARELLE] I implore you, sir – make her dumb again.

SGANARELLE. That's the one thing I can't do. The only thing I can do to help you is make you deaf if you like.

GÉRONTE. Thank you very much! [*To* LUCINDE] So you think –

LUCINDE. No. Nothing you say will make the slightest impression on me.

GÉRONTE. You'll marry Horace this very evening.

LUCINDE. I'll rather die first.

SGANARELLE [*to* GÉRONTE] For goodness sake stop. Let me deal with this business. It's her illness that's still affecting her, but I know what remedy to apply.

GÉRONTE. Is it possible, sir, that you can also cure a malady of the mind such as this?

SGANARELLE. Yes. Leave it to me. I have cures for every-thing. Our apothecary is the man to apply this one. [*To the apothecary*] One word. You see that her ardent affection for Léandre is entirely contrary to her father's wishes. There's no time to lose; the humours are fermenting and an immediate remedy for the trouble must be found – delay may make things worse. I see only one thing for it – a dose of run-away purgative mixed with two drachms of matrimony in pills as necessary. She may make some difficulty about taking it, but you know your job. You must bring her up to scratch and make her swallow it as best you can. Go and take her round the garden a bit just to put the humours into condition while I talk to her father. Above all, lose no time. To the remedy, quick, the one and only remedy for the case!

[*Exeunt* LUCINDE *and* LÉANDRE.]

GÉRONTE. What were those drugs you were referring to, sir? I don't seem to have heard of them.

SGANARELLE. Drugs one uses in emergency.

GÉRONTE. Did you ever see such insolence?

SGANARELLE. Daughters are often inclined to be head-strong.

GÉRONTE. You wouldn't believe how she dotes on this fellow Léandre.

SGANARELLE. It's the heat of the blood makes young people like that.

GÉRONTE. Ever since I discovered how madly she was in love I have kept her shut up in the house.

SGANARELLE. You did well.

GÉRONTE. I even prevented them from communicating with each other.

SGANARELLE. Excellent.

GÉRONTE. They would have been up to some folly if I had let them get together.

SGANARELLE. Undoubtedly.

GÉRONTE. I think she might even have run off with him.

SGANARELLE. Very prudently thought of.

GÉRONTE. I have been warned that he's making every effort to get in touch with her.

SGANARELLE. What a joke!

GÉRONTE. But he'll be wasting his time.

SGANARELLE. Ha ha!

GÉRONTE. I'll stop him seeing her all right!

SGANARELLE. He has no fool to deal with: you know the rules of the game better than he does. He'll have to be pretty smart to beat you.

[*Enter* LUCAS.]

LUCAS. Goodness me today! Here be a fine how d'ye do, maister. Your daughter be run off with that fellow Léandre. 'Twas he was the apothecary and it be Mr Doctor there that have done this 'ere fine operation.

GÉRONTE. What! You could stab me in the back like that! Here! Fetch a magistrate! Stop him from going out. Ah! You traitor! I'll have the law on you!

LUCAS. Upon my word Mr Doctor thou shalt be hanged now! Don't 'ee stir from there.

[*Enter* MARTINE.]

MARTINE [*to* LUCAS]. Oh my goodness! What a time I have had finding the house. Tell me, have you any news of the doctor I found for you?

LUCAS. There he be – a-going to be hanged!

MARTINE. What! My husband going to be hanged! Alas! What has he done to deserve that?

LUCAS. He'm arranged for our maister's daughter to be run away with.

MARTINE. Alas! Dear husband, is it really true that you are going to be hanged?

SGANARELLE. As you see. Oh!

MARTINE. Must you die with all these people around?

SGANARELLE. What can I do?

MARTINE. It wouldn't have been so bad if you had only finished cutting the wood.

SGANARELLE. Leave me. You are breaking my heart.

MARTINE. No. I'll stay and encourage you to die. I'll not leave you till I've seen you hanged.

SGANARELLE. Oh!

[*Re-enter* GÉRONTE.]

GÉRONTE. The magistrate's coming and they'll put you in a place where they'll be answerable for you.

SGANARELLE [*cap in hand*]. Alas! Couldn't it be settled with a few blows of a cudgel.

GÉRONTE. No, justice must have its way – but what's this I see?

[*Enter* LÉANDRE *and* LUCINDE *with* JACQUELINE.]

LÉANDRE. Sir, I come to produce Léandre for you and restore Lucinde to your keeping. We did intend to run away and get married but that intention has given way to a more honourable procedure. I don't wish to rob you of your daughter. I prefer to receive her at your hands. I am to inform you, sir, that I have just received letters from which I learn that my uncle is dead and I have inherited all his possessions.

GÉRONTE. Sir, I have the utmost consideration for your virtues. I give you my daughter with all the pleasure in the world.

SGANARELLE [*aside*]. A near shave for the medical profession.

MARTINE. Since you aren't going to be hanged you can thank me for having become a doctor: I was the one who procured you the honour.

SGANARELLE. Ay, and you who got me a terrible thrashing.

LÉANDRE [*to* SGANARELLE]. It's done you too much good for you to harbour resentment.

SGANARELLE. All right [*To* MARTINE] I pardon you the cudgellings in consideration of the dignity you have raised me to, but be prepared henceforward to show proper respect to a man of my consequence. Think how terrible the wrath of a doctor can be!

The Imaginary Invalid

LE MALADE IMAGINAIRE

A comedy with music and dances, the text revised from the Author's original manuscript omitting all spurious additions and scenes inserted without warrant in preceding editions.

Presented for the first time at the Theatre of the Palais Royal, on the tenth of February 1673 by the *Troupe du Roi*.

Prologue

After the glorious exertions and victorious exploits of our August Monarch, it is fitting that all whose concern is with writing should devote themselves to celebrating his fame or to diverting his leisure. That is what we have endeavoured to do here and this prologue is intended as a tribute to a great Prince and an introduction to the comedy of The Imaginary Invalid, *which was devised for his relaxation after his mighty achievements.*

The setting represents a charming rural scene.

ECLOGUE

Music and Dance

FLORA, PAN, CLIMÈNE, DAPHNÉ, TIRCIS, DORILAS, ZEPHYRS, SHEPHERDS, *and* SHEPHERDESSES

FLORA.   Come, leave your flocks
           Come hither, shepherds, come,
           Foregather here beneath these leafy elms,
           I bring you news propitious to these realms.
           Come leave your flocks
           Come shepherdesses, come,
           Foregather here,
           Foregather here beneath these leafy elms.

CLIMÈNE [*to* TIRCIS] *and* DAPHNÉ [*to* DORILAS].
           Shepherd refrain from talk of love
           'Tis Flora calls us, Flora 'tis who calls.

TIRCIS [*to* CLIMÈNE] *and* DORILAS [*to* DAPHNÉ].
           First, cruel fair, tell me whom love enthrals . . .

TIRCIS.   If my passion you'll approve . . .

DORILAS. If on deaf ears my pleading falls.

CLIMÈNE *and* DAPHNÉ.
           'Tis Flora calls us, Flora 'tis who calls.

TIRCIS *and* DORILAS.
           A word – 'tis all we ask – for us whom love
              enthrals.

TIRCIS.   Must I for ever see my true love slighted?

DORILAS. Can I dare hope one day with you to be united?

CLIMÈNE *and* DAPHNÉ.
       'Tis Flora calls us, Flora 'tis who calls.

        [*Enter Dancers.*]

[*Shepherds and Shepherdesses moving to music take their places around* FLORA.]

CLIMÈNE. Say, O Goddess,
          Say what news
          You bring for our rejoicing.

DAPHNÉ. We long to learn from you
          These mighty tidings.

DORILAS. We fain would know --

ALL.   We yearn to hear
          The news you bring.

FLORA.   Silence and hear the news
          For which you yearned!
          Your prayers are granted:
          Louis is returned
          And with him comes the reign of love and
            pleasure:
          Ended now are your alarms;
          The world submitting to his arms,
          He now can take his leisure.

ALL.   Oh joyful tidings
          Oh happy news for which we yearned
          Oh happy answer to our prayers
          Louis, Great Louis is returned.

        [*Second entry of Dancers.*]

[*All Shepherds and Shepherdesses express in dance the transports of their joy.*]

FLORA.   You shepherds, with your reeds
          Set every glade resounding,
          With echoes of his deeds
          Great Louis' fame expounding.
          From a hundred battles he
          Bears home the victor's guerdon,
          Let that your anthem be
          And Louis' fame your burden.

ALL.   Let that our anthem be
        And Louis' fame our burden.

FLORA.   These rustic lovers shall compete
        Who can best make a story,
        Set it to music meet
        And sing great Louis' glory.

CLIMÈNE. If Tircis should the victor prove . . .

DAPHNÉ. If Dorilas should gain it . . .

CLIMÈNE. I promise he shall be my love.

DAPHNÉ. He mine – I will sustain it.

TIRCIS.   Oh joyful hope!

DORILAS. Oh happy prospect!

BOTH.   What poet could fail to sing
        By such a theme inspired?
        What glorious fancies spring
        To one by love thus fired?

[*The violins play an air to encourage the two Shepherds to the contest while* FLORA *takes her position as judge at the foot of a tree in the centre of the stage accompanied by two zephyrs. The rest range themselves on either side of the stage as spectators.*]

TIRCIS.   Just as with winter snows
        A mighty torrent swelling
        O'er bears its banks and flows,
        Heedless of all restraint, compelling
        All barriers to cede,
        Brooks no deterrent to its speed –
        So sweeps onward from the frontiers of France
        Louis' proud and impetuous advance.

[*Shepherds and Shepherdesses on* TIRCIS' *side dance in a ring about him to express their applause.*]

DORILAS. The dreadful lightning,
        Which in its fury strikes through the thunderhead,
        Is not more frightening,
        Though it makes the boldest dread,
        Than is an army fighting
        With Louis at its head.

[*Shepherds and Shepherdesses on* DORILAS' *side dance as did the others.*]

TIRCIS.   All the deeds of ancient days
Handed down in song and story
Now we see surpassed in glory
By this hero of our time:
Deeds of heroes and immortals
With undying legend fraught
Mighty Louis sets at nought
Mighty Louis sets at nought.

[*Dancers on his side dance as before.*]

DORILAS. Seeing Louis' mighty deeds
We can credit ancient stories,
But who shall serve our grandsons' needs
As touchstone of Great Louis' glories?

[*Dancers on his side dance as before.*]

PAN [*attended by six Fauns*].
Vainly shepherds you aspire
To ape Apollo and his lyre
And seek with rustic strings to frame
What his noblest efforts claim.
'Tis to fly too near the sun
Thus to tempt comparison,
Thus his praises to essay,
With a simple rustic lay.
To depict Great Louis' glory,
Of such deeds to tell the story,
Is beyond the greatest pen
Task beyond the reach of men:
Better seek to charm his leisure
And contribute to his pleasure.

ALL.   Let us seek to charm his leisure
And contribute to his pleasure.

FLORA.   Though to such theme you could not rise
Still you may receive your prize
Both of you have proved deserving

And in such noble enterprise
Lies reward for him who tries.

[*Enter Dancers. The two Zephyrs dance with crowns of flowers and
then crown the two Shepherds.*]

CLIMÈNE *and* DAPHNÉ [*offering hands*].
In such noble enterprise
Lies reward for him who tries.

TIRCIS *and* DORILAS.
Oh! Sweet reward that we attain.

FLORA *and* PAN.
Nothing done in Louis' service
Can be done in vain.

ALL FOUR.
To the service of his pleasures we
Give ourselves again.

FLORA *and* PAN.
Happy these who can contrive
In his service so to live.

ALL.   Let us all with one accord
Join our pipes and voices;
Today the world rejoices;
Let us sing, with one accord
Until the welkin rings,
With praise of Louis, mightiest of kings!
Happy all who can contrive
In his service so to live.

[*Dance in which all join, Fauns, Shepherds, and Shepherdesses,
after which they go to prepare for the play.*]

Alternative Prologue

[*The scene is a wood. After the overture a Shepherdess appears. She laments her tribulations and her inability to find remedy for them.*]

[*Numerous Fauns and Satyrs assembled for their own celebrations meet the Shepherdess, listen to her plaints, and provide a diverting spectacle.*]

SHEPHERDESS.

       Vain and foolish doctors you
       Have no balm can cure my ills.
       Not your jargon, nor your skills
       Can relieve my heart's despair
       Can relieve my heart's despair.

       Alas, alas, how can a maid,
       How can a maid discover
       What it is that pains her heart
       To her shepherd lover?
       And what alone can mend it?
       You can ne'er presume to end it,
       Vain and foolish doctors, who
       Know no balm can cure my ills,
       Know no balm can cure my ills.

       All the remedies of which you boast
       And claim to know the uses
       For my ease can nought avail;
       Your foolish jargon can prevail
       Only with *imagined* ills;
       For all the rest they are *invalid*
       Hocus, pocus, sheer abuses –
       Howsoe'er you boast their uses!
       Vain and foolish doctors, you
       Know no balm can cure my ills
       Not your jargon, nor your skills
       Can relieve my heart's despair,
       Can relieve my heart's despair.

CHARACTERS IN THE PLAY

ARGAN, a hypochondriac
BÉLINE, his second wife
ANGÉLIQUE, his daughter, in love with Cléante
LOUISON, his younger daughter
BÉRALDE, his brother
CLÉANTE, in love with Angélique
MR DIAFOIRUS, a doctor
THOMAS DIAFOIRUS, his son, suitor to Angélique
MR PURGON, Argan's doctor
MR FLEURANT, an apothecary
MR BONNEFOY, a notary
TOINETTE, a servant

The scene is a room in Argan's house in Paris

Act One

ARGAN

ARGAN [*alone in his bedroom, seated at a table reckoning up his apothecary's bills with counters, and talking to himself as follows*]. Three and two make five, and five make ten and ten twenty. Three and two make five. Item, on the twenty-fourth, a small injection, preparatory, insinuative, and emollient to lubricate, loosen, and stimulate the gentleman's bowels. That's one thing I like about Mr Fleurant, my apothecary, his bills are so extraordinarily polite! The gentleman's bowels – thirty sous! All the same, Mr Fleurant, politeness isn't everything: you must be reasonable as well and not fleece your patients. Thirty sous for an injection? With all due respect, I've told you this before. You only charged me twenty in your previous bills and when an apothecary says twenty it really means ten, so there we are, ten sous. Item, on the same day, a good detergent injection compounded of a double catholicon, rhubarb, mel rosatum, etc., according to prescription, to flush, irrigate, and thoroughly clean out the gentleman's lower intestine; thirty sous. With your permission, ten. Item, the same evening, a hepatic, soporific, and somniferous julep to induce the gentleman to sleep, thirty-five sous. I've no complaint about that for it made me sleep well. Ten, fifteen, sixteen, seventeen, and a half sous. Item, on the twenty-fifth, a sound purgative and stimulating concoction of fresh cassia with Levantine senna as prescribed by Mr Purgon to expel and evacuate the gentleman's bile, four francs. Oh! Mr Fleurant, you can't mean that! you must give your patients a chance! Mr Purgon never told you to charge four francs. Make it three if you don't mind and we'll put down one and a half. Item, the same day, an astringent and soothing potion to help the gentleman to repose. Thirty sous – very well, put down ten, fifteen sous. Item, the twenty-sixth, a carminative injection to expel the gentleman's wind, thirty sous; call it ten, Mr Fleurant. The same thing repeated in the evening, thirty sous. No, Mr Fleurant, call it ten. Item, the twenty-seventh, a powerful dose to disperse, dissipate, and dispel the gentleman's ill humours, three francs. Right, twenty-thirty sous, I'm glad to see you so reasonable. Item, the twenty-eighth, a dose of clarified and dulcified whey, to purify, temper, tone up, and restore the gentleman's blood, twenty sous; good, we'll say ten. Item, a tonic compounded of twelve grains of bezoar, syrup of lemon and pomegranate, etc., according to prescription: five francs. Oh! Mr Fleurant, steady on, if you please! If you go on like that nobody will want to be ill any more. Be satisfied with four francs and we'll put down twenty, forty sous. Three and two make five and five, ten, and ten make twenty. Total – sixty-three francs, four and a half sous. That means that this month I've had one, two, three, four, five, six, seven, eight, lots of medicine and one, two, three, four, five, six, seven, eight, nine, ten, eleven, twelve injections and last month I had twelve lots of medicine and twenty injections. I'm not surprised that I'm not as well this month as last. I must have a word with Mr Purgon and get him to put that right. Come and take all this away somebody. There's nobody there. It's no use my talking: I'm always being left alone. There's just no way of keeping them here. [*Rings a bell to summon servant*] They don't hear. The bell doesn't make enough noise. Ting a ling, a ling, a ling. No use. Ting a ling, a ling. They are all deaf. Toinette! Ting a ling, a ling, a ling. Just as if I'd never rung at all. You jade! You slut! Ting a ling. It's infuriating. [*He rings no more but calls ting a ling a ling!*] The devil take her, the wretched creature! How can they possibly leave a poor sick man alone! Ting a ling, a ling! It's pitiful! Ting a ling, a ling! Oh my God! They'll leave me here to die! Ting a ling, a ling!

TOINETTE [*as she enters*]. I'm coming.

ARGAN. Ah! You wretch, you good-for-nothing!

TOINETTE [*pretending to have bumped her head*]. Bother your impatience. With your hurrying folk so I've gone and knocked my head against the window shutter.

ARGAN [*indignant*]. Ah! You faithless creature . . .

TOINETTE [*interrupting him each time*]. Ow!

ARGAN. It's a . . .

TOINETTE. Ow!

ARGAN. It's a whole hour . . .

TOINETTE. Ow!

ARGAN. You left me . . .

TOINETTE. Ow!

ARGAN. Be quiet, you slut, so that I can scold you.

TOINETTE. Upon my word! I like that – after what I've just done to myself!

ARGAN. You've had me bawling myself hoarse, you wretch.

TOINETTE. And you've made me bump my head and that's just as bad, so we are all square, I reckon.

ARGAN. What, you hussy!

TOINETTE. You scold me and I shall cry.

ARGAN. Leaving me alone like that, you . . .

TOINETTE. Ow!

ARGAN. You wretch, you'd . . .

TOINETTE. Ow!

ARGAN. What! Am I not to have the pleasure of scolding you if I want to?

TOINETTE. Scold to your heart's content, I'm not stopping you.

ARGAN. You *are* stopping me, you wretch, you interrupt me at every turn.

TOINETTE. If you are going to have the fun of scolding me, I'm going to enjoy a good cry. Everyone to his fancy. That's only reasonable. Ow!

ARGAN. No, no! I give in. Take this away. Take it away, you slut. [*He rises from his chair and gives her the bills and counters*]. Did my injection work well today?

TOINETTE. Your injection?

ARGAN. Yes, my injection. Did I pass much bile?

TOINETTE. Goodness! Don't ask me: let Mr Fleurant nose into that. He gets the profit from it.

ARGAN. Make sure that the hot water's ready for the one I'm due to have shortly.

TOINETTE. They're having fine games with your carcass,

Mr Purgon and that Mr Fleurant! They're making a milch cow of you. I'd like to ask them what's wrong with you that you need all these medicines.

ARGAN. Hold your tongue, you ignorant creature! Who are you to question the doctor's orders? Ask them to send my daughter Angélique to me. I've something to say to her.

TOINETTE. She's coming of her own accord. She must have guessed what you were thinking.

[*Enter* ANGÉLIQUE.]

ARGAN. Come over here, Angélique, you have come just at the right moment. I was wanting to talk to you.

ANGÉLIQUE. I'm all attention, father.

ARGAN. Wait. Give me my stick. [*Hurrying off*] I'll be back in a minute.

TOINETTE [*teasing him*]. Hurry master, hurry! Mr Fleurant *is* keeping us busy!

ANGÉLIQUE [*with a languishing look and confiding tone*]. Toinette!

TOINETTE. Well?

ANGÉLIQUE. Look at me.

TOINETTE. All right, I'm looking.

ANGÉLIQUE. Toinette!

TOINETTE. Well, what do you want of Toinette?

ANGÉLIQUE. Can't you guess what I'm wanting to talk about?

TOINETTE. I expect it's that young man of ours. For the last week we've talked of nothing else. You are never happy unless you *are* talking about him.

ANGÉLIQUE. Well, if you know that, why don't you begin first and spare me the trouble of introducing the subject?

TOINETTE. You don't give me time. You are so eager I can't get in first.

ANGÉLIQUE. I must admit that I'm never tired of talking about him. I love to take every opportunity of opening my heart to you. Tell me, Toinette, you don't blame me for feeling as I do about him?

TOINETTE. Not at all.

ANGÉLIQUE. Is it wrong of me to indulge in these fancies?

OINETTE. I'm not saying that it is.

NGÉLIQUE. Would you have me be indifferent to his protestations of love?

OINETTE. Heaven forbid!

NGÉLIQUE. You do agree with me, don't you, that there was something providential, something like destiny, in the unexpected way we made each other's acquaintance?

OINETTE. Yes.

NGÉLIQUE. Don't you think that the way he came to my help without knowing me was most chivalrous?

OINETTE. Yes.

NGÉLIQUE. He couldn't have behaved more generously, could he?

OINETTE. No.

NGÉLIQUE. And all done so charmingly.

OINETTE. Oh, yes.

NGÉLIQUE. Don't you think he's very nice looking, Toinette?

OINETTE. Of course.

NGÉLIQUE. And that he has a most attractive way with him?

OINETTE. No doubt about it.

NGÉLIQUE. And that there's something noble in everything he says and does?

OINETTE. Certainly.

NGÉLIQUE. And no one could talk more lovingly to me?

OINETTE. True.

NGÉLIQUE. And that the way they keep me under restraint and prevent any exchange of the tender affection that mutually inspires us is too annoying for anything?

OINETTE. Quite right.

NGÉLIQUE. But, my dear Toinette, do you think he loves me as much as he says he does?

OINETTE. Ah! That's where one needs to be cautious. Real love and pretending are so hard to distinguish. I have known some good actors in that line.

NGÉLIQUE. Oh Toinette! Whatever do you mean? Oh dear! Could he possibly talk as he does and not be telling the truth?

TOINETTE. You'll soon find out anyway. He wrote to you yesterday that he had made up his mind to ask for your hand and that's a pretty good way of letting you know whether he's in earnest or not. It'll be a good test.

ANGÉLIQUE. Ah Toinette, if he should deceive me, I'll never believe another man as long as I live.

TOINETTE. Here's your father back again.

[*Re-enter* ARGAN.]

ARGAN [*sitting in his chair*]. Well now, my girl, I've some news for you, something you were perhaps not expecting. I have received an offer of marriage for you. What's that? You are smiling. Ay, the word marriage tickles your sense of humour, does it? There's nothing rouses more merriment among young women. Ah! Nature! Mother Nature! From what I can see then, my girl, there's no need to ask you if you want to be married!

ANGÉLIQUE. It's my duty to obey you in everything, father.

ARGAN. I'm very pleased to have such an obedient daughter! It's all settled then. I've already promised he shall have you.

ANGÉLIQUE. It's for me to do without question whatever you wish, father.

ARGAN. Your stepmother wanted me to put you into a convent and your little sister, Louison, as well. She's always been set on that idea.

TOINETTE [*aside*]. The old cat has her reasons.

ARGAN. She wouldn't agree to the marriage but I carried my point and I have given my word.

ANGÉLIQUE. Ah, father, how grateful I am for your goodness!

TOINETTE. I really must give you credit for that. It's the most sensible thing you ever did in your life.

ARGAN. I haven't yet seen the young man himself, but they tell me I shall be pleased with him and you too.

ANGÉLIQUE. You may be sure I shall, father.

ARGAN. Why? Have you seen him?

ANGÉLIQUE. Now that your consent permits me to confess it I won't hesitate to tell you that we have already made each other's acquaintance a week ago and you have been asked for my hand because we fell in love at first sight.

ARGAN. They didn't tell me that but I'm very pleased to hear it. If that's how things are so much the better. They say he's a fine handsome young man.

ANGÉLIQUE. Yes, father.

ARGAN. Graceful.

ANGÉLIQUE. Undoubtedly.

ARGAN. Likeable.

ANGÉLIQUE. Certainly.

ARGAN. Nice looking.

ANGÉLIQUE. *Very* nice looking.

ARGAN. Steady – and comes of a good family.

ANGÉLIQUE. Absolutely.

ARGAN. A most trustworthy young man.

ANGÉLIQUE. Utterly trustworthy.

ARGAN. And he speaks good Greek and Latin.

ANGÉLIQUE. I don't know about that.

ARGAN. He's taking his degree as a doctor in three days' time.

ANGÉLIQUE. *Is* he father?

ARGAN. Yes. Hasn't he told you that?

ANGÉLIQUE. No indeed! Who was it told you?

ARGAN. Mr Purgon.

ANGÉLIQUE. Does Mr Purgon know him?

ARGAN. What a question to ask! Of course he knows him, since he's his own nephew.

ANGÉLIQUE. Cléante is Mr Purgon's nephew?

ARGAN. Cléante! What Cléante? Aren't we talking about the young man who's wanting to marry you?

ANGÉLIQUE. Yes, of course.

ARGAN. Very well then. He's Mr Purgon's nephew, son of his brother-in-law, Dr Diafoirus. The son's name is Thomas, not Cléante, and we arranged the marriage this morning, Mr Purgon, Mr Fleurant, and I. His father is bringing him over to see me tomorrow. What's the matter? You seem quite dumbfounded!

ANGÉLIQUE. Because I realize you have been talking about

one person, father, and I thought you meant someone
else.

TOINETTE. Why, master, however could you think of such
a ridiculous scheme? With all the money you have you
aren't going to marry your daughter to a doctor?

ARGAN. Yes I am. And what has it to do with you, you
impudent hussy?

TOINETTE. Heavens! Go easy! You start calling me names
straight away. Can't we discuss it without getting into a
temper? There now, let us talk calmly. What are your
reasons, if I may ask, for a marriage like this?

ARGAN. My reason is that in view of the feeble and poorly
state that I'm in I want to marry my daughter into the
medical profession so that I can assure myself of help in
my illness and have a supply of the remedies I need within
the family, and be in a position to have consultations and
prescriptions whenever I want them.

TOINETTE. Well that's certainly a reason and it's nice to be
discussing it calmly. But master, with your hand on your
heart now, *are* you ill?

ARGAN. What, you jade! Am I ill? You impudent creature!
Am I ill?

TOINETTE. All right then, you *are* ill. Don't let's quarrel
about that. You *are* ill. Very ill. I agree with you there.
More ill than you think. That's settled. But your daughter
should marry to suit herself. *She* isn't ill so there's no need
to give *her* a doctor.

ARGAN. It's for my own sake that I'm marrying her to a
doctor. A daughter with any proper feeling ought to be
only too pleased to marry someone who will be of service
to her father's health.

TOINETTE. Goodness me, master, will you let me offer you
some friendly advice?

ARGAN. What is your advice?

TOINETTE. Think no more of this marriage.

ARGAN. Why not?

TOINETTE. Why not? Because your daughter will never
consent.

ARGAN. She'll never consent?

TOINETTE. No.

ARGAN. My daughter?

TOINETTE. Your daughter! She'll tell you that she'll have nothing to do with Mr Diafoirus or his son, Thomas, either, nor any of the whole pack of Diafoiruses.

ARGAN. Yes, but *I* will, for the match is more advantageous than you think. Mr Diafoirus's son is his sole heir and what's more, Mr Purgon has neither wife nor children; he'll leave all his estate to the heirs of this marriage, and Mr Purgon is a man with eight thousand a year!

TOINETTE. He must have killed a lot of patients to have made all that money.

ARGAN. Eight thousand a year is a fair sum of money without counting his father's estate.

TOINETTE. That's all very well, master, but I stick to my point. My advice, between ourselves, is to choose some other husband for her. She's not cut out to be Mrs Diafoirus.

ARGAN. But I'm determined she shall be.

TOINETTE. Oh come, don't say that.

ARGAN. How d'ye mean 'don't say that'?

TOINETTE. Don't do it.

ARGAN. And why shouldn't I?

TOINETTE. Folk will say you don't know what you are talking about.

ARGAN. Let 'em say what they like. I tell you she'll do what I've promised.

TOINETTE. No, *I'm* sure she won't.

ARGAN. I'll jolly well make her.

TOINETTE. She won't do it, I tell you.

ARGAN. She will – or I'll put her in a convent.

TOINETTE. You will?

ARGAN. I will.

TOINETTE. Right!

ARGAN. How d'ye mean. 'Right'?

TOINETTE. You'll never put her into a convent.

ARGAN. I won't put her into a convent?

TOINETTE. No.

ARGAN. No?

TOINETTE. No.

ARGAN. Pooh! That's a good one! I won't put my own daughter into a convent if I want to!

TOINETTE. I tell you, you won't.

ARGAN. Who'll stop me?

TOINETTE. You yourself.

ARGAN. I will?

TOINETTE. You won't have the heart to do it.

ARGAN. Oh yes, I will.

TOINETTE. You are joking.

ARGAN. I'm not joking at all!

TOINETTE. Your own fatherly affection will stop you.

ARGAN. No, it won't stop me.

TOINETTE. A few tears, her arms around your neck, a 'dear kind daddy' in a loving tone of voice and it will be quite enough to soften your heart.

ARGAN. It won't.

TOINETTE. Oh yes, yes it will.

ARGAN. I tell you I won't budge an inch.

TOINETTE. Fiddlesticks!

ARGAN. Don't you say fiddlesticks to me!

TOINETTE. Heavens, don't I know you! You are far too kind hearted.

ARGAN. I'm not kind hearted at all. I can be thoroughly hard hearted when I want to.

TOINETTE. Go easy, master, you forget you are ill.

ARGAN. I absolutely command her to get ready to marry the man I have chosen.

TOINETTE. And I absolutely forbid her to do anything of the sort.

ARGAN. What are things coming to! The impudence! A slut of a servant talking like this to her master.

TOINETTE. When a master doesn't think what he's doing a sensible servant does right to correct him.

ARGAN [*running after her*]. Oh you insolent creature! I'll murder you!

TOINETTE [*dodging him*]. It's my duty to stop you disgracing yourself.

ARGAN [*stick in hand chasing her round the chair*]. Come here! Come here! I'll teach you to talk to me!

TOINETTE. I'm only doing my duty – and preventing you from making a fool of yourself.

ARGAN. You wretch!

TOINETTE. No, I'll never agree to this marriage.

ARGAN. You slut!

TOINETTE. I won't have her marry your Thomas Diafoirus.

ARGAN. You baggage!

TOINETTE. And she'll take notice of me rather than you.

ARGAN. Angélique! Won't you lay hands on this hussy for me?

ANGÉLIQUE. Oh father, don't make yourself ill.

ARGAN. If you don't stop her I'll refuse you my blessing.

TOINETTE. If she does, I'll never have anything to do with her any more.

ARGAN [*out of breath, throws himself into his chair*]. Oh dear! I'm done for. It's enough to finish me off altogether.

[*Exeunt* TOINETTE *and* ANGÉLIQUE. *Enter* BÉLINE.]

ARGAN. Ah, come in, wife, come in.

BÉLINE. Whatever's the matter, my dear.

ARGAN. Come and rescue me.

BÉLINE. What is it then, ducky?

ARGAN. My love!

BÉLINE. My dearest!

ARGAN. They have been annoying me.

BÉLINE. There, there! Poor little hubby! What is it, then, dearie?

ARGAN. It's that horrible Toinette of yours. She's getting more impudent than ever.

BÉLINE. Don't get excited.

ARGAN. She has infuriated me, my love.

BÉLINE. Quietly then, my dear boy.

ARGAN. She's been thwarting me in everything I wanted to do – this hour past.

BÉLINE. There, there, take it easy.

ARGAN. She had the effrontery to tell me I'm not ill at all.

BÉLINE. The impudence!

ARGAN. You know, dear heart, how bad I am.

BÉLINE. Yes, dearie, it's very wrong of her.

ARGAN. The jade will be the death of me.

BÉLINE. Now, now! there, there!

ARGAN. She's the cause of all the bile I'm secreting.

BÉLINE. Don't upset yourself so.

ARGAN. I've asked you to get rid of her I don't know how many times.

BÉLINE. Good Heavens, my dear! There are no servants without faults – men or women. We are forced to put up with their bad points now and again because of their good ones. She's clever, conscientious, and hardworking and, above all, she's honest; you know how careful we have to be with those we employ nowadays. Hey there, Toinette!

[*Re-enter* TOINETTE.]

TOINETTE. Madam?

BÉLINE. Why have you been annoying my husband?

TOINETTE [*sweetly*]. I, Madam? Dear me! I don't know what you mean. I always try to please the master in everything.

ARGAN. Oh! the deceitful creature!

TOINETTE. He was saying that he meant to marry his daughter to Mr Diafoirus' son and I said that though it seemed to me a very good match for her I thought he'd do better to put her into a convent.

BÉLINE. Well, there's nothing much wrong in that. I think she's quite right.

ARGAN. Ah! don't you believe her, my dear! She's a horrible wretch. She said no end of rude things to me.

BÉLINE. Well well, I believe you, my dear. There, pull yourself together. Toinette, if ever you annoy my husband again I'll sack you. There, give me his fur cloak and his pillows and I'll make him comfortable in his chair. You are all anyhow. Pull your night cap over your ears. There's

nothing like letting the air in at your ears for giving you a
cold [BÉLINE *arranges the pillows around him*].

ARGAN. Ah, my dear, how grateful I am to you for taking
such care of me.

BÉLINE. Get up and let me put this under you. We'll put this
one in to support you there and this one at the other side,
another one at your back and this one here to keep your
head up.

TOINETTE. And this one here [*dropping a pillow on his head
and running off*] to keep the dew off you.

ARGAN [*jumping up in a rage and throwing the pillows after
TOINETTE*]. Ah, you wretch, do you want to smother
me?

BÉLINE. There now, there now, what is it now?

ARGAN [*out of breath, throwing himself in a chair*]. Oh, Oh, Oh!
I can't bear any more of it.

BÉLINE. But why get so excited. She doesn't mean any harm.

ARGAN. My dear, you don't know what a wicked baggage
she is. She's completely upset me. It'll take eight doses of
medicine and a dozen injections and more to put me right
again.

BÉLINE. There, there, ducky, do calm yourself.

ARGAN. Ah my dear, you are my only consolation.

BÉLINE. Poor boy!

ARGAN. I want to try and show some recognition for the
love you bear me, my dear. I'm intending, as I was telling
you, to make my will.

BÉLINE. Please don't let's talk about that, dearie. I can't bear
the idea. The very word 'will' sets me trembling.

ARGAN. But I told you to talk to your lawyer about it.

BÉLINE. Yes, he's in there. I brought him along with me.

ARGAN. Ask him to come in then.

BÉLINE. Alas, my dear, when one loves one's husband as I
do one's in no condition to think of that sort of thing.

[*Enter* NOTARY.]

ARGAN. Come in, Mr de Bonnefoy, come in! Take a seat
please. My wife told me, sir, that you were a very trust-

worthy man and in her confidence so I asked her to have a
talk to you about this will I'm intending to make.

BÉLINE. Oh dear! I just can't talk about such things.

NOTARY. She has explained your intentions, sir, and what
you have in mind to do for her, but I'm bound to advise
you that you can't leave your wife anything in your will.

ARGAN. Why not?

NOTARY. It's contrary to customary law. If you were in a
district where statutory law prevailed you could do it but
here in Paris and the districts where customary law is in
force, or in the greater part of them, it cannot be done.
Any such provision would be null and void. The only
provision man and wife can make for each other is by
mutual gift during their lifetime: moreover, there must be
no children whether of that marriage or a previous one of
either party at the time of the decease of the testator.

ARGAN. Well that's a silly custom, that a man can't leave
money to his wife who loves him and cares for him. I
should like to take further opinion as to what I can do
about that.

NOTARY. It's no good going to a lawyer. They always
take a strict view of these things. They consider it a great
crime to dispose of anything to the prejudice of the law.
They are people who make difficulties and don't know the
ways of arranging things without prejudice to one's conscience, but there *are* other people you can consult who are
more accommodating and have means of quietly getting
round the law and adjusting things which aren't really
permitted, people who know how to smooth over difficulties and find means of evading the requirements of
customary law by indirect means. Where should we be if it
weren't so? There must be some flexibility otherwise we
should never get anything done and our job wouldn't be
worth the candle.

ARGAN. My wife had of course told me, sir, what a very
clever and reliable man you were. How can I manage,
pray, to give my estate to her and see that my children get
nothing?

NOTARY. How can you manage that? You can select some intimate friend of your wife, on the quiet, and make a will formally bequeathing to him whatever you can and the friend can hand it over to her later: or again, you can contract a number of obligations which will not give rise to suspicion to sundry creditors who will allow their names to be used on your wife's behalf and put into her hands a declaration that they handed it over to her as a gift, or again, you can, in your lifetime, hand over to her ready cash and such bearer bills as you may have on hand.

BÉLINE. Heavens, don't be bothering yourself with all that. If anything happens to you, my dear, I shan't want to go on living.

ARGAN. My dearest!

BÉLINE. Yes, my dear, if I were so unfortunate as to lose you . . .

ARGAN. My dear wife!

BÉLINE. Life would be worth nothing to me any more.

ARGAN. My love!

BÉLINE. I should follow you to the grave to prove how dearly I loved you.

ARGAN. Dearest, you are breaking my heart. Be comforted, do.

NOTARY. There's no occasion for tears. We haven't yet got to that stage.

BÉLINE. Ah sir, you don't know what it is to have a husband whom you dearly love.

ARGAN. My only regret if I were to die, my dear, is that I have no child by you. Mr Purgon promised me that he could make me able to beget one.

NOTARY. There's still time for that.

ARGAN. I must make my will, my love, in the way the gentleman says: but as a precaution I'm going to hand over to you twenty thousand francs in gold which I keep behind the wainscotting in my closet, and two bearer bills that are due to me, one from Mr Damon and the other from Mr Géronte.

BÉLINE. No, no, no. I don't want that at all. How much did you say you had in your closet?

ARGAN. Twenty thousand francs, my love.

BÉLINE. Please don't talk to me about money! What was the amount of the bills?

ARGAN. One is for four thousand and the other for six thousand francs, dearie.

BÉLINE. All the money in the world is nothing to me compared with you, my love.

NOTARY. Do you wish us to proceed to drawing up the will?

ARGAN. Yes, sir, but we shall be better in my study. Help me along there my love.

BÉLINE. Come, my poor boy.

[*Exeunt with* NOTARY.]
[*Enter* TOINETTE *and* ANGÉLIQUE.]

TOINETTE. There they are with the notary and I heard the word 'will' mentioned. Your stepmother isn't asleep. I don't doubt she's pushing your father into some sort of conspiracy against your interests.

ANGÉLIQUE. Let him do what he likes with his wealth so long as he doesn't dispose of my heart. You've heard the dreadful plans he has made for me. Don't desert me in this extremity, I implore you.

TOINETTE. Desert you? I'd rather die first. Your stepmother makes me her confidant and tries to get me on her side, but it's not a bit of use. I never liked her and I've always been on your side. Leave it to me. I'll do everything I can for you. But if I'm to help you effectively I must change my tactics, conceal my concern for your interests, and pretend to fall in with the wishes of your father and your stepmother.

ANGÉLIQUE. And do try, I implore you, to let Cléante know about this marriage they have arranged.

TOINETTE. There's only one person can do that for me and that's the old usurer, my lover Punchinello. It will cost me a few blandishments which I don't grudge on your behalf.

It's too late for today but tomorrow morning early I'll send someone in search of him and he'll be delighted to . . .

BÉLINE [*offstage*]. Toinette.

TOINETTE. She's calling me. Good night. Rely on me.

[*The scene changes to a street.*]

FIRST INTERLUDE

[*Enter* PUNCHINELLO, *come to serenade his mistress under cover of night. He is interrupted first by violins upon whom he vents his annoyance and then by the watch composed of dancers and musicians.*]

PUNCHINELLO. Oh love, love, love, love! Poor Punchinello what sort of silly idea have you got into your head now? What do you think you are doing, mad creature that you are? You leave your business and let your affairs go hang. You don't eat and you hardly drink and you lose your sleep at night and all for what? For a she-dragon, a veritable she-dragon, a she-devil in fact, who snubs you and makes game of everything you can find to say to her. But it's no good talking about it. If it's love you want, well then, you've got to be as silly as all the rest of 'em. It's not much use to a fellow at my time of life but what can I do about that? You can't always be sensible even if you want to and old heads can be turned as easily as young 'uns. I've come to see if I can soften my tiger cat's heart by a serenade. There are times when there's nothing so affecting as a lover singing his tale of woe to the keyhole or the door-knob at his mistress's gate. [*Picking up his lute.*] Here's the where-withal to accompany me – oh night, oh lovely night, carry my amorous plaints to the pillow of my inflexible mistress.

[*Sings*]*   Pity me your constant lover.
           Say but 'yes' and I recover;
           But if 'no' be your reply,
           Cruel fair, I needs must die.

               * The original is in Italian.

Hoping, despairing,
My heart is aching,
Absence, past bearing
Grieves me when waking.
Dreams are a fiction,
Sweetly denying
All my affliction
Ah, but they're lying!
For too much loving thus I pine and languish.

Pity me your constant lover.
Say but 'yes' and I recover;
But if 'no' be your reply,
Cruel fair, I needs must die.

Pity's a duty:
Be not unheeding.
'Tis through your beauty
My heart's a-bleeding.
One satisfaction
Though you disdain me;
Own yours the action
When you have slain me.
Only your mercy can abate my anguish.

[*An old woman appears at the window and ridicules* PUNCHI-
NELLO, *singing as follows.*]

Gallants all, who set store by am'rous glances
And false protestations
And sighing relations
And cunning advances
I 'faith you'd better leave me;
For you cannot deceive me.
I have learnt by trial –
Nay, there's no denial –
Your lies to discover.
She's but a madwoman who trusts in a lover.

Those sighs so flattering
Don't make me amorous,
Those vows so shattering
Cease to be glamorous.
I tell you truly.
Go home in misery
Though you weep mournfully;
My heart's at liberty,
Laughs at you scornfully.
Believe me, forsooth.

I have learnt by trial –
Nay, there's no denial –
Your lies to discover.
She's but a madwoman who trusts in a lover.

[*Music and dancing. Violins are heard.*]

PUNCHINELLO. What is this irrelevant harmony that comes
to interrupt my song?

[*Violins are heard.*]

PUNCHINELLO. Peace. Desist, you violins, leave me to
lament at my leisure the cruelty of my inexorable mistress.

[*Violins are heard.*]

PUNCHINELLO. Peace I say. I want to sing.

[*Violins again.*]

PUNCHINELLO. Quiet!

[*Violins again.*]

PUNCHINELLO. So ho!

[*Violins again.*]

PUNCHINELLO. Ah ha!

[*Violins.*]

PUNCHINELLO. Is this a joke?

[*Violins.*]

PUNCHINELLO. Ah! What a row!

[*Violins.*]

PUNCHINELLO. To the devil with you.

[*Violins.*]

PUNCHINELLO. I'm getting annoyed.

[*Violins.*]

PUNCHINELLO. Will you be quiet? Ah, Heaven be praised for that.

[*Violins.*]

PUNCHINELLO. Again?

[*Violins.*]

PUNCHINELLO. Confound these violins.

[*Violins.*]

PUNCHINELLO. What idiotic music it is!

[*Violins.*]

PUNCHINELLO [*making fun of them, with a lute which he only pretends to play, plin, plan, plan, etc.*]. La, la, la, la, la, a, and so on. Upon my word, this does amuse me. Go on, gentlemen, go on. You give me pleasure. [*Silence*] Come then, continue, I do implore you. That's the way to make you be quiet. Music never will do what you want it to. Now, let's get down to it! Before I sing I must have a little prelude and play a few notes to get myself in tune. Plan, plan, plan, plin, plin. This is tiresome weather for tuning a lute. Plin, plin, plin, plan, plan, plin, plin. The strings won't hold at all in this weather. Plin, plan. I hear a noise. We'll put the lute down beside the door.

ARCHERS [*passing along the street singing*]. Who goes there? Who goes there?

PUNCHINELLO. What the devil is it? That's the fashion now is it? Talking to music!

ARCHERS [*singing*]. Who goes there? Who goes there? Who goes there?

PUNCHINELLO [*alarmed*]. Me, me, me!

ARCHERS [*singing*]. Who goes there? Say, who goes there?

PUNCHINELLO. Me, I say, it's me.

ARCHERS. Who's me? Who's me? Who's me?

PUNCHINELLO. Me, me, me, me, me, me.

ARCHERS. Your name, your name, your name without delay.

PUNCHINELLO [*putting on a courageous air*]. My name is – go hang yourselves.

ARCHERS. Hither comrades, hither. Seize this fellow who thus insolently replies.

[*All the watch come on and search for* PUNCHINELLO.]
[*Music and dancing.*]

PUNCHINELLO. Who goes there?
[*Music and dancing.*]

PUNCHINELLO. Who are these rascals that I hear.
[*Music and dancing.*]

PUNCHINELLO. Hey, my lackeys, servants, here.
[*Music and dancing.*]

PUNCHINELLO. S'death!
[*Music and dancing.*]

PUNCHINELLO. S'blood!
[*Music and dancing.*]

PUNCHINELLO. I'll down them all!
[*Music and dancing.*]

PUNCHINELLO [*calling his servants*]. Champagne, Poitevin, Picard, Basque, Breton.
[*Music and dancing.*]

PUNCHINELLO. Bring me here my musquetoon.
[*Music and dancing.*]

PUNCHINELLO [*pretending to fire a pistol shot*]. Bang!
[*All fall and take to their heels.*]

PUNCHINELLO [*laughing at them*]. Ha ha! That's given 'em a shock. What a silly lot to be frightened of me when I'm frightened of them myself. Upon my word! Cheek is all you need in this world. If I hadn't put on airs, if I hadn't out braved 'em they would have nabbed me.
[*The Archers steal back and, hearing what he says, seize him.*]

ARCHERS [*singing*].
> Comrades we have him now
> We have him, have him, have him now.
> Quick bring a light here, a lantern.
> [*Dance – enter the watch with lanterns.*]

ARCHERS [*singing*].
> Traitor, scoundrel, so it's you.
> Villain, gaolbird, rogue audacious,
> Varlet, thief and fraud mendacious,
> You dared to scare us, you!

PUNCHINELLO. Gentlemen ... I was ... I was in liquor.

ARCHERS [*singing*].
> No use ... you should have known us quicker.
> No argument – we cannot listen.
> To prison with him, quick to prison.

PUNCHINELLO. Gentlemen I am no thief.

ARCHERS [*singing*]. To prison!

PUNCHINELLO. I am a citizen of this very city.

ARCHERS [*singing*]. To prison!

PUNCHINELLO. What have I done?

ARCHERS [*singing*]. To prison with him, quick to prison!

PUNCHINELLO. Good gentlemen, please let me go.

ARCHERS [*singing*]. No!

PUNCHINELLO. I do implore you.

ARCHERS [*singing*]. No!

PUNCHINELLO. Eh!

ARCHERS [*singing*]. No!

PUNCHINELLO. Please.

ARCHERS [*singing*]. No. No!

PUNCHINELLO. Gentlemen.

ARCHERS [*singing*]. No, no, no!

PUNCHINELLO. If you please.

ARCHERS [*singing*]. No, no!

PUNCHINELLO. For pity's sake.

ARCHERS [*singing*]. No, no!

PUNCHINELLO. For Heaven's sake.

ARCHERS [*singing*]. No, no!

PUNCHINELLO. Mercy, mercy.

ARCHERS [*singing*].

> No, no, no, no argument! We cannot listen.
> To prison with him, quick to prison.

PUNCHINELLO. Is there no means, gentlemen, of appealing to your hearts?

ARCHERS [*singing*].

> There is one way for those who know.
> We're more susceptible than you might think.
> Give us a shilling for a drink
> And we will let you – let you go.

PUNCHINELLO. Alas, gentlemen, I assure you I haven't a penny in my pocket.

ARCHERS [*singing*].

> If you haven't got a shilling
> You must choose what you propose
> Twelve slaps across your bottom
> Or thirty tweakings of your nose.

PUNCHINELLO. If it's absolutely necessary that I have one or the other I'll have the tweakings of my nose.

ARCHERS [*singing*].

> If that is what you choose
> Be ready with your nose.

[*Dance. The Archers each tweak his nose in time with the music.*]

PUNCHINELLO. One and two, three and four, five and six, seven and eight, nine and ten, eleven, twelve, thirteen, fourteen, fifteen.

ARCHERS [*singing*].

> Ha, ha! He missed one then.
> The forfeit is – begin again.

PUNCHINELLO. Ah, gentlemen, my poor head's had as much as I can stand – it's swelling like a roasted apple. I'd rather have the stick than begin again at the beginning.

ARCHERS [*singing*].

> Good, since the stick is what you prefer.
> We are quite willing, we aver.

[*Dance. The Archers beat him in time to the music.*]

PUNCHINELLO. One, two, three, four, five, six, ah, ah, ah,
I declare I can bear no more. Gentlemen here take my
shilling.

ARCHERS [*singing*].

> Ah, what a fine and generous fellow
> Good night, good night, good Punchinello.

PUNCHINELLO. Gentlemen, I give you – a very good
night.

ARCHERS [*singing*]. Good night, good night, dear Punchinello.

PUNCHINELLO. I'm much obliged.

ARCHERS [*singing*]. Good night, good night, dear Punchinello.

PUNCHINELLO. Your humble servant.

ARCHERS [*singing*]. Good night, good night, dear Punchinello.

PUNCHINELLO. Till we meet again.

[*Dance. They show their pleasure in the money they have received.*]
The scene changes back to Argan's room.

Act Two

TOINETTE, CLÉANTE

TOINETTE. What do you want, sir?

CLÉANTE. What do *I* want?

TOINETTE. Ah! It's you is it? What a surprise. What have
you come here for?

CLÉANTE. To know my fate: to speak with my lovely
Angélique, to learn her feelings, and ask her intentions
concerning this dreadful marriage I have just heard about.

TOINETTE. Yes, but you can't come and tackle Angélique
point-blank like that. These matters need arranging.
Moreover, you have heard how she is watched, not allowed
to go out or talk to anyone. It was only the curiosity of an
old aunt of hers that enabled us to go to the play where
you first fell in love with her and we have taken good care
to say nothing about that little adventure.

CLÉANTE. Yes, but I'm not here as Cléante or in the character of her lover but as the friend of her music master who has authorized me to say that he sent me here in his place.

TOINETTE. Here's her father. Withdraw for a moment and let me tell him that you are here.

[*Enter* ARGAN.]

ARGAN. Mr Purgon said I was to walk up and down my bedroom twelve times each way on a morning but I forgot to ask him whether he meant crosswise or lengthwise.

TOINETTE. There's a gentleman here, sir . . .

ARGAN. Speak more softly, you good-for-nothing; your voice goes right through my head: you never remember that you shouldn't speak loudly to people who are ill.

TOINETTE. I wanted to tell you, master, that . . .

ARGAN. Quietly, I tell you.

TOINETTE [*whispers*]. Master . . .

ARGAN. Eh?

TOINETTE [*as before*]. I wanted to tell you that . . .

ARGAN. What d'ye say?

TOINETTE. I was saying that there was a man here wanting to speak to you.

ARGAN. Let him in. [TOINETTE *beckons to* CLÉANTE.]

CLÉANTE. Sir.

TOINETTE. Not so loud. Your voice'll go right through the master's head.

CLÉANTE. Sir, I'm delighted to find you up and about and see that you are feeling better.

TOINETTE [*pretending to be angry*]. How d'ye mean feeling better? It's not true. He's still very poorly.

CLÉANTE. I heard that the gentleman was better and I thought he looked well.

TOINETTE. How do you mean 'looked well'? The master's very ill indeed and people who say he's feeling better don't know what they are talking about. He's never been as bad as he is now.

ARGAN. She's quite right.

TOINETTE. He can get about, sleep, eat, and drink, like anybody else but that doesn't mean that he isn't very ill indeed.

ARGAN. That's true.

CLÉANTE. I'm very sorry to hear it, sir. I have come on behalf of your daughter's music master. He has had to go out of town for a few days and as I'm a very close friend of his he has sent me in his place to continue the young lady's lessons lest the interruption might make her forget what she has already been taught.

ARGAN. Very well. Call Angélique.

TOINETTE. I think, master, it would be better if I took the gentleman to her room.

ARGAN. No, bring her here.

TOINETTE. He can't teach her properly except in private.

ARGAN. Oh yes he can.

TOINETTE. Master, it's bound to deafen you and you mustn't have anything to upset you in the state you are in. It'll go right through your head.

ARGAN. Not a bit of it. Not a bit. I'm fond of music and I shall be very pleased to ... ah, here she is. [*Enter* ANGÉLIQUE.] Off you go and see if my wife is dressed yet.

[*Exit* TOINETTE.]

ARGAN. Come in, my girl: your music master is out of town and here's someone he has sent in his place to give you your lesson.

ANGÉLIQUE. Heavens!

ARGAN. What is it? What are you so surprised at?

ANGÉLIQUE. It's ...

ARGAN. What? Why are you so upset?

ANGÉLIQUE. Such ... such a strange coincidence father.

ARGAN. What d'ye mean?

ANGÉLIQUE. I dreamed last night that I was in a most dreadful predicament when I met someone just like this gentleman and asked him to help me and he did – he managed to get me out of my difficulty. It was so surprising to come in here and meet unexpectedly the very person who had been in my thoughts all the night.

CLÉANTE. I'm very happy to occupy your thoughts whether waking or dreaming and should certainly count myself most fortunate, should you be in any trouble, if you thought me worthy of helping you. There is nothing I wouldn't do to . . .

[*Re-enter* TOINETTE.]

TOINETTE [*derisively*]. Upon my word, master, I agree with you now. I take back every word I said yesterday. Here are Mr Diafoirus, father and son, come to see you. You *are* going to have a fine son-in-law. Here's a good-looking, intelligent lad for you. He hasn't said more than a couple of words but I'm already delighted with him. Your daughter will be charmed by him.

ARGAN [*to* CLÉANTE, *who makes as if to go*]. Don't go, sir. The fact is I'm in the process of getting my daughter married, and they've brought the young man along. She's never seen him yet.

CLÉANTE. You do me too much honour, sir, in wishing me to witness so agreeable a meeting.

ARGAN. He's the son of a very brilliant doctor. The marriage is to take place in a few days' time.

CLÉANTE. Indeed.

ARGAN. Pass the word to the music master so that he can be at the wedding.

CLÉANTE. I won't fail to do so.

ARGAN. I hope you will be able to come too.

CLÉANTE. You are too kind.

TOINETTE. Come, make room, here they come.

[*Enter* MR DIAFOIRUS *and* THOMAS DIAFOIRUS.]

ARGAN [*putting his hand to his hat but not removing it*]. Sir, Mr Purgon has forbidden me to uncover. You are of the profession – and you'll understand why.

MR DIAFOIRUS. The purpose of our visits is ever to bring relief to our patients, never to incommode them.

ARGAN. Sir, I receive with . . .

[*They speak both at the same time, interrupting each other*].

DIAFOIRUS. We have come, sir . . .

ARGAN. With the greatest of pleasure . . .

DIAFOIRUS. My son, Thomas, and I . . .

ARGAN. The honour you do me . . .

DIAFOIRUS. To indicate to you . . .

ARGAN. And I wish I could . . .

DIAFOIRUS. Our pleasure in . . .

ARGAN. Have come to see you . . .

DIAFOIRUS. The kindness you have shown . . .

ARGAN. And assured you . . .

DIAFOIRUS. In receiving us . . .

ARGAN. But you know, gentlemen . . .

DIAFOIRUS. Into the honour, sir . . .

ARGAN. That a poor invalid . . .

DIAFOIRUS. Of your alliance . . .

ARGAN. Who has no alternative . . .

DIAFOIRUS. And to assure you . . .

ARGAN. But to tell you here and now . . .

DIAFOIRUS. That in anything to do with our profession . . .

ARGAN. That he'll take every opportunity . . .

DIAFOIRUS. As, indeed, in all other matters . . .

ARGAN. Of showing you, gentlemen . . .

DIAFOIRUS. We are always ready, sir . . .

ARGAN. That he is at your service . . .

DIAFOIRUS. To show our concern . . . [*Turning to his son*] Come along, Thomas, come forward, make your compliments.

THOMAS [*a great booby newly graduated from the schools, who does everything clumsily and at the wrong moment*]. Do I begin with the father?

DIAFOIRUS. Yes.

THOMAS. Sir, in you I come to salute, acknowledge, cherish, and revere a second father, but a second father to whom, I make bold to say, I am more indebted than to my original one. He begot me but you have chosen me out. He had to take me willy nilly: you have accepted me voluntarily. My kinship with him is physical – a product of the body: with you it is an effect of will and intention and so, inasmuch as the faculties of the mind surpass the faculties

corporeal, so am I indebted to you for, and in like measure
hold precious, this future affiliation, for which I come today
to offer you in advance, my humble and respectful thanks.

TOINETTE. Cheers for the colleges that send such clever
fellows into the world!

THOMAS. Was that all right, father?

DIAFOIRUS. *Optime.*

ARGAN [*to* ANGÉLIQUE]. Come. Make your greetings to the
gentleman.

THOMAS. Have I to kiss her?

DIAFOIRUS. Yes, yes.

THOMAS [*to* ANGÉLIQUE]. Madam! Rightly has Heaven
bestowed on you the title of mother since . . .

ARGAN. That's not my wife. That's my daughter you are
addressing.

THOMAS. Then where is your wife?

ARGAN. She's coming.

THOMAS. Do I wait till she comes, father?

DIAFOIRUS. Pay your compliments to the young lady in the
meantime.

THOMAS. Madam, even as the statue of Memnon used to give
forth a melodious sound at the moment when the sun's
rays first illumined it so do I find myself animated by
emotion when the sun of your beauty appears: even as the
naturalists observe that the flower named Heliotrope turns
ever to the star of day so will my heart henceforward and
for ever turn towards those resplendent luminaries, your
lovely eyes, as if to its own Pole Star. Permit me then,
madam, to offer this very day upon the altar of your
charms a heart which seeks no other glory than that of
being ever your obedient, humble, and devoted servant
and spouse.

TOINETTE [*mocking him*]. What it is to study, and learn how
to make fine speeches.

ARGAN [*to* CLÉANTE]. What do you say to that?

CLÉANTE. The gentleman's doing splendidly. If he's as good
a doctor as he is an orator it will be a pleasure to be one of
his patients.

TOINETTE. It will indeed. It'll be a wonderful thing if his cures are up to his speeches.

ARGAN. Quick, my chair and seats for all the company. You sit down here, my dear [*to* ANGÉLIQUE]. You see, sir, [*to* DIAFOIRUS] how everyone admires your son. You are very fortunate to have a boy like that.

DIAFOIRUS. Sir, it's not because I'm his father, but I can say I have good reason to be proud of him. All who know him speak of him as a most blameless young man. He has never shown the lively imagination or the sparkling wit one observes in some young men but that I have always taken to augur well for his judgement, a quality necessary for the practice of our art. In childhood he was never what one could call lively or pert but ever gentle and mild, never speaking a word or indulging in childish games. We had the greatest difficulty in teaching him to read: he was nine before he even knew his letters. 'Never mind,' I used to say to myself, 'the tardy tree oft yields the better fruit. One writes less easily on marble than on sand, but what is written there endures and this slowness of understanding, this sluggishness of imagination is the mark of sound judgement yet to come.' When I sent him to college he made hard going of it but he bore up against all difficulties and his tutors always commended him for his assiduity and hard work. At length, by dint of sheer persistence he succeeded in qualifying and I can say without boasting that in the two years since taking his bachelor's degree no candidate has made more noise than he in the disputations of our faculty. He has gained for himself quite a formidable reputation and there's no proposition put forward but he'll argue in the last ditch to the contrary. Firm in dispute, a very Turk in defence of a principle, he never changes his opinion and pursues his argument to the logical limit. But what pleases me most of all about him, and herein he follows my own example, is his unswerving attachment to the opinions of the ancient authorities and his refusal ever to attempt to understand or even listen to the arguments in favour of such alleged discoveries of our own times as the circulation of the blood and other ideas of a like nature.

THOMAS. I have prepared a thesis against those who uphold the circulation of the blood which, with your permission, sir, I venture to offer to the young lady as the first fruits of my genius. [*He draws a great roll of parchment from his pocket and presents it to* ANGÉLIQUE.]

ANGÉLIQUE. Such a thing would be no use to me, sir; I know nothing of such matters.

TOINETTE. Come on, give it to me. It's worth having for the pictures in the margin. It'll be nice to have in the bedroom.

THOMAS. With your permission, sir, I would invite her to come along one day and enjoy the pleasure of seeing a woman dissected and hearing my dissertation upon it.

TOINETTE. That *will* be amusing. Some young men take their young ladies to a play but a dissection is so much more entertaining!

DIAFOIRUS. To continue, so far as the qualities necessary for marriage and propagation are concerned, I assure you that by our medical standards he's everything that could be desired: he possesses in a laudable degree the qualities needed for proliferation and the proper temperament for engendering and procreating healthy children.

ARGAN. Don't you intend to promote his career at court, sir, and procure him a post of physician there?

DIAFOIRUS. To be quite frank I have never found the practice of our profession among people of great consequence very attractive. My experience has been that it's better for us to practise among the general public. They are less exacting. You don't have to answer to anybody for your actions and provided you keep to the beaten track of professional practice you don't need to worry what happens. The trouble about people of consequence is that when they're ill they absolutely insist on being cured.

TOINETTE. That's a good joke! Fancy expecting you fellows to cure them! That's not what you are there for at all. Your job is to collect your fees and prescribe the remedies. It's for them to get better – if they can!

DIAFOIRUS. That's quite true. We've no obligation beyond giving people the orthodox treatment.

ARGAN [*to* CLÉANTE]. Let my daughter sing a little, sir, for the company.

CLÉANTE. I'm at your service, sir. It occurs to me that it might be entertaining if the young lady and I were to sing a passage from a little opera composed just recently. [*Hands* ANGÉLIQUE *a piece of paper.*] Here is your part.

ANGÉLIQUE. Mine?

CLÉANTE [*to* ANGÉLIQUE]. Please don't say no. Let me explain to you the passage we have to sing. [*To the company*] I have no singing voice myself but it will be sufficient that I make myself heard. Perhaps you'll be good enough to make allowances for me in view of the fact that I must encourage the lady to sing.

ARGAN. Are the words interesting?

CLÉANTE. It is really a little extemporized opera. What you are going to hear is no more than rhythmical prose or a sort of free verse such as their feelings and the occasion might suggest to two people conversing together and speaking impromptu.

ARGAN. Very good. Let's be hearing it.

CLÉANTE. The substance of the scene is this. A certain shepherd was intent upon the beauties of an entertainment which had hardly begun when his attention was attracted by a disturbance near at hand: turning, he perceived a boorish fellow behaving rudely and insolently to a shepherdess. He immediately espoused the cause of the sex to whom all men owe deference and, after chastising the bully for his insolence, approached the shepherdess and beheld a young lady with the loveliest eyes he had ever seen. Her tears seemed to him the most beautiful spectacle imaginable! 'Alas!' he said to himself. 'How could any one offend so lovely a creature? What man, be he ne'er so barbarous, would not be moved by tears such as these?' He at once made it his business to stay them – those tears he found so beautiful – and the lovely shepherdess was at equal pains to thank him for the trifling service he had rendered her –

but in a manner so charming, so tender, so full of feeling that he found it quite irresistible. Every word, every glance went straight to his heart like a shaft of fire. 'How could anything,' said he, 'deserve a gratitude so charmingly expressed? What would a man not do, what service, what danger would he not undergo to earn for himself, even for a moment a gratitude so touching?' He paid no more attention to the rest of the play, which he found all too short since the end must separate him from his lovely shepherdess. From the very first moment he was as utterly and completely in love as ever man could be. He immediately began to suffer all the pangs of absence, the torments of separation from that which he had enjoyed for so short a spell. He tried by every means to catch another glimpse of that vision of which he retained so dear an image, sleeping and waking, but in vain! His shepherdess was kept under too close a restraint. Such was his passion that he determined to ask for the hand of the adorable creature without whom he could live no longer and he obtained her permission to do so by means of a letter which he contrived to have sent to her. But at that very moment he learned that her father had arranged to marry her to another and that all preparations were in train for the celebration of the marriage. Imagine the cruel blow to the affections of the unhappy shepherd! Behold him stricken with a deadly sorrow! The idea of his beloved in the arms of another is more than he can bear. With the desperation of love he finds means to enter her house, to learn her feelings and to hear his fate from her own lips. There he finds all is as he feared. He meets the unworthy rival whom the caprice of a father opposes to the tenderness of his own love. He beholds him, ridiculous but triumphant beside the lovely shepherdess as one already assured of conquest. The sight fills him with rage, which he can barely restrain. He exchanges despairing glances with the object of his love but consideration for her father's presence prevents her from speaking save with her eyes. At last, casting aside all restraint, in a transport of love he sings as follows:

Phyllis, this pain, this pain I cannot bear,
Break this cruel silence, reveal to me my fate.
Or life or death, which must I now await?

ANGÉLIQUE [*singing*].

Ah, Tircis, sad at heart am I,
Faced with a marriage which like you I hate,
I raise my eyes to Heaven but since it is my fate
What can I do but look on you and sigh?

ARGAN. Well, well. I didn't know my daughter was so clever as to sing at sight without hesitation like that.

CLÉANTE [*singing*]. Alas, fair Phyllis
How happy were your Tircis' part
Could he but claim as his,
A place within your heart!

ANGÉLIQUE. I may not hide it, what'e'er the event may prove,
'Tis you, O Tircis you, 'tis you, 'tis you, I love!

CLÉANTE. O blessed words.
To hear them am I fain.
Repeat, repeat, repeat them once again!

ANGÉLIQUE. 'Tis you, O Tircis, you I love.

CLÉANTE. Again, O Phyllis, yet again.

ANGÉLIQUE. 'Tis you, 'tis you, 'tis you I love.

CLÉANTE. Repeat, repeat, that blest refrain!

ANGÉLIQUE. 'Tis you, O Tircis, you I love.
'Tis Tircis – you – I love!

CLÉANTE. The Gods themselves are not more blest than I.
But Phyllis – say – say what is this thing I spy?
What is this new arrival –
This threat to all our bliss
Is it . . . Oh can it be a rival?

ANGÉLIQUE. O worse than death
His presence is to me.
Yes, worse than death I hate his loathed presence –

CLÉANTE. Yet to his suit your father lends complaisance!

ANGÉLIQUE. I'd rather die than to such fate consent.
I'd rather die,
I'd rather die than to such fate consent!

ARGAN. And what does her father say to all this?

CLÉANTE. He says nothing.

ARGAN. He must be a fool of a father to let all this go on and say nothing.

CLÉANTE [*singing*]. Ah dearest love . . .

ARGAN. No. No. No. We've had enough. Plays like this set a very bad example. Yon shepherd, Tircis, is a rogue and the shepherdess is an impudent baggage to talk like that in front of her father. Let me see the words. Heh? Where are they? Where are the words you've been singing. There's nothing here but the notes.

CLÉANTE. Don't you know, sir, that they've recently invented a method of writing notes and words all in one.

ARGAN. Very well. I'm your humble servant, sir. Good day t'ye. We could very well have done without your ridiculous opera.

CLÉANTE. I had hoped you would find it entertaining.

ARGAN. There's nothing entertaining in such silly nonsense. Ah, here's my wife.

[*Exit* CLÉANTE. *Enter* BÉLINE.]

ARGAN. Here's Mr Diafoirus's son, my love.

THOMAS [*starts on the speech he has learned by heart but breaks down and can't go on*]. Madam, rightly has Heaven bestowed on you the title of mother because . . . in your visage we behold . . .

BÉLINE. I'm delighted to have come in time to have the honour of seeing you, sir.

THOMAS. Because in your visage we behold . . . madam, you have interrupted me in the middle of my sentence and now I can't remember . . .

DIAFOIRUS. Keep it for another time, Thomas.

ARGAN. I wish you had been here a while ago, my dear.

TOINETTE. Oh madam! What you've missed by not being here for the second father and the statue of Memnon and the flower called Heliotrope.

ARGAN. Now come along, my girl, give the gentleman your hand and plight him your troth as your husband to be.

ANGÉLIQUE. Father!

ARGAN. Why 'father'? What d'ye mean?

ANGÉLIQUE. I beseech you not to hurry things. At least give us time to get to know one another and see arise between us the mutual inclination which is so essential to a perfect union.

THOMAS. As far as I'm concerned, madam, the inclination is there already and I have no need to wait any longer.

ANGÉLIQUE. You may be quick to act, sir, but I'm not, and I must confess your virtues haven't yet made all that impression on me.

ARGAN. Oh well! There will be plenty of time for that when you are married.

ANGÉLIQUE. Ah father, please give me time. Marriage is a bond which shouldn't be imposed on anyone by compulsion. If the gentleman is an honourable man he will not wish to take a wife who is forced to marry him.

THOMAS. *Nego consequentiam*. I deny your conclusion, dear lady. I could very well be a man of honour and still accept you at the hands of your father.

ANGÉLIQUE. To force yourself upon a girl against her will is a poor way of making her love you.

THOMAS. We read how in ancient times, madam, it was customary for the men to carry off the young women they intended to marry by force so that it shouldn't appear that they flew to a man's arms of their own volition.

ANGÉLIQUE. Ancient times are all very well, but we are living in modern times. In our age there is no need whatever for such pretences. When marriage is congenial to us we know how to play our part without being dragged into it. Be patient. If you really love me, my wishes should be yours.

THOMAS. True, madam, excepting where my love is concerned.

ANGÉLIQUE. But the test of love is willingness to give way to the wishes of one's beloved.

THOMAS. *Distinguo*, madam. I make a distinction. Where love is not involved *concedo*, I concede the point, but where love is involved *nego*, I cannot agree.

TOINETTE [*to* ANGÉLIQUE]. It's no use your arguing. The gentleman is fresh out of college. He's too good for you every time. What is the point of resisting and refusing the honour of being attached to the faculty?

BÉLINE. Maybe she has some one else in mind.

ANGÉLIQUE. If I had, madam, it would be one such as reason and modesty would approve.

ARGAN. Ay well! A nice figure I'm cutting now!

BÉLINE. If I were you I wouldn't insist on her marrying, but I know what I *would* do.

ANGÉLIQUE. I know what you mean, madam, and I am aware of your good intentions towards me but it may be that your hopes won't be realized.

BÉLINE. Because clever and well brought up daughters like you scorn to submit to their father's wishes. Things were different at one time.

ANGÉLIQUE. There are limits to a daughter's duty, madam. Neither in reason nor justice can it be extended to cover every circumstance.

BÉLINE. You mean to say that your mind's set on marriage but you want to choose a husband to suit your own fancy.

ANGÉLIQUE. If my father won't allow me the husband of my choice, I beg him at least not to insist on my marrying one I could never love.

ARGAN. I'm very sorry about all this, gentlemen.

ANGÉLIQUE. Women marry for different purposes! For my own part, since I intend to marry for love and I regard it as a life-long attachment I must, I assure you, approach it with caution. There are women for whom a husband is no more than a means of escape from the control of their parents and obtaining freedom to do whatever they wish. There are others, madam, for whom marriage is merely a matter of material advantage. They marry with an eye to a settlement, and becoming rich by the death of their husbands, run through a succession of them, collecting their wealth without the slightest scruple or conscience. Such women don't, of course, stand upon ceremony and they show little consideration to the husbands themselves.

BÉLINE. You are very eloquent today. May I ask what you mean by all that?

ANGÉLIQUE. What do I mean, madam? Just what I have said.

BÉLINE. Your silliness is becoming unbearable, my dear.

ANGÉLIQUE. No doubt you would like to provoke me to rudeness, but I warn you I don't intend to give you that satisfaction.

BÉLINE. I never heard such impertinence.

ANGÉLIQUE. No, madam, you can say what you like – but it will do you no good.

BÉLINE. You are a public laughing stock with your absurd pride and presumption.

ANGÉLIQUE. It is no use, madam. You cannot provoke me, and I'll spare you any prospect of doing so by taking my leave.

ARGAN. Listen! Either you marry this gentleman within four days or you go into a convent, one or the other. Make your choice. [ANGÉLIQUE *goes out.*] Don't worry I'll bring her to heel.

BÉLINE. I'm sorry I must go too, my dear. There's business in town I have to attend to. I'll be back again shortly.

ARGAN. Go along my love and call and see the notary so that he gets on with you know what.

BÉLINE. Good-bye, dear heart.

[*Exit* BÉLINE.]

ARGAN. Good-bye, my darling. How that woman loves me! It's incredible!

DIAFOIRUS. We must also take our leave of you, sir.

ARGAN. Please tell me how I am, sir, before you go.

DIAFOIRUS [*taking his pulse*]. Thomas. Take the gentleman's other hand to show that you can take a pulse properly. *Quid dicis*. What sayest thou?

THOMAS. *Dico*, I say, that this is the pulse of a man who is – not at all well.

DIAFOIRUS. Good.

THOMAS. Strongish not to say strong.

DIAFOIRUS. Very good.

THOMAS. Falling off a little now.

DIAFOIRUS. *Bene.*

THOMAS. Even a little erratic.

DIAFOIRUS. *Optime.*

THOMAS. Indicative of a disturbed state of the splenetic parenchyma – that is the spleen.

DIAFOIRUS. Excellent.

ARGAN. No. Mr Purgon says it's my liver that's wrong.

DIAFOIRUS. Oh yes! When one talks of Parenchyma it covers both because of the close accord between them by way of the *vas breve* of the *pylorus* and the *meatus cholodici*, the bile ducts of the *duodenum*. No doubt he tells you to eat plenty of roast beef?

ARGAN. No, only boiled.

DIAFOIRUS. Oh yes! Roast or boiled – same thing. He's very wise. You couldn't be in better hands.

ARGAN. Tell me, sir. How many grains of salt should one take with an egg?

DIAFOIRUS. Six, eight, ten, and so on – always even numbers just as with pills you always take odd numbers.

ARGAN. Until we meet again, sir.

[*Exeunt* DIAFOIRUS *and* THOMAS.]
[*Enter* BÉLINE.]

BÉLINE. I looked in, my dear, before going out to let you know there's something you ought to keep an eye on. As I was passing Angélique's door I saw there was a young man with her. He slipped away as soon as he saw me.

ARGAN. A young man with my daughter!

BÉLINE. Yes. Little Louison was with them. She'll be able to tell you about it.

ARGAN. Send her in here, my love, send her in here. Oh, the brazen hussy! No wonder she was so obstinate.

[*Exit* BÉLINE, *enter* LOUISON.]

LOUISON. What do you want, daddy? Stepmother said you were wanting me.

ARGAN. Yes. Come here. Come nearer. Turn this way. Look up. Look at me. Well?

LOUISON. Well what, daddy?

ARGAN. Now!

LOUISON. What is it?

ARGAN. Have you nothing to tell me?

LOUISON. If you like I'll tell you the story of the Ass's Skin or the Fable of the Fox and the Crow. I have just been learning them.

ARGAN. That's not what I'm asking about.

LOUISON. What is it then?

ARGAN. Ah, you cunning little thing! You know well enough what I want.

LOUISON. Excuse me, daddy, I don't.

ARGAN. Is this how you obey me?

LOUISON. What do you mean?

ARGAN. Haven't I told you to come and tell me everything you see at once.

LOUISON. Yes, daddy.

ARGAN. And have you seen nothing today?

LOUISON. No, daddy.

ARGAN. Nothing?

LOUISON. No, daddy.

ARGAN. Sure?

LOUISON. Sure.

ARGAN [*taking a cane*]. Then I shall have to make you see something.

LOUISON [*seeing the cane*]. Oh, daddy!

ARGAN. Oh! you brazen little witch. You didn't tell me you'd seen a young man in your sister's room.

LOUISON. Oh, daddy!

ARGAN. This will teach you to tell lies.

LOUISON. Forgive me, daddy. Sister told me I wasn't to tell you but I will, I'll tell you everything.

ARGAN. You must be whipped first for fibbing. Then we'll deal with the rest.

LOUISON. Forgive me, daddy.

ARGAN. No, no.

LOUISON. Dear daddy, don't whip me.

ARGAN. Oh yes, I'm going to.

LOUISON. For Heaven's sake, don't whip me, daddy.

ARGAN. Come along, come along. [*Takes hold of her to whip her.*]

LOUISON. Oh daddy, you've hurt me. Stop – I'm dying. [*Pretends to be dead.*]

ARGAN. Hey! Whatever is it? Louison! Louison! Good Lord! Louison. Oh, my child! Ah, wretched father! Oh accursed stick! A plague on all sticks! Ah, my poor child, my poor little Louison.

LOUISON. There, there, daddy. Don't take on so. I'm not quite dead yet.

ARGAN. Ah! You little scamp. Well, well I forgive you this time provided you tell me the whole truth.

LOUISON. You won't tell my sister I told you!

ARGAN. No.

LOUISON. A man came into her room, daddy, while I was there.

ARGAN. Well?

LOUISON. I asked him what he wanted and he said he was her music master.

ARGAN. Ah ha! So that's the game! And then?

LOUISON. Then sister came.

ARGAN. Go on.

LOUISON. She said, 'Go, for Heaven's sake, go: you'll drive me to despair.'

ARGAN. Yes?

LOUISON. He didn't want to go.

ARGAN. And what did he say to her?

LOUISON. Oh. All sorts of things.

ARGAN. And then what?

LOUISON. He told her this and that and how he loved her dearly and that she was the most beautiful girl in all the world.

ARGAN. And after that?

LOUISON. After that he went down on his knees.

ARGAN. And then?

LOUISON. Then he kissed her hands.

ARGAN. And then?

LOUISON. And then my stepmother came to the door and he ran away.

ARGAN. And is there nothing else?

LOUISON. No, daddy.

ARGAN. But my little finger is whispering something. Sh! Eh? Ah, Yes! Oh! Oh! My little finger says there's something else you saw, something you haven't told me about.

LOUISON. Then your little finger's a fibber.

ARGAN. Be careful.

LOUISON. No daddy, don't you believe it. It's a fibber, I assure you.

ARGAN. Well, well, we'll see about that. Run along now and keep your eyes open. Be off. Children aren't children any more. Ah! What troubles I do have. I haven't even time to think about my illness. I'm just about done for. [*Sits in chair.*]

[*Enter* BÉRALDE.]

BÉRALDE. Now, brother, what's the trouble? How are you?

ARGAN. Ah brother, I'm bad, very bad.

BÉRALDE. Bad? In what way?

ARGAN. You wouldn't believe how feeble I am.

BÉRALDE. That's a pity.

ARGAN. I've hardly strength enough to speak.

BÉRALDE. I came here with an offer of marriage for my niece Angélique.

ARGAN [*with vehemence, rising from his chair*]. Don't talk to me about that wretched creature! She's a brazen-faced, impertinent baggage and I'll have her in a convent before many days are out!

BÉRALDE. Now that's better. I'm glad to see you are stronger. My visit's doing you good. Well, well, we can talk about business later. I've brought you an entertainment that'll cure your ill-humour and make you better disposed for what we have to talk about. There are gypsies in Moorish costume to dance and sing for us. I'm sure you'll enjoy it.

It'll do you just as much good as one of Mr Purgon's prescriptions. Come along.

SECOND INTERLUDE

FIRST MOORISH GIRL [*singing*].
>   Rejoice in the spring time of beauty
>   Rejoice while you're young,
>   While you're young,
>   When loving's a duty;
>   So rejoice while you're young
>   Rejoice in the spring time of beauty.
>
>   Life holds no pleasures like love;
>   Without it you'll find
>   No content for the mind;
>   Life holds no pleasure like love
>   So rejoice while you're young
>   Rejoice in the spring time of beauty.
>
>   Delay not love's pleasures to prove,
>   For once beauty's graces,
>   Time's cold hand effaces,
>   And age youth replaces,
>   You'll find no more pleasure in love.
>   So rejoice while you're young
>   Rejoice in the spring time of beauty.

SECOND MOORISH GIRL.
>   When to love a man invites you,
>   Why be coy?
>   If love's the way of truth
>   Then nothing can, in sooth,
>   Bring such joy.
>
>   If such is Cupid's power,
>   And you find
>   Love so wholly charming,

And its pleasures so disarming,
Why should you ever look behind?

Yet all I have heard tell
Suggests that in its train
Love brings both grief and woe,
And store of sorrow so
That it isn't worth the pain.

THIRD MOORISH GIRL.

How sweet when one is young and pretty
To have a lover
Plight his troth!
But should he fickle prove
Alas, the pain of love!

FOURTH MOORISH GIRL.

Alas, when love has proved a rover
The worst is not that all is over,
That grief is keen or anger sharp
But that the heart bereft for ever
Itself from loving can't dissever.

SECOND MOORISH GIRL.

Then when she's young and pretty
What should a maiden do,
Avoid the grief and woe
And the sorrows that may rend her
Or to love's joys surrender?

ALL TOGETHER.

Oh follow love's pleasures
Though its joys be capricious,
Though its trials be hard,
Its delights are delicious.
Though its trials be hard
Its delights are delicious.

[*Enter dancers leading monkeys. They dance with the Moorish Girls and make the monkeys leap and perform.*]

Act Three

BÉRALDE. Well brother, what d'ye say to that? That's better than a dose of senna isn't it.

TOINETTE. Hm! Don't you say too much against a dose of senna.

BÉRALDE. Well now, shall we have a little chat?

ARGAN. Wait a minute, brother. I'm coming back.

TOINETTE. Wait, master, you are forgetting you can't walk without your stick.

ARGAN. Ah! How right you are!

[Exit ARGAN.]

TOINETTE. Please don't desert your niece's interests.

BÉRALDE. I will do anything I can to get her what she desires.

TOINETTE. We must at all costs prevent this absurd marriage that's he's so foolishly set on. I've been thinking that it would be a good plan to produce a doctor of our own, set him against Mr Purgon, and ridicule his methods. If there's no suitable person available I have a good mind to see what I can do myself.

BÉRALDE. What do you mean?

TOINETTE. It's a fantastic idea, but it might come off better than a sensible one. Leave it to me. You do what you can on your side. Here he comes.

[Re-enter ARGAN.]

BÉRALDE. Will you allow me brother to ask you above all not to excite yourself during our conversation?

ARGAN. Agreed.

BÉRALDE. And answer the questions I put to you without asperity?

ARGAN. Right.

BÉRALDE. And treat whatever we have to discuss together in a spirit of entire detachment?

ARGAN. Lord, yes! What a preamble!

BÉRALDE. Then why is it brother when you have all the money you have and only the one daughter – for I'm not counting the little one, why, I ask, are you talking of putting her into a convent?

ARGAN. Why? Because I'm the master in my own house and intend to do what I think fit, brother.

BÉRALDE. Your wife won't fail to advise you to dispose of both your daughters that way. I don't doubt that in the goodness of her heart she would be delighted to see them both become nuns.

ARGAN. Now we are coming to it! My poor wife's brought into it again. She's the cause of all the trouble and everyone's against her.

BÉRALDE. All right, brother, we'll leave her out of it. She's a woman with the best of intentions towards your family, absolutely disinterested, wonderfully attached to you, and shows inconceivable affection and good will towards your children. That's all beyond question. We'll say no more about that and come to your daughter. What's your idea, brother, in wanting to marry her to a doctor's son?

ARGAN. The idea is, brother, for me to have the sort of son-in-law I'm in need of.

BÉRALDE. But that's no concern of your daughter's and, moreover, there's someone available who would suit her much better.

ARGAN. Yes, but this one happens to suit *me* better.

BÉRALDE. But is she to take a husband for her own sake or yours?

ARGAN. For both brother – hers and mine and because I want to have people in the family who will be useful to *me*.

BÉRALDE. I suppose on the same principle if the little one were a bit older you'd marry her to an apothecary?

ARGAN. Why not?

BÉRALDE. How can you possibly continue to be so infatuated with apothecaries and doctors? Are you determined to go on being ill in spite of all that your friends and nature itself can do for you?

ARGAN. What do you mean by that, brother?

BÉRALDE. What I mean is that I don't know anybody who's less ill than you are. One couldn't wish for a better constitution than yours. One proof that there's nothing wrong with you and that your health is perfectly sound is that in spite of all your efforts you haven't managed to damage your constitution and you've survived all the medicines they've given you to swallow.

ARGAN. But don't you know, brother, that that's just what keeps me going. Mr Purgon says that if he left off attending me for three days I shouldn't survive it.

BÉRALDE. He'll be attending you into the next world if you aren't careful.

ARGAN. Let's pursue this question a bit further. You don't believe in medicine at all then?

BÉRALDE. No, brother, and I don't see that it's necessary to my salvation that I should.

ARGAN. What! You don't accept the truth of what is universally accepted and has been treated with respect and reverence all down the ages.

BÉRALDE. Far from accepting it as true, I look upon it, between ourselves, as one of the greatest follies of mankind. Looking at it philosophically I don't know any more absurd piece of mummery, anything more ridiculous, than for one man to set up to cure another.

ARGAN. And why won't you admit that one man may cure another?

BÉRALDE. Because, brother, the nature of the human organism is still a mystery about which we know very little, because nature has drawn too thick a veil before our eyes for us to understand anything of the matter.

ARGAN. So according to you doctors know nothing?

BÉRALDE. Precisely. Most of them know their classics, talk Latin freely, can give the Greek names of all the diseases, define them, and classify them, but as for curing them – that's a thing they know nothing about.

ARGAN. Yet you must agree that doctors know more about such things than other folk.

BÉRALDE. They know what I've told you, which doesn't

amount to much when it comes to curing people. All that their art consists of is a farrago of high-sounding gibberish, specious babbling which offers words in place of sound reasons and promises instead of results.

ARGAN. All the same, brother, there are other people as wise and as clever as you and we find that everybody has recourse to a doctor when he's ill.

BÉRALDE. That's evidence of human frailty not proof of the doctor's skill.

ARGAN. But doctors must believe in their art because they have resort to it themselves.

BÉRALDE. That's because there are some of them who share the popular errors from which they profit. There are others who don't share them but still take the profit; your Mr Purgon for example makes no bones about it. He's a doctor through and through, a man with more faith in his rules than anything capable of mathematical proof. He would think it a crime even to question them. Medicine has no obscurities for him, no doubts, no difficulties. Full of headlong prejudice, unshakeable self-confidence, and no more common sense and reasoning than a brute beast he goes on his way purging and bleeding at random and hesitates at nothing. It's no good bearing him ill will for the harm that he does you – he'll send you into the next world with the best of intentions and in killing you off do no more for you than he would do for his own wife and children or, if need arose, for himself.

ARGAN. You have your knife in him, brother. Let's come down to facts. What is one to do when one's ill?

BÉRALDE. Nothing, brother.

ARGAN. Nothing?

BÉRALDE. Nothing. Rest. That's all that is necessary. Nature, if we will but leave her to it, will find her own way out of the disorder into which she has fallen. Our restlessness, our own impatience is the ruin of everything. Most men die of their remedies not of their diseases.

ARGAN. But you must agree, brother, that there are ways and means of assisting nature.

BÉRALDE. Good heavens, brother, that's the sort of delusion which we all like to indulge in! Men have always tended to entertain these credulous fancies because they flatter their self-importance and because they would like them to be true. When a doctor talks to you about aiding or assisting or relieving nature, or removing what is harmful and restoring what is lacking to it, renewing and reviving its functions; when he talks about purifying the blood and settling the bowels or soothing the brain, reducing the spleen, restoring the lungs, and cleansing the liver, strengthening the heart and re-establishing or maintaining the natural heat, prolonging your life or lengthening your days, he's just telling you the fairy tales of medicine. When you get down to the truth of the matter and the test of experience you find there's nothing in them; they are just like those beautiful dreams which leave you on awakening with nothing but a feeling of regret for having believed in them.

ARGAN. What you mean is that all the knowledge of the world is contained in your head and that you know more about these things than all the greatest doctors of the day.

BÉRALDE. Your great doctors are two quite different sorts of people according to whether you judge them by their words – or their deeds. Listen to them talking and they are the cleverest fellows in the world. See them at work and they are the most ignorant of mankind.

ARGAN. Ay well! You are a great doctor I can see. I only wish some of those gentlemen were here to answer your arguments and cut your cackle.

BÉRALDE. I'm not taking it upon myself to attack medical science, brother; not at all. Everybody can believe what he likes at his own risk and peril. All I'm saying is just between ourselves and I only wish I could have taken you, both for your amusement and to convince you of the error of your ways, to one of Molière's plays on this subject.

ARGAN. I've no patience with your Molière and his plays. It's all very amusing I must say to be holding up worthy people like doctors to ridicule.

BÉRALDE. It's not the doctors themselves he makes fun of but the absurdities of medical science.

ARGAN. It's very becoming I must say for him to take it on himself to put medicine in order. A fine sort of simpleton he must be, a good conceit he must have of himself to mock at consultations and prescriptions, set himself up against the whole faculty and put respectable people like doctors on the stage.

BÉRALDE. What could he do better than put on the stage men of all professions? Princes and kings are put on the stage every day and they aren't of less consequence than doctors.

ARGAN. The devil! If I were a doctor I'd have my own back on him for his impertinence. If he were ill I wouldn't help him though he were at death's door. He wouldn't get the slightest bleeding or the smallest injection however much he begged and prayed for 'em. 'Die and be damned,' I'd say, 'and that'll teach you to make fun of the doctors!'

BÉRALDE. You *are* down on him aren't you!

ARGAN. He's a very foolish fellow and if the physicians are wise they'll do what I've told you.

BÉRALDE. He'll be wiser than the doctors and not ask them for help.

ARGAN. So much the worse for him if he has no medicines to help him.

BÉRALDE. He has his own reasons for not wanting to have anything to do with them. He thinks that only the strongest and most vigorous of men can stand up to malady and medicine at the same time and that, so far as he's concerned, it's as much as he can do to bear his illness.

ARGAN. What ridiculous arguments! Come, brother, don't let us talk any more about the fellow. It rouses my bile. You'll be making me ill.

BÉRALDE. Very well, brother, to change the subject, let me say that you ought not to take any violent decision to put your daughter into a convent purely because of her showing some slight opposition to your wishes and when it's a question of choosing a son-in-law you shouldn't let yourself be carried away by your impetuosity, but try to make some concession to your daughter's wishes, since marriage is a matter of a whole lifetime and her entire happiness depends on it.

[*Enter* MR FLEURANT, *syringe in hand.*]

ARGAN. Ah, brother, excuse me.

BÉRALDE. Why? What are you going to do?

ARGAN. Just take a little injection. It won't take very long.

BÉRALDE. You are mad! Can't you manage a minute without injection or dosing? Put it off to another time and enjoy a little bit of peace.

ARGAN. This evening, Mr Fleurant, or tomorrow morning then.

MR FLEURANT [*to* BÉRALDE]. What do you mean by interfering with the doctor's orders and preventing the gentleman from having his injection? The audacity!

BÉRALDE. Go away, sir, it's evident you aren't used to addressing yourself to people's faces.

MR FLEURANT. You've no business to be making fun of medicine and wasting my time. I came here on specific instructions and I shall tell Mr Purgon how I've been prevented from carrying out his orders and performing my professional duties. You shall see! You shall see.

ARGAN. This is going to be very unfortunate, brother.

BÉRALDE. Unfortunate! To miss one of Mr Purgon's injections! I ask you again, brother, is there no curing you of this disease of being doctored? Are you going to be the victim of their remedies all the rest of your life?

ARGAN. My God! You talk like a man who's well, but you'd change your tune if you were in my position. It's easy to talk against medicine when you're in good health.

BÉRALDE. Well then, what *is* your trouble?

ARGAN. You'll be getting me annoyed. I only wish you had it! We'd see if you'd still talk such rubbish. Ah, here's Mr Purgon.

[*Enter* MR PURGON.]

MR PURGON. Fine news I have been hearing downstairs!
I hear that you are making a joke of my orders and refusing
to take the remedies I have prescribed!

ARGAN. Ah sir, it isn't . . .

MR PURGON. The audacity! A patient in rebellion against his
doctor! Unnatural!

TOINETTE. Shocking!

MR PURGON. An injection which I had deigned to make up
myself!

ARGAN. It wasn't me . . . I . . .

MR PURGON. Compounded and concocted according to
formula!

TOINETTE. He did wrong!

MR PURGON. An injection which would have had a wonderful effect on the bowels.

ARGAN. My brother . . .

MR PURGON. To send it away with contempt . . .

ARGAN. *He* did it . . .

MR PURGON. Outrageous behaviour!

TOINETTE. That's true enough!

MR PURGON. An enormity, a crime against medicine!

ARGAN. He's the cause . . .

MR PURGON. Flat treason against the whole Faculty! No
punishment could be sufficiently severe!

TOINETTE. Quite right!

MR PURGON. I declare I'll have nothing more to do with
you!

ARGAN. It was my brother . . .

MR PURGON. I renounce all connexion with you.

TOINETTE. You do right!

MR PURGON. And to show that I'm entirely finished with
you, there's the marriage settlement I made in favour of
my nephew. [*Tears it up.*]

ARGAN. It was my brother who caused all the trouble.

MR PURGON. To despise my injection!

ARGAN. Bring it back again and I'll take it at once.

MR PURGON. Just when I was going to cure you!

TOINETTE. He didn't deserve to be cured!

MR PURGON. I was about to give your system a thorough clean out and completely detoxicate you!

ARGAN. Ah, brother!

MR PURGON. Another dozen doses and I should have bottomed the trouble . . .

TOINETTE. He's not worthy of your attention.

MR PURGON. Since you don't choose to be cured at my hands . . .

ARGAN. It isn't my fault.

MR PURGON. Since you've failed in the obedience a patient owes to his doctor . . .

TOINETTE. He deserves all he gets!

MR PURGON. Since you've dared to rebel against my prescriptions . . .

ARGAN. Ah! I never did.

MR PURGON. I declare that I abandon you to your evil constitution, to the disorder of your bowels, the corruption of your blood, the bitterness of your own gall, and the feculence of your humours.

TOINETTE. You've done right.

ARGAN. Oh Lord!

MR PURGON. I foretell that within four days you'll be in an incurable condition.

ARGAN. Oh mercy!

MR PURGON. You'll fall into a state of bradypepsia.

ARGAN. Mr Purgon!

MR PURGON. From bradypepsia into dyspepsia.

ARGAN. Mr Purgon!

MR PURGON. From dyspepsia into apepsia.

ARGAN. Mr Purgon!

MR PURGON. From apepsia into diarrhoea and lientery.

ARGAN. Mr Purgon!

MR PURGON. From lientery into dysentery.

ARGAN. Mr Purgon!

MR PURGON. From dysentery into dropsy.

ARGAN. Mr Purgon!

MR PURGON. And from dropsy to autopsy that your own folly will have brought you to.

[*Exit* MR PURGON *and* TOINETTE.]

ARGAN. Oh my God! I'm dying. Brother, you've done for me.

BÉRALDE. What's the matter?

ARGAN. I'm finished. I feel already that medicine is taking vengeance upon me.

BÉRALDE. Upon my word, brother, you are crazy! I shouldn't like anyone to see you in the state you are now. Take yourself in hand. Do pull yourself together! Don't give so much rein to your imagination!

ARGAN. You heard the awful maladies he threatened me with.

BÉRALDE. What a simpleton you are!

ARGAN. He said I should be in an incurable condition within four days.

BÉRALDE. And what does it matter what he said? He's not an oracle is he? Anyone would think, to hear you going on, that he held your life in his hands and had absolute authority to prolong your days or cut them short as he fancied. Do understand that the living principle is within you and that Mr Purgon's wrath is as powerless to kill you as his medicines are to keep you alive. Here's your chance to be rid of the doctors, if you'll take it, or if you really are so constituted that you can't manage without them you can easily get another and run less of a risk.

ARGAN. Ah, brother, but he understands my constitution and knows just how I ought to be treated.

BÉRALDE. You are terribly obstinate, I must say and you have a strange way of looking at things!

[*Enter* TOINETTE.]

TOINETTE. Master, there's a doctor wanting to see you.

ARGAN. What doctor?

TOINETTE. A doctor of medicine.

ARGAN. l asked who he was.

TOINETTE. I don't know who he is but he and I are as alike as two peas. If I were not sure my mother was an honest woman I should say he was a younger brother she'd produced for me since my father died.

ARGAN. Show him in.

TOINETTE. That's the very thing that you wanted. One doctor leaves you. Another turns up.

ARGAN. I'm only afraid you've let me in for a lot of trouble.

BÉRALDE. Going back to that again are you?

ARGAN. What I'm worrying about is all those ailments I never heard of before.

[*Enter* TOINETTE *disguised as a doctor.*]

TOINETTE. Permit me to call upon you, sir, and offer my humble services for any blood-lettings and purgings you may be needing.

ARGAN. I'm greatly obliged to you, sir. My goodness! He's the image of Toinette.

TOINETTE. Excuse me a moment, sir. I have forgotten to give instructions to my servant. I'll be back in a moment.

BÉRALDE. There's certainly a remarkable resemblance but I've come across similar cases before and one often reads about such freaks of nature.

ARGAN. Well, I must say, I'm astonished . . .

[*Re-enter* TOINETTE *as herself.*]

TOINETTE. Were you wanting something, sir?

ARGAN. What's that?

TOINETTE. Weren't you calling me?

ARGAN. Me? No.

TOINETTE. My ears must have been burning.

ARGAN. Stay a minute and see how like you this doctor is.

TOINETTE. Not I! I'm too busy downstairs. I've seen enough of him. [*Exit.*]

ARGAN. If I hadn't seen both of them I should have thought it was one and the same person.

BÉRALDE. I've read about some surprising cases of resemblance of this kind. One has known cases where everybody was deceived.

[*Re-enter* TOINETTE *as doctor.*]

TOINETTE. I'm very sorry to keep you, sir.

ARGAN. It's remarkable.

TOINETTE. I hope you will forgive my curiosity, sir, in wishing to see so celebrated an invalid as yourself. Your widespread reputation may, I hope, excuse the liberty I have taken.

ARGAN. I'm at your service, sir.

TOINETTE. I see you are staring at me, sir. How old would you think I was?

ARGAN. I should think you wouldn't be more than twenty-six or twenty-seven at most.

TOINETTE. Ha, ha ha! I'm ninety.

ARGAN. Ninety!

TOINETTE. Yes. That's one of the secrets of my art – how to keep oneself young looking and vigorous.

ARGAN. Upon my word! But you are a young looking ninety!

TOINETTE. I'm a travelling physician. I go from place to place, province to province, and country to country seeking opportunities for the exercise of my talents, patients worthy of my attention, cases which call for the profound discoveries I have made in the field of medicine. I scorn to bother with the dull ordinary run of minor ailments, rheumatism, coughs, fevers, vapours, headaches, and such-like. I want serious illnesses, nice fevers of long duration, with spells of delirium, interesting scarlet fevers, plagues, advanced cases of dropsy, pleurisies, and inflammation of the lungs – that's the sort of thing I like and that's where I show my skill. I only wish, sir, you had every malady I've just mentioned, that you were given up for lost by all the doctors, despaired of, at death's door, so that I could demonstrate the excellence of my remedies and my anxiety to be of service to you.

ARGAN. I'm very grateful to you, sir, for your kind consideration.

TOINETTE. Let us have your pulse! Come along now! Let's have you beating properly! Ah. I'll put you in order. Hey! Here's an impudent pulse. It doesn't know me yet, I can see that. Who's your doctor?

ARGAN. Mr Purgon.

TOINETTE. He's not on my list of the great physicians. What does he say is wrong with you?

ARGAN. He says it's my liver – others say it's my spleen.

TOINETTE. They are all ignoramuses. Your lungs are the trouble.

ARGAN. My lungs?

TOINETTE. That's it. What are your symptoms?

ARGAN. I have headaches from time to time.

TOINETTE. Exactly. Lungs!

ARGAN. Sometimes I seem to have a sort of mist before my eyes.

TOINETTE. Lungs!

ARGAN. At other times I've a pain at my heart.

TOINETTE. Lungs!

ARGAN. At other times I'm weary in every limb.

TOINETTE. Lungs!

ARGAN. Then I have pains in my stomach – as if I had colic!

TOINETTE. Lungs! Have you an appetite for your food?

ARGAN. Yes, doctor.

TOINETTE. Lungs! Fond of a drop of wine?

ARGAN. Yes, doctor.

TOINETTE. Lungs again! Sleepy after a meal? Feel you want a nap?

ARGAN. Yes, doctor.

TOINETTE. Lungs! Lungs I assure you. What diet does your own doctor prescribe?

ARGAN. He says I can have – soup.

TOINETTE. The ignorance!

ARGAN. Chicken.

TOINETTE. Ignorance!

ARGAN. Veal.

TOINETTE. Ignorance!

ARGAN. Stew.

TOINETTE. Ignorance!

ARGAN. New laid eggs.

TOINETTE. Ignorance!

ARGAN. And a few prunes in the evening as a laxative.

TOINETTE. Ignorance.

ARGAN. And above all I'm to take plenty of water with my wine.

TOINETTE. *Ignorantus, ignoranta, ignorantum!* You must never take water with your wine, and to strengthen your blood, which is too thin, you need to eat good prime beef, fat pork, and plenty of good Dutch cheese, rice puddings, chestnuts, and dry biscuits to make your blood thicken and conglutinate. Your doctor's an ass. I'll send you one of my own choice and I'll look in and see you myself from time to time when I'm in the town.

ARGAN. I shall be very much obliged to you.

TOINETTE. What the deuce are you doing with this arm?

ARGAN. How d'ye mean?

TOINETTE. I should have that arm off at once if I were you.

ARGAN. Why?

TOINETTE. Don't you see how it takes all the nourishment and prevents the other one from thriving?

ARGAN. Ay, but I need my arm.

TOINETTE. I should have that right eye out too if I were in your place.

ARGAN. Have my eye out?

TOINETTE. Don't you see how bad it is for the other one? It deprives it of sustenance. Take my advice, have it out as soon as you can. You'll see a lot better with the left.

ARGAN. There's no hurry.

TOINETTE. Well, good-bye. Sorry to leave you so soon but I must be at a consultation on a man who died yesterday.

ARGAN. On a man who died yesterday?

TOINETTE. Yes – to see what should have been done to cure him. Till we meet again.

ARGAN. You'll excuse my not showing you to the door.

[*Exit* TOINETTE.]

BÉRALDE. He seems to be a pretty clever sort of doctor.

ARGAN. Yes, but he's in a bit too much of a hurry for me.

BÉRALDE. Great physicians are all like that.

ARGAN. Wanting to cut one arm off and take out an eye so that the other would get along better! I'd much rather they didn't get on so well. A fine operation that would be, wouldn't it, to leave me one-eyed and one-armed!

TOINETTE [*offstage*]. Be off with you! That sort of thing doesn't amuse me, thank you very much.

ARGAN. What's the matter?

TOINETTE. That doctor of yours – he was wanting to feel *my* pulse.

ARGAN. Did you ever! At ninety!

BÉRALDE. Well now, brother, since your friend Purgon has fallen out with you, won't you let me talk to you about the young man who's a suitor for my niece?

ARGAN. No, I mean to put her into a convent since she won't do what I want. I can see well enough that there's an intrigue going on somewhere. I found out about a certain clandestine meeting she thinks I don't know about.

BÉRALDE. Well, brother, if she has a little inclination for someone, what's wrong about that? It's all quite honourable and intended to end in marriage so why should it worry you?

ARGAN. No. She shall take the veil now whatever happens. I have made up my mind.

BÉRALDE. There's one person who'll be pleased.

ARGAN. I know what you mean. You keep coming back to it. It's my wife you are thinking about.

BÉRALDE. Well, to be frank, I do mean your wife. I can no more bear your infatuation where she's concerned than your obsession with doctors. I can't see you walk straight into every snare that's set for you.

TOINETTE. Ah sir! Don't talk like that about the mistress. No one can say a word against her. She's a woman without guile and she loves the master – how she does love him! There's no telling how she loves him.

ARGAN. Ask *her* how fond she is of me.

TOINETTE. It's quite true.

ARGAN. How worried she is by my illness.

TOINETTE. No doubt about that.

ARGAN. What care, what trouble she bestows on me.

TOINETTE. That's certain. Would you like me to prove to

you, to convince you immediately just how much she loves him? Master, let me show him how little he knows – and convince him of his mistake.

ARGAN. How?

TOINETTE. The mistress is just coming in. Lie down in that chair and pretend to be dead. You'll see how she'll grieve when I tell her the news.

ARGAN. All right.

TOINETTE. Don't keep her too long in a state of despair. It might be the death of her.

ARGAN. Leave it to me.

TOINETTE [*to* BÉRALDE]. You hide yourself in the corner.

ARGAN. I suppose there's no risk in pretending to be dead?

TOINETTE. No. No. What risk could there be? Just stretch yourself out so. [*Whispering*]. It'll be a pleasure to show your brother how wrong he is. Here comes the mistress. Keep still.

[*Enter* BÉLINE.]

TOINETTE [*crying out*]. Heavens! How terrible! What a dreadful thing to happen!

BÉLINE. What is it, Toinette?

TOINETTE. Oh, mistress!

BÉLINE. What's happened?

TOINETTE. Your husband is dead.

BÉLINE. My husband is dead?

TOINETTE. Alas, yes! The poor soul is gone.

BÉLINE. Are you sure?

TOINETTE. Quite sure. No one knows it has happened yet. I was all by myself. He just expired in my arms. See here he is – stretched out in his chair.

BÉLINE. Heaven be praised for that! What a relief! Don't be so silly, Toinette. What are you crying for?

TOINETTE. I thought that was what we ought to do, madam.

BÉLINE. Go on! It's nothing to worry about. Who's going to miss him? What use was he anyhow? He was a nuisance to everybody, dirty, disgusting, always wanting an injection, or another dose of medicine in his belly, for ever snivelling, coughing, spitting, dull, boring, bad tempered, tiresome to everybody, and grumbling at the servants at all hours of day or night.

BÉRALDE [*aside*]. A nice funeral oration, I must say.

BÉLINE. You must help me to carry out my plans, Toinette. You can rely on me to see that you are rewarded. Luckily no one knows what has happened so we'll carry him to his bed, and keep his death quiet until I've done all I want to. There are papers and money I want to get hold of. I've given him the best years of my life and I deserve some reward. Come along Toinette. Let's get his keys first of all.

ARGAN [*rising hastily*]. Steady on!

BÉLINE. Ah!

ARGAN. So my lady! That's how you love me!

BÉLINE. He's not dead after all!

ARGAN [*to* BÉLINE *as she runs out*]. I was very pleased to see just how much you love me and to hear your fine panegyric. I shall be wiser in future.

BÉRALDE [*coming out of hiding*]. Well, brother, you see how it is.

TOINETTE. My goodness! I would never have believed it. But I hear your daughter coming. Get back where you were and see how she'll take the news of your death. It's easily done and while you are at it you might as well know what your family think about you.

[*Enter* ANGÉLIQUE.]

TOINETTE. Heavens! What a dreadful thing to happen. Oh, unhappy day!

ANTÉLIQUE. What's the matter, Toinette? What are you crying for?

TOINETTE. Alas! I have sad news to tell you.

ANGÉLIQUE. What is it?

TOINETTE. Your father – is dead.

ANGÉLIQUE. My father is dead, Toinette?

TOINETTE. Yes. There he is. He's just had a fainting fit and – expired.

ANGÉLIQUE. Oh Heavens! How terrible! What a cruel misfortune! Alas! To lose my dear father, who was all the world to me, and what makes it even more dreadful, lose him at a time when he was angry with me! What will become of me? Unhappy daughter that I am! What consolation can I find for such a loss?

[*Enter* CLÉANTE.]

CLÉANTE. What's the matter my dear Angélique? Why are you weeping?

ANGÉLIQUE. Alas, I weep for the dearest, the most precious thing I had to lose. I weep for my father's death.

CLÉANTE. What a dreadful misfortune! Alas, I had implored your uncle to speak to him on my behalf and I was just coming myself to endeavour by my own prayers to persuade him to accord me your hand.

ANGÉLIQUE. Oh Cléante, no more of that! Let us give up all thought of marriage. I have no more interest in the world now that I've lost my father. I renounce it for ever. Yes, father, if I opposed your wishes before I will comply with them now and make amends for the grief which I so reproach myself for having caused you. Let me give you my promise now, father. Let this kiss be a token of my repentance.

ARGAN [*rising*]. Ah, my daughter.

ANGÉLIQUE [*startled*]. Oh!

ARGAN. Come. Don't be frightened. I'm not dead. There you *are* my own daughter, my own flesh and blood, and I'm delighted to find you behave as such.

ANGÉLIQUE. Ah, father, what a relief! Since Heaven, in its goodness, restores you to my love, let me now throw myself at your feet and implore one favour of you. If you can't approve my heart's desire, if you can't give me Cléante for a husband don't, I beg you, force me to marry another. That's all I ask of you.

CLÉANTE [*on his knees*]. Sir, let her prayers and mine move you. Don't oppose our mutual inclinations.

BÉRALDE. Brother can you refuse?

TOINETTE. Master. How can you resist such affection?

ARGAN. Let him become a doctor and I'll consent to the marriage. Yes, become a doctor and I'll give you my daughter.

CLÉANTE. Willingly, sir. If that's all that's required to become your son-in-law I'll turn doctor, ay, even apothecary if you like. That's no great matter. I'd do far more than that to win my fair Angélique.

BÉRALDE. An idea occurs to me brother. Why not turn doctor yourself? It would be even more convenient to be able to provide yourself with everything you need.

TOINETTE. That's true. And it's the very way to get better quickly. What disease could have the audacity to attack the doctor himself?

ARGAN. I think you are making fun of me brother. Am I of an age to start studying?

BÉRALDE. Study! That's a good one! You know enough about it already. There are lots of them who know no more than you do.

ARGAN. But you need to know Latin, diagnose the various complaints, and know the remedies for them.

BÉRALDE. Once you put on the cap and gown of a doctor the rest comes of itself. You'll find you have all the skill you require.

ARGAN. What! One can discourse on disease once one puts on the robes?

BÉRALDE. That's it. Once you have the cap and gown all you need do is open your mouth. Whatever nonsense you talk becomes wisdom and all the rubbish, good sense.

TOINETTE. Just think, master – if it were nothing more than your beard that goes quite a way – the beard is more than half the physician.

CLÉANTE. Anyhow, I'm ready for anything.

BÉRALDE. Would you like it arranged right away?

ARGAN. Right away? How d'ye mean?

BÉRALDE. Here and now. In your own house.

ARGAN. In my own house?

BÉRALDE. Yes, I have a number of friends in the Faculty

who'll come at once and perform the ceremony here in your own room. And it won't cost you a penny.

ARGAN. But what shall I have to say? What answers shall I give?

BÉRALDE. They'll reduce it to a few words for you and put down on paper what you have to say. You go and get yourself suitably dressed while I send for them.

ARGAN. All right then. Let us see it. [*Exit.*]

CLÉANTE. What *are* you talking about? What's all this about your friends in the Faculty?

TOINETTE. What have you got in mind?

BÉRALDE. Just something to amuse us this evening. I have actors available who have used the ceremony for conferring a doctor's degree as the basis for a little burlesque with music and dances. I want us all to take part and my brother shall play the leading role.

ANGÉLIQUE. But it rather seems to me, uncle, that you are making fun of father too much.

BÉRALDE. No, it's not so much making fun of him as playing up to his fancies. And it's all among ourselves. We can each take a part and so give the play for each other's amusement. After all, it's carnival time. Come along, let us go and get things ready.

CLÉANTE. Do you agree?

ANGÉLIQUE. Yes, since it's uncle's idea.

FINALE

A burlesque ceremony of the conferment of a doctor's degree
[*Enter dancers.*

Attendants come in and prepare the hall and set out the benches to music. Then enter the whole assemblage, including eight men bearing syringes, six apothecaries, twenty-two doctors, and the candidate with eight surgeons dancing and two singing. All take their places according to their rank.]

PRAESES. Sçavantissimi doctores,
Medicinae professores,
Qui hic assemblati estis;

Et vos, altri messiores,
Sententiarum facultatis
Fideles executores;
Surgeons and apothecaries,
Atque tota compania also,
Salus, honor, and argentum,
Atque bonum appetitum.

Non possum, docti confreri,
In me satis admirari,
Qualis bona inventio,
Est medici professio;
How rare and choice a thing it is
Medicina illa benedicta,
Quae suo nomine solo
Marveloso miraculo
Since si longo tempore;
Has made in clover vivere
So many people omni genere.

Per totam terram videmus
Grandam vogam ubi sumus;
Et quod grandes and petiti
Sunt de nobis infatuti:
Totus mundus currens ad nostros remedios.
Nos regardat sicut deos,
Et nostris ordonnanciis
Principes and reges submissive videtis.

'Tis therefore nostrae sapientiae,
Bonus sensus atque prudentiae,
Strongly for to travaillare,
A nos bene conservare
In tali credito, voga and honore;
And take care to non recevere
In nostro docto corpore
Quam personas capabiles,
Et totas dignas fillire
Has plaças honorabiles.

That's why nunc convocati estis,
Et credo quod trovabitis
Dignam matieram medici,
In sçavanti homine that here you see;
Whom in things omnibus
Dono ad interrogandum,
Et to the bottom examinandum
Vestris capacitatibus.

FIRST DOCTOR.

Si mihi licenciam dat dominus praeses,
Et tanti docti doctores,
Et assistantes illustres,
Learnidissimo bacheliere
Quem estimo and honoro,
Domandabo causum and rationem, quare
Opium facit dormire.

ARGAN.   Mihi by docto doctore
Domandatur causum and rationem, quare
Opium facit dormire.
To which respondeo,
Quia est in eo
Virtus dormitiva,
Cujus est natura
Sensus stupifire.

CHORUS.   Bene, bene, bene, bene respondere,
Dignus, dignus est intrare
In nostro docto corpore.
Bene, bene respondere.

SECOND DOCTOR.

Cum permissione domini praesidis,
Doctissimae facultatis,
Et totius his nostris actis
Companiae assistantis,
Domandabo tibi, docte bacheliere
Quae sunt remedia,
Quae in maladia
Called hydropisia
Convenit facere?

ARGAN.   Clisterium donare,
          Postea bleedare,
          Afterwards purgare.

CHORUS.   Bene, bene, bene, bene respondere,
          Dignus, dignus est intrare
          In nostro docto corpore.

THIRD DOCTOR.
          If bonum semblatur domine praesidi
          Doctissimae facultati
          Et companiae praesenti,
          Domandabo tibi, docte bacheliere,
          Quae remedia eticis,
          Pulmonicis atque asmaticis
          Do you think a propos facere.

ARGAN.   Clisterium donare,
          Postea bleedare,
          Afterwards purgare.

CHORUS.   Bene, bene, bene, bene respondere:
          Dignus, dignus est intrare
          In nostro docto corpore.

FOURTH DOCTOR.
          Super illas maladias,
          Doctus bachelierus dixit maravillas:
          But if I do not tease and fret dominum praesidem,
          Doctissimam facultatem,
          Et totam honorabilem
          Companiam hearkennantem;
          Faciam illi unam quaestionem.
          Last night patientus unus
          Chanced to fall in meas manus:
          Habet grandam fievram cum redoubleamentis
          Grandum dolorem capitis,
          Et grandum malum in his inside,
          Cum granda difficultate
          Et pena respirare.
          Be pleased then to tell me,
          Docte bacheliere,
          Quid illi facere.

ARGAN.   Clisterium donare,
          Postea bleedare,
          Afterwards purgare.

FIFTH DOCTOR.
          But if maladia
          Opiniatria
          Non vult se curare
          Quid illi facere?

ARGAN.   Clisterium donare,
          Postea bleedare,
          Afterwards purgare.
          Rebleedare, repurgare, and reclysterisare.

CHORUS.   Bene, bene, bene, bene respondere:
          Dignus, dignus est intrare
          In nostro docto corpore.

THE PRESIDENT [*to* ARGAN].
          Juras keepare statuta
          Per facultatem praescripta,
          Cum sensu and jugeamento?

ARGAN.   Juro.

THE PRESIDENT.
          To be in omnibus
          Consultationibus
          Ancient aviso;
          Aut bono,
          Aut baddo?

ARGAN.   Juro.

THE PRESIDENT.
          That thou'lt never te servare
          De remediis aucunis,
          Other than those of doctae facultatis;
          Should the patient burst-O
          Et mori de suo malo?

ARGAN.   Juro.

THE PRESIDENT.
          Ego cum isto boneto
          Venerablili and docto,
          Dono tibi and concedo

Virtutem and power
Medicandi,
Purgandi,
Bleedandi,
Piercandi,
Carvandi,
Slashandi,
Et occidendi
Impune per totam terram.

[*The surgeons and apothecaries do reverence with music to* ARGAN.]

ARGAN. Grandes doctores doctrinae,
Of rhubarb and of senna:
'Twou'd be in me without doubt foolish,
Inepta and ridicula,
If I should engage myself
Your praises donare,
Et pretendebam addare
Light to the sun,
Stars to the sky.
Ondas to the oceano,
Rosas to the springo.
Agree that in one wordo
Pro toto remercimento
Rendam gratiam corpori tam docto.
Vobis, vobis debeo
More than to nature, or than to patri meo;
Natura and pater meus
Hominem me habent factum:
But vos me, that which is plus,
Avetis factum medicum.
Honor, favor, and gratia,
Qui in hoc corde,
Imprimant ressentimenta
Which will endure in saecula.

CHORUS. Vivat, vivat, vivat, vivat, for ever vivat
Novus doctor, qui tam bene speakat,

Mille, mille annis, and manget and bibat,
Et bleedat and killat.

[*All the surgeons and apothecaries dance to the sound of the
instruments and voices, and clapping of hands, and apothecaries'
mortars.*]

FIRST SURGEON.
May he see doctas
Suas praescriptionas
Omnium chirurgorum,
Et apotiquarum
Fillire shopas.

CHORUS. Vivat, vivat, vivat, for ever vivat
Novus doctor, qui tam bene speakat,
Mille, mille annis, and manget and bibat,
Et bleedat and killat.

SECOND SURGEON.
May all his anni
Be to him boni
And favourable ever
Et n'habere never
Quam plaguas, poxas,
Fievras, pluresias
Bloody effusions and dissenterias.

CHORUS. Vivat, vivat, vivat, vivat, for ever vivat
Novus doctor, qui tam bene speakat,
Mille, mille annis, and manget and bibat,
Et bleedat and killat.

[*While the chorus is singing, the doctors, surgeons, and apothecaries
go out all according to their several ranks, with the same
ceremony as they entered.*]

Notes on the Plays

THE MISANTHROPE. The original title under which Molière sought licence to print the play was *Le Misanthrope ou L'Atrabilaire amoureux*. The play was first performed at the theatre of the *Palais Royal* in Paris (the Court being still in mourning for the Queen Mother, Anne of Austria) on 4 June 1666. Molière wore breeches and doublet of striped gold brocade and grey silk lined in shot silk with green ribbons, a waistcoat of gold brocade, silk stockings, and garters. The recorded list of properties was 6 chairs, 3 letters, a pair of riding boots (presumably for Du Bois).

THE SICILIAN. This comedy-ballet was first played for the King at Saint-Germain-en-Laye in January 1667 as part of a series of spectacular *divertissements*, the *Ballet des Muses*. The first public performance was at the *Palais Royal* the following June. Molière played Don Pedro, his wife the slave girl Zaide. Isidore was played by Mlle de Brie. In the Court performance the King himself took part in the ballets with Mlle de la Vallière and distinguished members of the nobility. Molière wore Sicilian dress – breeches and cloak of violet coloured satin embroidered in gold and silver, lined with green silk, a tunic in gold satin with sleeves of silver with lace and silver-gilt trimmings, a night cap, a periwig, and sword.

The original scene 'Messina, a public square' implies the characteristic setting of Italian farce, a street of houses with practicable doors and windows. Molière did not make any division into acts but there is, clearly, a point at which the action moves indoors and another, rather less clearly defined, where it returns to the street. Some producers may prefer to delay the scene change until after Climène's final exit leaving only the scene with the Magistrate to be played out of doors again.

TARTUFFE. Tartuffe was first played in three acts as part of the *Plaisirs de L'Île enchantée* at Versailles in 1664, again in September, for the King's brother at Villers-Cotterets and in November at Raincy. According to La Grange who kept the records of the company, the play performed at Raincy was in five acts. In August 1667 while the King was in Flanders Molière put on a revised version under the title of *The Imposter* at the *Palais Royal*. It was at once proscribed although the King had given permission for it to be played (or Molière understood him to have done so). From 6 August to 20 September Molière's theatre was closed. This was the lowest point of the play's fortunes. The third (or fourth) and final version was played at the *Palais Royal* on 5 February 1669. Molière played Orgon, his wife Elmire. Tartuffe was played by the florid Du Croisy. Molière wore a doublet, breeches, and cloak in black satin lined with shot silk trimmed with English lace and lace on his garters and shoes.

A DOCTOR IN SPITE OF HIMSELF. This joyous farce immediately followed *The Misanthrope*. It was first played on 6 August 1666 at the *Palais Royal*. It was an immediate success: hence perhaps the common belief that it was deliberately written and put on to support a less popular *Misanthrope*. As a matter of fact Molière had already played what was probably a less polished version of the same theme under the title of the Woodcutter (*Le Fagotier*). Molière played Sganarelle in a doublet with collar and ruff, breeches, waistband with wallet suspended from it, wool stockings, the costume as a whole being in yellow serge trimmed with sateen: as a doctor he wore a satin gown, velvet breeches and very high pointed hat. The property list included faggots, a large bottle, two sticks, three chairs, a piece of cheese, counters, and a purse.

THE IMAGINARY INVALID.* The first performance was at the *Palais Royal* on 10 February 1673. Molière played Argan, his wife Angélique. He wore slippers, thick stockings, narrow breeches, a red jacket with some braid or lace, an old braid neckerchief carelessly tied, a night cap with a lace crown.

The stage directions provided for a bedroom with an alcove up-stage. Properties were – Act I: a chair, table, bell, purse, counters, a fur cloak, six pillows, a stick. First interlude: a guitar or lute, four muskets, four dark lanterns, four sticks, and a bladder. Act II: four chairs, a switch, paper. Second interlude: four tambourines. Third interlude, i.e. Finale: throne for the presiding doctor, benches, eight syringes, four balances, four pestles, four mortars, six stools, robes, gowns, etc.

Molière was taken ill during the fourth performance on 17 February 1673 and died the same evening. He was fifty-one and had been actively engaged in the theatre for thirty years.

* Those who prefer to be exact may like to go back to the title of *The Hypochondriak* used by Baker and Miller in their edition of 1739.

MORE ABOUT PENGUINS
AND PELICANS

Penguinews, which appears every month, contains details of all the new books issued by Penguins as they are published. From time to time it is supplemented by *Penguins in Print*, which is a complete list of all titles available. (There are some five thousand of these.)

A specimen copy of *Penguinews* will be sent to you free on request. For a year's issues (including the complete lists) please send 50p if you live in the British Isles, or 75p if you live elsewhere. Just write to Dept EP, Penguin Books Ltd, Harmondsworth, Middlesex, enclosing a cheque or postal order, and your name will be added to the mailing list.

In the U.S.A.: For a complete list of books available from Penguin in the United States write to Dept CS, Penguin Books Inc., 7110 Ambassador Road, Baltimore, Maryland 21207.

In Canada: For a complete list of books available from Penguin in Canada write to Penguin Books Canada Ltd, 41 Steelcase Road West, Markham, Ontario.

MOLIÈRE

THE MISER AND OTHER PLAYS

Translated by John Wood

A new translation of Molière was overdue: the version most familiar to English readers dates from the early eighteenth century and its idiom is far removed from contemporary English. Lack of effective translations may account, in part, for the neglect of Molière which has long been a reproach and a loss to the English theatre. There are signs that the tide may have turned. If so, it will be to our common pleasure and advantage for his is, above all, a comedy which in George Meredith's words, 'springs to vindicate reason, common sense, rightness, and justice'.

A selection within the compass of one volume must be arbitrary and personal: it can offer no more than a taste, a first sample, of the power and range of Molière's genius as displayed in the thirty or more plays which are extant. Of those included here, three are major works, *The Would-be Gentleman, The Miser,* and *Don Juan*; the other two, *Scapin* and *Love's the Best Doctor,* are happy examples of Molière's delight in pure entertainment.

The translation keeps close to the original and seeks to retain something of the vigour and felicity of Molière's language in an English which is at once readable – and actable.

JEAN-JACQUES ROUSSEAU

CONFESSIONS

Translated by J. M. Cohen

In his posthumously published *Confessions* Jean-Jacques Rousseau
(1712–78) describes the first fifty-three years of his life. With a
frankness at times almost disconcerting, but always refreshing,
he set out to reveal the whole truth about himself to the world,
and succeeded in producing a masterpiece which has left its
indelible imprint on the literature of successive generations,
influencing among others Proust, Goethe, and Tolstoy.

J. M. Cohen's translation provides a clear, easy rendering
in contemporary English of this fascinating panorama of
eighteenth-century continental life, which ranges freely from
the *haut monde* to the picaresque.

Also available

THE SOCIAL CONTRACT
Translated by Maurice Cranston

VOLTAIRE
CANDIDE

Translated by John Butt

Candide, the wittiest of Voltaire's novels, might almost have been written for us today instead of for the eighteenth century. Though we no longer declare in the face of human suffering that 'all is for the best in the best of all possible worlds', we are in danger of taking an equally callous and hopeless point of view. *Candide* may serve as a corrective even while it makes us laugh. The characters in this novel suffer extraordinary tortures and humiliations, but they show that 'hope springs eternal in the human breast'. And Voltaire's famous recipe for banishing boredom, vice, and poverty – 'we must go and work in the garden' – deserves remembering in an age among whose greatest problems, we are told, is the possibility of world famine.

This translation was made by John Butt, the Professor of Rhetoric and English Literature at Edinburgh University.

Also available

PHILOSOPHICAL DICTIONARY